Tom Holland is the author of *The Vampyre,*
Supping With Panthers, Deliver Us From Evil
and *Attis*. He lives in London.

The SLEEPER in the SANDS

TOM HOLLAND

An *Abacus* Book

First published in Great Britain by Little, Brown and Company 1998
First published by Abacus 1999

A CIP catalogue record for this book is available
from the British Library.

ISBN 0 349 11221 5

Map artwork by Venture Graphics
Typeset in Bembo by M Rules
Printed and bound in Great Britain by
Clays Ltd, St Ives plc

Abacus
A division of
Little, Brown and Company (UK)
Brettenham House
Lancaster Place
London WC2E 7EN

To Mattos,
A Pharaoh amongst friends

Ring found by Howard Carter, El Amarna, 1892.
Original drawing from *Tell El Amarna*
by W.M. Flinders Petrie.

CONTENTS

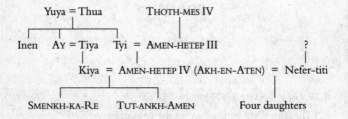

The Late Eighteenth Dynasty

Author's Note
There are many ways of spelling Egyptian names.
Throughout this novel, I have copied Carter's own.
The names of Pharaohs are capitalised.

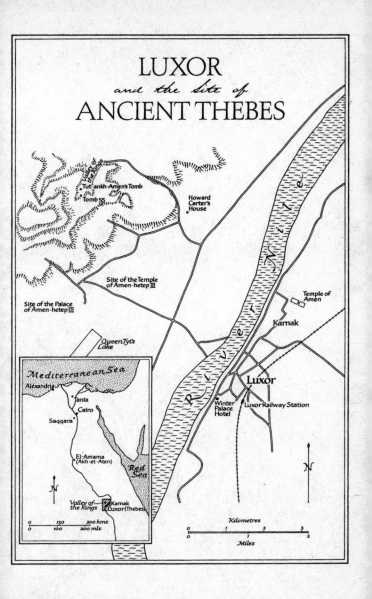

LUXOR
and the site of
ANCIENT THEBES

Valley of the Kings

Tut-ankh-Amen's Tomb

Tomb 55

Howard Carter's House

Site of the Temple of Amen-hetep III

Site of the Palace of Amen-hetep III

Queen Tyi's Lake

Temple of Amen

Karnak

Luxor

Winter Palace Hotel

Luxor Railway Station

River Nile

N

Inset map

Mediterranean Sea

Alexandria

Tanta

Cairo

Saqqara

El-Amarna
(Akh-et-Aten)

Red Sea

Valley of the Kings

Karnak
Luxor (Thebes)

N

| 0 | 150 | 300 kms. |
| 0 | 100 | 200 mls. |

Kilometres

| 0 | 1 | 2 | 3 |

Miles

| 0 | 1 | 2 |

Say: I seek refuge with the Lord of the Dawn,
From the mischief of created things;
From the mischief of Darkness as it overspreads;
From the mischief of those who practise Secret Arts;
And from the mischief of the envious one as he practises envy.

'Surah al-Falaq' (The Daybreak), from the Koran

The
TALE
of the
GOLDEN
BIRD

ll night he dreamed he was searching. He imagined himself lost in a labyrinth of stone, where there was nothing to be found save for shreds of mummy wrapping, and papyri from which the writing had long since been erased. Yet always, even as he stumbled through the darkness and the dust, he knew that ahead of him, buried somewhere in the rock, there was a chamber waiting, a wondrous, hidden tomb; and it was this certainty alone which kept him from despair. Still he stumbled on; and he imagined, as he did so, that he was drawing near the tomb. He reached out with his arms, as though to part the rock. For a moment he imagined that he caught a glint of gold, and at once he felt a joy that seemed to justify his life. When he looked again, though, the glint had disappeared, and he knew that the mysteries of both his life and a far more distant past remained in darkness. He reached out a second time. He thrashed with his arms. But still no sign of gold – only rock and sand and dust . . .

All at once, Howard Carter jerked awake. He sat up, breathing very hard – and yet realising, as he did so, that he felt almost refreshed. He blinked. The early morning sun, still warm despite the lateness of the year, was already casting a bright rectangle across the far side of the room – and yet it was not the sun which had woken him. Carter blinked again, and rubbed his eyes. As he did so, he heard it: the singing of a bird.

He gazed across the room. He had brought the canary with him from Cairo just a week before, a golden bird inside a gilded cage. He rose from his bed, and crossed to it. He remembered what the workmen had cried when he had first arrived back to start the season's digging, his servant carrying the gilded cage behind him. 'A bird of gold,' they had proclaimed, 'it will surely bring us luck! This year we will find, *inshallah*, a tomb of gold!'

Howard Carter certainly trusted so. Yet even as he bent down to feed the canary, his smile was grim. For he did not need reminding that he was in desperate need of luck – more luck, certainly, than he had been granted in the past six years. So much effort – and for so little return. His patron, he knew, was already losing faith; it was only with difficulty that Lord Carnarvon had been persuaded to fund one further, final season. If they were to locate the tomb, the sealed tomb of gold, the tomb which might win them an undying renown, then it would have to be within the next few months. The next few months . . . or not at all.

And yet, no matter that an unplundered tomb had never been found in the Valley before, he knew that it was out there. Not once had he doubted it. Howard Carter paused a moment, gazing at the bird; then he rose suddenly and crossed to a desk, where he reached for a key and unlocked the bottom-most drawer. From its depths he drew out a sheaf of faded papers. His grip on them tightened as he pressed them hard against his chest.

Suddenly, the bird began to sing again, and the music that it made, in the clear light of the Theban dawn, did indeed seem golden.

Howard Carter returned the papers to their place and locked up the drawer. He had work to do. An excavation was awaiting him in the Valley of the Kings.

The water-boy grimaced and settled down his load. The day's work on the site had only just begun, and the great earthen jar was still full up to the brim. The boy rubbed his shoulders, then gazed enviously about him. He wanted the chance to dig, the chance to find the hidden tomb of gold. Carrying water about all day, running and fetching for the older men, what hope did he have of finding anything at all?

He scuffed the dirt before him idly with his toes. Scratching at it, he felt flat rock just beneath. He crouched down and began to sweep more energetically, using his hands. As he exposed it, the rock seemed to fall suddenly away.

One of the workmen called out to the boy, demanding water, but the boy ignored him. The workman crossed to him, angry, his hand upraised. Then all at once his arm dropped back by his side as he gazed in silence at what the boy had exposed.

There was a step. It had been hewn from the rock. It seemed to lead downwards, down into the earth.

The silence still lay thick in the air, like the haze of white dust, when Howard Carter arrived at the site. The labourers were all staring at him, and he knew at once that something had been found. Ahmed Girigar, his foreman, stepped out from the crowd. He bowed, his face set, and pointed with his arm.

For a moment, Carter imagined that his heart had

stopped: that all the Valley, the very sky, were melting and plunging into that single moment.

Then he nodded brusquely. Still silent, he passed through the line of workmen. As he did so he heard it muttered amongst them, rising fast into cries of excitement and awe, that what had been found was 'the tomb of the bird'.

He had ordered the canary brought to the site, to encourage the workmen as they cleared away the rubble. It was also – Carter could not deny this to himself – a feeble attempt to calm his own raging nerves, for since his boyhood he had always been a lover of birds, and found in their singing a source of great comfort. But although his expression, that first long day and the next, appeared perfectly composed, his thoughts remained a tumult of terrors and wild hopes, and he barely heard the canary's song. Nothing filled his ears but the chink of spade upon rock, as slowly, step by step, a stairway was revealed.

It was almost sunset when the first part of a doorway was at last exposed. Howard Carter stood at the top of the steps, barely able to move, every nerve numbed by his sudden doubts. To be so close to a miraculous success . . . and then to be disappointed – the horrible possibility shadowed all his imaginings. Yet his step remained measured as he slowly descended towards the door, and his face as granite-calm as it had been throughout the day.

His hands, though, were unsteady as he reached out to brush the dirt from the doorway. There was a seal upon it, he realised suddenly; and he began to shake so much that he had to rest his palms upon the ground. As he did so, he inspected the seal. He recognised it at once: a jackal triumphant above nine bound captives – the motif of the necropolis of the Valley of the Kings.

Carter breathed in deeply. He had seen the symbol often enough before, stamped upon the other tombs of the Valley – but they had all been plundered. He reached out to touch the block of stone before him now, to trace with his fingertip the pattern of the seal. Elsewhere, the guardianship of the jackal had been in vain; what reason to believe that it might not have been so here? Again, Carter began to sweep at the dirt upon the doorway, and as he did so he observed a heavy wooden lintel at the top of the block. At once he called for a pick and, using its point, very delicately began to carve out a peephole. When it was completed, he pulled a flashlight from his pocket, then narrowed his eyes and peered through the gap.

He could make out rubble. It was blocking a passageway. Stones had been tightly packed from the floor to the ceiling. There appeared no evidence of the rubble having ever been disturbed. Whatever lay beyond it was surely still in place.

Slowly, Carter lowered his flashlight. He rested his forehead against the dusty block of stone.

Something, clearly, was waiting to be found. Something which had been immured with the utmost care.

But what?

What?

Carter rocked back with sudden impatience on to his haunches. He had to know; he had to make certain. He began to sweep at the doorway again, examining it carefully for a different seal, one which would identify the owner of the tomb. It seemed impossible that it could not be there, for it had been the remembrance of a name, he knew, in the Ancients' philosophy, which had served to keep the soul of the departed alive. And who was to say, Carter thought with a sudden lurch of wonder, that such an assumption had not been correct – that fame was indeed the truest immortality?

Still, though, he could find nothing exposed to his view, and even as he continued to sweep, he grew suddenly frantic with uncertainty. He began to scrabble at the dirt with his fingers, seeking to lay bare a further portion of the door – and then, as he did so, he suddenly froze. He had felt his fingers brush something and as he began work again, clearing the dirt now with all the care he could muster, he saw that he was exposing a tablet of baked clay. It appeared to be intact, stamped along one side with a line of hieroglyphics. Carter eased the tablet free. He rose to his feet, studying it carefully, his lips mouthing the words as he sought to make sense of the script.

It seemed to the workmen, studying their employer, that the colour had suddenly drained from his face.

'Please,' Ahmed Girigar, the foreman, asked, 'what is it, sir, what does it say?'

Carter appeared to start, and then his expression grew as frozen as it had been all that day. He made no reply but, climbing the steps, reached for a cloth and carefully swaddled the tablet in its folds. Then he turned to the foreman as he gestured at the stairway. 'Fill it in,' he ordered. 'We can proceed no further until Lord Carnarvon has arrived. Fill it to the surface, then conceal the site with rocks. I want it to seem as though the tomb was never here.'

Not until late had Howard Carter ridden home. The cliffs had loomed steepling against the brightness of the stars, and upon the winding road which led from the Valley, lonely and abandoned, the shadows had seemed black with the silence of the dead. There had been no one to observe him, no one to glimpse the expression on his face. Yet only as he drew near to his house did Carter permit himself to relax the muscles in his jaw, to betray with a sudden smile his sense of triumph and joy. He remembered the guards he had left up on the site, the most trustworthy of his workmen, how excited they had seemed – almost, he thought, as excited as himself. He smiled once again. Almost – but not quite.

As he swung down from his saddle, he glanced about him as though to make certain that he was not somehow still lost within a dream. All, though, was just as he had left it that morning: his house a fragile oasis of green amidst the jagged rocks and dust, as near to the ancient realm of death as it was possible for any man to live. All still seemed silent, but Carter knew that here, away from the Valley, amidst his lovingly tended trees and straggling flowers, the night would be filled with the motions of life. He glanced up. He had heard the sudden beating of wings and saw a bird swooping at great speed, then turning intricately, in pursuit of insects. It was well disguised, but Carter could recognise the mottling of the nightjar all the same, for there was not a bird in all Egypt which he did not know. '*Teyr-el-mat*,' he murmured to himself, employing the phrase which the local Arabs used. 'Corpse-fowl', it meant – a bird of ill-omen.

And at once he remembered what he had in his bag. He tried to look for the nightjar again, but it was gone, and so he turned instead into the house, carrying the bag. Feeling the weight of what lay wrapped up in its folds, he flushed with sudden uneasiness. He had always been proud to follow the highest standards of his profession, he thought, to work to illumine, not purloin, the hidden past – for what other justification could there be for the excavation of tombs, save that of the cause of enlightenment and science? Certainly, he reflected, he had never before removed an object from a dig, unlike many of his colleagues, richer, more amateur, less scrupulous than he. Yet on this one occasion, surely, he had been justified in his action? He knew how superstitious the natives could be. He could not afford to lose them now, not when his goal was so tantalisingly near – not on account of foolish rumours and fears.

His servant appeared and at once Carter found himself gripping his bag more tightly, almost clutching it to his chest; then, muttering a brief salutation to the man, he hurried past. He continued briskly on his way through the house into the study; once arrived there, he closed the door and lit a lamp. All was silent. The canary, brought back earlier that evening, appeared asleep, and nothing stirred save the flickering shadows. Carter stood motionless a moment more in the wash of the lamp, then carried it to his desk and pulled up a chair. He laid his bag down before him and unfastened it; he reached inside. Very gently, he drew the tablet out.

He parted back the folds to expose it. As he did so, he realised that his heart was beating fast and that he had begun to twist the end of his moustache. Furious with himself, he sought to steady his nerves. Such folly! He was a professional, a man of science! Had he fought so hard to gain that status for himself only to betray those efforts now, at the very climax of their success? Carter shook his head impatiently. He began to study the line of hieroglyphics again, tracing the pattern of each one with his finger. When he had finished, he sat back in his chair.

'"Death",' he whispered, '"on swift wings will come, to whosoever toucheth the tomb of the Pharaoh".'

The words still seemed to linger in the silence which followed.

He repeated the translation aloud once again – and then, despite himself, he glanced suddenly round. He was certain he had heard something. A blind was stirring very gently in the breeze, but the room was empty and there was no one there. Carter rose briskly and crossed to the window. Outside everything was still, save for the twinkling of the stars in the warm velvet sky.

Carter returned to his chair. As he sat down again, his attention was caught by a statue on the desk, silhouetted by the flickering of the lamp. He reached for it. The statue was only small, carved from a block of the blackest granite, but the detail was exquisite – as fresh, so Carter imagined, as when it had first been fashioned, almost three and a half millennia before. He gazed at the figure. Its face was a young man's, no more than twenty at the very most; yet for all its youth there was an implacability to the statue's stare, and a timelessness to its features, which made it seem a thing of death, barely human at all. In his hands the young man grasped the symbols of immortality, and upon his head he wore the regalia of a Pharaoh of Egypt. Carter gazed at the cobra still preserved upon the head-dress: the sacred *uraeus*, hooded and raised, poised to spit poison at the enemies of the King. *Wadjyt* – the guardian of the royal tombs.

And suddenly, even as he thought this, Carter felt his dread start to evaporate and his mood of triumph and excitement to return. He laid the statue aside, and turned to inspect the tablet again. What could its imprecations mean, after all, save that what he had discovered was indeed a Pharaoh's tomb – nor just any Pharaoh's, but the very one he had long sworn to find? He glanced at the statue again, then felt in his pocket and drew out his keys. When he unlocked the bottom drawer of his desk, he saw to his relief that the faded papers were lying folded as he had left them. He drew them out and placed them gently on the tablet, then laid them back with the tablet at the rear of the drawer. He secured the lock. There they would stay until such time as Lord Carnarvon could arrive in Egypt. For now that the tomb had been located at last, there was much, Carter knew, he had sworn he would explain – to his patron at least, if to no one else. The secret had always been a burden to shoulder, and Carter realised – almost with surprise, for it was his custom to think of himself as a self-sufficient man – that he would welcome the chance to share its weight at last.

He reached for a scrap of paper, then unscrewed the lid from the top of his pen. 'NOVEMBER 4TH,' he wrote down. '1922. TO LORD CARNARVON, HIGHCLERE CASTLE, HAMPSHIRE, ENGLAND.' He paused a moment, then continued to write. 'AT LAST HAVE MADE WONDERFUL DISCOVERY IN THE VALLEY. A MAGNIFICENT TOMB WITH SEALS INTACT. RECOVERED SAME FOR YOUR ARRIVAL. CONGRATULATIONS. CARTER.' He blotted the message. He would have the cable sent the following morning – as early as possible. Carter smiled grimly. He could endure to wait, but he had no wish needlessly to extend the torture of delay.

Before he retired to bed, he reached once again for the statue of the king and placed it upon the message to serve as a paperweight. He was gazing into its face, holding the lantern aloft, when all of a sudden the eyes appeared to blink. A trick of the light, though – for even as Carter inspected the face more closely, he saw how its stare grew blank once again, the blackness deeper and more pitted by shadow.

There was much to keep him busy in the following days. Lord Carnarvon had wired back promptly: he would be arriving in Alexandria within the following fortnight, accompanied by his daughter, Lady Evelyn Herbert. He had lately been ill, he confessed, and was still somewhat under the weather; yet news of the tomb had been just the tonic he had needed. Both he and Lady Evelyn were filled with the utmost excitement.

That they might not be disappointed in their anticipation, Carter filled the two weeks with meticulous planning. There was equipment to be gathered and experts to be recruited, problems to be foreseen and opportunities second-guessed. Planning was all. Carter had not come so far, nor endured so long, to rush and stumble at the final fence. The steps to the doorway were buried under rubble; the tablet and his papers were locked within his drawer. In his mind too, he sought to keep them hidden, where they could not be disturbed nor even beheld.

In his sleep, though, in his nightmares, the bonds of self-restraint were easier to slip. Again and again, Carter would dream that the steps had been unearthed. He would imagine himself standing before the doorway, now wholly exposed. In his hands would be the tablet, and its curse would seem written in symbols of blood. He would know that the seals had to stay unbroken – but he would order the doorway opened all the same. As he did so, the tablet would shatter in his hands, and Carter would think himself suddenly awake. But the dust of the tablet would linger in the darkness, and seem to form the shadows of strange figures in his room.

Such nightmares, when he truly awoke from them, angered Carter. Drawn so near at last to the object of his quest, he discovered that he could not endure to be reminded of that mystery which had led him to the very doorway of the tomb, and which he had chosen to keep locked within the drawer of his desk. He began to blame his sense of guilt that he had ever removed the tablet from the sands; yet he knew he could not return it there, nor announce its discovery, for he was still unwilling to provoke the workmen's fears. Nor could he keep it upon his person, for he did not care to feel that he was somehow grown a thief. A vexing problem, exceedingly vexing – and yet Carter knew that a solution had to be found.

For all the while, as the date of Lord Carnarvon's arrival drew nearer, so his dreams were growing steadily worse.

He had regretted bringing it almost at once. As it had done before, when he had brought it from the site of the discovery, the tablet weighed heavily in his bag. Carter shifted it from one hand to the other. A boy approached him, offering to take the portmanteau; but the very prospect of surrendering his precious burden made Carter grip it all the more tightly. He ordered the boy away.

He watched as the rest of his luggage was loaded upon the felucca. Only when all was readied did he prepare to board the vessel himself. He clambered along the gang-plank and for a brief moment, just the briefest, he thought of turning round, taking the bag and its load back to his house. But he knew there could be no delay: he could not afford to miss the train, for Lord Carnarvon was expecting him in Cairo, and he only had three days to spare in the capital – there was no time to lose. So Carter continued up the gang-plank, greeting the captain and then taking his seat. He nestled the portmanteau by his side, and watched as the boat began to drift out from its moorings to join the widening flow of the Nile.

Carter shifted and looked about. He could see a night heron above him, soaring gracefully through the early-morning light, still abroad in the last half-hour before sunrise. Nervously, even as he watched the bird, Carter began to fiddle with his bag and, despite not meaning to, pressed on the catch. He opened it; peered inside; felt with his hand to support the evidence of his eyes, that the sheaf of papers were still where he had placed them, sealed within an envelope at the bottom of the bag.

Then, almost by accident, he brushed against the tablet with his fingertips. At the same moment he glanced round guiltily, to make certain that no one had been observing him. As stealthily as he could, he drew out the tablet and rested it upon his lap, then stared over the side of the boat. The Nile was flowing deeply, its waters very dark.

Carter sat hunched a long while, frozen by his feelings of

doubt and self-reproach. He knew that what he was planning was an act of cowardice, and worse – a dereliction of all he had ever sought to be, a betrayal of every standard he held dear. He glanced back inside his bag, at the thick, sealed envelope, and shook his head. For almost twenty years the contents of that envelope had served to draw him on, strengthening his resolve, granting him self-belief, even when direct corroboration had been lacking. Now at last, so it seemed, proof of the manuscript's value lay upon his lap – for what, after all, had its argument been, if not that the Pharaoh's tomb was indeed beneath a curse? Carter smiled to himself ruefully, and stroked his moustache. He knew, of course, that there was no need to take such nonsense literally. Indeed, it had been the very presence within the manuscript of fantastical wonders, and secrets born of long-abandoned superstitions, which had first persuaded him that it might hint at something more, for he had long since learned how the myths of an age can be as distinctive as their tombs, and just as important for the archaeologist to date.

Why then, knowing all that as he did, had he found himself so unsettled by the warning on the tablet? He glanced down at it once again. Had he simply lived too long with the manuscript, he wondered, with its worlds of mystery, and impossible powers? Had it touched him more than he had ever dared to think?

Carter sighed. It was the dread that his reason might indeed have been affected, the dread that it might even come to inhibit his work, which had decided him in the end. He had been presumptuous in his fears of the workmen's superstitions; for his own, it appeared, were far more insidious a threat. Carter smiled faintly. If it took a single sacrifice to put them to rest, to appease them, well . . . the Ancients at least might have understood.

He glanced round again, to make certain that he was still not being watched. Satisfied, he raised the tablet from his lap. He rested it on the boat's edge . . . then let it drop. There was a soft splash. Carter stared behind him at where the tablet had sunk, as the boat glided on. The waters of the Nile flowed as silently as before. Only the night heron, disturbed by the noise, wheeled and cried in a startled manner as it flew away before the coming of the dawn.

At the same moment, in Carter's house, his servant was sitting on the front porch, listening to the notes of the canary in its cage, when suddenly there rose a faint, almost human cry. It was followed by a silence and the servant, straining to hear more, realised that even the canary's song had been stilled. He rose to his feet, then hurried to the room from where the scream had seemed to come. It was Mr Carter's study and upon entering it, almost instinctively, the servant turned to gaze at the cage.

It seemed filled by a monstrous form. As the servant drew nearer, he recognised the hood of a cobra, and saw that the canary was already limp within its jaws. A flicker passed through the cobra's coils, and it began to sway its head as though to strike once again. But then it reduced its hood and, dropping the bird, slipped out between the bars. As it glided towards him the servant backed against the desk, then watched in horror as the cobra drew nearer still. Fumbling desperately behind him, he found a small figurine; turning again, he raised it in his hand, but the cobra was already slipping past him, coiling up around the leg of the desk, then out through the window until, with a final, dismissive flicker of its tail, it was gone.

The servant pushed the desk aside, and hurried to the window to mark the cobra's progress across the empty yard outside. But he could see no trace of it, not even a trail left upon the dust. He shuddered suddenly, and muttered a prayer – for it was as though the cobra had vanished into air.

He turned back and crossed to the cage. Reaching inside it, very gently, he scooped out the corpse of the bird. It was only as he did so that he realised he was still clutching the tiny figurine in his other hand, and as he inspected it, so his knuckles whitened even more. For he could recognise the statue now: it was a figure of the King whose tomb had been found, and was soon to be disturbed; whose head-dress bore the figure of a cobra upraised – the King whose name, he had learned, had been Tut-ankh-Amen.

The
TALE
of the
SLEEPER
in the
SANDS

Letter from Howard Carter to Lord Carnarvon

The Turf Club,
Cairo,
20 November 1922

My dear Lord Carnarvon,
  You will know how I have ever enjoyed my time spent with you, and yet on this occasion above all others, how pleasant, how gloriously pleasant, has been the cause of our meeting with each other once again! Even so the best, I may venture to hope, is still to come and I shall duly await, with the keenest sense of anticipation, your following me onwards within the next two days. By then, I trust, all should be readied for yourself and Lady Evelyn, for my preparations here in Cairo have gone exceedingly well, and everything is now purchased which we shall require to complete our excavation. I am therefore confident that between your arrival in Thebes and the commencement of our work within the Valley of the Kings, there will be no cause for delay.
  You asked me last night what I thought we might discover beyond the doorway of our – as yet – unidentified tomb. I hesitated then, in the company of others, to reply with due

confidence; but now, putting pen to paper, I dare to proclaim that we are indeed on the threshold of a magnificent discovery, one which may grant us immortality in the annals of archaeological science. Anything – literally anything – may lie beyond the passageway. I do not speak only of artefacts or gold but of treasures, it may be a hundred times more valuable. For unless I am much mistaken, the tomb we have uncovered is that of King Tut-ankh-Amen; and if such should indeed prove to be the case, then we shall discover within it, I prophesy, the proofs of a great and ancient mystery. Once the tomb has been opened and its contents examined, our understanding of the past may be remarkably and forever changed.

You will doubtless wonder what inspires me to make such a boast, and all the more so when you recall the six years of failure we have had to endure – barren, it must have seemed to you, of even the faintest promise. Yet you will recall as well my assurances, made with all the earnestness and vigour I could muster, that the Valley of the Kings had *not* been exhausted, and how when, this summer, you finally contemplated abandoning our work, I swore that I was certain that a tomb lay undisturbed. You did not then press me to justify myself, but did me the honour instead of accepting my word. I shall ever be grateful for that mark of trust, since it is certain that, but for your untiring generosity and constant encouragement, our labours would long ago have come to naught.

Now, though, let us trust, the hour of triumph is at hand. At such a moment, my continued silence can no longer be justified. Yet as you read the papers which I have given to you, it may be you will understand my former reticence, for the story they tell is certainly a strange one. I would not have cared to stake my reputation upon it – and yet without it, as you will see, I would never have dared to believe that a

Pharaoh's tomb could indeed lie undiscovered. Therefore – please, if you can find the time, read the papers enclosed with this letter. Some are my own: biographical reminiscences composed over the course of the past month or so, once I had learned for certain that this season – unless successful – would be my last in the Valley. The other stories have a stranger origin. They have been in my possession now for many years – and yet you are the first to whom I have ever shown them. I do not, of course, need to ask you to keep silent about their contents. As you will doubtless understand once you have completed your perusal of them, the papers raise matters of considerable interest. Let us discuss them in confidence once you have joined me again at Thebes.

Until then, conserve all your energy and keep yourself well – for I do not doubt we have a good deal of hard work still ahead of us! Yet how mightily we have laboured, and how long we have searched – and now at last journey's end is drawing very near!

Look after yourself, my dear Lord Carnarvon. These papers are yours – for so also is my success.

H.C.

Narrative composed by Howard Carter, early autumn 1922

Castle Carter,
Elwat el-Diban,
The Valley of the Kings.

I am not a man who thrives upon company, and yet tonight I feel — not despair, I would say — but rather the strangest compulsion to share my confidences and to justify the unfulfilled exertions of my career. Of course, should I finish this account I shall have to keep it locked from any prying eye, and yet even so it would do me good, I believe, tonight and over the course of succeeding nights, to imagine a colleague or a friend — Lord Carnarvon, perhaps — seated opposite me, able to listen to my words even as I commit them to paper.

Nor, I must hope — even at this eleventh hour — will they moulder forever in my drawer unread. It is true that King Tut-ankh-Amen and his tomb still defy my excavations — yet though my final season in the Valley approaches, I remain confident. He shall be found — *he must be found* — for to think otherwise would indeed be to despair of my entire career. I shall never marry, I fear, and yet in truth I have been married for a long while to my hunt for this tomb. For I realise now that I had been set upon Tut-ankh-Amen's trail,

24

without my ever knowing it, within the earliest months of my arrival in Egypt – and indeed, it may be before even that occasion, for I recollect now an event in my youth, seemingly trivial and yet serving, so it strikes me at this distant remove, almost as a portent of much which was to come. It is not surprising that I failed to understand this at the time, for my prospects then were limited and circumscribed, and my passions confined to a self-taught knowledge of birds – not a great deal of use, sadly, to one having to make his way in the world. Indeed my education, as I have always regretted, was miserably incomplete, and yet there was no help for it, for there were bills to be paid and I had been set to earn my living at a very tender age. I did so at first as an assistant to my father, who worked as an illustrator in London and a portraitist in the country, a mode of employment which necessitated staying at many grand country residences. My favourite, and the one where my father was most employed, was Didlington Hall in the county of Norfolk – for the family who lived there possessed both great talent and great taste, nor did they believe that quality need necessarily be determined by good birth. Certainly, they were gracious enough to recognise within me certain talents as an artist, and so to give me the run of much of their house, for they were wonderful collectors and their every room and corridor seemed adorned with treasures. To my youthful eyes, such a trove of riches seemed a fairy tale made true, and it soon became my ambition – no, my most passionate dream – to hunt out and recover such marvels for myself.

Yet though generous and open in all other matters, there was one room to which the family barred me entry, for I was warned that its contents were especially precious. Naturally, I sought to respect their wishes – but equally naturally my interest was piqued, for human nature, I suppose, is always what it is, and all the more so when that nature is a child's.

So it was that in the end, like Bluebeard's wife, I could no longer hold out against my curiosity and crept away, while my father was occupied with his painting, to inspect the secret room. I discovered, to my surprise, that the door was unlocked and, opening it stealthily, I passed inside. The room beyond was in darkness, and for several seconds I could make out nothing at all. Feeling my way along the side of the wall, therefore, I reached for a curtain and pulled it aside, allowing a shaft of sunlight into the room. At once I gasped in wonder and surprise, as I viewed the collection of objects before me. Never had I seen such strangeness before! There were figures of stone and clay and gold, pictures painted on panels of wood, and the body of a mummy swathed in tight cloth – laid out within its coffin, for all the world as though it were asleep. The idea inspired in me a remarkable fascination, and a shiver of mingled dread and delight. I approached the mummy and gazed at it in stupefaction for a long while, then went from object to object, inspecting each one with the minutest attention. What a bizarre nature these people must have had, I thought, what bizarre patterns of behaviour, and assumptions, and beliefs, to have created such things – and yet, as was evident, they had been human just like me!

Of course, lost in my astonishment, I was at length discovered in the room – and yet, such was the kindness of my hosts and so evident, no doubt, the brightness in my eye, that I was not punished but encouraged in my enthusiasm. During the next few years, such became my taste for Egyptian art that I came to have the greatest longing to visit Egypt itself. It was now that I regretted my poverty all the more, and my lack of education too, for in truth I knew nothing of Egyptology save what I had seen at Didlington Hall, and so my understanding of it continued very small. Yet in the end, at the age of seventeen, it was to be my skill in draughtsmanship which gave me my chance to journey there, for it had been decided that a survey was required of all that country's monuments before the art upon their walls began to crumble into dust, and I was recommended by the kindness of my patrons for the post. It was not as an excavator, then, nor as anyone with any claims to specialist knowledge, but rather as a humble copyist that I first of all entered an Egyptian tomb.

What paintings I discovered there! And again, in the next tomb, and again after that – endless galleries of wonder and beauty! Alone amidst such work, with the darkness illumined only by a feeble torch, I felt all those emotions I had experienced years before amidst the private collection at Didlington Hall, yet multiplied now a thousand times, for I was standing where the Ancients had once stood themselves, and this affected me more strongly than I had ever imagined possible. I found myself impressed by a profoundest sense of timelessness, so that I would almost forget the long roll of centuries and imagine that the figures before me were freshly painted – or even, sometimes, alive upon the wall!

I recall, for instance, one example in particular which somehow served to place all my feelings on the matter into focus. It happened one afternoon that I had been copying the painted image of a hoopoe. When I had finished my work for the day, I walked to the entranceway to the tomb where I saw, to my astonishment, a living example of the very same bird – its plumage, its posture, the angle of its head, precisely the same! I felt almost shaken by the coincidence; and all the more so when, having mentioned it to my superior on the surveying team, Mr Percy Newberry, he told me that to the Ancients the hoopoe had been a bird of magical significance. I answered him that I could well believe it – for indeed, I had felt a little touched by magic myself! The idea that both I and an artist who had lived more than

4,000 years before my time could have observed and represented the same species of bird struck me with the force of a thunderclap – and I felt once again the strangest sense of how the present and the distant past might yet be linked. Inspired by such fancies, I found my own work steadily prospering and my fascination with the world of ancient Egypt, my concern to penetrate its mysteries, growing all the more. Nor did I ever cease to be struck, copying the figures before me, by how familiar they seemed – and yet, at the same moment, how very haunting and strange.

I mentioned this seeming paradox to Mr Newberry one day. He gazed at me narrowly, then asked me what I thought the explanation might be. I answered him, somewhat hesitantly, that it was perhaps a reflection upon the formalised nature of the art: that we soon grew to recognise the conventions which had governed it, while never ceasing to find them exotic. Newberry nodded slowly. 'And yet the strangest Egyptian art,' he replied, 'certainly which I have seen, is also the art in which the conventions are most radically overthrown. Some have called the result life-like.' He paused, then made a face. 'I call it grotesque.'

'Indeed?' I asked, intrigued.

'Yes,' said Newberry hurriedly. I wanted to ask him more; but he rose to his feet, and even as I opened my mouth he cut me short. 'Grotesque,' he repeated, then walked briskly away. I watched him leave, puzzled by his abruptness – for I had always found him a most communicative man. I wondered what the art could be which had affected him in such a way, but in the days which followed I chose not to press him, and Newberry himself did not mention it again. But then, shortly before Christmas, when we were due for a break from our work upon the tombs, Newberry approached me in a confidential manner and asked me if I would care to make a short trip across the desert. Not yet having left the cultivated borders of the Nile, I replied that nothing would give me greater pleasure, and indeed I felt flattered, for I was only one of three assistants upon the site and Newberry had sworn me, in offering the invitation, not to repeat it to the other two. Still, though, it seemed I was not altogether trusted, for when I asked him what our destination was to be, Newberry would only tap the side of his nose. 'You shall see,' was all he would add.

We left that same afternoon upon camels. I had never ridden upon such a beast before, and my body was very soon aching all over. Newberry must have observed my discomfort, for he laughed at me and told me I would soon be distracted from all thoughts of my bruises. Again, I pressed him to tell me by what, but he continued reticent. Instead, he urged his camel onwards and together, lumbering and swaying along the dusty track, we had soon left the palm groves of the Nile behind and passed into the desert. I was astonished by the suddenness of the transformation: one moment there had been cattle, and crops, and trees, the next nothing but a vast expanse of rock and sand. The dunes would sometimes be skimmed by a blast of hot wind, the dust lifted in a momentary veil, but otherwise all was deathly still. It was as though the very world had ended, and I at once understood, gazing out at the fiery sands, why for the Ancient Egyptians the colour of evil had been red.

Certainly, the landscape through which we rode – savage and barren, and littered with boulders – might have seemed a fitting haunt for restless demons, and I felt something almost like relief when we suddenly joined the edge of a cliff and saw the ribbon of the Nile once again below us, fringed with the green of fields and trees. We continued to follow the edge of the cliff, until at length it curved away from the river and we saw before us, hollowed out to form a natural amphitheatre, the crescent of a sandy plain. There appeared nothing of great interest upon it, only scrub and the odd low pebble-strewn mound; but I could see, toiling in the centre of the plain, gangs of white-clad workmen and, just beyond them, a line of baked-mud huts. We began to descend the cliff towards them, and as we did so, unable to restrain my curiosity any further, I demanded to know from Newberry what it was we had come to see. He answered me by sweeping outwards with his arm. 'This is known today as the plain of El-Amarna,' he replied, 'but its ancient name was Akh-et-Aten, and there once stood here, though for barely fifteen years, the capital city of a Pharaoh of Egypt.'

'Indeed?' I pointed towards the workmen. 'Then that is what is being excavated here?'

I saw a gleam of excitement in Newberry's eyes as he nodded.

'Who is leading it?' I asked.

'Mr Petrie,' he replied.

'Not Mr Flinders Petrie?'

'The very same.'

I heard this with considerable interest. Of course, I had known of that celebrated archaeologist even before my arrival in Egypt, for he had long been the dominant figure in his field. In Cairo, though, during the few days I had passed there, I had been fortunate enough to meet with him and to learn some of his opinions on Egyptology. He had struck me then as a man of considerable eccentricity, but also of remarkable discernment and vision, and so I welcomed the chance to see him at his work. As we approached the line of mud huts, Newberry called out his name and I saw – emerging from the doorway, his black beard vivid against the glare of the sands – the figure I remembered so well from before.

Yet he greeted us with no particular show of enthusiasm, making it perfectly plain that we had distracted him from his work, and asking us brusquely what our purpose was. Newberry answered that he had heard reports of a find. Petrie grunted noncommittally. 'Well,' he muttered, 'since you have ridden all this way, you had best come and see it.' First, though, he demanded that we descend from our mounts, for it was an eccentricity of his that he would never ride anywhere but always go on foot, and I, for one, was glad to leave my camel behind. We trudged together towards some distant mounds, Petrie muttering as we did so about the iniquities of the French. This was a favourite topic of his, it seemed, for the French, then as now, had a vice-like grip upon the country's *Service des Antiquités* and were determined, so Petrie claimed, to thwart his projects at every turn. 'Can you believe it,' he muttered, 'but they almost denied me the concession to dig here? *Me – Flinders Petrie!* And even as it is, I cannot excavate anywhere but here, upon the plain.' I noticed that Newberry grew pale at this and gazed around at the cliffs, almost as though he feared to see them crawling with Frenchmen. There was no one there, of course – but I found myself wondering all the more what his interest in this strange site could be.

I was soon to find out, and soon to discover what it was he hoped to find. Here, though, let me pause, for I have suddenly realised how it is grown very late, and there is work – hard work! – to be done in the morning. Let me resume, then – if my labours have not been too exhausting! – when I can, tomorrow night.

So then – to continue – the plain of El-Amarna. As we drew near to our destination, Petrie began to break into a trot. 'This was once the Great Palace,' he proclaimed as he ran up the side of the mound, then back down again to seize me by my arm. 'You, Carter,' he said. 'Are you not a painter?' But he did not wait for an answer, and I found myself being tugged across a series of mounds, still at a trot, until we came to a halt at last before a walkway of planks. It had clearly been raised with meticulous care, and I remembered Petrie's dictum, delivered to me in Cairo, that an archaeologist's duty was not only to uncover but also to be the guardian of the past. 'Come,' he said, still tugging on my arm. I followed him on to the walkway. 'There,' he said, jabbing downwards with his forefinger. 'If you are truly an artist, then tell me – what do you make of that?'

I gazed down in wonder, and not a little awe, at a pavement painted with the most exquisite designs. They had all been drawn from the beauties of nature: fish swam in lotus-filled pools, spotted cattle gambolled through fields, and cats lay stretched with eyes half-closed in the sun. Above such beasts, everywhere, seated on trees or rising up on the wing, were birds, and it was these which attracted my particular attention, for I found that I could identify almost every one. Swallows were there, and kingfishers, geese and ducks, ibises and hoopoes, all the varied birdlife which characterised the Nile. And with what freshness had they been represented, with what vivid accuracy! Certainly, in my limited experience of Egyptian art, I had seen nothing to compare with these paintings, neither for the pleasure they suggested in the world of living things nor for their exquisite naturalism of style. I turned in surprise to Newberry. 'But these are not grotesque!' I exclaimed. 'These are very miracles of delicacy!'

'Naturally,' Petrie grunted. 'It is the most important discovery, artistically, which I have ever made.'

Newberry nodded slowly. 'Then it must suggest,' he murmured, 'that the Pharaoh who commissioned such a work, the Pharaoh who desired to live in such a place, was even more extraordinary a man than we had hitherto thought.

For see – no chariots, no armies, no violent scenes of war. Only – yes . . .' – his eyes grew wide – 'the richness of life.'

Still rapt, he continued to gaze at the floor and even Petrie, surveying his find, seemed to lose some of his former gruffness. He suddenly smiled, with something almost like pride. 'He was clearly a most extraordinary man.'

I glanced at him. 'Who was?'

'Why, the Pharaoh.'

'Which Pharaoh?'

Petrie's eyebrows bristled with evident surprise 'Why, Newberry,' he exclaimed, 'you mean you have not told your assistant of Akh-en-Aten?'

'He is very new to Egypt,' answered Newberry defensively. 'You know full well that I do not tell just anyone of my hopes for this place.'

'Your hopes?' Petrie laughed dismissively. 'You are wasting your time on that particular score.'

'I cannot believe so.'

'I tell you, the French have the concession to all the cliffs hereabouts. They will have got to the tomb.'

There was an angry silence.

'Got to what tomb?' I dared to ask.

Newberry glanced at me, hesitation still in his eyes.

'Please,' I protested. I turned back to gaze down at the floor. 'If there is a mystery relating to this Akh-en-Aten, then I would dearly love to hear more about it.' I gestured towards the exquisite paintings. 'For anyone who could have delighted in the beauty of such animals and birds is surely worthy of further study.'

Petrie laughed suddenly, and clapped me on the shoulder. 'Well, you are a good-natured lad,' he exclaimed, 'and if you are concerned to know more about the Heretic King, then I shall tell you what I can, for so much at least is public property.'

'"The Heretic King"?' I asked.

'Indeed,' Petrie answered. 'For it was not in his taste alone that Akh-en-Aten was a rebel.' He clapped me on the shoulder again; then, with a sideways glance at Newberry, he began to steer me down the side of the mound and towards a further series of planks and tents. 'We found it this morning,' he said, as he lifted a flap and gestured towards a fragment of stone resting against the far side of the tent. 'Sadly damaged, but not without interest all the same.'

I approached it uncertainly, Newberry with an eagerness he did not bother to conceal. We gazed at it together in silence; and then, after an interval of several moments, Newberry glanced at me. 'You see?' he whispered. 'Did I not tell you it was remarkably grotesque?'

I did not reply, but continued to stare at the carving with astonishment. It represented a group of figures, clearly Egyptian but unlike anything I had ever seen before. There was a Pharaoh – I could tell as much from the insignia of his rank – but this one did not seem like a hero or a god. Instead he appeared strangely, almost cruelly deformed: his belly and thighs were rounded like a woman's, his calves and arms preternaturally thin, while his skull was domed and his face very long, his lips very fleshy, and his eyes like almonds. Gazing upon this extraordinary figure, I felt the touch of something icy running down my spine, for it seemed more like the portrait of a eunuch than a man, and I could not deny that it was indeed repellent and – yes – grotesque. Yet its grotesqueness did not fully explain my response to it; for there seemed something more, something which was serving to counter my initial feelings of disgust. It took me a moment to realise what this was – and then I understood. For the Pharaoh was not the only figure represented on the tablet; he was surrounded by three girls, strange-skulled like himself, two by his feet, and one in his arms, whom the Pharaoh was kissing very gently on her brow. I thought of the tombs in which I had been working, and of the books I had studied; and of how I had seen nothing in Egyptian art, nothing at all, to compare with such a tender and domestic scene of love.

'They are his daughters?' I asked.

Petrie nodded. 'Affection for his family, it would appear, was held up as the Pharaoh's great ideal of life. In the context of royal portraiture, that is something utterly extraordinary and new.'

'And why is the style of art so very strange?'

Petrie shrugged. 'Who can know what the reason was? Something remarkable, certainly, to have overturned the ancient traditions of his people.'

'There are clues,' said Newberry hurriedly. 'Scattered all about us.' He glanced at Petrie. 'Is that not so?'

'Why' – Petrie swept with his hand – 'this whole vast site is a clue.'

'Indeed?' I gazed out through the tent at the sands and scrub of the plain beyond. 'But I can see nothing.'

'Exactly!' Petrie nodded, then swept his hand again towards the barren plain. 'You can see nothing – just as Akh-en-Aten himself would have seen nothing when he first arrived here to have his city built. Yet he already had a rich and splendid capital in Thebes, beautified by his fore-fathers over many years – for Akh-en-Aten was the heir to Egypt's greatest kings, and Thebes itself was at its very apogée of wealth. Why, then, did Akh-en-Aten choose to abandon it? Why come to this barren spot, more than two hundred miles from any city at all?'

I gazed at him in bemusement, then shook my head. 'I confess, I cannot imagine a reason.'

Petrie narrowed his eyes. 'You have not yet, I assume, had the chance to visit the site of Thebes?'

'Not yet.'

'Then I trust that one day you will have the opportunity. For when you go there, you will discover that its crowning glory is the temple of Karnak, a place of stupefying, overwhelming size, a place still so vast, despite the ravages of time, that you will wonder by what power it was ever built. And yet indeed, the answer is quite simple – it was built with the tribute paid to superstition. Karnak was the home to Amen-Ra, the King of Egypt's great galaxy of gods – and therefore the focus of all the country's hopes and fears.'

'And yet Akh-en-Aten . . .'

'Abandoned it.' A faint smile flickered beneath Petrie's moustache as he knelt down almost tenderly beside the fragment of stone. 'For did I not tell you,' he asked, looking up again, 'that he had been a rebel against more than just the conventions of art?'

'What . . .' I frowned – 'so he abandoned the worship of Amen-Ra as well?'

'Proscribed him. Erased his name throughout the length of the land. That of Amen, and Osiris, and all the gods, all the ancient and myriad divinities – save only one . . .' Petrie paused and turned again to gaze at the carving. 'Save only one.' He pointed to the top of the stone, where a fragment had broken away. There were still traces there of what appeared to be hands raised in blessing over the head of the King, the arms radiating downwards like the spokes of a wheel. 'These represent the rays of the sun,' said Petrie, pointing to what I had mistaken for arms. 'The other half of the stone would have portrayed its disk.'

I gazed at the fragment's broken edge. 'So that was Akh-en-Aten's god?'

Petrie nodded. 'The sun – the Aten – the life-giving Aten, in whose honour the Pharaoh even changed his name. For once, like his father, he had been Amen-hetep – "Amen is content" – but when he came here such a title would no longer do. "Akh-en-Aten".' Petrie gazed a moment more at the figure of the King, then lumbered back to his feet. 'Which means, very simply – "the Glory of the Sun".'

He stepped out from the tent. Newberry and I joined him, and we stood there together in silence for a while. Beyond the dust-humped mounds of El-Amarna and the silhouetted palm trees of the distant Nile, the sky was clouding into dusk, and I knew that all of us were gazing at the red disk of the sun. '"Living in Truth",' murmured Petrie at length, 'that was Akh-en-Aten's motto – "*Ankh em maat*". And truthful, I think, he could indeed claim to be, when he chose to enshrine the sun's radiant energy. There is not a rag of superstition or of falsity to be found in such a worship, but rather a philosophy which our own modern science can confirm. For what is the sun indeed, if not the source of all life, power and force in our world?'

Newberry shivered suddenly. 'And yet still,' he said, pointing, 'you see how it sets.'

Petrie glanced at him strangely. 'Yes.' He grunted. 'Yet only so that it may rise once again.'

Newberry did not answer, and we left soon afterwards, for the shadows were indeed beginning to lengthen. Petrie accompanied us to our camels, and as we walked Newberry extracted solemn promises from our host that he would keep nothing from us of what he might find. Yet still the precise object of Newberry's ambitions was kept veiled from me, and I began to despair that it might ever be revealed. Once we had mounted our steeds, however, he did not retrace the path by which we had arrived but rather spurred his camel along the side of the cliffs, so that he remained upon the plain, following the edge of its curve. I assumed that this meant he had something more to show to me, and so I urged my camel after him and, once by his side, dared to ask him again what it was he hoped to find.

Newberry shifted in his saddle to inspect the distant tents and mounds of the excavation. 'Petrie is a great archaeologist,' he said at last. 'He has a flair for the minutiae of history. He can erect whole structures of understanding from the fragment of a pot. And yet . . .' – he turned again to face me – 'there are those who hunt prizes much greater than pots.'

'You are one of them, I presume?'

Newberry nodded abruptly; and I could see how, despite the shadow of the cliff, his eyes were glinting brightly. 'My God, Carter,' he exclaimed suddenly, as though his words were a torrent barely dammed until that moment, 'have you ever thought, ever considered, how little we understand of the Ancients? Yes, Petrie digs his mounds, and temples, and pots, but what do they truly tell us? No more than a skull can tell us of what a dead man once dreamed. And what dreams – what wondrous dreams! – the people who dwelt in this land must have had. Those are what I hunt!' In his passion he had reached across from his saddle, and now he pulled upon my arm. 'The long-forgotten mysteries of those ancient times!'

'Mysteries?' I frowned at him. 'I don't understand. What can you mean?'

Newberry checked himself as though suddenly embarrassed. 'The Greeks spoke of them.' His tone was more reserved and sober once again. 'Even the Egyptians themselves, in dark, uncertain hints, in terms of nervous awe. Of the wisdom possessed by the priests – something ancient, very ancient, and impossibly strange.' He swallowed, then looked away. 'Nor, I believe . . .' he swallowed again – 'the rumours that I spoke of . . . they are not altogether dead.'

'What do you mean?' I exclaimed a second time.

'The peasants hereabouts – the *fellahin* . . .' – he turned back to me – 'they too have strange stories.'

'Of what?'

Newberry shook his head.

'I am intrigued,' I continued, 'but I can scarcely believe . . .'

'What? That the past might run so deep?'

I did not answer him, astonished by the sudden violence of his tone. Newberry must have observed my look of surprise, for he reached out again and gently squeezed my arm. 'History around here is like the Nile itself,' he said, more calmly now. 'An eternal, ceaseless flow. Statues and pots lie preserved beneath the sands. Why should not traditions linger on as well?'

I trusted that my expression did not betray my feelings of doubt. 'And what is the particular tradition you have heard?'

'That there is a tomb hereabouts, still hidden, the object of a curse.' Newberry paused. 'A tomb which had once belonged to a King.'

'Akh-en-Aten?'

Newberry shrugged very faintly. 'This is what the folk tales report of the King. He had not been a worshipper of idols like the other Pharaohs, but rather a true Muslim; for he had believed in Allah, the one and only God. In the name of this God, the King had driven all the demons from the land, and their priests from the temples which they had stained with living blood. But the ambitions of the King betrayed him in the end, for he was afraid of death and wished to live for ever; and so he sought to discover the hidden name of God. He fell like Lucifer, whom the peasants hereabouts know as Iblis, Prince of the Jinn. A curse was laid upon his tomb that he, who had sought eternal life, should now for ever be restless in death. And so he remains even to this day, a demon whose breath is the winds of the desert — and the womenfolk scare their children with his tale.'

He paused, then smiled. 'I apologise,' he murmured,

suddenly diffident, 'for the perhaps melodramatic nature of my tone. Yet it is an intriguing story, I think you will agree.'

'But . . .' I frowned, and shook my head. 'A myth, surely?'

'And what are myths, if not the expression of some hidden or forgotten truth?'

'Yet . . . the vast length of time we are talking about – what exactly were Akh-en-Aten's dates?'

'He reigned, it is thought, around 1350 BC.'

'Then how could the tradition possibly have been preserved from such a time?'

'Oh, with the greatest ease,' answered Newberry airily. 'Arab folk tales are directly descended from the traditions of Ancient Egypt. If you do not believe me, then you need only compare the Westcar Papyrus with the cycle of "The Arabian Nights".'

Never then having heard of the Westcar Papyrus, I did not know how to reply to this assertion; but I must still have looked doubtful, for Newberry began impatiently to list the parallels between Akh-en-Aten and the peasants' folk tale king – how they had both sought to overthrow an ancient priestcraft, how they had both been the worshippers of a single god . . .

'And his end?' I interrupted him. 'What did happen to Akh-en-Aten in the end?'

'We cannot be certain,' Newberry answered promptly. 'But his revolution' – he shifted in his saddle, to gaze back at the dusty, abandoned plain – 'it clearly did not last.'

'And his children?'

Newberry frowned. 'What do you mean?'

'In the fragment Petrie showed us – the King appeared surrounded by his children. He must have had heirs.'

'Two sons, Petrie thinks.'

'Then what happened to them? Why did they not carry on their father's work?'

'Again' – Newberry shrugged – 'we cannot be certain. The first son, it would appear from the evidence of Petrie's excavations, reigned here no more than two or three years. And then in the second son's reign – we can be confident of this much at least – El-Amarna was abandoned, and the court restored to Thebes.'

'Why can we be so confident?'

'Because, just as his father had changed his name, so did this King as well. He had first been known as Tut-ankh-Aten – or in English, "the Living Image of the Sun". But when he returned to Thebes, and to the influence of the priests of Karnak, such a title was clearly impossible to keep. So you can imagine what new name he chose to adopt.'

'Indeed?'

'Think, Carter, think.'

I shook my head.

'Why, what else could it have been' – Newberry paused to smile – 'but Tut-ankh-*Amen*? "The Living Image of Amen" – you see?' His smile grew wistful. '*Tut-ankh-Amen*.'

And so I heard, for the first time, the name of that King who was one day to shadow all my ambitions and hopes, and become in due course the very object of my life. And indeed, almost as though in witness of the moment, even as Newberry pronounced the fateful name so we rounded an outcrop of jagged rock and I saw ahead of us, guarding the entrance to a narrow ravine, a carving hewn out from the wall of the cliff. Newberry gestured to it. 'You can see here,' he proclaimed, 'what on Petrie's fragment had been incomplete.' I gazed up at the carving. Although still seated in my saddle, the figures it portrayed rose high beyond my eye-level. I recognised the Pharaoh, Akh-en-Aten, at once: his appearance was, if anything, more grotesque than it had seemed upon the earlier frieze. He was standing with arms outstretched to greet the welcoming rays of the sun. Two girls were behind him, very small, their appearance likewise even more bizarre than before. But there was also a second adult figure, a woman, who wore upon her head the crown of a queen; and she, although just as distorted in her features as the others, did not seem, for all that, grotesque in the least. Far from it – for the strangeness of her appearance lent her a loveliness which was both unsettling and profound, a beauty which seemed almost to be not of this world. I strained to inspect her more closely, puzzled by this mystery; and even as I urged my camel closer to the carving, so the angle of the sunlight changed and all the figures were stained a dark red, and then the beam itself was gone and the carving cast into darkness.

'We must hurry,' said Newberry. 'We do not want to be out in the desert late at night.' Yet even as he said this, he continued to stare up at the weird carving of the Pharaoh, as though he could not bear to look away. 'It would be a grand thing,' he whispered, 'to discover the tomb. A grand thing indeed.'

'And if we were successful' – I paused – 'what then? What do you hope to discover inside?'

It took Newberry a moment to reply. 'A darkness rendered light,' he answered at last, 'a mystery solved. For that the fate of Akh-en-Aten is a mystery, both science and legend can agree.'

I laughed. 'Legend claims that he never even rested in the tomb.'

Newberry glanced round at me irritably. 'In the end,' he muttered, 'who knows what we may find?' He stared up at the carving one final time, then urged his camel onwards. 'For that is the mystery – the great mystery, and the prize.'

We began our search early the next morning. I had been sworn once again to the profoundest secrecy, and we left the camp as quietly as we could, for Newberry could not endure the thought that others should learn of our ambitions. I doubted, though, that our departures would long remain concealed, for the camel is not the most discreet of beasts, and I knew that my colleagues, Blackden and Fraser, were both observant men. When I mentioned this to Newberry, however, and suggested we bring them into the search, a look of near panic passed across his face. 'No, no,' he insisted, 'we must keep this to ourselves'; and he began to speak to me again of his hopes of the tomb, of the many mysteries it might prove to contain. 'We must keep this as quiet as we can.' And in truth, I was content to do as he said, for the passion of his enthusiasm was infecting me strongly and I was experiencing for the first time what I had long desired to feel – the thrill of a quest.

We concentrated our efforts on the rocks above the plain. Whenever we passed into the desert, I was filled, leaving the Nile behind and gazing at the red sands piled against the sky, with the strangest sense that the world had been ended, that all was silent, and empty, and vast. As we laboured in our search, poking about amidst gullies and clefts, Newberry would tell me of the legend of Seth, the ancient god of darkness and evil, who had once sought to seize the throne of the world from Osiris, his brother. The resulting conflict had been terrible and long; but Seth, in the end, had been overthrown and banished to the deserts which stretched beyond the Nile. There he had reigned as the spirit of confusion, eternally restless, and hungry for revenge. When the fiery winds began to blow across the river, and the fields be lost to the encroachments of the sands, then the Ancient Egyptian would pray with fear in his heart that Seth was not seeking to return from the desert, that the realm of darkness might not be restored. At night, when the gales swept in from the endless deserts, he would pray all the more; for he would know that he was hearing the devil-god's screams.

'Remarkable,' I commented. 'Just as the peasants today, in the story you have told me, hear the screams of the spirit of the restless King.'

'Remarkable indeed.' Newberry smiled at me. 'The persistence of these myths never ceases to amaze.'

Nor, so far as Newberry himself was concerned, to inspire. His excitement may well be imagined when, on the third day of our search, we were approached by three *bedawin* who spoke to us of tombs buried deep within the desert. The *bedawin* had clearly learned of Newberry's obsession, for when he mentioned to them the folk tale of the restless King, they smiled and nodded: 'Yes, yes, that King!' We mounted our camels in a flurry of excitement, and the *bedawin* led us for several hours across the sands, until at length we discovered an ancient road. Following this for a couple more hours, we arrived at a deep and extensive gorge where veins of salmon pink ran through gleaming white calcite; and we could see, piled against these cliffs, heaps of rubble and limestone chippings. Newberry dismounted from his camel and hurried across to them. He picked up a handful, inspected them for a moment, then flung them down again. 'But this is a quarry!' he exclaimed. The disappointment on his face was almost painful to behold. 'Nothing but a quarry!'

He strode across to the *bedawin*, and spoke angrily with them. I saw the *bedawin* point, and then Newberry reach into his pocket for more coins. He handed them across impatiently, as one of the *bedawin* dismounted and began to pass further into the ravine.

I hurried after Newberry. 'What did he say?'

'He claims – so far as I could make him out – that the King made sacrifices here, when he succumbed to temptation and became a servant of Iblis.' Newberry paused, his doubt and disappointment still evident on his face. 'He claims there are inscriptions marking the site.'

'What about the tombs?'

Newberry's lips tightened, and he pointed to mine shafts dug into the cliffs. 'Those are the so-called tombs.' He shrugged in despair. 'So God knows what the inscriptions will turn out to be.'

I looked ahead at the *bedawin*. He had stopped by a fork in the ravine, and when we joined him he pointed into the shadows of one of the clefts. Newberry ordered him to lead on; but the *bedawin* shuddered and shook his head. He muttered a garbled prayer, then suddenly began to scamper back the way he had come. Newberry watched him go with undisguised contempt. 'These people!' he muttered, passing into the cleft.

I followed him; and the moment I did so felt suddenly cold. We had been walking in shadow before, but the darkness now seemed icy and black, and I found myself shuddering just as the *bedawin* had done. I called out to Newberry to ask him if he felt it. He turned round impatiently. 'Feel what?' he barked. But I could not reply. My throat felt hoarse – parched with a baffling, unaccountable fear.

As I joined Newberry at the end of the cleft, I asked him again if he could not sense something strange about the place. But he was too distracted even to have heard me, and pointed instead to the innermost wall of the cleft. 'Well,' he muttered despondently, 'there it is.' I gazed at where he was pointing. There was an inscription, clearly visible, chiselled out from the rock, and above it the disk of a sun with its rays curling downwards. Two figures could just be made out squatting underneath it; both were very worn, but seemed to represent a man and a woman.

For a moment my heart had leapt, but then, as I studied the inscription itself, I frowned in disappointment and puzzlement. 'Is it Arabic?' I asked, for my knowledge of that language was as yet rudimentary. I reached up to trace the inscription with my finger, then glanced back at Newberry. 'Can you read what it says?'

He shook his head. 'I'm afraid my knowledge of the lingo's only good enough to know when the beggars want more *backseesh* out of me.'

'Should we note it down, then?'

Newberry frowned. 'Why should we do that?'

'Well' – I pointed to the figure of the sun – 'it seems so similar to the portraits of the Aten.'

'I suppose there is a superficial resemblance. But it is clearly of a piece with the Arabic inscription. That is hardly going to lead us to Akh-en-Aten's tomb.'

'But you said yourself . . .'

'Yes?'

'How history in Egypt runs very deep.'

'Not that deep, old man.' Newberry gazed reproachfully up at the sun once again. 'Why, at the very earliest, it must date from almost two thousand years after Akh-en-Aten's death. No use at all. No, no – this whole damn place is a busted flush.' He kicked at a stone with sudden violence. 'Come on, Carter. Let's get out of here.' He turned and walked briskly back down the ravine. I pulled out a piece of paper and quickly scribbled the inscription down, then hurried after him, almost at a run. It will sound queer, I know, and it is hard to explain, but I had no wish to be left on my own in that place, for even as we rode back across the desert I imagined that the chill of its shadows lingered upon my skin. As a wind began to blow, the sand rising in whirls upon its shriek, I remembered the ancient superstitions and could almost believe that I was listening to Seth, stirred from

46

his rocky sleep, and risen once again to claim back the world.

We arrived back at last, feeling weary and depressed. Not surprisingly in view of our state, Blackden and Fraser asked us where we had been. I told them about our discovery of the quarry, but nothing more. I noticed, however, that they both exchanged glances, and I knew that our purpose would not remain a secret for long. Newberry himself was growing steadily more frantic as the days slipped by and nothing more was found; and the more frantic he grew, so the more hap-hazard our search came to seem.

At length, the period of our holiday came to an end and I prepared to return to my work in the tombs. Newberry, however, had other plans, for he told me he had arranged with my sponsors that I should move to El-Amarna, where Petrie had offered to train me up as an excavator. Of course, I knew full well what Newberry's motive was in all this: he wanted his own man in residence on the site, so that he would learn at once of any significant finds. But what did I care? Petrie was the greatest archaeologist of the age – and now he had offered to teach me all he knew. Me! – a mere draughtsman – in Egyptological terms, the lowest of the low! What would I not have done to be granted such a chance? I had been in Egypt a bare few months, but already it had confirmed me in all my boyhood fascination, and I knew that it had become my great love and perhaps, I thought, my fate. The lure of its mysteries had me in their grip – and it had grown my profoundest hope that I too, one day, would be an archaeologist myself.

I trusted that Petrie, who was self-taught himself, would understand this ambition – and yet it was just as well that I possessed it, for he was not to prove an easy taskmaster. I had learned before of his eccentricities; now I was to suffer their full effect. My first day he put me to building a hut; for I found that – like furniture and linen – servants were sternly tabooed. The result of my efforts could hardly rank as luxury – nor could the conditions under which I was then set to work. There was to be no galloping about in the pursuit of lost tombs now; rather, a painstaking sifting of rubble and dust; no searching for hidden mysteries or treasure; rather for shattered statues, the fragments of pots, and all the scattered pieces of an impossible jigsaw. How I loathed my teacher, for he was a pedant of the most ruthless and bloody-minded kind. And yet how I reverenced him as well, for he was certainly a genius as Newberry had claimed, with the most extraordinary aptitude for interpreting history out of chaos. I began to understand, as I sweated and toiled beneath the midday sun, how archaeology is dependent upon meticulous research – not the giddy pursuit of some dramatic find, but rather the labour of months, perhaps even years, and the mapping of an infinite number of clues. Petrie taught me, in short, the ABC of my profession – how an excavator must be a man of patience and of science.

Yet for all the enthusiasm with which I accepted these lessons, I sometimes found myself missing Newberry – his faith in the extraordinary, the sense of passion he had brought to his quest. Petrie, I knew, mistrusted such emotions, and it was with something almost like relish that he informed me one morning, as I was panning mounds of dirt, that some French officials had been seen upon the cliffs. 'I won't let them come *here*,' he proclaimed, extending his arms outwards to gesture at the plain, 'for all this site has been allocated to me, and to me alone. But if the French want to come and have a poke amongst the cliffs, then, well . . .' – he paused, and stroked his beard – 'I think we can guess what it is they hope to find.'

I was not surprised that same afternoon when Newberry joined us, for his expression made it clear that he had also heard the news. He told us that he was planning to pay a visit on the French, and asked us if we would care to accompany him. The three of us duly set off into the desert, Newberry appearing much distracted, when suddenly he froze and his face grew pale. 'There,' he said, pointing. We looked – and saw the prints of boots in the sand. Such a sight in the desert is a rare enough thing, and so we at once set off in pursuit of the trail. It led us for several miles over the sands, and then into a jagged and savage ravine. Down ahead of us we could see two figures, and as we slithered after them the mystery was solved. It was Blackden and Fraser – both leading mules which were loaded down with spades.

Newberry greeted the two men with barely suppressed fury. 'What do you think you are doing?' he exclaimed. When Blackden muttered an inaudible reply, Newberry seized him by his shirt. '*What have you been doing?*'

Blackden suddenly laughed. 'Why,' he answered coolly, 'hunting for the tomb of Akh-en-Aten.'

Newberry breathed in deeply. 'And did you not realise,' he hissed, 'that I was hunting for the tomb myself?'

'Oh, indeed,' Blackden replied. 'But one man may observe what another man overlooks. For instance' – he drew out from his pocket a sheaf of papers – 'we have completed a survey of the quarry in the desert. You missed some intriguing Middle Kingdom graffiti.' He handed the papers across. 'I have taken the liberty of publishing the details myself.'

Newberry gazed at the papers in disbelief. 'But . . . but I discovered the quarry,' he stammered.

'Not the graffiti though,' Blackden replied. 'Some of it is really very interesting indeed.'

'Of course,' Fraser added, 'we perfectly understand that you were . . . *preoccupied* . . . with your search for Akh-en-Aten's tomb. But that need not concern you any more. For we have just discovered' – he smiled maliciously – 'that the tomb has been found.'

'Wha . . .' Newberry mopped at his brow. 'Where?' he whispered. 'Where?'

Fraser pointed. 'At the end of the *wadi*.'

Newberry gazed at him in fury and disbelief. A spasm seemed to pass across his face, before he turned and hurried off.

'There is no point in calling on them,' Blackden called out. 'We have just been there ourselves, and they are not allowing anyone to look at the tomb.' But Newberry, if he had heard him, gave no sign of it but continued to storm his way up the valley. Neither Petrie nor I sought to follow him.

I heard later that he had abandoned his work altogether and left for England, vowing that he would never return to Egypt. A few months previously, perhaps, I would have been astonished at such a display of intemperance, and not believed that the search for a tomb could grow so desperate and obsessive, nor that it could breed such heated rivalries. Now, though, already I could understand it, perhaps even almost share in it myself. Certainly, as Petrie expressed it one evening, the affair did not leave a pleasant taste in the mouth. 'Learn your lesson,' he advised me. 'Do not focus your energies on a single goal, for then you run the risk of missing much else.' I nodded: the point was well made. But then I reached inside my pocket and felt the paper with the inscription I had copied from the quarry. There was another lesson too, I thought, which one could draw from the affair: if you have picked up a trail, then keep it to yourself. In Egypt, closeness did not have to be a fault.

Some days later, in early January, Petrie gained permission to visit the much-searched-for tomb. I accompanied him in a mood of considerable excitement, for I was still intrigued to know what wonders it might prove to contain. My imaginings, however, were to be sorely disappointed. The tomb itself seemed empty, and even the paintings on the wall had been vandalised. I gazed about me in puzzlement. Was this what Newberry had sought so desperately to find? I wondered again what he had been expecting to uncover. I could recall vague talk of a secret wisdom: a deadly secret, faintly remembered – transcribed into the folk tale of a restless King. I turned to the Frenchman who was showing Petrie round. 'What of the mummy?' I asked as I peered into the darkness. 'Have you found any trace of Akh-en-Aten himself?'

The Frenchman answered my question with the wryest of smiles, and beckoned us to follow him. We passed into the darkness, along an endless corridor and then, descending steeply, down a flight of stone steps; beyond lay a chamber, pillared around its edges, and as the Frenchman lifted his torch I gazed about me at the burial room.

Everywhere there was evidence of the most violent destruction. Reliefs on the walls had been literally defaced, for wherever the heads or names of figures had been painted, the plaster on the stone had been gouged away. The floor was covered with rubble, and as we picked our way across it I recognised a shattered sarcophagus, its base barely distinguishable, for its sides, like the plaster, had been smashed into pieces. I bent down and picked up a fragment of the stone. Holding it to the light, I recognised it as granite. 'What an effort it must have cost to shatter this,' I exclaimed. I looked about me again at the debris in the chamber. 'It is as though someone wished to obliterate the very memory of the person who was laid here.'

'Yes,' nodded Petrie. 'I do not think there can be much doubt on that score.' He turned to the Frenchman. 'Can you even be certain this was Akh-en-Aten's tomb at all?'

The Frenchman replied in his own language, which I did not understand, but I saw him pointing to a cartouche – the traditional oval which framed the name of every Pharaoh – still preserved above the door. Petrie inspected it closely, then turned back to me. 'Well' – he shrugged – 'a single cartouche, and that is all which has endured. It must have been overlooked in the general destruction.'

I shook my head, and gazed again about me at the ruin. 'But why all this effort to destroy his name?'

'Who can say? He was, after all, the Heretic King – and heresies, by their nature, endanger established powers.'

'You think, then, it was the priests of Amen who caused this to be done?'

Petrie picked up a fragment of the sarcophagus. 'Doubtless,' he answered, inspecting it closely. 'He had closed down their temple, and threatened their power. They certainly had reason to execrate his memory.' He paused, then crossed to a figure whose face had been obliterated. 'And yet . . .' he murmured, frowning. 'And yet . . .' He traced the hole which had been made in the plaster, and then a second. 'The violence of the loathing is most certainly extraordinary. As though it expresses not just hatred, but almost a fear – as though even his appearance could inspire them with terror. And not just Akh-en-Aten's. For look . . .' He pointed to a further painting on the wall. 'See. Here are his children represented. They have all been defaced. And everywhere – not only here, but throughout the length of Egypt – we find the same thing repeated: an attempt to wipe out all memory of Akh-en-Aten and his line.'

'Indeed?' I gazed at him in surprise. 'I had not realised that. Surely his dynasty was the royal one?'

'So it was.' Petrie nodded to himself. 'One which had borne a countless number of Pharaohs. And yet Akh-en-Aten's two sons, so it seems, were the last.'

I struggled to remember what Newberry had told me of them before – and especially of the King who had altered his name. 'Tut-ankh-Amen?' I asked.

'Yes.' Petrie glanced at me. 'I am surprised you know of him.'

'I know of his name and nothing more.'

'Then you know all there is to know. And of his predecessor, Smenkh-ka-Re, there is even less known. They reigned, they died – the rest is shadow. Such was the extent of the priests' success. Before this century, and the first excavations here, no one even knew that such a king as Akh-en-Aten had ever reigned.'

'I had not realised that the oblivion had been so complete.'

Petrie nodded. 'Oh, yes. There is not a single mention of him in an extant Egyptian record. It seems that even his name was laid beneath a curse.'

'Yes,' I said softly. I thought of the legend of the restless King; and then I looked once again at the abandoned sarcophagus. 'A terrible curse indeed.'

And certainly it was a relief, after our inspection of the chamber, to climb back to the doorway and catch a glimpse of the bright blue sky beyond. Petrie, I think – just like myself – had been strangely disturbed by our visit to the tomb, for he brooded in silence as we walked back to the plain and seemed lost all that evening in a spirit of melancholy. Later, as we sat around the fire, he spoke of Akh-en-Aten, and the mysteries of his reign, in terms which reminded me almost of Newberry. 'I imagined,' he told me, 'standing in the tomb, that the very air was infected with an ancient desolation. It is not my usual habit to acknowledge such a fancy, and yet – in the darkness of that chamber – how the shadows seemed to linger!' He reached forward and prodded the fire, a trail of orange sparks rising and then fading into the night. 'What secrets might that tomb not conceal,' Petrie exclaimed suddenly, 'to cause such an aura of evil and despair? For if any Pharaoh deserved a better memorial it was surely Akh-en-Aten. Not for him the ambitions of his conquering forefathers – their plundering, self-glorifying, pompous cruelties. Only the light, and the truth, and the life of the sun. And yet . . .' – Petrie paused, then frowned – 'I wonder . . .' He rose to his feet; and gazed towards the distant silhouette of the cliffs. 'How to explain what I felt in the tomb?' He stood in silence a long while, then shrugged impatiently. 'So many mysteries – so few answers, it seems.' His expression, I thought, appeared almost weary. 'But such is ever the nature of our profession, I am afraid.'

Even so, it seemed that Petrie had still not wholly despaired of finding out more. Some days later he told me that he had gained permission for me to copy the reliefs from the walls, and so I found myself, for the second time, in Akh-en-Aten's tomb. Petrie had not needed to tell me to keep my eyes open; yet although I had my own curiosity to satisfy as well as his own, I could discover nothing which struck me as especially strange. It was true that the ruin of the frescoes had not been as total as had at first been assumed: in one of the side-chambers especially, entire scenes could be made out, barely damaged at all. The most striking was also the most pathetic and affecting: the King and Queen were shown in mourning for a child, a little girl, laid out upon a bier. The King was clearly weeping and I was affected – studying this portrait of love, this outgushing from the heart of a man long dead and gone – with the strangest sense that he was not dead at all but behind me, bent low across his daughter, casting the funeral dust into the air. I spun round, startled – there was no one there, of course. But at the same moment, even as I turned, my eye was caught by something else and, as I saw it in my torchbeam, I felt my heart seem to stop.

Painted in the corner, so far back in the shadows that I might easily have missed it, was the figure of a sun. But it was not in the style of the other frescoes: rather it had been painted roughly, as though in a great hurry, and had I not seen the same design before, I might never have recognised it. Yet as I stepped forward, I knew I was not mistaken: it was identical to the sun I had seen carved in the quarry, and below it were the same two squatting figures, and then a line of Arabic script. Such resemblances, I knew, could not be mere coincidence; and it was with a shaking hand, and much excitement, that I reached for my pen to copy them out.

Once I had finished, I laid my drawing board aside and would have turned away, save that as I started to do so my torch caught something more, a touch of colour, very faint, upon the wall. I strained to inspect it more closely until I could just make out, beneath the rough strokes of the painted sun, the figure of a woman. As I studied it, and realised what it was, so again I felt a sudden shock. The portrait was clearly of a piece with the other artwork on the walls, for it had been painted in the familiar style of Akh-en-Aten's reign; but, whether as a consequence of its obscure position or for some other reason, it had survived the fanatic zeal which had destroyed so much else within the tomb. Certainly, I thought, gazing upon the face of the woman, there was a quality which might well have served to hold a desecrator's hand, for so great was her beauty, and so unsettling its nature, that it almost froze me to gaze upon it. Her head, impossibly massive upon a slender neck, seemed like a monstrous orchid swaying upon its stem; her black-rimmed stare was exalted and cold; her lips, half-formed between a smile and a frown, appeared to hint at deathly and unfathomable depths. Only these lips had retained their former brightness, for despite the passage of millennia they were still a fresh and vivid red – the same colour, I realised suddenly, as the graffito of the sun.

I had suspected at once whom the portrait portrayed. I bent down closer to search for a script, and found it, almost obliterated beneath a brush-stroke of red paint, by the side of the head. I had been learning the rudiments of hieroglyphics, and was able to trace, very haltingly, the syllables painted on the wall. *Nef-er-ti-ti*. I smiled to myself. So my supposition had been correct. 'Nefer-titi' – 'She-Who-Comes-In-Beauty'. Akh-en-Aten's Queen.

There were more hieroglyphics running in a line down the wall. I permitted myself a second smile. Petrie, I knew, would be exceedingly intrigued, for Nefer-titi, like her husband, was a figure of great mystery, and I too, ever since my first glimpse of her carved upon the cliff, had found myself haunted by the image of the Queen. She had come in beauty – so much her name had proclaimed; but almost nothing else about Nefer-titi was known. Although it had been the infallible custom for a Pharaoh to take his own sister as Queen, Akh-en-Aten as ever had trampled on tradition. Who Nefer-titi really was, and where she had come from, were questions still unanswered. Certainly, she had not belonged to Egypt's royal line. Petrie, I knew, had his own ideas – but there was a sorry lack of proof. I reached once again for my drawing board. I could not read the hieroglyphs, but if I copied them, Petrie would be able to. Who knew what information they might not prove to contain?

Who indeed? Even as I sit here almost thirty years later, in the afternoon warmth of the Theban sun, such a question must serve to chill me still. I am not, I think, by nature an over-imaginative man, and let me state, in mitigation of my youthful folly, that it taught me a lesson I have always remembered. It is all too easy for an archaeologist, eager in the pursuit of knowledge, to forget that a tomb is something more than a mere repository of historical details. It is also a place where the dead have been laid; and although, of course, I have no time for such fancies as ghosts, it is possible all the same for the dead to surprise those who would ignore them altogether.

Certainly, I was taught so that day. For I imagined, in the darkness of the tomb as I gazed at the face of Nefer-titi, that I saw her smile start to broaden, and her eyes to gleam; and I felt such a horror that I was paralysed. I thought suddenly how I had never seen a look so terrible; and even as I imagined that she was coming alive, so also I knew she was not human at all but something alien, and monstrous, and terribly dangerous. Of course I recognised, even as I conceived this, that such a fantasy was nonsense, and I forced myself to turn and rub my eyes. When I gazed upon the portrait of the Queen once again, all was as before, save that in the light of the torch her lips seemed somehow fuller than before. Intrigued despite myself, I brought the torch closer; yet even in the full glare of its beam, my hallucination persisted. So startled was I by this delusion, that I – God, but I blush even to set this down – I bent down lower, as though to kiss the lips with my own, and reached out with my finger to touch the portrait's cheeks. As I did so, the whole frieze seemed to shimmer before my gaze, like a true ghost indeed – a veil of infinite shimmering points, risen from the wall and hung upon the air. Then it collapsed and the image was gone, crumbled into a powder of fine dust upon the floor. Where the portrait had been there was only naked rock.

I never told Petrie. My sense of shame and guilt was too great. I sought instead, during the course of the following weeks, to make amends for my folly by uncovering something else – some object of great beauty, perhaps, or historical worth; but alas, my efforts were to little purpose, and I found nothing to compare with the find I had destroyed. However, I did, towards the end of our excavations on the site, show Petrie my copies of the Arabic inscriptions. He was briefly intrigued by the image of the sun and its worshippers, but just as Newberry had done, he scoffed at the idea that an Arab might have copied the art of Akh-en-Aten's reign. 'Such a theory,' he told me, 'although very original no doubt, has not the slightest foundation. Inspect the evidence more closely, Carter, and you will see how the idea must melt into air.' Such a reproof was more painful than he could know, and so I pressed him no more. However, despite the brusqueness of Petrie's rejection, I could not believe that the inscriptions were without significance at all – and it amused me sometimes, in my more extravagant moments, to believe them a mystery of great significance indeed.

Two late discoveries in particular encouraged me to persist with this view. The first was the translation of the two lines of Arabic, which I had initially feared to be without meaning at all. Petrie himself, although reasonably versed in the language, had been unable to make sense of the copies I had made, and when he approached one of the nearby village elders and showed the two lines of Arabic to him, the old man had frowned and shrugged his shoulders. Such a disappointment might have seemed decisive – save that I had observed how, when the old man had first gazed upon the lines, he had appeared to start and his face had grown pale. The next day, while Petrie was away elsewhere upon the site, I approached his foreman, and asked him if he could translate the two lines for me. The foreman, who spoke tolerable English, agreed willingly enough; but the moment he inspected them, he too grew pale and began to shake his head. But he could not, as the village elder had done, deny to me that he recognised the lines, and so I was determined to know what their meaning might be.

'Very bad,' the foreman stammered. 'Very bad indeed. Not good to know.'

'Why not?' I asked, growing more and more intrigued.

The foreman gazed about him as though searching for help, but none was forthcoming, and so he shook his head once more and breathed in deeply. 'This,' he whispered, 'this is a curse.' He pointed to the line I had copied from the quarry. 'The curse of Allah. "Leave forever," it says. "You are damned. You are accursed." So it is written in the Holy Koran.'

'And who is the object of Allah's curse?'

Now the foreman began visibly to shake. 'Iblis,' he stammered. 'Iblis, the Evil One, the angel who fell. And so, you see, please, sir – it is not good to know.'

I ignored his plea and pointed to the second line. 'And this one?' I asked him. 'Is this one too from the Holy Koran?'

The foreman's nervousness now was almost painful to behold. He muttered something softly, then moaned and shook his head.

'I am sorry,' I pressed him. 'I did not quite catch that.'

'No,' he whispered. 'It is a very wicked verse. Not a verse from the Holy Koran at all. The Holy Koran was written by Allah. But this' – he pointed – 'it was written by Iblis . . . written to deceive.'

'What does it mean?'

Again he shook his head, but with the assistance of a considerable financial inducement, I was able to help him to overcome his qualms. He took the sheet of paper, and in a ghastly whisper he traced the meaning of the script. '"Have you thought upon Lilat," he read, "the great one, the other? She is much to be feared. Truly, Lilat is great amongst gods."' He stared at me wide-eyed. 'That is what it says.'

'Who is Lilat?'

The foreman shrugged.

'You must know.'

'It is forbidden to know.'

I tried to offer him more money, but this time he would not accept it, and again he shook his head. 'Truly,' he protested, 'I do not know. A great demon – much to be feared – but otherwise, sir . . . truly – I cannot say. I am sorry, sir. *I cannot say.*'

I believed him; and indeed, hearing his talk of demons, I was suddenly gripped by a sense of the ridiculousness of it all. I dismissed the foreman and, left alone, smiled ruefully at the thought of how my careful investigations, pursued with such hope and with such high ambitions, had led me into nothing but a morass of superstition. Iblis! Lilat! Verses from the Koran! What had I to do with such mumbo-jumbo? The very thought of it served to fill me with shame. I returned to my excavations; and as I resumed the hard work of sifting fragments from the sands, I vowed to banish all wild conjectures from my mind for ever.

I stayed true to this resolution for the next few weeks – and indeed, would willingly have continued to do so had I not made, in the final days of our excavations at El-Amarna, a second and far more startling find. I say it was I who made the find – but that is not strictly true, for as summer came on and the temperatures rose, so also I began to suffer from the heat and then to grow quite ill. It was while I was seeking to recuperate one midday beneath the shelter of some palm trees that a workman came to me. He held out his hand and I saw, gleaming upon his palm, a beautiful golden ring. I took it with no especial show of enthusiasm, for I was still feeling faint, when suddenly, gazing upon it, all my strength was restored. I inspected the design on the ring with disbelief, rubbed my eyes, then inspected it again. Yet there could be no mistake – I had recognised it at once: two figures crouching beneath the disk of the sun. I paid the workman, then hurried to my tent. I drew out my papers, and found the copies I had made of the two Arabic designs. I compared them with the ring. I breathed in deeply . . . they were the same in every way.

I returned to search out the workman. He led me to where he had made the discovery and I realised, inspecting the stratum of rubble, that the ring was certainly an artefact from the age of Akh-en-Aten, for it had been found amidst brickwork and shards of pottery all dateable to Akh-en-Aten's reign. Yet despite the evidence before my own eyes, I could still barely credit it, even less explain what it appeared to suggest. For how *could* the designs – separated in time by more than two thousand years – be so clearly identical? Was it just a coincidence? Or maybe, somehow, something more? I had no way of answering these questions – yet at least I could now be certain that they needed to be asked.

Not at El-Amarna, though, for soon after the excavation was brought to a close, and with the end of the season I left the site for good. What I had learnt there, however, was to alter the entire course of my life. Under Petrie's supervision, I had begun my transformation into an archaeologist, a true professional, able to dig and examine systematically, and to temper the wildness of my untutored enthusiasms. But I had also, so I thought, stumbled upon the evidence of a remarkable and puzzling enigma – one which was to haunt me, as it proved, for the length of my career.

After leaving El-Amarna, I was fortunate, in the autumn of 1893, to obtain a post which kept alive my concern with the mystery. Indeed, I was fortunate to obtain a post at all, for I had briefly feared that I would be left unemployed and with no alternative but to depart Egypt altogether. However, with the assistance and recommendation of my former patrons, I was able not only to continue at work in the country, but to do so in that part of it I had most desired to visit. Ever since Petrie had spoken to me of its magnificence, I had longed to behold the great temple of Karnak and to inspect the environs of ancient Thebes. The post I had obtained gave me just such a chance – and brought me to that place where I sit writing even now.

Nor, despite the many years I have spent here, has it ever ceased to excite my wonder. For it is the spot, perhaps, more than any in Egypt, where past and present can seem most annihilated; even the Nile, the palms, the very crops in the fields, when they are outlined by the brilliance of the midday sun can appear like the features of a timeless architecture, unchanging, unchangeable, so distinct and stilled they seem. I can remember being struck by this thought on my very first arrival at Thebes, leaning from the window of my train and then, a moment later, seeing a flash of stone above the distant palms, stone and yet more stone, and knowing that I was glimpsing the great temple of Karnak. I visited it that same afternoon and imagined, lost amidst its stupendous and grandiloquent bulk, that the centuries might indeed have learned to dread such a monument. Courtyard after courtyard, pylon after pylon, the temple appeared to extend without end, and I could not help but contrast it with the sands and barren waste of El-Amarna 200 miles away to the north. Certainly, I felt the mystery of Akh-en-Aten's revolution all the more keenly now, for I could understand, gazing about me, that in seeking the destruction of Karnak, he had been attempting what Time itself is yet to achieve. What dreams could have inspired him to challenge so awesome a place? What dreams, what hopes – or, it may have been, what fears?

I would have welcomed the chance to stay in Karnak and

consider further such mysteries. My post, however, required me elsewhere, and so that same evening, as the twilight began to deepen, I crossed the Nile to the western bank. Mud-rich fields soon gave way to tawny sands and beyond me, its peaks dyed red by the setting of the sun, arced a low range of mountains. Here, in the ancient mythology, had lain the boundary between the worlds of the living and the dead; just as the sun each evening would disappear beneath the western horizon, so also, it was conceived, would the spirits of the departed journey west towards the desert. I had come to work within the shadow of this boundary, for it was marked by monuments of unparalleled romance and interest, built as gateways to the underworld and forming, to this very day, one vast and fabulous city of the dead.

Here, over the next six years, I laboured hard to become the master of my chosen calling. I had been employed to work upon the greatest of the Pharaonic mortuary temples, barely visible when I first arrived upon the site but gradually revealed to be a masterpiece of art. The excavation was a back-breaking one, and I found nothing which could shed any direct light upon the mysteries of El-Amarna. But I was not impatient, and indeed I have ever looked back upon those years with the most cheerful of reminiscences. I have often considered how, if life had dealt me some other hand of cards, I might have made an excellent detective: not a Sherlock Holmes, perhaps, producing solutions with some great flash of insight, but rather one who accumulates his evidence with a steady care, hunting out every scrap of information, observing and analysing every clue. Certainly, I had realised that to pursue my ambitions I would need all the grounding I could possibly obtain – and this I drew from my six years' work upon the temple. For I learnt more there about the Ancient Egyptians, their history and their way of life, than in any other place or time; and it left me well equipped for the great adventure of my life.

Not that I had wholly neglected – during this period of my apprenticeship – to explore those mysteries which had first set me out on such a course. Beyond the temple on which I was working there rose a mighty cliff; and beyond that cliff there stretched a bleak and wild ravine, remote from every mark or sound of life. The Valley of the Kings! Of all Egypt's wonders, there is none, I suppose, which makes more instant appeal to the imagination. Here in ancient times whole dynasties of Pharaohs had been entombed within the rock, and still to this day, thousands of years after its abandonment, it can seem an awesome, holy, death-haunted place. One might almost believe that one is on another world, and the very paths which wind across the contours of the valley, whiter and more blinding than the sand and rocks themselves, can seem like the veins of some calcified monster, the beat of its life long since drained and turned to stone. Certainly, it is hard to explain those impressions which go to make the entering of the tombs themselves so unsettling, for one cannot adequately express the silence, the echoing steps, the dark shadows, the hot, breathless air; nor describe the aura of vast Time, and the penetrating of it which stirs one so profoundly.

Yet although the tombs of the Valley possessed an incomparable magnificence and beauty, I found nothing on the walls which could compare with the portrait of Nefer-titi, whose face, beauteous and deathly, still rose on occasion before my mind's eye, surprising my fancy, or sometimes my dreams, as though luring me onwards to some unglimpsed goal. Nor did I discover any of those strange symbols and Arabic inscriptions which I had traced at El-Amarna; yet in truth, the finding of such marks would have surprised me more than their absence did. For the Aten had never been the guardian of the Valley; it was not the radiant image of a single god who had kept watch upon the tombs, but rather the ancient divinities of the underworld – those same divinities Akh-en-Aten had been so desperate to suppress.

Above all, reproduced again and again upon the walls, I found the image of Osiris – Osiris, the first King of Egypt, whom his own brother Seth had sought to overthrow. Inspecting the artwork, I would recall the legend which Newberry had related to me; how twice the god of evil had murdered his brother, first by sealing him within a sarcophagus, then by dismembering and scattering his limbs across the world. Yet I was also reminded of how Osiris had then been brought back from the dead by Isis, his sister, the Great Goddess of Magic, to reign for ever in the Underworld; and it was in this role that he had been portrayed upon the walls of the tombs, as the eternal King of the realm of the Dead. The legends did not reveal how Isis had achieved the mystery of his resurrection; and yet his presence as a guardian over the royal sarcophagi – his expression inscrutable, his lips faintly smiling – appeared to hint that the secret had somehow been vouchsafed, to the souls of the Pharaohs at the very least. Again, thinking of this, I would find myself puzzling over Akh-en-Aten; at what had persuaded him to abandon such a god, and the prospect of an eternity of life after death.

Regrettably, without the opportunity of excavating in the Valley I had little chance of discovering answers to such questions. Indeed, only one faint avenue of investigation suggested itself. Recalling Newberry's discovery of the legend of the restless King, it struck me that there might perhaps be similar folk tales abroad in the neighbourhood of Thebes. Certainly, there was one tradition which had been preserved from time immemorial amongst the villagers of the area, for the Valley remained what it had been since the age of the Pharaohs, the profitable hunting-ground of tomb-thieves and robbers. Evidence of their labours was everywhere to be found: open or half-filled mummy pits, heaps of rubbish, great mounds of rock debris with, here and there, fragments of coffins and shreds of linen mummy-wrappings protruding from the sand. Surely, I thought to myself, the accumulated wisdom of such professionals might contain some fragments of information which I could put to my own use. By this time I was able to converse in Arabic with tolerable ease, and on the darker nights, when the pestilential gnats and midges had tired me out of all patience, I would sometimes rise from my quarters and visit the head-man of a neighbouring village. It is true my inquiries met with no immediate response, but I was neither surprised nor especially disheartened by this. For I had the impression, when I asked about the legends of the ancient tombs, that something was being kept back from me, and I found evidence enough that such legends might indeed be still alive. Sitting by the coffee-hearth of the headman of a village, one could often listen to reciters of romances who, without any books at all, had committed their subjects to memory, and afforded the villagers wonderful entertainment. Their recitations contained a good deal of history and ancient lore, and I would occasionally hear, with reference to the Valley, vague allusions to some great and wonderful secret, pro-tected, so it seemed, by a terrible curse. It was hard to make anything specific of such stuff, but it certainly served to pique my curiosity, and I would often find myself wonder-ing what more the village poets might not know.

While I was being employed upon the mortuary temples, away from the Valley, such a question might not have seemed an urgent one. But then in the autumn of 1899, towards the end of my sixth year of field work at Thebes, a dramatic upturn in my fortunes occurred which was to place the question into the sharpest of focus. It appeared that my efforts to prepare myself for the excavator's life had not gone wholly unnoticed, for I was suddenly offered, as though from the blue, the post of Chief Inspector of Antiquities. This was a doubly unexpected honour, for not only was I still very young – a mere 25 years old – but I had the far worse disadvantage of not being French. Petrie's prejudices had influenced me strongly: I had always assumed the worst of the *Service des Antiquités*. But the head of that organisation, Monsieur Gaston Maspero, was in reality a man of remarkable discernment, and it may be, indeed, all the more so for his not being English – only a Frenchman, I suspect, would have appointed a man of my humble background to the post. I accepted it, of course, with the utmost alacrity, and with a sense of excitement intermingled with the utmost anticipation; for henceforth I was to be responsible for the antiquities of the whole of Upper Egypt – and in particular, for the exploration of the Valley of the Kings.

At last, then, I reflected with a measure of satisfaction, I could count myself a true archaeologist. Nevertheless, in those first few months of my appointment, I remembered the lesson I had learned years before when I had seen the portrait of Nefer-titi dissolve before my eyes, and I bore in mind how the pre-eminent virtue of my chosen calling must ever be patience, patience, patience. Of course, I longed to plunge into excavations and make great discoveries, but the over-riding requirement, as I saw it, was first to make a close inspection of the already discovered tombs. And so it was, in my favoured character of a detective investigating a crime, that I began my hunt for clues.

Almost straight away, I uncovered something startling. It appeared that someone had already been around the tombs before me: in all the most recently uncovered ones tiny amulets had been left, either upon the breasts of the mummies in their sarcophagi or at the feet of paintings of Osiris on the walls. The amulets themselves appeared to be of recent manufacture, and yet the image they bore made my heart begin to pound, for although very roughly reproduced, it was unmistakably a portrait of the sun, with the two familiar worshippers crouching underneath. Here was a pretty puzzle to be sure! What a copy of the Aten was doing in Thebes, many hundreds of miles away from El-Amarna, I could not begin to imagine – nor what the natives might be up to, manufacturing an image of such a clearly pagan nature. Yet I was certain, remembering the graffiti I had found at El-Amarna – similarly by a Muslim, similarly of the sun – that the parallels were exact, and that such a correspondence, perhaps, was the greatest puzzle of them all.

Some faint light at least was shed upon the mysterious affair by the supervisor of my workmen, Ahmed Girigar. He was a man in whom I had an absolute trust, for he had worked under a succession of excavators and possessed an integrity which was rivalled only by his knowledge of the Valley's terrain. One day, when I had found another amulet laid upon a mummy, I handed it over to him. Ahmed inspected it suspiciously.

'Do you recognise it?' I asked.

He shrugged with disdain. 'It is a proof,' he answered me, 'that folly is still alive and flourishing.'

Intrigued, I asked him to explain himself.

Ahmed shrugged a second time. 'It is believed, when a tomb is uncovered in the Valley, that one of these symbols must be left upon the mummy, so that the spirits of the Kings will not be woken from their sleep.'

I frowned. 'Why would they be woken?'

'It is nonsense, sir, all nonsense.'

'Naturally,' I pressed him, 'but what do people say?'

'There is an old story . . .' Ahmed paused to glance down at the mummy – 'a very old story . . . that, long, long ago, a tomb was discovered. Great treasures were found inside it – unimaginable wealth – but also a secret of terrible evil . . .' He swallowed and paused again, appearing suddenly uncomfortable; but I could not permit him to halt now, so I insisted that he continue. 'The secret?' I demanded. 'What was the secret?'

Ahmed frowned at me, then suddenly laughed. 'Why, sir, what do you think? In these foolish stories of ours, wherever there is treasure there must also be a demon. This particular demon had once been a Pharaoh, buried in his tomb. When he was disturbed, he punished those who had released him, for he had the power to summon up the spirits of the dead.' Ahmed paused again, and bent down closer by the mummy in its coffin. 'The demon, by Allah's grace, was destroyed in the end. And so it was, you understand, sir, that the tomb which had been disturbed was sealed up once again, and for many years the Valley was left well alone – for it was feared that wherever treasure might be uncovered, there also the demons would certainly be found.'

'Whereas now . . .'

Ahmed glanced up at me inquiringly.

'Whereas now,' I repeated, 'people no longer seem afraid of any demons.'

'Oh no, sir,' Ahmed whispered, his face suddenly solemn, 'they are still afraid.' He raised his candle to inspect the amulet. 'But has it not ever been this way?' He smiled faintly. 'That greed, in the end, will always conquer fear?'

Well, I reflected later, that was a pertinent enough warning for any Chief Inspector to be offered, and I certainly had no intention of ignoring it. I duly installed gates upon the most prominent tombs, but, alas! – Ahmed's words were to return to haunt me all the same. Barely months after he had spoken them, the very tomb in which we had been standing together was brutally ransacked, with even the wrappings being torn from the mummy. Fortunately, there had been no valuable objects left upon the body, and the damage to the tomb itself was only very slight. I could not help but understand fully now, however, what a task of conservation I had before me, and so I was careful to fit the gates even more securely than before, and to install electric lights. I also stepped up my night patrols and to be sure, roaming across the cliffs alone and unarmed, always on the lookout for the marks of clandestine excavations, did not want for excitement. At such moments, with the blaze of the stars above me and the tombs all around, it did not seem so hard to believe in demons after all!

Nor, if truth be told, had the proof of the tomb-robbers' continuing interest in the Valley altogether disappointed me. I had been in the area of Thebes long enough now, and grown sufficiently familiar with the habits of its natives, to have developed a healthy respect for their lore. I could not, of course, readily admit this to my colleagues in the government service, who would have viewed such a trust as both degrading and foolish – yet I had grown convinced that superstitions might sometimes veil the germs of fact. Certainly, the tradition to which Ahmed Girigar had alluded – that a tomb filled with treasure had once been found by the villagers – appeared exceedingly plausible; and if one such tomb had already been found, then why should not a second be uncovered in the future? On this point, at least, the logic of the tomb-robbers struck me as being perfectly sound – so sound, indeed, that I was eager to follow it myself.

Yet it was not merely the prospect of treasure which served to preoccupy my thoughts. Despite Ahmed's explanation of their function, the amulets I had discovered within the royal tombs continued to perplex me, for the mystery of their origin, and of their apparent connection to Akh-en-Aten's sun, appeared beyond explanation. I was tempted to dismiss them as either a hoax or coincidence; yet there was, after all, one other explanation which presented itself. Suppose a tomb with treasure had indeed once been found – might not the image of the Aten have been uncovered with the gold?

Such a solution, of course, could only be tentative. Nevertheless, it was confirmed for me by one particular episode, which may strike the reader as trivial, but which affected me strongly. It happened one night, as I was out patrolling the cliffs above the Valley, that I heard a muffled scrabbling sound such as I knew could mean only one thing. The noise was coming from a narrow ravine just below me; and so, as quietly as I could, I descended the cliff and walked up the ravine. Just ahead of me, and illumined by the very faint flickering of a torch, I could make out the doorway of a hitherto unrecorded tomb. The scrabbling was coming from within it, and as I paused by the doorway I could make out two voices whispering together. One was a man's, very peremptory and impatient; the other, shrill and almost hysterical with fear, seemed to belong to a boy.

I peered round the corner of the doorway. Two figures, one very slight, both cloaked in black, were standing in a passageway; ahead of them, its doorway half-sealed by a pile of dust and stones, loomed the darkness of a further chamber. The man, so it appeared, had ordered his companion to pass through the gap, but the boy was wailing and shuddering with dread. Through his sobs, I could make out choking references to demons – for it seemed he was afraid he might disturb the sleeping dead. Then he turned and raised his arm to point at an image painted on the wall, and as he did so, I caught the glint in his eyes and I started, for I thought I had never before seen a look of such fear. Unfortunately, my sudden movement disturbed a trickle of pebbles and the two thieves were alerted to my presence. I attempted to apprehend them, but the elder at least was a seasoned villain and, by the simple expedient of producing a knife, was able to effect a speedy escape for himself and his boy. I was disappointed, naturally, but relieved as well to have secured a fresh tomb. Summoning Ahmed Girigar, I ordered him to prepare it for excavation, and placed well-armed guards on either side of the door.

In the event, the tomb proved to have been plundered in antiquity, for there was little to be found in the burial chamber save only the fragments of funereal furniture and jars. Certainly, I discovered nothing which might have justified the expression of terror I had glimpsed upon the youthful tomb-robber's face; yet so striking had it been, so evident and vivid his fear, that I could not believe it had been caused merely by shadows. Had he known of the tale which I had heard from Ahmed Girigar? Was it that which had caused him to seem so afraid? The evidence was circumstantial; but present all the same. For the image on the wall which had so startled him proved to be a figure of Osiris – that same god who, in the Ancients' mythology, had been the King of the Dead, and before whom, in all the other tombs, an amulet with an Aten had been carefully laid. And sure enough, some two days after my initial discovery of the tomb, the same thing occurred: entering the passageway I found, placed before the figure of Osiris, an amulet stamped with the figure of the Aten. As to who might have laid it there, I could find no clue at all.

Nevertheless, I was strongly encouraged, for I was almost certain now that my initial hypothesis had been correct and that the natives, however long ago, must indeed have found a tomb adorned with the Aten. The discovery could only have had a profound effect upon them – how else to explain the continued use of the Aten as a charm into the present day, against the demons imagined to lurk within the tombs? It amused me to think that these demons were associated by the natives with the figure of Osiris. What had led them to make such a connection I could not imagine, but I was sure that Akh-en-Aten's spirit at least would not have disapproved!

Of course, I could not be certain whose resting-place it had been which the natives had disturbed. One candidate, indeed, was already known to archaeology – the tomb of Akh-en-Aten's father, Amen-hetep the Third, long since plundered and abandoned as empty. That still left other possibilities, however, which had not been found: the tombs of Akh-en-Aten's mother, his children, perhaps even his wife. If only one of these had been broken into by the natives, then the others, so I trusted, might still be intact. All I needed now were time and resources, and I felt hopeful that I might indeed make a wonderful discovery, so that my name would be rendered famous in my chosen field for ever more. Time, I supposed, would not be a problem; only resources appeared to threaten my plans, for the *Service des Antiquités* did not pay well and, of course, I had no private funds of my own. I could not, though, endure to have my ambitions frustrated; and, indeed, eager and almost confident as I was, I had already cast my eyes upon a possible solution.

The moon tonight is full. As I sit here at my desk, I can see through my window that the very mountains seem touched by a ghostly silver. On a night such as this, one might almost believe in the spirits of the dead: that they are gliding along the road as it curves past my house, in sheeted, silent crowds, towards the pass which leads into the Valley of the Kings. Of course, it is not the custom for archaeologists to admit to such fancies; yet if they are honest, I think, they will not deny altogether that they have them. For what, after all, is the great hope of our calling if not the faith which we share with the Ancients themselves – that the past may be restored to the dimension of the living, that life may be breathed into that which is gone?

Certainly, although it has often angered me in its more idiotic manifestations, I have never despised that lure of romance which attracts so many to this land. Why should I? It is a foolish man who would ignore a source of income. For indeed it was upon a night just like tonight, when the moon shone full upon the temple of Karnak and cast the monstrous structures a pale and deathly silver, that I secured the funding I had been so desperate to obtain. In my role as a guide to the rich, I had long since discovered how there is nothing like mystery to open up a wallet; and Karnak more than anywhere, when lit by a spectral gleam, can seem a place much haunted by the spectres of the past.

My companion on that night, wandering through the empty courtyards and halls, was an American by the name of Theodore Davis. A retired lawyer, he had come originally to Egypt for the sake of his health but, having rapidly grown fed up with lingering on his house-boat, he had taken instead to poking about Thebes. He had soon become a familiar sight in the Valley as he strode between the tombs, his white moustachioes bristling, a cigarette forever clenched between his teeth. He was a tiny, restless, eccentric man – but he was also, it so happened, both bored and very rich.

It is scarcely to be wondered at, then, that his interest in the Valley had not gone unnoticed by me. Indeed, I had always been most careful to guide him through the freshest discoveries and had lately begun to observe, as I discussed my work with him, how fiercely his bright eyes had taken to gleaming. 'But there must be more to discover!' he would bark at me impatiently. 'There must be more to find out!' I had never denied it; nor, though, until that night at Karnak, had I done more than hint at my own private speculations. I had preferred to leave the bait dangling – and thereby make all the more certain of pulling in my catch.

I could tell, as we stood amidst the temple's massive columns that evening, that he was impatient to bite. 'Dammit, Carter,' he exploded suddenly, 'dammit to hell but this whole damn place seems a mystery.' He waved his arms expansively, his cigarette scattering sparks as he did so. 'What business does it have with being so vast?' He glared at me accusingly, as though he were in some courtroom again and I an obstructive witness. 'Well,' he pressed me, 'what do you say?'

'We know,' I shrugged, 'that it was sacred to Amen, the greatest of the gods.'

'But look at it . . .' – he waved with his arms again – 'this was sure as hell something more than a temple. This was . . . well . . . a whole damn city!' He began to walk forward, past the silhouettes of obelisks and tumbled granite blocks. 'Imagine it, Carter! The wealth, the power those priests must have had! Where did it come from?'

'It is true,' I answered, accompanying him, 'that Amen was a somewhat mysterious god.'

Davis's eyes darted beadily back at me. 'How so?'

'How?' I smiled faintly. 'Because mystery was the very heart of his cult.'

'What do you mean?'

I stared into the darkness of the ruins ahead. 'The name of Amen,' I murmured, 'translates into English as "the hidden one". His titles too – "unknown", "unknowable", "mysterious of form" – all appear to suggest the same thing: that his true identity could never be revealed; that his hidden nature was incalculably strange.'

Davis frowned at me. 'How do you mean?'

'It is clear enough, I think, that his priests imagined themselves the guardians of some secret – some magical source of wisdom and power, derived from an incalculably ancient source.'

'Your evidence for this, Mr Carter?'

'We have a papyrus,' I shrugged, 'found some forty years ago, which relates how Isis, the sister of Osiris and Seth, became "*Weret Hekau*", or "Great of Magic". It appears that she achieved this by blackmailing Amen, and gaining from him the knowledge of the secret of his name. But what was that secret? The papyrus does not say. Nor is it the only one to drop such tantalising hints. In another papyrus, a hymn to Amen, it is proclaimed how the god is "too great to be inquired after, too powerful to be learned", that "people fall down all at once for fear, lest his true name be revealed". Evidently it was believed that, in the whole of the universe, there was nothing of greater or more magical power. That was what the priests of Amen claimed to guard. And that was the source' – I gestured – 'of the splendour of this place.'

Davis stared at me in wide-eyed silence for a moment, then snorted impatiently. 'Yes, but that's only old stories and myths,' he complained. 'What about hard facts? Isn't that what your own profession's for? What light has archaeology been able to shed on all this?'

'Remarkably little,' I replied straight away.

'Well dammit, Carter,' he barked, gesticulating at the ruins with his arms once again, 'there must be some clues in a place this damn size!'

'Yes,' I answered, 'but though the complex was vast, the innermost shrine was remarkably small.' I began to walk forward again, Davis accompanying me, almost, I thought, as though I were some ancient priest, and he an eager acolyte, drawn by me into great mysteries. We passed the shattered base of a mighty gate, and then I turned to gaze back at the route we had taken. Gateway after gateway, hall after hall, the ruins stretched away. 'The most magnificent processional route in the world,' I murmured. 'And yet where does it lead us? It leads us to – here.' I turned again, and gestured. I saw how Davis frowned. For where I had pointed, there was nothing to be seen: nothing but dust and fragments of stone.

Davis's frown deepened. 'What are we looking for?'

I bent and scooped up a handful of the dust. 'If only we knew.'

'What are you saying, Carter? That this is where the shrine of Amen once stood?'

'The most sacred place in Egypt, Mr Davis – the veritable Holy of Holies. Yet as you can see . . .' – I flung the dust away, so that it was scattered on the breeze – 'there is not a trace of it left. No hint of what the mysteries of Amen could have been.'

Davis stared at me in silence a long while, then, with great deliberation, he finished his cigarette and ground the butt into the dust with his heel. 'So tell me, Carter . . .' – he narrowed his eyes – 'what exactly is it you are getting at?'

'You were a lawyer, Mr Davis,' I answered him slowly. 'It is a principle of law, is it not, that the testimony of the prosecution must be as valid as that of the defence?'

Davis reached in his pocket for another cigarette. 'Go on,' he nodded, striking a match.

I watched as the flame hissed and spurted. 'You have asked me,' I murmured softly, 'what might have been the secret guarded by the priests. Certainly, we know that whoever – whatever – Amen may have been, even the greatest of the Pharaohs stood in awe of such a god. All the Pharaohs . . .' – I paused – 'save only one.'

Davis breathed out a thick plume of smoke. 'You are referring, I presume, to King Akh-en-Aten?'

'Very good,' I nodded, 'so you know of him. Then you will also know, perhaps, how after his death his name, his religion, his very line were extirpated utterly by the vengeful priests of Amen. Yet the oblivion which fell upon his family, the attempt to wipe them from the record of history, may have served by great irony to have kept their tombs intact.'

Davis puckered his brow. 'You have proof of this?'

'Let us say, I have weighed the probabilities.'

'And in these tombs – supposing they are indeed unplundered – what exactly is it you'd be hoping to find?'

I breathed in deeply. From far away I heard the sudden crying of a jackal, faint but distinctive, its mournful tones borne across the sands on the wind. 'What might we find in the tombs?' I murmured. 'Secrets, perhaps. Clues as to the power which the priests of Amen worshipped, and which Akh-en-Aten sought to destroy. Clues long buried, these three thousand years.' I paused, for the jackal had started to howl once again, and this time so unearthly did it sound that it served to freeze my tongue. Then the breeze dimmed; and I felt myself oppressed by an unexpected sense of closeness, as though the stars were crowding the rubble-strewn dust and the gateways behind us were breaking like a wave. A nausea clouded my thoughts, so that I half-stumbled and had to support myself against a toppled column. I had not felt such a strange and irrational horror, I thought, for a long while – not since I had stood in the chamber of Akh-en-Aten's tomb and gazed upon the face of the painting of his Queen. Yet even as I recalled this, I felt the horror fade, and I could hear, not the howling of a jackal now, but the more comforting noises of an Egyptian night, the whispering of palm trees, the swaying of crops. I turned back to Davis. 'In truth,' I said softly, 'who knows what we may find? For a mystery must stay a mystery until brought into the light.'

Davis did not answer me. His face was pale and, when I suggested we conclude our trip to Karnak, he agreed with great readiness. We neither of us spoke on our journey back across the Nile, but I suspected, studying his face, that he too had experienced some strange clouding of his senses, for his brow appeared creased with mingled puzzlement and fear. Only once we had reached the far bank of the river did his wonted animation return; and as we crossed the fields towards the Theban hills, he began to question me further about the mysteries of Akh-en-Aten's reign. I did nothing to dampen his enthusiasm but rather, with precise deliberation, began to list the tombs still waiting to be found. 'It is a great pity, though,' I concluded, 'that excavation requires funds. I wish that someone would buy the concession to the Valley of the Kings, so that I might then conduct a search on their behalf . . .'

Of course, Davis bit – as I had known that he would. With my advocacy, it was not hard for him to secure from the Service des Antiquités the concession to the Valley of the Kings, and with funding now assured I at once began to dig. I had already long decided on which stretch of the Valley would be the most profitable to explore; and so, under the expert supervision of Ahmed Girigar, my newly hired workmen were set to clearing the area. We were to be rewarded, in one sense, with almost continuous success, for during the course of the next two years' excavations we were to bring to light a good number of tombs. One in particular I was briefly much excited by, for it proved to be that of Akh-enAten's royal grandfather, King Thoth-mes the Fourth. Alas, however! – as so often happened, disappointment soon followed the first rush of hope. For once again, we found that nothing had survived the depredations of the tomb-robbers: there was neither treasure nor gold, nor anything capable of shedding light upon the past. Even the immense quartzite sarcophagus had not been spared; its massive lid, weighing many tons, had been prised away and flung to the ground, and its contents despoiled. I had begun to fear I was deluded in my hopes, save that some days after our initial discovery of the tomb, when I was working within the funeral chamber, I saw from inside the sarcophagus a dull, cheap glow and, crossing to inspect it, found an amulet. It had evidently been placed there just a few hours before, but by whom, and for what reason, I could still not imagine. It had been stamped, though, with the familiar icon: two crouching figures beneath the disk of a sun.

I did not show it to Davis, nor mention it, for I preferred to keep the details of the mystery to myself. Not that Davis needed encouraging by now – with each successive discovery, his obsession had grown apace, and with his obsession his self-confidence as well. I had been observing for some while the changes in his relationship with me: whereas at first he had been perfectly content to acknowledge my superior expertise, now increasingly he treated the Valley as his own private fiefdom and myself, it sometimes seemed, as a mere employee. I was obliged constantly to remind him of my status: that it was I who was the Inspector, I who was the official director of excavations. Davis accepted this only with great reluctance – and indeed, the more we quarrelled, so the more cocksure and dictatorial he grew.

It was with some alarm then, in the autumn of 1904, after more than two years' excavations in the Valley of the Kings, that I learned I was to be transferred to the post of Chief Inspector based at Cairo. Davis, however, greeted the news with undisguised glee. He clearly trusted that my successor would be easier to control than I had been, and I suspected that his optimism might prove to be well founded. In such a case, I feared for the future of archaeology in the Valley, for Davis's interest in the science of excavation had always been slight, and with my own departure could only grow even slighter still. Knowledge for its own sake was of no concern to him; rather, his obsession was with the discovery of treasure, and the Valley, in his eyes, might as well have been a Klondike. I dreaded to think, in the face of such a gold-lust, what details and clues might go forever unrecorded, and I began to wonder – like the man in the tale who freed a genie from a bottle – what it was I had uncorked.

Time, in the event, was to show me soon enough.

Perhaps not surprisingly, as the moment neared for my departure to Cairo, so my own work grew touched by a sense of mounting frustration. Finds continued to be made and tombs to be explored, but they were never from the period of Akh-en-Aten's reign, and the sheer size of the Valley, and the roughness of its terrain, ensured that it was impossible to cover every inch. However, I had not lost hope utterly, and wherever a site appeared to offer some encouragement there I would order my labourers to explore. In my final week in the Valley, I had no fewer than four groups of them at work, and I would stride impatiently between them, praying that a great find might yet be made – the tomb of Nefer-titi perhaps, or that of the shadowy pharaoh Smenkh-ka-Re, or that of his brother, the equally shadowy Tut-ankh-Amen. There was nothing, however – neither a tomb nor even a hint that a tomb might lie nearby – and all the while, my final week in Thebes was slipping by.

Then, on my very last afternoon of work, even as the sky was darkening and the labourers were preparing to leave the Valley for their homes, I was startled by a scream. Since the spades and picks had by now been laid aside, and the din of excavation largely ended, the sound echoed across the rocks with a horrid clarity – horrid, I say, for the scream's tone had been one of extraordinary fear. I could only think that an appalling accident had occurred, and so I hurried as fast as I was able towards the source of the scream. As I approached it, I was relieved to see no obvious marks of a disaster: three of the labourers were gathered about a fourth, who appeared to be gripping something tightly in his hands. As I neared him, however, and he turned to face me, I had little doubt that it was he who had screamed, for his eyes were bulging and his face was chalky white, and he started, then shuddered and shrank from my approach.

I took a step nearer him and demanded to know what the matter was. He stammered something unintelligible but I suddenly saw, with a lurch of excitement, that the object in his hand had an edging of gold. I asked him to show it to me. He shrank back even further, and as I stretched out my hand to remove it from him, his stammerings rose into a dread-haunted wail. At the same moment I heard footsteps behind me and, glancing round saw Ahmed Girigar. I gestured to the workman. 'For God's sake, sort him out.' The man screamed wildly at Ahmed, then fell by my feet as though begging for something. I felt almost embarrassed – and yet in truth, not greatly so, for as I took the object from the labourer's hand I at once grew oblivious to everything else.

The find appeared to be the plaque of a bracelet of gold. It had been beautifully crafted from carnelian, yet it was the design rather than the workmanship which had made my heart begin to pound. For within the golden edging was the portrait of a queen: not Nefer-titi, as I had briefly thought at first, but a ruler if anything of even greater power, the very Queen of Queens indeed, wife to Amen-hetep the Third, Akh-en-Aten's mother, Tyi. In an age of mighty rulers, there had been none more powerful nor more splendid than she, and it filled me with a sense of awe just to hold her portrait in my hands. Certainly, there could be no doubting her identity – I recognised not only her features but also her favoured incarnation, a sphinx with feathered, outspread wings. But although I had seen several such portraits of Tyi elsewhere, I had never come across anything to compare with the one I held now, neither for delicate loveliness nor for sinister power. Indeed, it was the exquisite femininity of the Queen's face and breasts, mounted as they were upon the body of a lion, which served to render the portrait so unsettling and give it a look at once so monstrous and cruel. Like a true lioness Tyi crouched, her hindlegs tensed and her forearms outstretched: as though reaching for her victim; as though greedy for prey.

I glanced at the workman still shuddering before me. What had he seen in the portrait to reduce him to such a state? I beckoned Ahmed across and showed him the ornament. He frowned as he inspected it. His uneasiness, although he sought to conceal it, was immediately apparent.

'Goodness,' I exclaimed, 'but you are all an ungallant lot, to be so unsettled by the portrait of a lady!'

Ahmed, however, did not answer my smile. 'It is said,' he muttered, 'when the tomb was found – the one which held the demon who guarded the treasures – that just such a thing was discovered by its door: the image of a lion with a woman's head.'

'The sphinx,' I whispered, almost to myself. 'Guarding the portal which leads the way to treasure . . .' Again I felt a sudden lurch of excitement, and to restrain it I clapped my hands and gave the order to continue at once with the dig. No one moved, though, and Ahmed, I saw, was gazing at the mountain peaks behind us, as they were dyed dark red by the setting sun. He turned back to me. 'It will be night-time soon, sir.' He shuffled uncomfortably. 'Would it not be better to continue in the day?'

I shook my head. 'You know, if nothing is found tonight, then I must leave here tomorrow. No, no – we must continue digging now.'

Ahmed gestured to the workmen. 'You have seen, sir, how these four will not dig here, not on this site.'

'Then find me others!' I exclaimed impatiently. 'And do it fast! We have no time to lose!'

Ahmed hesitated a moment more, before bowing his head and hurrying off. I watched him go, then inspected the ornament closely again. As I did so, my excitement was at once renewed. It appeared to me, studying how Tyi's features had been represented, that they confirmed a theory I had heard long before from Petrie: that the great Queen of Egypt had not herself been an Egyptian. Petrie, I knew, believed that Tyi had been of Semitic origin; but on the evidence of the portrait I now held in my hand, it struck me as likelier that she had been of Nubian descent. I frowned. Though I had come to it myself, I found this conclusion a hard one to accept. For it had been the universal custom of the Pharaohs, I knew, to pick a Chief Wife from amongst their own family; more than custom, indeed, it had been a cast-iron religious decree, affirmed and imposed by the priests of Amen, who had feared lest the royal blood-line be polluted. Where, then, had Tyi come from? If she had been not only a commoner but a foreigner as well, how could she possibly have risen to become the great Queen of Queens, indeed the first Queen in all of Egypt's long history to be portrayed as the equal of her husband, the Pharaoh? She must have been as formidable as her portrait suggested, to have seduced King Amen-hetep so utterly, and then to have prevailed over the priesthood of Amen. In that success, I wondered suddenly, what clues might there not be towards the character of Akh-en-Aten, her son – clues, perhaps, which lay buried in the very sands beneath my feet?

It was in a fever of anticipation, then, that I waited to continue with the dig. I was disappointed, though, when Ahmed returned, to see that he had brought no more than ten men with him and that these, to judge by the expressions on their faces, had been summoned much against their wills. 'There is a great fear,' Ahmed whispered to me, 'and much superstitious nonsense abroad. For everyone has heard of the find that was made, of the lion with the woman's head. And so they are afraid lest they disturb the tomb which it guards, and set the demon free a second time.'

'There is no demon,' I answered loudly, for the benefit of the workmen gathered before me. 'No demon, and nothing to fear. Now . . .' – I reached in my pocket and brought out a coin – 'this for the first man who comes across a find.'

The labourers reached for their picks and set to work; yet I could see, in the flickering light of the torches, that their faces were still tense and twisted with dread. Even I, affected no doubt by the labourers' mood, began to feel strange flickerings of tension and rather than continue with my perusal of the portrait of Tyi, I covered it carefully and set it aside, as though to inspect it by moonlight might somehow bring bad luck. I picked up a spade and set to digging myself; and indeed, if I am honest, I must admit that I welcomed the chance to work off my nerves – for there is nothing like labour to keep one's fancyings at bay.

Or so at least I have always found; yet the case of my workmen was to suggest the contrary. We had been digging for a couple of hours, clearing the sand and loose rubble from the site, when there arose – just as there had done before – a sudden, piercing scream. I looked up. One of the workmen had dropped his pick and was shrinking backwards, his mouth set in a twisted grimace of fear as he pointed at something he had clearly just exposed. The others too had all paused in their work, and then, as their fellow had done, begun to shrink backwards. I heard a low, dreadful moan, and one of the workmen turned on his heels. 'Stop!' I cried out, 'stop!'; but there was no holding him. I stepped forward, to try to persuade the others to remain, but they too were flinging their tools upon the ground and scrabbling out of the trench they had dug. 'Stop them!' I yelled at Ahmed, but though he tried his best, there was nothing he could do. The men had soon vanished for good into the dark, and the two of us were left in the abandoned trench alone.

I swore angrily, and stepped forward to see what could have caused such a stampede. At first, I could make out nothing at all: when I shone my torch, there was no glint of metal, nor any sign of the stonework which might have marked a tomb. But then, as I bent down closer, I saw what appeared to be a clawlike human foot and, brushing the sand away, I realised that we had indeed found a corpse.

I glanced up at Ahmed. 'The stories,' I asked him, 'do they speak of such a thing?'

Ahmed paused a moment, his eyes very wide. 'I have told you, sir,' he said at length, 'all those stories are nothing but nonsense.' He forced himself to smile; but I noticed, as he bent down beside me, how he darted a glance behind him, and then to his left and right, as though he imagined there might indeed be something lurking in the dark.

Nothing disturbed us, however, as we began our work of sweeping the sand from the cadaver. It soon became clear, as first a second foot and then the two legs were exposed, that the body had been mummified naturally by the dryness of the sands. The process had not been total: in certain places the skin had given way to the bone, and despite my best hopes, it proved impossible to determine the sex of the mummy. I was able to assume, though, from certain wisps of rich fabric which had been preserved upon the limbs, that our cadaver had once been a person of high rank; yet it puzzled me that he or she had been buried in the sands, when even the meanest of Egyptians would have hoped to be laid to rest within a tomb.

An answer to this mystery, however, was not long in coming. As we continued to work up the length of the cadaver, sweeping the sand from first the pelvis and then the ribs, I began to realise that the body was twisted, as though from the agonies of a violent death. I wondered if Ahmed too had observed the same thing, for I noticed his hand had started to shake. At length, as I prepared to expose the neck of the corpse, he dropped his brush altogether and sat as though frozen, a look of mingled horror and fascination on his face. I met his stare fleetingly, before continuing with my work. Then I too suddenly stopped, and rocked back in surprise.

There could be no doubting now what the cause of death had been. Preserved against the passage of the centuries by the sands, twin flaps of flesh could still be made out, torn in opposite directions along the length of the throat. The victim's hands were still clutching at the wound, the vain clawing of the fingers preserved for ever by the sands. And even as I considered that, I leaned forward again and began to work with a renewed, half-nervous energy, clearing the rocks from over the head, then sweeping back the sands to expose the corpse's face. As I did so, I heard Ahmed gasp, and so also – or was it only my imagining? – I heard a noise from beyond the trench. But I did not pause, not until the face had been wholly exposed. As I finished, I realised how badly my arm had begun to shake. I glanced at Ahmed. 'My God,' I muttered. 'You see what the power of imagination may be. This hellish thing has made me as nervous as you.'

Ahmed smiled, but his teeth were bared like the grin of a dead thing, and so wide and bulging were his eyeballs in their sockets that they seemed like baubles placed within a mask. His face appeared, in short, like a living skull; yet ghastly though it was, it was not so ghastly as the thing I had exposed. I could barely bring myself to look at the hideously preserved thing a second time, and when I did so – how it ashames me to admit it! – I began to shudder terribly once again. Never had I seen such a human face before, so vilely, so loathsomely mutated and deformed! The skull seemed so vast that it quite overshadowed the face, which in turn appeared strangely shrunken, as though the cheeks had been pinched between two giant thumbs. There was very little to counter this impression of something barely human: some few tufts of hair remained upon the skull, and a layer of scaly skin stretched taut across the bone, yet no clues as to the living individual had endured, no hint as to what its sex, or age or race had been, for all that had been mortal had shrivelled utterly away, and only the strangeness of its form had been preserved.

'Sir!' Ahmed's sudden cry was almost a scream. He pointed towards the darkness beyond the edge of the trench. 'A noise. I heard a . . . noise.'

I strained my ears. All seemed quiet; deathly quiet. I was about to laugh – to chide Ahmed for imagining ghosts – when suddenly I too heard something. A shuffling, very faint but unmistakable; and drawing nearer to us all the time.

Ahmed glanced at me, his eyes still very wide. Then he seized one of the torches, and raising it aloft, scrambled up the side of the trench. I called out to him to wait, but he did not pause, and with an impatient curse I hurried after him. As I did so, I heard the shuffling again. I could tell now that it was coming from behind me. I spun round, flashing my torch, but still I could see nothing. I crept forward. All had gone silent once more. Then suddenly, still from behind me, I heard footsteps, running now, and even as I turned I knew it was too late. I caught the briefest glimpse of my assailant – an Arab, his eyes very cold, his smile very thin – and then I felt a crimson pain across the side of my head before everything went black.

How long I remained unconscious I am still uncertain. I was revived by Ahmed splashing water on my face, but I knew even before he told me that he too had been attacked, for I could see how his hair was still matted with blood. Of the man who had struck me there was not a sign, save only a jumble of footprints; nor was he the only thing to have disappeared. For as I staggered to my feet, Ahmed pointed grim-facedly in the direction of the trench. I hurried across to it, but alas! – my worst forebodings were to prove all too correct. The mummy had gone; so too the ornament which I had wrapped and laid aside so carefully. Of all my hopes and finds of that night, not a single trace remained.

My disappointment cut me especially deep, since I knew now that I would have no choice but to leave the next day for Cairo. I had briefly hoped that Ahmed might have recognised our assailants; but he, like me, had been caught by surprise, and when I attempted to describe the man that I had glimpsed he could only shrug and give a shake of his head. He promised, though, that he would launch a full investigation, to track down not only our mysterious assailants but also the mummy and the portrait of Tyi. Even as he vowed this, of course, I knew that he had little prospect of success; but I slipped him money all the same, and made him promise to keep me informed of any news.

Then I thanked him for all his many years' service, and would have bade him farewell save that I could sense he had something he still wanted to say. He appeared strangely reluctant, however, to spit it out, and indeed, I was almost losing patience when he finally cleared his throat. 'The tomb, sir,' he asked me. 'What about the tomb?'

'Tomb?' I frowned.

'The tomb, sir, in the story, with the demon inside. I told you of the lion with the woman's head – how that was supposed to have been found beside the unopened door. But in the story, sir – there was . . . yes – there was something else as well. A withered body, with its throat torn apart.'

I narrowed my eyes and, with great deliberation, began to stroke the ends of my moustache. 'Indeed?' I said at length.

Ahmed cleared his throat again. 'You cannot, sir, stay a few more weeks?'

I considered this option, then shook my head slowly. 'No. Not with the present lack of definite proof.'

'And . . . Mr Davis, sir?'

I glanced at him sharply.

'Will you tell Mr Davis of what happened here tonight?'

As I gazed around me at the level sands, I thought of all the secrets, the treasures they might contain. I glanced at Ahmed again; I did not reply.

'You will be back, sir,' he whispered. '*Inshallah*, the chance will come, and you will dig in the Valley of the Kings once again.'

I shrugged very faintly. 'Let us hope so,' I said.

It goes without saying, of course, that I profoundly regretted my transfer from Thebes; and yet for all my disappointment, I could not suppress a certain mood of excitement at taking up my new post. After the solitude and quiet of my former Inspectorate, how vast Cairo seemed, how impossibly full of colour and noise! In the desert, I might well have heard nothing for hours save the crying of a jackal or a hawk, but in Cairo the sounds of the streets formed an endless backdrop to my day. Even at night, the tramping of feet would never cease, nor the hubbub of conversation, nor the shouting of traders and the howling of dogs. And sometimes too there would come the summonings to prayer, a chorus as ancient as the city itself, so that standing upon my roof, scanning the minarets as they speared into the haze, I would imagine Cairo's centuries melted by the cry. But then I would turn and stare towards the southern horizon, and see a skyline more vastly ancient by far. The pyramids of Ghiza, viewed from the roof of my house, appeared strangely insubstantial, as though afloat upon a mist; yet they would outlive, I suspected, all of Cairo itself. Nor did it cease to stir me, nor to fill me with pride, that it was I who had been charged with their continued protection – for the pyramids had been ancient even in Akh-en-Aten's time.

Not that my interest in that King, nor in the mysteries of his reign, had been in any way diminished by my transfer to Cairo. I knew, of course, that the trails I had been following in Thebes would now be difficult to pursue. There were no sites near Cairo to excavate, nor any source of those folk tales which I had relied upon before. Indeed, only one faint line of inquiry still seemed open to me, for it would be my duty in Cairo, as it had previously been in Thebes, to keep a track of any smuggling of antiquities. With so many dealers in the capital, I feared that this would prove a near impossible task; but I also knew that the finest of Egypt's many plundered treasures, all the richest loot of the Valley of the Kings, would infallibly end up in Cairo's bazaars, where European collectors might then have their pick. When my other duties spared me the time, I began to visit these shops, making myself known to the antiquity dealers and closely inspecting their assembled wares. I particularly hoped to trace the portrait of Tyi, but that was not the only object I sought, for indeed I was interested in anything dating from

Akh-en-Aten's reign. Above all I hunted images of the sun, images with two worshippers praying underneath.

As I had suspected would be the case, however, I had little luck at first. Yet my calls upon the dealers were not wholly without point, for they served to establish my name amongst them and to establish theirs with me. I had soon come to identify where the true heart of the antiquities industry lay, in a souk just south of the Khan el-Khalili, the great covered market of the medieval city. It was there, accordingly, that I centred my search. And indeed, I thought, it was a fitting enough place in which to hunt for treasure; for the narrow, winding streets, with their spices and bright silks, their porters and donkeys, their cross-legged merchants and slowly-moving crowds, seemed a vision conjured from some oriental fantasy, some children's book version of 'The Arabian Nights'.

Several months after my arrival in Cairo, however, I was starting to grow discouraged. But then, just as I was on the point of abandoning my search altogether, I had a piece of luck – one which was to lead me, as though I might truly have been Aladdin or Ali Baba, into a world full of dark and fabulous mystery. It happened one evening, as I was passing through the trinket-laden byways of the souk, that I observed a shop-front I must have overlooked before, for it was very narrow and stood in the shadow of a high, crumbling wall. I crossed to it and, brushing aside the curtain which had veiled the contents from my view, passed inside. There were two men sitting there. One was stooped and very old; his companion, however, seemed little more than a boy, and it was he who rose and came forward to greet me. I asked him if he had any antiquities for sale. He nodded, and beckoned me to follow him. Although he was only carrying a single lamp, I had already caught the gleam of metal ahead and, as I passed further into the shop, I began to make out goblets, jewellery and swords piled randomly amidst blocks of decorated stone. I soon realised, however, that the artefacts were all of an Islamic date. My disappointment must have been evident on my face, for the old man now came forward to see if he could help.

I described to him what I was looking for. As is ever the way of the Orient, the old man could not bring himself to admit that he did not have what a customer might want, and so he allowed me to continue with my questions, nodding and smiling and shrugging all the while. Then I asked him if he had any portrayals of the sun, and at last his smile seemed one of relief. He took me by the arm, still smiling broadly, and led me across to the blocks of stone. He pointed at one of them, but I shook my head, for I had seen at once that the decorations on its side were like all the others, of an early Islamic origin. But the old man insisted I look closer and so, for the sake of form, I bent down to inspect it.

At once, I felt my heart leap into my mouth. I stared up at the old man, wide-eyed, then back at the artwork on the side of the stone. For there could be no doubting that it was a portrait, not just of the sun but quite specifically of the Aten – and beneath the disk were the figures of two crouching worshippers. It was identical, in almost every way, to the image I had found in the quarry with Newberry, and although the one before me now bore no inscriptions, it clearly dated from a similar period. Seeing my excitement, the old man began naming his price, but although I was perfectly willing to pay, it was information I wanted, not the piece of stone itself. I asked where it had come from. The old man shrugged and smiled, but then, when I pressed him, his smile suddenly dissolved into a look of fear. I pulled more money from my wallet.

'All I want to know,' I repeated, 'is the source of this stone.'

But the old man, for some reason now terrified of my intentions, had declined with great suddenness into the most remarkable funk, and would say nothing at all. Instead he began to flap at me, as though to shoo me away. I tried once again to calm his nerves by pulling out more money, but the old man appeared barely to see it, so abject was his terror, and still he flapped at me, moaning all the while. At length, accepting that I would get no sense from him, I turned and left, as infuriated by his terror as I was also intrigued.

I began to stride in a tense fury through the crowded souk. To be so close to such a remarkable breakthrough . . . and then to be denied! But it so happened, just as I was resolving to turn and go back, that I felt a tugging upon my jacket and, swinging round, found the lad from the shop. He grinned up at me. 'The piece of stone, sir,' he whispered, 'it came from a mosque.'

'What mosque? One here in Cairo?'

The boy's grin broadened.

I reached inside my pocket for a roll of bank-notes and handed a couple over.

The boy inspected them disdainfully. 'You must know, sir, the information that you want, it is very dangerous.'

'Why?'

'A very bad mosque – a very bad reputation.'

I counted out more bank-notes, and handed them across.

The lad slipped them into the pocket of his robe, then took my arm and led me in a conspiratorial manner towards the darkness of a side alley. 'The mosque, sir, you want is that of al-Hakim. He was a Caliph, a great King, who ruled over all the Arab lands long, long ago. But he was evil, sir, and mad, and it is said he worshipped not Allah but Iblis, for he was a servant of darkness.'

'How did the old man come by the stone?'

'The mosque, sir, is abandoned – so it was an easy matter for my uncle to remove the stonework where it crumbles.'

'But why was he so terrified that he could not tell me that himself?'

The lad glanced sideways into the night shadows. As he turned back to me, he fingered a charm which hung around his neck. 'To carve a sun, sir,' he hissed, 'and upon the walls of a mosque, it is a terrible crime. If anyone should know that my uncle had found it . . .'

'But who would know? I thought you said that the mosque was abandoned?'

The lad shrugged. He appeared almost as nervous now, I thought, as his uncle had been. 'I must go, sir,' he said.

'Wait,' I called out, 'wait! Where can I find this mosque of al-Hakim?'

The lad glanced back at me over his shoulder. 'By the Bab al-Futuh,' he cried, 'the Northern Gate. And may Allah guard you, sir!' Then he turned and was gone.

I stared after him a moment before glancing up at the sky. The stars were already prickling brightly and, remembering the fear which the mosque had inspired in both the old man and the young lad, I was almost tempted to postpone my visit there. But I had business the next day away from Cairo, and when I asked, I found it was not a great distance to the Bab al-Futuh. Accordingly, I left the souk and began to walk northwards, forcing my way through the still-crowded bazaars, and smiling ruefully to myself as I did so at the thought of how superstition could infect even my own, rational mind. But as I left the covered markets behind, so the crowds began to thin, and the darkness gradually to seem more close and intense. Certainly, the piles of refuse in the street were growing higher, but so also were the crumbling buildings on either side, so that when I looked up I could see only a narrow strip of stars, barely glimpsable through the balconies which projected from the walls. No lights shone from behind either windows or doors, nor – a strange thing in Cairo indeed! – could I hear any noise at all; yet I had the most powerful sense of being watched, as though there were hidden eyes behind every latticed front. Even as I thought that, I began to observe eyes painted on the walls, staring out from within the palms of open hands – the traditional Egyptian charm against an imagined curse.

As the street widened again, so the number of eyes upon the walls began steadily to increase. Peering ahead of me now, I could just make out the silhouette of a massive gateway – the Bab al-Futuh, I assumed, where the mosque was said to stand. I stopped and looked about me. I could see nothing, however, save for a dilapidated wall with an archway to my right, so decayed and littered with rubble that I was astonished the authorities had not already pulled it down. Even in comparison with the rest of the street, it seemed a wasteland of particular desertion and shadow; yet although I sought to tear my gaze from it, I found myself strangely drawn by its aspect of ruin. Almost despite myself, I crossed to the archway and gazed through it to see what lay beyond. I could just make out a courtyard, its crumbling marble lit silver by the moon; but as I approached it, so the gleam began to fade and grow mottled by the withered tangles of weeds, as though the desolation were stifling the light. I continued to walk forward. Ahead of me now, I could see more debris: collapsed walls, abandoned boxes, piles of toppled stone. I could also see, to the left and right of me, two minarets stabbing upwards, perfectly silhouetted against the star-emblazoned sky. At the same moment, I felt a strange blackness settle on my heart; and I knew that I had surely found the mosque of al-Hakim.

★

Conquering my quite irrational sense of oppression, I began to walk towards a doorway beneath the nearest minaret. The stonework there appeared better preserved, and I was hopeful that I might discover something worthy of my study. Above the doorway, when I inspected it, I found a line of Arabic text, but so weathered had it become that I could barely make sense of it. 'Al-Vakhel', I read – that seemed to be a name – and then faded stonework, and then 'this place', and then, on the other side of the archway, only the one word 'darkness'. I frowned. It was impossible to read any more but certainly, whatever the text may originally have said, it did not seem to allude to a long-dead Pharaoh, and I shook my head to think I had ever hoped that it might have done. How, in God's name, when Akh-en-Aten's reign had been buried utterly in oblivion, would his name have been known to a Muslim Caliph? And how, even if by some extraordinary coincidence it had been known, would the evidence of such a heresy – carved upon the stonework of a mosque, no less – ever have been preserved these many long centuries? And yet . . . I frowned. I remembered the carving of the Aten in the old man's shop. I had seen it with my own eyes. And I had seen his terror as well, his abject fear; and that had certainly been real enough . . .

When I pushed at the door, it swung open easily. I peered into the darkness beyond it, and could just make out steps. Feeling my way carefully, I began to walk up them. I soon realised that they had been built in a spiral, and that I was climbing the centre of the minaret. My journey, though, was very slow, for the darkness remained pitch until suddenly I saw a thin beam of silver ahead of me, slanting across the stairway, and when I looked out through the slit of the window I realised that I had climbed higher than I had thought. I inspected the shell of the mosque laid out below me for a while, then continued with my ascent. Soon there came another window, and then another, and then, just beyond the fourth, there came a heavy door. Unlike the first one I had passed through, it appeared newly fitted and I could see, in the pale moonlight, how the stonework around it had been reinforced. I tried the handle. It wouldn't turn. I sought to force it, but without much hope. At length I stepped back, frowning. What could possibly lie beyond it which had led it to being secured with so much evident care? I inspected the door again, and then the stonework more closely. As I did so, the angle of the moonlight must have changed, for I suddenly caught something I had not observed before; and at once my heart seemed to stop.

Above the highest part of the arch there was a carving of the Aten. But I could still barely make it out, and so I reached up to trace the lines with my finger. I could feel that the disk was full and that two worshippers knelt beneath it, reaching up to greet its rays.

I breathed in deeply and at the same moment – very faint and far below – I imagined I heard a noise like that of a door creaking open. I froze and stood motionless a while, straining my ears. But I could hear nothing more, and so I assumed it had been a trick played upon me by my nerves. I breathed in again, this time with relief, and turned back to inspect the carvings on the arch above the door.

I could see now that there were two lines of script on either side of the sun. "'Have you thought upon Lilat'," I quoted aloud, as I copied down the first inscription, "'the great one, the other? She is much to be feared. Truly, Lilat is great amongst gods"'. So it had been written in the tomb of Akh-en-Aten, by the portrait of his Queen; and so again it had been written down here.

I turned to the second inscription. This too I had seen before, in the quarry I had explored with Newberry. I shuddered as, again, I began to copy it down, for this verse suddenly struck me as a warning aimed forcibly at myself. And even as I thought this I heard it spoken, rising from the steps behind me, spoken by a voice as silver as the moonlight and as cold as when it shines upon the sand dunes of the desert. '"Leave for ever",' the voice whispered. '"You are damned. You are accursed". *Leave for ever.*'

I turned round to see a man standing on the step below me, dressed in the robes of an Arab scholar, which flowed long and white like his beard and moustache. His shoulders were stooped and his face very lined; yet though in appearance he seemed fabulously old, there was nothing of weakness or frailty in his manner. Quite the opposite, for he gazed at me with such an unblinking and luminous stare that I could barely endure to continue meeting it; and indeed, so brightly did it glitter and so hollow and impassive did his thin face appear, that it seemed more a serpent's than that of a man. And as I thought that, despite myself I shuddered; for I could not think how the old man had come to be standing behind me, when I had not even heard him climbing the steps.

'What is your business here?' I asked, attempting to disguise my unease beneath a show of brusqueness.

The old man smiled very palely. 'I might more fittingly ask that question of you.'

'I am . . .' I paused, then sought to draw myself up more fully. 'I am the Chief Inspector of Antiquities,' I announced.

The old man's stare seemed to flicker. 'Does that give you jurisdiction over a Holy Place of God?'

'This . . .' – I pointed to the figure of the sun above the door – 'it is the image of a God once worshipped by a Pharaoh.'

'Pharaoh?' The old man took a step closer to me. 'But it is said in the most Holy Koran that Pharaoh proclaimed there was no God but himself. So how can what you tell me possibly be the truth?'

'That is what I wish to find out.'

The old man laughed very faintly. 'But you have no right to find out anything at all.'

'I have told you,' I repeated. 'I am the Chief Inspector of Antiquities!'

'And yet, for all that, you do not belong here. Go! Go, sir – and do not come back!' The old man gestured suddenly with his arm, and indeed I almost did start to leave, for in his voice I had heard a note of terrible warning and almost of appeal. But I stood my ground, for I sensed that I might be near some revelation, some extraordinary secret, and it was my hope that the old man might unlock it after all. But he merely shook his head at me; and the look in his eyes was a chilling one. 'What can you hope to know of Egypt?' he whispered. 'As fears lie buried in the nightmares of our sleep,' I heard him murmur, 'so secrets lie buried in the past of this our land. Do not disturb them, Mr Carter. Do not disturb them. *Be warned!*'

The sudden and unexpected use of my name had quite served to freeze my tongue. I gazed wide-eyed into the old man's own unblinking stare, deep into its strange reptilian glitter. Still I tried to speak, but it was as though my mind were no longer my own but rather the thing of the old man's eyes. I imagined I saw within them – strange as it must sound! – a waste of sands, and treasures scattered, abandoned on the dunes. Here a half-shattered bust of stone lay, there a glittering of gold, and sometimes, exposed and then buried by the action of the wind once again, ancient, brittle parchments, suggestive of secrets which I could not make my own. Upon these stinging winds I was blown like dust myself, blown across the old man's dream, which seemed to stretch before me like the very wilds of Egypt. A shadow was lengthening. It seemed to be rising from beyond the horizon. It fell cold upon me and then, as I gazed ahead, I could see the form of a temple much like Karnak, half-submerged beneath the sands, but still so monstrous that it towered high above me and its shadow, as I neared it, was growing colder all the time. Then at last I had passed the outermost line of capitals, and was being blown ever deeper into the dark, and yet the temple still seemed to stretch away like infinity. There was something ahead of me, though; something buried within the place's deepest sanctuary; some awful presence, still veiled by the dark but drawing nearer, drawing nearer all the time, as though infinity might indeed be pierced after all; and the terror was like nothing I had ever known before. I longed to scream. I had imagined I was only a second away from it now. I would behold it; for it was as though the curtain which had veiled it were being raised before my eyes. I tensed and jerked back my head; then opened my eyes. The hallucination had vanished, and I was standing alone at the summit of the stairs. Of the old Arab scholar there was not a sign.

Of course, I reflected later, there need not have been anything supernatural or mysterious about my experience. I had been the victim of a skilful hypnotist, that was all. I had heard of such conjuring tricks before, and indeed sometimes seen their practice when sitting by the fire of a headman back in Thebes. Never, though, had I imagined that I might be susceptible to them myself – for I have always considered myself to have a fairly solid grip on things – and so, I do not mind confessing it, the experience had unsettled me to a fair degree. I chose not to linger in the mosque that night, for the door was still barred to me and I doubted I would be able to find out anything much more – but nor will I deny that I was relieved to get back home. I lay a long while on my sofa, still feeling strangely haunted by the images I had seen, and grateful for the companionship of the birds I had brought with me from Thebes. As it ever did, the music of their song served to comfort me, and the sight of the beauty of their plumage and flight. Yet my mood of oppression was not altogether lifted, for I still felt with a novel sense of regret how lonely I had become, and began to dread what the pursuit of my ambitions might not bring. Even so, it was only after many hours that I was lulled upon the song of my birds at last to sleep.

I woke the next morning after a night of bad dreams. I had a great deal of pressing business ahead of me, yet I could not get thoughts of the mosque from my mind. I felt certain now that I was on the trail of something very strange indeed: a secret long buried but somehow still alive; a conspiracy, perhaps, which had spanned more than 3,000 years. Where it might lead to I could not begin to imagine – for indeed, even now, I could barely believe it might exist. Nor, in truth, was I any nearer to resolving the mystery, for the door of the minaret had remained locked in my face, and though the old man had hinted at secrets, he had told me nothing more. It struck me as being a cruel feature of my quest that the more I discovered, the more there still seemed to find – that frustration seemed the fruit of every success.

All morning, as I went about my business, I pondered this apparent paradox. Yet events that same day were to render it even more pressing. It happened, as I was supervising work by the desert at Saqqara, that news was brought to me of a drunken affray. A group of Frenchmen, it seemed, had grown rowdy and offensive while visiting the nearby tombs, and started to create trouble for my native staff. Naturally, I hurried to investigate the matter as fast as I could and, upon arriving, discovered what appeared to be a virtual fracas. My appeals for calm were so much wasted breath, for it was not only the Frenchmen who were threatening my staff but also a group of their servants, as vicious a collection of thugs as one might ever care to encounter. It was immediately apparent to me that it was these servants who were the true cause of the trouble, and so I summoned up reinforcements and ordered them disarmed. The Frenchmen, realising that they were outnumbered, at once retreated from the confrontation, but continued to protest most vociferously when my men persisted with the attack upon their own. They demanded that their servants be left alone and, upon the condition that they would immediately withdraw, I reluctantly agreed. As my men fell back, however, I was able to study the ruffians more closely – and one in particular, their evident ringleader, whose face as yet I had been unable to glimpse. I moved forward. As I did so, he turned to glance at me; and I shuddered at once with recognition and surprise.

There could be no mistaking him. I had seen him only for the barest second before, when he had come at me from the darkness of the Valley of the Kings and laid me out cold – but still I knew him, that thin smile, that glittering stare. I pointed and, shouting to my staff, ordered him to be taken. But the Frenchmen, outraged by what they may have seen as my bad faith, reacted by threatening to join the fight themselves; and it was all I could do to hold them back. In the chaos of the ensuing scuffle, the villain I had hoped to seize was able to make his escape, he and all his band. I was left with nothing to show for the episode save the injuries to my staff, six affronted Frenchmen – and a potentially fatal threat to my career.

For the Frenchmen, with that arrogance so typical of their nation, had the nerve to complain to my superior – doubtless in the knowledge that he was a Frenchman himself. I must acknowledge here once again, however, that the head of the Service, Monsieur Gaston Maspero, was a man of rare discernment and honour who, having appointed me as Inspector in the first place, was now unwilling to dismiss me upon a trumped-up cause. He knew me well enough to accept that I had not been to blame and, despite the mounting protests from the French establishment in Egypt, he continued to stand by me. Nevertheless he wished me, for the sake of form, to offer an apology, and seemed to imagine I could do so with good grace. Naturally, however, I found such a request an insulting one, and indeed, felt the humiliation to an exceeding extent. I had carried out my duty, as I had always sought to do – how then could I apologise for other people's faults?

Nevertheless I accepted that, although my pride and my very honour were at stake, so also were other, perhaps more threatening concerns. For who could the Arab have been, I wondered, who had first attacked me in the Valley of the Kings, and then orchestrated the brawl which had so damaged my reputation? What was the reason for his campaign against me? And was it just a coincidence, or something far more sinister, that he should have intruded again into my life on the very day after my visit to the mosque of al-Hakim? I remembered the old Arab scholar and his parting words to me: '*Be warned!*' Well, so I was now – warned and prepared. For indeed, it seemed probable to me that I was closer to a breakthrough than I had ever dared to hope – for why else would anyone be seeking to drive me from my post?

This conviction came to seem all the more certain when I received a letter a few days after the brawl with the Frenchmen, posted to me from the Valley of the Kings. It had been scribbled, evidently in great excitement, by Theodore Davis; and it told of the discovery of a treasure-laden tomb. My emotions on reading this news were mixed in the extreme: I felt a keen interest, obviously, but also – I must confess it – a certain degree of resentment that it was not I who had made the find. Indeed, my initial fear was that

Davis might have stumbled upon the site which I had been excavating on my final evening in the Valley of the Kings, but a hurried reading of his letter reassured me on that point, for it seemed clear that he had been digging upon a quite different slope. Nevertheless, the find was still of an especial interest to me – for the tomb had belonged to the parents of Queen Tyi. 'There can be no doubt about it,' Davis asserted in his letter, 'although I was surprised at first, for I had never heard of noblemen being buried in the Valley of the Kings. But their names have been preserved upon the lids of their coffins – Yuya, the father, and Thua, his wife. The mummies too have survived – and Yuya especially is in an excellent condition. I know you thought that he might have been a Nubian, but he don't look like no nigger I've ever seen. In fact, he's the image of a Jew politician I knew back on Rhode Island – same beaked nose and long, scrawny neck. A wonderful find, Carter – and a damned shame you can't be here. You dig the Valley all those years, and then the moment you're gone we find this amazing tomb!'

A damned shame indeed. Yet although Davis had clearly been relishing his chance to have a gloat, it appeared that our former partnership still meant something to him. The finds, he reported, would shortly be on their way to the Cairo Museum, the treasures first and then the mummies a few months after, and Davis would be needing watercolours for his projected book upon the tomb. 'I've seen for myself,' he wrote at the bottom of his letter, 'how you're the finest artist in Egyptian studies today. Would you consider, then, once the finds from the tomb have arrived in Cairo, painting them for me? Naturally,' he added in a scribbled postscript, 'I would reimburse you for your efforts.'

I wrote back at once accepting his offer. The time might come, I thought ruefully, when I would need such employment; for although I had not yet been asked to resign, neither could I bring myself to apologise for something that had not been my fault. Maspero, clearly searching for some way out of the impasse, seemed determined to exile me far away from Cairo. I knew that by dispatching me to a back-water, he hoped to allow the storm I had raised to blow itself out; yet even so, I felt the indignity of my demotion very keenly. I could not bring myself to abandon Cairo, not at such a time, not when the trail seemed suddenly so promis-ing – and yet to keep my post, I would clearly have to leave. With the greatest reluctance, therefore, I bowed to the inevitable and left for Tanta, the hell-hole which had been appointed as my new headquarters. A more miserable town I had never come across, for it was dull and hot, and pos-sessed the most appalling drains. Even my poor birds were affected by the stench, and with every breath I took I grew more tempted to resign. Yet still I could not bring myself to take the fateful step, for it was not only my income I would lose but also, perhaps crucially, my Chief Inspector's powers. Who knew when I might not need them? Patience, I reminded myself, as I had always sought to do – patience, patience, always patience.

At last, during the very height of an unbearable summer, I received the news that the artefacts from Yuya's tomb had arrived in Cairo. I took a couple of weeks leave as soon as I could and travelled to the Museum, relieved to have escaped Tanta, and excited at the prospect of what the treasures might reveal. Just as Davis had asserted, they were of a magnificent quality, and it was evident that Yuya must have been a man of very great importance indeed, for he was described upon several artefacts as being 'a man made the double of Pharaoh', and his wife as 'the Superior of the Harim'. Certainly, as Davis had already pointed out to me in his letter, no other commoner was known to have been buried in the Valley of the Kings – and yet I could discover nothing which might explain such a remarkable honour. The sarcophagi, for instance, usually such a prime source of detail, appeared virtually without decoration at all, and certainly without those elaborate portraits of the gods which it was the custom for the ancients to paint upon their coffins. More frustratingly, however, I could find no hints as to who Yuya might truly have been, and how it was – in direct contradiction of traditional royal custom – that his daughter Tyi had come to marry the Pharaoh. It had long been clear to me that these puzzles might be of a crucial significance, and so it was all the more dispiriting to find them still unresolved.

But I had not given up hope altogether. The treasures had been displayed in a public gallery and it had proved impossible, surrounded by crowds of gawping tourists, to give them the attention they so clearly deserved. With the written help of Davis, I therefore secured permission to paint the treasures after gallery hours; and indeed, studying them late at night, with the silence and darkness of the museum all around me, my sense was heightened of the mysteries they might veil. Still, though, that veil remained drawn and I grew all the more certain, as I continued with my painting, that I was glimpsing the surface and nothing more. What, then, was I missing?

One event in particular served to make me wonder this. I had arrived at the gallery early one evening, perhaps half an hour before the closing time. I stood for a while amongst the last few tourists, admiring the treasures as though I were one of their number. Then I laid down the painting equipment I had brought with me and wandered off to inspect the further galleries, until I could be certain that the museum had finally been closed. Only then did I return to Yuya's coffins, back through the now empty halls, their exhibits shrouded in an unillumined gloom. Where I was working, however, a light had been left on — and it was this which enabled me to see the amulet straight away. Others might not have observed it, for it had been leaned unobtrusively against the coffin's side — but perhaps, after my experiences in the Valley of the Kings, I had been almost expecting it. I crossed to the amulet and picked it up. I scarcely needed to inspect the design, but there it was all the same: two worshippers kneeling in prayer beneath a sun. I looked about me; I strained my ears. All was quiet. I hurried through the galleries, searched the whole museum . . . but still I could find no sign of an intruder. Someone must have been there, though — someone must have placed the amulet by Yuya's coffin. If only I could find him! If only I could hunt the conspiracy down, with its web of strange secrets and long-buried legends — and its apparently centuries-old dread of a terrible curse! But my period of leave was coming to an end; and in Tanta there would be nothing to hunt down at all.

Even so, I went back there to my exile. I still had hopes of a recall to my former post in Cairo, and for as long as that remained a viable prospect, I was reluctant to jeopardise my career in the Service. But my sense of frustration now was damnable, and the longer I spent smelling the drains of Tanta, so the less appealing their odour became. By the autumn my patience was wearing pretty thin, and when Davis wrote to me reporting the arrival in Cairo of Yuya's mummy and his wife's, it was more than I could endure to wait for an official spell of leave. Instead, I caught the earliest train available and arrived, that same night, by the gates to the museum. Only a sleepy foreman was on guard, and he must have recognised me, for he waved me through. Fortunately, I had brought my keys with me, and I was able to enter the museum unattended. I did not, though, pass into the Main hallway, but took a side door which led upstairs to the first floor. It was here, I knew, that the mummies were exhibited, the bodies of some of Egypt's greatest kings – and also, I trusted, those of Yuya and Thua too.

Not wishing to draw attention to myself, I was reluctant to switch on the overhead lights, and so instead I drew out my torch and flashed its beam across the exhibition room. Mummy after mummy stretched away into the dark, their withered forms preserved not in gold coffins now, not beneath the watchful gaze of Osiris, but under panes of labelled glass. I began to walk past them, my footsteps echoing through the silence. I continued to sweep my torch, peering into the face of each long-dead man until I saw, at the very end of the hall, two human-shaped objects swathed in sheets. I quickened my stride towards them, then stepped over the rope which was marking them off and approached the first body. By its side a sheaf of notes had been left: 'Thua,' I read, 'the mother of Queen Tyi.' I glanced behind me once more, to make certain I was alone, then raised the sheet and took a glance underneath.

The gaze of a centuries-old woman met my own. I could not help, though, but feel a stab of disappointment, for her features had been not at all well preserved and her face seemed little more than a skull. There was something blank about her expression, something inhuman and strange, which I found oddly unsettling; so much so that when I heard a sudden scurrying from the far end of the room, I started violently and gazed about me, as though expecting to glimpse some horror lurking in the shadows. But there was no more noise, and nothing to be seen, and so I assumed I had heard some nocturnal rodent. I glanced about me once again, then crossed to the second body. As I had done before, I grasped the edge of the sheet, raised it and took a look underneath.

This time, however, I could barely restrain a gasp of astonishment. Where the face of Thua had been sadly decayed, that of her husband was astonishingly preserved. Davis had not exaggerated, for it was, I thought, the finest mummy I had ever seen. There was nothing distorted about his features, and they enabled me to see that once again Davis had been right in his assertions, for it was evident that Yuya might indeed have been a Semite. He had a shock of white hair, a great hooked nose, a prominent, determined jaw – a man, even in death, of commanding presence still. Gazing upon his powerful and dignified face, I could not help but wonder whether I had perhaps found the originator of that great religious movement, that elevated worship of a single god, which the old man's grandson was to institute as Pharaoh. But then, even as I considered that possibility, questions crowded in on me again. For who could Yuya have been? How had he married his daughter to a king? And how – when he had not even been Egyptian, still less a king himself – had he come to be buried in the Valley of the Kings?

My consideration of these mysteries, however, was suddenly interrupted again by a scuffling, very faint but unmistakable now. I swung round and this time, in the beam of my torch, I caught the silhouette of a human form. It stood frozen a moment in the doorway to the hall, and although I could not make out the man's features I knew at once who he was, for I could see the glittering of his eyes, and I remembered them from Saqqara and the Valley of the Kings. 'Stop!' I cried out; but the man was already running down the stairs. 'Stop!' I called again, starting to pursue him and hoping that some of the guards would hear me. But by the time I had reached the bottom of the stairs, all was silent again; and though I searched with my torch, I knew I would never find my quarry, for in a place as vast and cluttered as the museum, there were an infinity of places where a man might hide himself. Indeed, I doubted he would even still be lurking in the place. Where might he have gone to, then? Where might such a man have his secret base?

I left for the mosque of al-Hakim at once. My cab made good speed at first, for it was by now very late and the streets of Cairo, although they are never empty, were not as crowded as they might have been. As we drew nearer to the mosque, however, I could sense my driver's mounting unease until at length, while we were still some streets from our destination, he pulled in his horse and refused to go further; nor could all my exhortations or inducements serve to change his mind. In a fury, I gave up on him at last and continued on foot, for I knew, in truth, that it was not too far to the mosque. But although I had thought that I recognised the way, I soon found myself lost. The streets seemed to wind and double back upon themselves, like a maze in a nightmare which never comes to an end, and by the time I stumbled upon the mosque at last, I knew it was too late – I would never be able to surprise my man now. Nevertheless, I climbed the stairway of the minaret and, reaching the door, cried out for it to be opened. But there was only silence; and the door remained shut. I ran back down to the courtyard of the mosque. It was bleached a sickly white, as on my previous visit, by the moon. I could see that it was empty. Still, though, I called out for my quarry, for the old man, for anyone at all. But nothing answered me. The mosque would not speak.

I returned to my old house in Cairo for a few hours' sleep, then took the train back to Tanta. I arrived there in the late evening, dispirited and tired, wanting nothing so much as an undisturbed night. As the cab which had brought me from the station drove away, however, my servant came running out through the door, moaning and sobbing unintelligibly, and though I sought to get him to make some sense, all he could do was point towards the house. I hurried in through the front door. Everything appeared to be as I had left it, but then, just as I was about to turn to my servant and demand an explanation, I saw that the door into my study had been smashed.

Feeling somewhat tense myself now, I crossed over to it. In the doorway I stood rooted to the spot, suddenly frozen by what I saw in the room beyond. 'Damn them,' I whispered. 'Damn them to hell.' I realised to my surprise that my eyes had begun to water and, not wishing to be seen by the servant, I had to pause a moment more to brush the tears away. Only then did I enter the study and, bending down, pick up my dead birds. So light and small they were that I could hold all their bodies in my hands . . . my birds, my beautiful, beautiful birds. Their tiny bodies had been ripped open; their blood had been used to scrawl a warning on the wall. It was one I had already been given before. 'Leave for ever,' I read. 'You are damned. You are accursed.' And then behind me, above my desk, had been daubed a second verse. 'Have you thought upon Lilat, the great one, the other? She is much to be feared. Truly, Lilat is great amongst gods.'

It was evident they hoped to frighten me with their voodoo spells. In my case, though, I thought, they had got the wrong man, for I have always had that tenacity of purpose which the unfriendly will call obstinacy, but which I call resolve. I had been given, as it seemed to me, not a warning but a declaration of war. That same evening, I sat down at my desk and, writing to Monsieur Maspero, informed him of my immediate intention to resign.

I left for Thebes. I had no firm plan of action; I knew only that I needed to order my thoughts. In the Valley of the

Kings I might find fresh clues, discoveries of which Davis had not thought to inform me. I would also need to provide for myself, and I hoped that in Thebes, where I had been well known amongst the wealthy tourists, I would be able to scrape a living as a painter and guide. But above all, after the shock of what had happened in my study at Tanta, I wanted nothing so much as to feel secure – and Thebes, more than anywhere, had come to seem like home.

Even so, I suspected that there was nowhere in Egypt, and certainly not by the Valley of the Kings, where I could be truly safe from my unknown enemies. My most urgent consideration was to warn Ahmed Girigar of the danger, for he had been with me when I had first been attacked, and I had heard nothing from him since that night in the Valley. Accordingly, when I arrived at Thebes, my first port of call was the village where he lived and I was much relieved, as I approached his house, to see him sitting hale and hearty, puffing on his pipe. He rose to greet me, his face radiating that expression of unfeigned welcome which is so typical of your Egyptian. 'Mr Carter!' he exclaimed, bowing low, then shaking my hand. 'I am so glad to see you – and so sorry to hear that you have resigned your post.'

'How did you hear it?' I frowned. 'The news is not yet public.'

Ahmed's smile did not falter. 'You know this country, sir. Secrets always travel very fast.'

'Not every secret,' I answered.

'Ah.' Ahmed gazed at me closely. 'Then you are still on the trail of your mysteries, I see.' He gestured at me to sit down as he called for coffee; then, once it had been brought to us, he began to tell me of the latest developments in the Valley. I found it hard to concentrate, however, even on such news, for I could not help but continue wondering how Ahmed had heard of my resignation. But I knew that I should accept his explanation: not only had it been a credible one – all too credible – but in my present mood I was afraid that I was coming to scent conspiracies everywhere. And so I sipped my coffee, and sought to banish my suspicions, and listened with more attention to all that Ahmed had to say. He must have observed my change of mood, for he suddenly paused and leaned over to me. 'Is it not as I foretold, sir?' he smiled. 'Did I not say how, Allah willing, you would dig here once again?'

I was touched by his loyalty, but I could scarcely share in his expectations. For he had little of much value to tell me: he had not been working on Davis's excavations, and was even uncertain as to whether the amulets were still appearing in the tombs. From Davis himself I could expect few favours, and certainly not the chance to renew my own excavations. Having originally secured the concession to the Valley for him, I knew that I would now have to wait for him to retire from archaeology before I could hope to dig there once again – and Davis, unfortunately, did not seem in a retiring mood at all. 'Why, Carter,' he would crow, 'I'm digging up a tomb or two every goddam season! At the rate I'm going, it won't be long before the whole Valley is exhausted!' And then, despite myself, I would know that my frustration was all too visible upon my face, for he would lean across to me and pat me on the arm. 'Don't worry, though – when I find the tombs of Queen Tyi, and Smenkh-ka-Re, and Tut-ankh-Amen, you'll be the first to hear of it.' Then his grin would slowly broaden. 'Why,' he would sometimes add, 'I'll do more than just inform you! After all – who better than Howard Carter to paint my finds for me?'

I took this with all the good humour I could muster. At least I could reassure myself that the Valley was not yet entirely exhausted, and I was careful, in an unobtrusive manner, to study Davis's work there as closely as I could. There were certain areas – very promising, I thought – which he had excavated in only the most cursory way, and so I duly noted these for future reference. But there were also areas where Davis still had to dig – and one of these, the most promising of all, was the site where I had uncovered the portrait of Queen Tyi. It was this which caused me the greatest worry. I was almost certain – remembering the corpse we had exhumed, and the attack which had followed my attempt to dig further – that a tomb lay buried there – and not just any tomb. For if it was in any way linked to the folklore of the area, then it might surely be linked to something much more – to those secrets which the Mosque of al-Hakim appeared to shelter, and to a conspiracy which seemed almost vertiginously old. What, then, might happen if Davis did find the tomb? And if he opened it, what might be waiting there inside?

But I knew that there was nothing I could do to hold him back. Indeed, so tense and frustrating did the situation grow that I sometimes found it hard to continue in Thebes. There was still research to be done in Cairo, of course, and since I did not have the money to pay for even a servant, I had to carry out all the work there myself. During my time in the capital, I was able to map out the mosque as carefully as I could. I found little new of any great significance save that, above the doorway to the second minaret, I was able to trace the script of a second inscription. Like the first, it mentioned the mysterious word 'al-Vakhel', but this time I could make sense of the phrase as a whole. 'Al-Vakhel,' I read, 'had this warning inscribed, that by sheltering the darkness, the light might be preserved.' As I read this, I glanced up at the opposite minaret. 'The darkness,' I wondered. What darkness? What was it which lay locked away there, behind a door surmounted by the sun of Akh-en-Aten?

As to the identity of al-Vakhel himself, I could find no further clues. I had been hopeful at first, for I had discovered many traditions relating to the Caliph al-Hakim, sixth of the Fatimid rulers of Egypt, who had ruled at the turn of the tenth century and whose cruelty and displays of blasphemy, even at such a distance, were still spoken of by the Faithful in terms of horror and awe – certainly, it did not surprise me that his mosque should be considered cursed. Yet though it appeared that such had his madness been that he had ended up proclaiming himself a god, I found there were also those who proclaimed the Caliph a saint; who insisted that he had never died; who whispered that he had discovered the very elixir of life. Certainly, it appeared that his assassination – for such, according to the history books, had been the Caliph's ultimate fate – had in truth been an exceedingly mysterious affair, and I began to wonder, in the context of such a busi-ness, what the role of al-Vakhel might not have been, for wherever there was mystery there I would look out for his name. But I could still find no mention of him – nor, although I continued with my research month after month, could I discover any lead at all.

And then one evening, when I had returned disconsolate to my shabby hotel room, I found a letter waiting for me, scrawled in Arabic, and laid upon my bed. 'Mr Carter, sir,' I read, 'come quick. The tomb of the buried demon has been found. Urgent.'

It had been signed in the name of Ahmed Girigar.

I left for Thebes at once. For the whole length of my jour-ney I was plagued by the strongest doubts and fears, not only on account of the uncovered tomb but also by the letter which Ahmed had sent, for I had not given him my address, and it perturbed me to wonder how he might have obtained it. When I arrived at my destination, therefore, I did not, as I had formerly done, approach Ahmed for the latest news from the Valley, but headed off there myself at once. Passing through the narrow gorge which formed its entrance, I met with the archaeologist hired by Davis to conduct his excavations, an Englishman like myself and a decent enough fellow, if lacking in expertise. I asked him if it were true that a fresh tomb had been found. He nodded, but appeared exceedingly flustered and tense as he did so. Intrigued, I asked him what the matter could be. The poor man breathed in deeply. 'Davis,' he hissed.

He began to explain to me, as he escorted me to the site, that everything about it was a puzzle and a mess. The tomb had been plundered; but there were countless objects still scattered on the floor. It clearly dated from the time of Akhen-Aten; but every name on the walls had been chiselled away. There was a corpse inside a coffin; but the face on the lid had likewise been destroyed. Even the skeleton was a mystery. 'Davis, though,' my colleague explained, 'is convinced he has found the remains of Queen Tyi.'

'Any particular reason?'

'We found a large gilded shrine within the tomb – partially dismantled, it is true, for it had been used to block off the entrance to the chamber, but nevertheless clearly marked with Tyi's cartouche.'

I frowned. 'Then why do you think that the body isn't hers?'

'Because we had a doctor come up this morning, and he says that it was a man's – probably adolescent, certainly not more than early twenties.'

'Ah. And what has Davis said to that?'

'You know what he's like. You might as well try to stop an avalanche as try to get him to change his mind.'

I nodded sympathetically. By now we were emerging

from the ravine into the broader expanse of the Valley of the Kings. My companion pointed to the new tomb and I recognised it at once, with a sinking of my heart, as the site where I had found the portrait of Queen Tyi. The entrance-way had been only partially cleared, but even as I stared at it I saw a couple of workmen emerging from the darkness, carrying various objects in their arms. I turned to my companion in disbelief. 'What the hell are they doing?' I demanded. 'Don't you realise that if you empty the contents before you've inspected the tomb, you may be destroying critical evidence?'

'Of course I realise it,' my companion snapped back. 'But as I said – Davis has ordered it, and Davis must have his way.'

I snarled an imprecation and hurried to the tomb. Inspecting the doorway very hurriedly, I could see there was evidence of the original brickwork having been breached and then repaired, but could find nothing to indicate when this might have happened. Nor were things any better in the chamber beyond, for there, just as I had feared, the objects had already been hopelessly scattered and dispersed. I sought to find some proof of the legend I had heard from Ahmed, that the tomb had been entered in the Muslim period, but even as I did so I could tell that it was already too late. I cursed again, startling the hapless workmen with the violence of my language, then emerged from the darkness into the blinding brightness of the day.

Yet I was not so dazzled that I was unable to see, standing upon the facing cliff, the figures of two Arabs. As I emerged from the tomb entrance, they had both turned away; yet even as I inspected them, one of them glanced round again and I knew him at once. It was my old adversary from Saqqara, the man I suspected of killing my birds; and I straight away began to run towards the path which climbed the cliff. As I did so, both men started back and I realised, to my shock, that the second of the natives was Ahmed Girigar. They both turned and then, as I reached the path, I lost sight of them. By the time I had reached the top of the cliff, there was no sign of either man, and though I sought to follow their tracks, the sands soon gave way to a bare expanse of rock. I pressed onwards, however, to Ahmed's village. His house was empty, and as I walked away from it I felt that sense of disquiet, of brooding menace, which so often seems to wait upon silence in the East, bred from heat and stillness, and the gaze of veiled eyes.

Uncertain now as to what I should do, and feeling oddly perturbed, I made my way back towards the tomb. But as I approached it I heard Davis's voice, and immediately I froze. As though it were a coating of fine white dust, lassitude and disappointment had settled on me; and I could not face any meeting with my erstwhile patron. Turning and retreating from the Valley of the Kings, I walked as firmly as I could back down the track; but it was hot now, unbearably so, and my knees felt weak from the pounding of the sun. All around me the landscape was shimmering, and the brightness blinded me. I would find nothing now, I thought. Why bother to continue with the search? Where, and for what?

I walked the several miles back to my quarters. I had the dingiest room in the town's dingiest hotel and the air, like myself, was sticky with dust. I crossed to my bed. Not bothering to remove my clothes, I pulled back the sheet. There it lay. Had I been expecting it? It may well be – for how else to explain my lack of surprise? I picked it up and for a moment inspected it – an amulet stamped with the image of the sun.

Then I dropped it on to the floor. Vaguely I heard it clatter on the boards, but I must already have been drifting away into sleep for it seemed to echo and echo as though amplified by my dreams. Yet all the while I thought myself awake, for it was still too hot to fall truly asleep. And thus it was that I was claimed by the onset of fever, bred from my exhaustion, and my disappointment, and the heat; and still, all the while, I believed myself awake.

When I saw reliefs upon the walls of my room, then, it was with the keenest sense of their verisimilitude. They were carved in the style of Akh-en-Aten's reign, grotesque and deformed. As I watched them, they began to emerge from the plaster, their swollen heads swaying and their thick lips parted in imbecilic grins. They were soon crowding my bed. As they reached for me, so their limbs seemed to crackle and their heads began to sway all the more, like those of insects of a monstrous size. It struck me now that I was surely dreaming; and so I sought to open my eyes.

When I did so, I imagined that I was alone again in my room – until I saw, at the foot of my bed, a single figure standing motionless. I met the figure's stare. He seemed much like the others had been, thin-limbed and swollen-skulled, save that he wore upon his head a Pharaoh's double crown, and his smile was not greedy but blank, just very blank. And then he was gone; and I started suddenly. I opened my eyes. Where the figure of the King had been in my dream, there was now another man.

Although he was standing in a silhouette, I knew him at once. 'Have you come to kill me,' I asked him slowly, 'as you killed my birds?'

The man did not answer immediately. Only as I stirred and sat up did he speak at last, as though he were afraid I might otherwise rise to my feet. 'I have never willingly,' he whispered, 'harmed any human soul.'

And indeed, such was the effect of his voice, such its tone of weariness and seeming despair that I did sit motionless on the side of my bed. I had not expected him to speak in such a way, not this man who had assaulted me and destroyed my career, and scrawled violent threats against me in blood. I frowned as I sought to make out his expression, but his face remained in shadow. 'What is your business with me, then?' I asked. I reached for the amulet where I had dropped it on the floor. 'What does this mean?'

'It is not for me to say,' the man whispered at last.

'Then who can tell me?'

'In the mosque of the Caliph al-Hakim, there you will find your answers.'

'What will I find there, which I have not found already?'

The man sighed. 'Go there,' he shrugged. 'Go, and find out.'

He turned and, as he did so, at last I rose to my feet. 'Wait!' I called; but the man did not look round. I followed him and reached out to seize him by the arm, for I could not allow him to depart, not with so many questions still unanswered. He turned to confront me – and at once I was struck dumb. Never, I thought, had I seen such an expression of defeat before, such a compound of anger and violent despair; yet although it was twisting the man's face grotesquely, in his eyes there was still a glare of deep warning. 'Ask as I have told you,' he hissed. He met my own stare fleetingly, then turned and passed from the room. I did not seek to follow him, for my fever was too bad. Instead, I could only wonder what could have occurred, what dark and unforeseen event, to have opened the way when all had seemed so lost – to have unlocked the door to the minaret.

So indeed I continued to wonder, even as I climbed the steps to the door several days later, even as I knocked upon it and heard it being answered. I was met by the aged scholar who had confronted me before. He gestured at me to enter. I passed him and, as I did so, I was able to see how on his face too, as there had been on his lieutenant's, there appeared the mark of some defeat. His eyes, which had affected me so remarkably before, had nothing of their former brightness; his skin hung loosely in folds off his skull; he appeared old, and shabby, and not impressive at all. He said nothing as he led me up a further spiral of steps and then guided me, at their summit, into a tiny square room. I looked about me but I could see nothing of any interest. My bemusement must have been evident, for the old man smiled very bitterly and gestured towards the far corner of the room, where I realised in the shadows stood a further door. 'There,' the old man whispered, and as he spoke I felt a soft chill, a flickering of that effect which he had induced in me before. He grinned, but very horribly, curling back his lip to expose his blackened teeth. 'In there is what you seek.'

I attempted to smile back. 'I am not sure what it is that I am seeking.'

'The secret of Pharaoh.' The old man's eyes slowly narrowed into slits. 'The secret of al-Vakhel.'

'And what might that secret be?'

Still lower the old man's eyelids drooped, so that it seemed he was almost drifting into sleep. 'A burden,' he whispered at last. 'One which I have guarded in this mosque these many long years. And so, before me, another did the same, and before him another, in an unbroken line, stretching back to that time when the True Faith was young.'

'Is it so terrible, then,' I asked him, 'this secret which you keep, that it cannot be betrayed?'

The old man parted his eyelids a fraction. 'It is a secret,' he murmured, 'from the realms beyond death.'

I frowned. There was an uneasy silence, for I felt embarrassed by such talk, and uncertain how to respond. At length, I cleared my throat. 'In that case,' I asked him as casually as I could, 'why have you permitted me to come here now?'

'I have been persuaded,' the old man answered, 'that I had no choice.'

'By whom?'

'By those who understand the way the world now behaves.'

He paused and I waited in silence, not wishing now to interrupt him, for I could sense that he was wrestling with powerful scruples and fears. Lower still his eyelids flickered. 'You have heard,' he said at length, 'the story of how a tomb was disturbed long ago. Since that time, in the place which you know as the Valley of the Kings, there have always been those who have guarded the tombs, to ensure that they could never be disturbed again.'

'Ahmed Girigar?' I asked.

The old man nodded his head imperceptibly. 'He is, much like me, one in a very long line of guardians. Yet now, so he says, the times have changed. There are strangers in the Valley. These strangers have new methods, new ambitions. They cannot be stopped.' He paused a moment. 'Men like yourself.'

I raised my hands. 'I do not dig for gold,' I protested, 'nor to desecrate long-buried secrets, but in the name of science and knowledge alone.'

The old man smiled very faintly. 'So you say.' He paused. 'And so Ahmed Girigar says as well.' He reached suddenly for my hands and, taking them in his own, squeezed them tightly. 'He says that, of all the foreigners at work in the Valley, you are the best. The most likely to believe in the dangers which lie buried – and the least likely to be corrupted by greed.'

'Then I am flattered,' I answered him, 'more flattered than I can say . . .'

But the old man dismissed my effusions with a sweep of his hand. 'Tell me it is true,' he whispered. He fixed me with his stare. Again, I felt myself falling into its depths and I struggled to free myself.

'Tell me it is true,' he repeated.

'It is true,' I replied.

The old man shuddered; he gripped my hands more tightly. 'Then I hold you to your claim,' he whispered. 'For be warned how it is written in the words of the All High, that every soul will be held in pledge for its deeds. There have been those like you, long before your time, who have sought to gain knowledge, and yet still have been damned.'

He dropped my hands and, reaching inside his robes, drew out a key. Without glancing at me again, he crossed to the door and unlocked it. He passed inside and then I saw, from the darkness, the flickering of a candle. I moved over to the door. 'Close it behind you,' the old man ordered. I did so, blinking for a moment to adjust to the light before looking about me. There were shelves along the walls, and upon each shelf a row of bottles. The bottles were filled with a clear, thick substance, and floating in the liquid were the parts of various limbs. I inspected them more closely. Here there was a foot, there a fragment of a forearm, the flesh very black and shrivelled on the bone.

'*Mummia*,' the old man whispered in my ear. I glanced round at him. 'Mummy,' he grinned, using the English word.

I nodded, but could not restrain a frown of disappointment. Such fragments of blackened corpses were two a penny in the bazaars, for it was a common native superstition, I knew, that they possessed medicinal powers. But where was the great secret in nonsense of that kind? I pointed to a bottle. 'Is this all you wanted to show me?' I asked.

The old man grinned again. 'It is true,' he answered, 'that they will never suffer from the breath of putrefaction, as other flesh must do, but will endure instead for as long as time itself. Were the secret of their ageless state to be revealed to you, then would you not consider that a wonder enough?'

'It is no wonder to me,' I retorted, 'not in the slightest. For the secrets of the mummification process, the embalming techniques employed by the priests, are scarcely mysteries to modern science.'

The old man's grin broadened into a hideous grimace. 'Is that so?' he nodded. 'Is that truly so?' He swept up his robes and then, still holding the candle aloft, crossed to the darkest corner of the room. I saw him reach for another key. He inspected it by the candle light, then glanced back at me. 'Your science cannot know it all,' he said. 'For there are mysteries known only to the wisdom of God, lest the sight of them should blast our feeble, clay-bred minds. Yet if you dare, sir . . .' He beckoned. '*If you dare.*'

I crossed to join him. I could see in front of me a tiny grille, clearly guarding a niche in the wall. As I bent closer to inspect it, I breathed in deeply, for I could see that there was an image upon it, painted in the Muslim style but derived, it was evident, from a far more ancient source. '"Those who believe not in the Hereafter",' the old man muttered, '"name the angels with female names".' I glanced at him, then back at the painting. 'But she is not an angel,' I answered him. 'Her name was Nefer-titi, and she was a Pharaoh's queen.'

The old man laughed hollowly, and opened the grille to reveal a second one. Painted upon it was the familiar image of the sun with two worshippers kneeling beneath. The old man pointed to one of them. 'This Pharaoh?' he asked me. He paused a moment, as though in mockery, before his finger crossed to the second worshipper. 'And this queen?'

I shrugged, and shook my head. 'How can I know?'

'You will know soon enough.'

'The secret?'

'Here it is.' The old man fitted a key into the second grille; he turned the lock; he swung the grille open. Burning with impatience, I stared inside. There seemed to be nothing but a tattered manuscript. The old man glanced at me; then he reached for the manuscript reverently, and lifted it out. 'Guard this well,' he ordered. 'For the worth of it may not be told, and its weight in diamonds would not purchase a thousandth part of it.'

I took it. How fragile it seemed, and stained with age! 'But what is it?' I asked.

'Read it,' the old man answered me sharply. 'Why else would I have given it to you? Read it, Mr Carter – read it and understand.'

And so I did.

Of course I did – for why else would I be sitting here now?

A copy of the manuscript lies before me on my desk. I pick it up, I glance at the first line. And then I raise my eyes, to see the stars where they burn above the Valley of the Kings.

I wonder. I wonder and hope – and sometimes feel afraid.

Manuscript, copy made by Howard Carter of an original of uncertain authorship and date, discovered by him in the mosque of al-Hakim, March 1905

IN THE NAME OF ALLAH, THE MERCIFUL,
THE COMPASSIONATE, IN HIM I TRUST

Praise be to Allah, the Creator of All, who raised the Heavens and peopled the World, there is no guidance save in Allah! For want of His protection, the City of Brass was overthrown, even from the very height of its pride, and all its great works made as silent as the tomb, so that now, across its monstrous expanse, its giant statues of metal, its domes of lighted jewels, only the owls can be heard to lament. Or think upon that city of the worshippers of fire, they who failed to heed the mighty voice of Allah, and all of whom, save one, were transformed into stone. Or think upon Pharaoh of the vast domains: none was mightier than he, and in his pride he proclaimed himself a god. Yet still there is a Master who breathes upon armies, and who builds a narrow and dark house for Kings, and his name is Death. Where, then, is Pharaoh? Fallen, forever fallen, for want of Allah's grace. Truly, there is no guide, save for Allah alone.

★

127

It is related – but Allah alone sees and knows what lies hidden – how the Commander of the Faithful, al-Aziz, fifth of the caliphs who reigned over Egypt, was a prince whose foresight was the equal of King Solomon's. One evening, feeling much troubled, he summoned to his presence Haroun al-Vakhel, his most trusted servant and intimate friend, who was as great in wisdom as his heart was good.

'Come,' said the Caliph, 'let us walk together, and breathe in the sweet scent of roses and jasmine – for there is nothing more restful than the cool of a garden, when the day is hot and the soul ill at ease.'

Haroun rose from his couch and followed his master. Together, the two men strolled amidst the fountains and flowers until at length, approaching a marble bench beside a pool, they sat down. The Caliph sighed deeply, then turned to his friend.

'You must know,' said the Caliph, 'how I am mortally sick. Do not think I fear Death on its own account, for it is the inexorable, the inevitable, the builder of tombs. Yet all men must have their regrets – those things undone which they would hope to see complete. And so it is, O Haroun, that I would put two requests to you before I die.'

'Even were you not my Prince, your merest whim, O Commander of the Faithful, would be to me as a command.'

The Caliph smiled softly, as though suddenly lost in his memories, and rested his hand upon the hilt of his sword. 'Together, O Haroun,' he murmured, 'what conquests have we made! Not for our own sake, but for the glory of our Faith!'

He glanced at his friend. Haroun had clasped his hands together, and appeared to be staring far away at nothing. The Caliph frowned. 'Tell me, what is the matter, for you do not reply.'

Haroun appeared to hesitate, for he did not wish to say what was really the truth, that he was exhausted by bloodshed and sickened of war. 'Your lands, O Caliph, are all at peace,' he said at last. 'Every nation praises the wisdom of your rule.'

The Caliph shook his head. 'You know, O Haroun, how there are those unbelievers who will welcome the news of my death, and see in it their chance to take up arms once again.' The Caliph clasped his servant's hands. 'Be to them, O Haroun, my unsheathed sword! Do not rest until their idols are broken, and you have proclaimed within their shrines how there is no God but the one God, and Mohammed is His Prophet!'

Haroun met his master's eye. 'To hear is to obey,' he murmured at last. He turned away again. 'And what, O Commander of the Faithful, is your second request?'

The Caliph opened his mouth to reply, but at that very moment there came a sudden scream, and then a sound like that of a young girl weeping. Both the Caliph and Haroun rose at once to their feet and hurried through the gardens, concerned to discover what the cause of the weeping might be. They found, standing in the shadow of an overspreading tree, the young Prince al-Hakim Bi-amr Allah. He was a boy of extraordinary beauty and grace, with a waist as fine as silken thread, cheeks as lovely as the hue of anemones, and eyes with the brightness of coloured agate. But in his hand was a whip, and his arm was upraised, and by his feet was a girl with the clothes torn from her back. Her shoulders were bleeding, and her heaving sobs were pitiful to hear. As the Caliph approached her, she turned her head and he recognised his daughter, the Princess Sitt al-Mulq.

'What is the meaning of this?' the Caliph demanded in a fury.

The Prince turned round. 'I am punishing her for her

impudence,' he answered, as he brought down the whip once again across her back. 'She denied me certain requests.'

'She is your elder,' the Caliph frowned. 'She is entitled to command you.'

'But she is a girl, O Father – a compound of sticky slime and unclean blood! Is it not written in the Koran, how a man should never be subject to a woman?'

'You are not yet a man.'

The boy stared at him very strangely. 'But soon, O Father, I shall be. For my sister has told me' – he lashed at the girl again – 'that you are dangerously ill, and I shall soon be Caliph myself.'

His father's frown deepened, and his eyes began to blaze. He struck the whip suddenly from the Prince's hand, and flung it away as far as he could. But the effort made him gasp and clutch at his heart, and he would have fallen had Haroun not been able to catch him in his arms. As he gazed at his father, Prince al-Hakim narrowed his eyes, and a very cold smile began to touch his thin lips. Then he hurried away down the path, and as he did so his sister stumbled to her feet. Still choking back her sobs, she did not even glance at her father but turned and ran in pursuit of the Prince. The Caliph watched them both go. He sighed very deeply. 'My son,' he whispered, 'who will be your master very soon.'

Haroun shook his head. 'As Allah wills it,' he replied, 'you will live for many years yet.'

'But if He does not will it . . .' The Caliph tottered back to his feet. 'You must swear you will always look after my son. He is wild, Haroun, wild and very rash. He will need good friends, to keep him upon the way of Allah's path.'

'You know, O Caliph, that I will always be the loyal servant of your house.'

'You will always be true to him?' The Caliph grasped his

friend's hands and pressed them very eagerly. 'You swear you will never raise your hand against him?'

'I swear it,' he answered, 'in Allah's name.'

The Caliph smiled, then kissed both the cheeks of his friend. 'At last,' he whispered, 'I can die in peace. Three of my servants and friends have I appointed here in Cairo to serve as guardians to my son – my brother, my Vizier and my Master of Horse. But of all my servants, you, O Haroun, are the most precious to me, and of all my many friends, you are the one whom I most trust to keep his word. Allah bless you, then, O Haroun. Praise be to Allah.'

So it was, in obedience to the wishes of the Commander of the Faithful but in conflict with his own, that Haroun al-Vakhel left Cairo, journeying as though he were the breath of the wind, and with his bright sword unsheathed to be the terror of the infidel. For even as he rode, there had come a messenger with the news of the Caliph's death, and then the next day a second reporting how the faithless had risen in revolt, from the mountains of Khurasan to the deserts of Shem, and from the islands of Kamar to the bright sea of Rum. But Haroun al-Vakhel was nothing daunted, for he had the courage and the strength of a hundred lions, and there was no one living who could match his sword in battle. Many were the captives, and much the gold which he won for the greater glory of his Faith, and which he sent in mighty trains to the Caliph al-Hakim. But the Caliph, all the while, sent him back no reply.

Seven long summers and seven winters passed, until at last such were the victories of Haroun al-Vakhel that all the Caliph's lands seemed at peace once again. 'Now Allah be praised,' said Haroun to himself, 'for the time has arrived for me to journey back to Cairo, the unrivalled city, the Mother of the World! Too long I have been a stranger to her streets, and all her arts of peace.' And he thought with pleasure of how he would sit amidst his gardens and take a wife to himself, since although no longer young, he was still without a child, that most perfect blessing which Allah can afford.

First, though, before his sword could be sheathed, he knew that he would have to gain the blessing of the Caliph. Arriving in Cairo, he journeyed at once to the Palace. Above the gates, he saw a man upon a stake. 'Is that not the brother of the former Caliph?' he asked in astonishment. The guard nodded very faintly, but seemed reluctant to speak. Instead he led Haroun in silence through a second gate. Above that one too, Haroun saw, there was a man upon a stake, and when he inspected the poor wretch's face he gasped and cried out aloud, 'Is that not the Vizier of the former Caliph?' Again the guard nodded, but again he did not speak, and he led Haroun instead through a further gate. Above this gate there was a third man on a stake, and his groans and cries for mercy were pitiful to hear. Haroun cried out a blessing upon him. 'Is that not the Master of Horse of the former Caliph?' he asked the silent guard. Still, though, the guard would say nothing, but when they passed through a fourth gate he pointed to a stake which had no one yet upon it. Haroun gazed at this in silence. 'Walk on,' he said at last.

The guard led Haroun into the throne room. Straight away, all who were gathered there fell silent, as Haroun approached the throne and prostrated himself.

'Rise,' the Caliph ordered him.

Haroun rose back to his feet.

'Draw near,' the Caliph ordered.

Haroun did as he was commanded. He could see now that al-Hakim had grown into a tall and shapely youth, and that his beard was trimmed and fine like silk. Upon his knees sat his sister, the Princess Sitt al-Mulq, and she too was no longer a child but arrived upon the bloom and loveliness of womanhood. Curved and supple were her limbs, sweetly swelling her breasts, and upon one of them the Caliph had laid his slim-fingered hands.

For a long while he gazed at Haroun in silence. 'Tell me,' he said at last, 'why you have returned to us here when your work is not yet done.'

'But all your lands, O Prince, now stand at peace, from the western ocean to the borders of Hind.'

'You lie.'

So startled was Haroun, and so angered as well, that his hand reached at once for the hilt of his sword. But then he thought upon his oath to the father of al-Hakim, and so he swallowed back his fury and humbly bowed his head. 'Tell me, O Commander of the Faithful, what enemy yet remains unconquered by your slave.'

The Caliph smiled very thinly. 'Did you not,' he inquired, 'recently despoil the city of Iram?'

'Indeed, your Highness, Iram of the Many Columns, far beyond the furthest reaches of the desert.'

'From which you sent me many captives and slaves?'

'For your greater honour and contentment, O Prince.'

The Caliph nodded very faintly, then clapped his hands together. 'Here is one of them.' At once from the shadows there stepped a blackamoor of a hideous ugliness and massive size, so that he seemed more like a demon than a mortal man, for his eyes were ablaze with a hell-like fire and his white teeth grinned with a terrible menace.

'Make known to him, O Masoud,' the Caliph ordered, 'what you have lately made known to me.'

The blackamoor stepped forward, so that he was gazing directly down at Haroun. 'Learn, O General, that beyond Iram there lies a yet further city, by the name of Lilatt-ah,

133

and it is rich in treasure and all wondrous things, for no man has ever lived to breach its high-towered walls. For this city is known as the City of the Damned.'

'Why,' asked Haroun, half-caught between dread and a sudden curious wonder, 'what is the nature of this city, that it has been given such a name?'

'It is claimed,' replied the blackamoor, still grinning vilely, 'that the dwellers of that city have surrendered their souls.'

'But to whom?' The Caliph twitched. 'Tell him! To whom?'

The blackamoor folded his two massive arms. 'In their temples,' he answered, 'they worship not Allah but Lilat, whom they call the Great Goddess, the authoress of all. They claim – may Allah preserve me! – that even man was the creation of this goddess, moulded and granted life through the discharge of her blood.' The blackamoor paused, then glanced back at the Caliph. 'And all this I affirm and swear to be true.'

'Well?' the Caliph asked, his voice very thin. He gripped his sister's breasts as though clinging to them, and a shudder of rapture passed across his face. 'I would know,' he whispered, 'what prize could ever have induced this City of the Damned to sell its soul.' He glanced down at his sister and again he cupped her breasts, the same look of ravishment as before upon his face. 'It would needs have been something wonderful.' He bowed his head slowly. 'Wonderful indeed.'

Then all at once he shuddered, and even as he gazed at his sister once again, he narrowed his eyes, as though it were the first time he had ever truly seen her, and his face seemed to darken with a violent disgust. 'Well?' he screamed, rising to his feet, so that the Princess was flung from his lap and dashed down on the floor. 'Am I not the Commander of the Faithful?' he shrieked. 'Should not the treasures of this city be my own? Should not its walls be levelled with the sands? And should not its idols be shattered into dust?' He jabbed with his finger. 'How can you rest here, O Haroun al-Vakhel, when you know that such a city still stands, proclaiming that man was fashioned by a harlot, created not from dust but from unclean blood, from the foul, oozing blood of a woman's secret parts? It is not to be endured!' His eyes began to roll, and foam to fleck his lips, as he pointed to the gates. 'Go,' he screamed, 'go! *It is not to be endured!*'

Haroun bowed his head and did as he was ordered, for still he felt bound by the oath he had sworn, that he would obey the son of his late master in all things. Yet he wondered, even as he saddled up his horse once again, and rode from Cairo, his bright sword hanging by his side, at the memory of how the Caliph had caressed his sister's breasts, and at how a man so fervent in the cause and name of Allah should at the same time appear so vicious and depraved. 'But there is much in this world which must be a mystery,' Haroun thought, 'for only Allah has the knowledge of all things.' And so he sought to banish such confusion from his mind, and to think instead upon the City of the Damned.

For forty days and nights, then, he led his soldiers through the desert, until at length he arrived before the city of Iram. But his view of it this second time was very different from his first, for the city's walls and columns were nothing now but ash, and its people beggars camped amidst the ruins. And seeing them, Haroun felt a terrible shame to think that it was he who had reduced them to such a state. And he ordered that food and alms be given to them.

But when he offered even greater gifts to anyone who would guide him to Lilatt-ah, all who heard him grew pale and shrank away. 'Turn back,' they cried, 'turn back, for not even your matchless sword, O General, will be proof against the curse of the City of the Damned!'

Haroun demanded to know what this terrible curse might be; but the people if anything grew even paler still, and they cried that no one had ever returned to say. But when they saw that Haroun remained undaunted, and his resolve as firm as before, they agreed to tell him a certain means by which the city could be found. 'Drop a shower of blood upon the sands,' they advised, 'and mark the direction in which it flows, for it will always be drawn towards the idol of Lilat. And in that way – may Allah guard your head! – you may discover the secret of the curse for yourself.'

So Haroun continued with his men far into the desert, travelling across the sands for a further forty days, until at last one evening he saw a column of black stone. Drawing nearer to it, he observed how there were letters in Arabic carved upon its side, and what appeared to be a demon bound by burnished chains upon its base. This demon was buried in sand up to the chest, and it was withered and dry like an afrit or a ghool. Suddenly, though, with a scream which seemed to chill the very air, the monster cried out the holy name of Allah and a single tear began to trickle down its cheek. But it could say nothing more, for its tongue was shrivelled, and it could only wave its arms despairingly as though to break the chains which bound them, until at last the tear dropped and fell upon its tongue. Then the demon met Haroun's eye and spoke the single word, 'water'; and Haroun, feeling pity, poured water down its throat.

'Tell me,' he then demanded, rising back to his feet, 'in the name of He who rules the seen and the unseen, what nature of thing you are.'

'I will not answer you,' said the demon, 'until you have sworn that you will drive your sword through my heart.'

'That is a strange request indeed.'

'Swear it!'

'I will slay no living thing,' Haroun answered, 'not without just cause.'

The wretched creature moaned in anguish. 'I shall give you cause enough.'

And so ghastly was his tone, and so pitiable to hear, that Haroun again felt a sudden rush of pity for the creature. 'Give me the cause, then,' he vowed, 'and I shall do as you request.'

'I was once a man,' the demon answered, 'and a Muslim like yourself, the leader of an army of glittering swords. It was my hope to discover the city of Lilatt-ah, and to proclaim within its temples the One and Only Faith. But there is a curse upon that place far too great to overcome, and it was I who was vanquished and overcome myself. In mockery of the Prophet, I was chained and buried here, and a verse in monstrous letters was carved above my head.'

Haroun stepped back. '"Have you thought upon Lilat",' he read out aloud, '"the great one, the other? She is much to be feared. Truly, Lilat is great amongst the gods".' As he pronounced this, Haroun shook his head in disbelief. 'There is no god but Allah!' he cried. 'And yet this Lilat, I fear, must be a jinni of monstrous powers indeed!' He knelt again by the side of the buried demon. 'Tell me,' he asked him, 'what is the secret of her greatness? What is the curse which has brought you to this state?'

'Why,' the creature answered, 'a prize which some have called the philosopher's stone, and for which they have ransacked every corner of the world.' He laughed bitterly, so that all who heard it were chilled to their bones. 'For although I was once a mortal like you, yet I have been chained to this column now for three hundred years.'

Haroun gazed at him in astonishment. 'And are the people of Lilatt-ah all as long-lived as yourself?'

'Indeed,' the wretch grimaced, 'for though their heads be lopped from their necks, and their stomachs slit open and their guts spilled in the dust, yet still they will rise and fight another day.'

'And in what does the secret of this miracle lie?'

At once, the wretched creature began to shudder and moan. 'In an elixir,' he answered, 'very bitter to the taste, which I and all my captured men were forced to drink, so that we would suffer torture through the centuries and never gain release.'

'And how is this elixir prepared?'

'That is the darkest of all dark mysteries. For it is guarded by the priests, who are the rulers and founders of Lilatt-ah and who came, it is said, in very ancient times, from the land of Egypt when the pagan Pharaohs reigned.'

'From Egypt?' Haroun frowned with puzzlement and gazed about him at the endless waste of sands. 'But why would sages of such power ever have left that rich and happy land?'

The chained creature grinned horribly. 'Why do you think, O General? So that they might not be disturbed by the likes of you and me.' And even as he said this, so he started to writhe in his chains, screaming and foaming like a lunatic. 'Turn back,' he shrieked, 'turn back, turn back! For why else was I left here, if not to serve as a warning and a monstrous wonder? *Turn back, I beg you, turn back from here at once!*'

Haroun stood bowed in silence, thinking of his vows to the Caliph al-Aziz. 'No,' he said firmly, 'I cannot turn back.'

At once the chained demon slumped and was still. 'Then it may be,' he said at last, 'when you and all your power have been overthrown, that you will be brought here to hang and suffer in my place.'

But Haroun shook his head and slowly drew out his sword from its sheath. He placed its sharp point upon the creature's withered chest. 'You have said it yourself,' he smiled, 'that even the cursed of Lilat may be brought to Allah's grace. *La Ilaha Illallah!* There is no God but Allah!' And so saying he drove the point of his sword into the wretch's chest, and the demon shrieked and writhed in his glittering chains as he clutched at the blade with his naked hands.

'Are you dying?' Haroun cried. 'Do you feel your immortality begin to fade and slip away?'

The demon froze for a moment, then plunged the blade deeper and yet deeper still, until a spume of black liquid spurted out on to the sands. 'Yes,' he whispered suddenly, 'yes, I remember . . .'

'But how?' Haroun pressed him. 'How can this be happening, when you said you could not die?'

'Upon the walls . . . the same thing . . . I remember – the last man I fought with before they captured me . . . I pierced his heart, and watched him seem to die.' He began to cough, and more black liquid spattered on the sands. 'All these many years . . .' Suddenly he smiled. 'These many long centuries . . . I have wondered . . . I have dared to hope . . . whether I had slain that enemy indeed. And now, it seems . . . it seems . . . I know.' And even as he said this, so his eyes began to roll and their light to dim, and then the very sockets which framed them to crumble. Soon the man's body was nothing but a cloud of fine dust, and it was borne away upon the breath of a breeze, and the chains hung empty from the column of rock.

Haroun knelt before them, his head bowed in prayer, and then he lifted the fetters and turned to his men. 'Truly Allah is great!' he cried. 'For what have we been given, if not a portent and a sign that even the damned in the city of Lilattah may be slain? Praise be to Allah! For to Him and to His power there is nothing impossible!'

★

Nor was the faith of Haroun to prove misplaced. A great horror, it was true, had settled upon the hearts of his followers, and the next evening, when they first saw the distant towers of the city, lit a blazing red by the setting of the sun, it was all Haroun could do to keep his men from flight. Monstrous it spread before them, as though formed from living fire, the tips of each flame a vaunting, jagged tower, while around it stretched a wall of colossal, burnished stone which gleamed, and then was lost, as the sun was swallowed by the west. Of the form of Lilatt-ah, now that nightfall had come, only a looming weight of blackness could be glimpsed against the stars, at one with the barren and featureless plain; and Haroun drew out his sword and commanded his men to stand prepared.

It was well that he had done so, for the first assault soon came. Again there was panic and cries of despair, for the enemy seemed wraiths with eyes of burning silver, and with skin which glimmered palely even in the blackest dead of night. Yet by the grace of Allah the Muslim line stood firm. Gradually, with the approach of dawn, the attacks began to fade until at last, as the sun's first rays rose golden above the east, the enemy retreated to behind the city walls. Some few of them lay still where they had been felled, none of them dead despite their hideous wounds, and a murmur of terror and despair arose amongst the Muslims that their foes could not be slain. But Haroun walked amongst the injured things, stabbing them through their hearts with the point of his sword, and as he did so they shrieked and melted into dust.

Then, without delay, the march was begun upon the walls. Very briefly, entering within their massive shadow, Haroun paused and gazed up in silent wonder, stupefied by the radiance of the city's glittering towers, its temples encrusted with gold and fiery jewels, its arches, and pyramids, and alabaster domes. But it was not only awe which had served to freeze Haroun, for along the length of the battlements could be seen the bodies of men impaled upon hideous instruments of torture – yet though the tortures seemed deadly, the men were still alive. And Haroun, gazing upon them, felt a desperate surge of anger at the thought of how long they might have suffered in that way, bound upon the torments of endless centuries; and so he stood frozen no more, but drew his gleaming sword and, galloping forward, he raised the cry of battle.

Like a raging lion he fought, he and his men, to breach the gleaming walls of Lilatt-ah, for the conflict was bloody and the enemy strong, and the result stood doubtful all that fierce morning. Yet as the sun climbed ever higher and blazed brighter in the sky, so the strength of the enemy began to ebb and Haroun knew himself borne upon the tide of victory. By midday the streets had been drowned beneath blood, and the dust of the slain lay thick in the air; but still Haroun pressed into the heart of the city. A temple stood there of stupendous size, with gateways of gold and towers of black marble, carved with the portraits of loathsome-headed demons; and it was to the courtyards of this temple that the injured had sought to crawl. Haroun paused in almost pity, gazing upon their wounded, mutilated forms; but then he turned to look up at the midday sun, and he thought how soon it would start to sink into the west. 'Kill them all!' he cried – for he feared that with the darkness their strength might be restored. 'Not one must be spared! Not one must survive!'

Yet already he felt sick with the sight and stench of slaughter. Up and down his sword arm stabbed, up and down, as he passed from courtyard to hallway and to yet further hall, deeper and deeper into the darkness of the temple until at last, it appeared, there were no hearts left to stab, and no one left in all that monstrous place alive. But still Haroun could not be certain, for although the hallways before him seemed empty now, he had not yet reached the very heart of the temple; and the further he pressed, so the darker it grew, as the roof grew ever lower and each hallway still more small. The air was heavy now with incense, but also with a foetid, strangely sweet smell, and Haroun could feel it lying thick upon his lungs. He stopped suddenly. Gazing ahead, he could make out wisps of brown smoke curling through the gap left by two bolted doors, and beyond them what seemed to be a flickering orange glow.

Haroun crept forward, then all at once hurled his weight against the doors, which splintered and gave. Gingerly, he made his way through the wreckage and into the room beyond. Along either side of it, stacked up to its ceiling, there lay long rows of bodies. They appeared dry and with-ered, but since they had been bound very tightly with thin swathes of cloth, it was impossible to make out anything of what lay beneath their wrappings. Haroun approached the nearest corpse. Of its face, only the profile of a nose could be distinguished through the cloth, and indeed it appeared barely a human thing at all. Haroun reached out to touch it, yet when he did so he discovered that the head rolled from the neck on to the floor, for the entire body had been dis-membered into many parts. At the same moment, from the smoke-wreathed, furthermost end of the hall, he heard a soft hiss of laughter and then a voice as withered, so it seemed, as the dried head by his feet. 'Do you presume to touch the mystery of the gods?'

Haroun turned. With one arm, he sought to disperse the brown smoke, and with the other he lifted his glittering sword. Slowly he advanced down the length of the hall. He could make out the silhouette of a man now – shaven-headed, so it seemed, and dressed in the flowing robes of a priest – standing behind a brazier which was filled with soft flames. A shallow pan had been laid across it, and it was from this that the brown smoke was billowing upwards. As Haroun approached the brazier, he saw a thick black liquid bubbling within the pan.

'There are no mysteries,' said Haroun, 'which the sight of Allah cannot pierce.'

The priest laughed again, an awful, crackling, desiccated sound. 'Yet I am older than your god by many thousands of years.'

Haroun stretched his arm across the brazier. 'A vaunting claim indeed.' He placed the tip of his sword upon his adversary's chest. 'Let us hope, then, that it has served to prepare you for your death.'

Haroun felt the priest tense. He jabbed in the point of his sword a fraction deeper, and as he did so he swept at the veil of smoke again, so that he could see what lay beyond it clearly for the first time. A stare as bright and cold as moonlight met his own, and a face drained utterly of all emotion. Once, Haroun thought, it might have been handsome – once long ago, before the mutilations, for the priest had no ears and his nose had been slit.

'Death,' the priest whispered. He smiled suddenly, and Haroun observed that on his brow there were now beads of sweat. 'I had almost forgotten it, and what it might be.' Then he closed his eyes. He cried out suddenly, some strange foreign prayer, as he let his body drop forward and drove the sword deep into his heart. 'Tyi,' he whispered; then he screamed the same word, 'Tyi!' Still he stumbled forward. He crashed into the brazier, so that coals were scattered in an arc across the hall and the pan with its contents was knocked into the air.

Haroun flinched and stepped back as splashes of the liquid fell across his cloak. They seemed without effect, but he had no time to inspect them, for fire was starting to spread through the hall and by his feet the corpse was already a pool of dust and spreading blood. Higher and higher now the flames began to reach, but still Haroun lingered, for he had seen how the blood was flowing fast away into the flickering shadows of the far end of the hall. He recalled the advice of the people of Iram, which had enabled him never to grow lost in the desert, and to discover the fateful city of Lilatt-ah, and so he stepped beyond the brazier to seek the idol out.

He discovered it set against the furthermost wall, but as he approached it he felt his courage start to fail. He could not explain this effect, for the idol was nothing, in the darkness, but a silhouette. Impatient with himself, Haroun muttered a prayer beneath his breath, then turned and reached for a brand of burning wood. He turned back to the idol, and raised the flames up to its face. His first thought, on gazing upon it, was that he had never before seen a woman of such beauteous perfection, for the statue had been sculpted with unearthly skill, so that the marble appeared softer than the softest skin and he was almost tempted, gazing upon her lips, to crush them with his own. But then he blinked and shook his head, and when he gazed at them again he saw — as he had not done before — how the curl of their smile was mocking and cruel, as though hinting at secrets too monstrous to pronounce and depravities too terrible for mortal contemplation. Even her head-dress of gold appeared deadly, for it bore the image of a spitting cobra and Haroun, gazing upon it, suddenly imagined himself trapped, as though he were nothing but a morsel of prey. He began to feel himself melting with the strangest thoughts, desires which he would never have known that he possessed. Nearer and nearer to her bright mouth he drew, more and more he felt himself lost . . . and then he closed his eyes and brushed her lips with a kiss. At once, though, he shrank back in horror and wiped at his mouth, for the statue had been cold and damp to the touch, so that to kiss it had seemed like kissing a serpent indeed; and Haroun struck it with his sword, and sent it toppling to the ground.

Still it smiled up at him, but all Haroun's desire had now been transformed into disgust. He could see how the flagstones on to which it had fallen were a glistening crimson, and when he glanced round it was to find that the hallway was damp with a flowing tide of blood, lit every shade of orange and red by the flames. Haroun turned back to the idol. For a moment his arm was frozen by its gaze, but then he shuddered and brought his bright sword swinging down. The neck was shattered by the impact, and the head rolled across the floor. Haroun followed it and again he brought his arm down, this time hacking at the smile. Only when it had been obliterated did he turn and hurry from the hall, wading through blood, passing between twin walls of roof-beating fire.

Returned to the streets, he issued his commands. 'Burn the city and all its dead. See that its foundations are sown with salt. Let nothing be left to show where it stood.' Then he turned and rode out through the gates of Lilatt-ah. For a long while he stood upon a nearby hill, gazing at the inferno of the City of the Damned, as its towers were consumed by red lashes of flame, its walls and pyramids and alabaster domes, until at last all was blackened, and silent, and still.

'It is done,' Haroun whispered. He bowed his head in prayer. 'But never more, I here swear it, shall I spill such blood again.' And pulling out his sword, he snapped the blade in two.

In the throne room of the palace of the Caliph al-Hakim, Haroun al-Vakhel bowed low before the throne. 'In obedience to your wishes, O Commander of the Faithful, I have destroyed the city of Lilatt-ah, so that not a brick of that monstrous place survives. Its treasures, loaded upon a caravan of many camels, have been brought to you here, that you may employ them to succour the sick and the poor.'

'The sick and the poor?' The Caliph raised an eyebrow. 'I had not thought, O General, you were grown so compassionate.'

'I serve you best, O Caliph, by serving your people.'

'You serve me best, O General, by fighting my wars.'

Haroun bowed his head, but then from under his cloak drew out the pieces of his sword.

'What is the meaning of this?' the Caliph demanded.

'I am sworn, O Commander of the Faithful, by a terrible oath, never again to shed mortal blood.'

Once again the Caliph raised a single eyebrow. 'Then we must consider,' he murmured in a silken tone, 'some new and fitting position for you.'

'It is my ambition now, O Prince, to study the ancient sciences, that I may grow wise in the magic of the Angels and bring life, Allah willing, where before I brought death.'

For a long while the Caliph did not reply, but rose instead to his feet and crossed to a window, where he gazed out at the gateways which led to his palace. Upon three of them corpses could be seen, almost skeletons now, exposed to the hunger of the vultures and crows. Upon the fourth gate there stood a stake which was still without a corpse. The Caliph shuddered violently through all his frame. 'I cannot think clearly on this matter,' he exclaimed in sudden anger, 'not now, not now!,' and then he stamped his foot and stormed out from the room.

Haroun was left alone. All that day, he was in hourly expectation of being seized and taken to his death. At last, late in the afternoon, he was approached by two guards. For a moment he felt that all was over, and he committed himself to Allah's grace, but the guards bore only a command from the Caliph that he was to wait by the gateway to the palace gardens. Haroun did as he had been ordered. Afternoon deepened into purple dusk, and then dusk into beauteous and star-encrusted night. At last, when the moon stood full in the sky, he heard the gates behind him open, and he turned. It was the Caliph, heavily cloaked. He had with him only a single companion, Masoud, the black-amoor.

'Come,' said the Caliph, taking Haroun's arm. 'For there is nothing finer, nor more instructive, than to walk through the night and trace the ways of man.' So saying, he began to lead the way out past the palace wall, and then down into the maze of the city's narrow streets. Soon all was stench, and clamour, and filth, and yet the Caliph's eyes shone – to Haroun's mind at least – much brighter than they had ever done amidst the splendours of his palace. 'So,' he hissed suddenly, pinching Haroun's arm, 'you would no longer kill?' He gestured towards a row of butcher's shops. Although it was night, there was still a cloud of flies shimmering above the shopfronts, the visible particles of an even thicker cloud of odours, formed from the sweetness of rotten meat and spices. The Caliph laughed with delight, and clapped his hands. 'All must kill!' he exclaimed. 'For have you not understood, O General, how the lesser must ever be the prey of the greater? Why, it is the eternal law of this world! And so it is that I order you' – he pointed to a butcher – 'to kill that man now!'

Haroun frowned. 'What harm, O Caliph, has he ever done you?'

'Ask rather, what harm he has done to the innocent cows, the wide-eyed calves who now lie dismembered across the flagstones of his shop.' The Caliph paused, and his eyes began to roll. 'Kill him!' he shrieked suddenly. 'Kill him, kill him now!'

But Haroun shook his head. 'O Prince, I cannot.'

A shudder passed all the way through the Caliph's body. He turned to Masoud; he clapped his hands, and the black-amoor at once bared his teeth in a grin. He crossed to the butcher who, turning round and seeing such a giant, let out a cry of terror and sought to back into his shop. But Masoud seized him easily and, having gripped him by his hair, forced his face into a slab of stinking meat. The Caliph, as he had done before, clapped his hands with delight, then crossed to the shop and picked up a cleaver. He brought it down hard upon the butcher's head, and did not cease to wield it until the dead man's corpse had been riven in two and hung amidst the other carcasses from hooks. Only then did he turn to the watching Haroun. 'You see,' he shrugged, 'what an easy matter death can be. Had you done as I ordered, I would have granted you half of the treasure which you brought from Lilatt-ah. As it is, however, you shall have not a dinar.'

They continued to walk together through the streets. After a short distance, they passed by a further row of shops. A large crowd had gathered around one of them, and it soon appeared that a baker had been discovered employing false weights. Again, the Caliph pinched Haroun's arm. 'Redeem yourself,' he ordered. 'For here is a thief, caught in the very act of his villainy. Kill him!' he shrieked suddenly, 'kill him, kill him now!'

But again Haroun shook his head. 'O Prince, I cannot.'

The Caliph stretched and shook himself like a hungry cat. He turned to Masoud, who once again began to grin. He crossed to the baker and seized him by the hair, then forced his face into the mud by the Caliph's feet. The Caliph stepped upon the wretched man's head, stamping upon it very hard, then nodded to Masoud. The blackamoor at once raised the hem of the baker's robe and then, having loosed the cord which bound his trousers, began to inflict upon the baker that sin which should never be named. The wretched man shrieked uncontrollably until Masoud, with the vigour of his assault, succeeded in rending the baker in twain. He then dropped the body into the mud, and stuffed its mouth with a loaf of bread.

The Caliph turned to Haroun. 'Again,' he shrugged, 'you see what an easy matter death can be. Had you done as I ordered, I would have spared you your home, your slaves and all your worldly goods. As it is, however, you shall have not a dinar.'

They continued to walk until at last they neared the city's most northerly wall. Here, by the Bab al-Futuh, there came the sudden sound of women laughing and shouting. The Caliph froze at once, and his face grew black with indignation and rage. 'What is this?' he cried. He turned towards the source of the noise, and saw a bath-house tiled with many-coloured marble and fretted with delightful patterns of gold. 'How can it be,' the Caliph shrieked, 'that women should dare to stain a place of such beauty with their filth? Have I not ordered them never to leave their homes? Have I not, to make good this command, forbidden the manufacture of shoes for them to wear? How could I have served to make my desires more clear?' He turned to Haroun. 'I am the Caliph, the Beloved of Allah! I shall be obeyed!' He pointed to the bath-house. 'Kill them!' he screamed. 'Kill them, kill them all now!'

But again Haroun shook his head. 'O Prince, I cannot.'

The Caliph chewed upon his lip, and his face grew pale. 'Beware, O General, for you have nothing left now to forfeit, nothing in all the world save only one thing.'

But Haroun bowed his head and did not reply, and so the

Caliph turned to the blackamoor. 'Do it!' he shrieked. Masoud went to a brazier by the Bab al-Futuh and seized a brand from it. He crossed to the bath. First he locked the doors, then circled the building, setting fire to all he could. The laughter of the women soon began to change to screams and Haroun, who had been standing in motionless disbelief watching the actions of Masoud, could endure to watch no more. He ran to the doors. Unlocking their bolts and venturing into the bath-house, he was able to save some few of the women who had been trapped inside, but many more were already in their death throes, boiled alive within the hissing waters of the baths. Desperately, Haroun sought to reach them through the flames, but even as he did so, he was seized by Masoud and dragged back to the Caliph.

'In Allah's name,' Haroun cried, 'O Prince, what are you doing?'

The Caliph drew himself up tall but made no reply.

Haroun gestured back wildly at the blazing bath-house. 'Are you not the Commander of the Faithful?' he cried. 'Is it not your duty to protect those weaker than you? Are we not, all of us, the children of Allah?'

A flicker seemed to pass through the Caliph's every limb. He motioned Haroun to be silent, but still Haroun spoke.

'The women you have boiled alive, O Prince, were mortals just like you. They could have been your own flesh and blood.' He shook his head in disbelief, then exclaimed at the top of his voice, 'Why, they were like your sister, the Princess Sitt al-Mulq!'

The Caliph's face twitched violently, and again he was racked by a strange convulsion. He bit very hard on his lower lip, so that blood began to flow, and then he moaned and hit his head with his hands. He gazed up at the black-amoor. 'Well,' he screamed suddenly, 'what are you waiting for, you accursed lump of offal, you dog bred from whores?

Extinguish the flames!' Then, still shuddering, he reached for his purse. Opening it up, he began to hurl coins at the survivors of the fire, where they stood shivering beneath the archway of the Bab al-Futuh, desperately clutching scraps of clothing to themselves. The Caliph gazed at them, his eyes very wide, and then he turned back to Haroun. 'Who would have thought,' he murmured, 'that flesh could look so sweet?'

Haroun did not answer, for he had turned and averted his gaze. The Caliph followed him, and took him by the arm. 'O Haroun al-Vakhel,' he said, 'do not leave my side, for I would sooner be parted from a man of your wisdom than from my own existence.'

Haroun gazed at him in surprise. 'I had thought it was your intention to impale me on a stake, and abandon me to the crows.'

'So I would have done, had you broken your vow and spilt blood, for a man untrue to his own words will surely prove untrue to his Prince. But now you shall discover how I value good faith. I here grant you the treasures of Lilatt-ah, and then I double them again.'

But Haroun shook his head. 'O Commander of the Faithful,' he replied, 'I cannot accept.'

Again the Caliph's brow began to grow dark. 'What do you mean?'

'You have said that a man should be true to his vows. I am sworn, from this point on, to be a student of the high and magical arts, for it is my wish to have the power to banish all mortal sickness and to heal the injuries of all those who are wounded. What need shall I have for wealth in such a life?'

Still the Caliph frowned, but then suddenly he seized Haroun in his arms and kissed him on both cheeks. 'Blessings be upon you,' he cried, 'for as Joseph was to Pharaoh, so you have been to me! I shall indeed grant the treasures of Lilatt-ah to the poor. And here, so that my memory may be ever more preserved and my goodness recalled, I shall build a holy mosque, where the Faithful may hourly offer praises to my name.'

He pointed to the ruins of the bath-house. The flames had been extinguished, and men were starting to sift through the steaming, blackened rubble. One heaved up a corpse on to his shoulder, and Haroun would have turned away, but the Caliph was gazing at the body with fascination, his eyes gleaming brightly. Then suddenly, as he had done before, he began to shudder and turning to Haroun, clung to him with an implacable grip. 'O Prince amongst counsellors,' he whispered, 'tell me the magic which you hope to seek out.'

'That magic which King Solomon possessed, by virtue of his knowledge of the Secret Name of Allah.'

'And what powers did it bring him?'

'The power to command the Jinn, and all those spirits made of fire.'

'And what could he order the Jinn to perform?'

'Anything, O Prince, for there is no limit to their power.'

The Caliph glanced across at the ruins of the bath-house, where another blackened corpse was being pulled out from the rubble. 'Anything?' he whispered.

'Anything at all.'

The Caliph breathed in deeply. 'Then when you have discovered the Secret Name of Allah,' he ordered, 'you shall spell it out to me, and I shall have its letters inscribed upon the stonework of my mosque. For though I am the Caliph, yet there is a traitor abroad, who plots against the happiness of my sister and myself, threatening to rack our bodies with cruel tortures, and to imprint the marks of his vile fingers on our forms.' He paused and once again glanced across at the bath-house, where corpses were now being laid out in a line. 'He breathes upon delight, this traitor, he throws down palaces, he raises up tombs where once palaces stood. And his name, O Haroun – his name is bitter Death!'

Across the lands where once he had ridden as a proud and mighty conqueror, Haroun now wandered as a humble student. Everywhere he sought out those who might best teach him wisdom, both true believers and infidels, whether they dwelled amidst the towers of Constantinople, or in the far-off temples of fabled Peking, or in lands across the oceans, where men abide beside the Angels. At the feet of a thousand and one different sages Haroun sat, so that at length he grew to be a mighty sage himself, and in the practice of the healing of the sick he had no rival. Such was his success that those whom he cured proclaimed him a sorcerer, for it seemed impossible to explain his skill in any other way. Never, it was declared, had there been a magician such as Haroun. He was proficient, it was whispered, in every hidden science. He could read the language of the stars, and of the beasts and of the birds, and the fire-bred jinn were held at his command. And some spoke of secrets more terrible by far, and when pressed would hint that he had the mastery even of the grave.

Rumour, then, was the constant herald of Haroun. Long before his arrival back in Cairo, it had announced his return to his native land and the Caliph, who had been awaiting him impatiently, ordered guards to be placed on every city gate. At length Haroun was glimpsed upon the northern road, and an escort rode out at once to meet him and take him to the Commander of the Faithful. Haroun accompanied them wordlessly, although he was observed, as he passed the half-completed mosque by the Bab al-Futuh, to smile very faintly and shake his head just once. But still he remained silent until at last, in the throne room, he was left alone with the Caliph, who rose to kiss him and hold him in his arms.

'O Prince amongst magicians,' the Caliph exclaimed, 'the fame of your sorcery has spread across the world!'

But Haroun shook his head. 'O Commander of the Faithful,' he replied, 'I have no knowledge whatsoever of the magical arts.'

The Caliph gazed at him in disbelief. 'But it is said you can cure almost every disease.'

'It needs no sorcery, O Prince, to tend and heal the sick.'

The Caliph's stare hardened. 'You have failed, then, to uncover the Secret Name of Allah?'

'His name, O Prince, cannot be uncovered by mortal hand, not without the guidance of the celestial Angels, may peace and blessings be forever on their heads!'

The Caliph clenched his fist and brought it down hard, once, then twice. 'You are certain?' he demanded.

'Certain, O Prince. For when I left you, I travelled through many far countries and many strange lands, until at last I reached the Mountains of Káf, where the Jinn will often walk amongst men and talk to them of the mysteries of this and far off worlds. It is for this reason that the people of the Mountains of Káf are accounted the wisest of men, for there is little they do not know or understand. Yet even they have never learned the Secret Name of Allah – and when I asked them, they shuddered and seemed suddenly to grow pale.'

The Caliph gnawed at his lower lip, then brought down his clenched fist violently again. 'It seems, then,' he whispered, 'that the stonework of my mosque will stay blank after all.' He spun round and strode across to a window where he stood in silence a long while, gazing out at the garden below. 'My sister . . .' he murmured at last. He turned to Haroun, and beckoned him across. 'My sister.' The Caliph pointed through the window and Haroun saw, seated by a fountain, the Princess Sitt al-Mulq, lovelier than the fairest of the flowers of the garden. 'Must she die?' the Caliph whispered. 'Must she truly grow old and pass into the grave?'

'She is a rose, O Prince. Roses must fade.'

'No.' The Caliph had whispered this very softly, so that when he suddenly swung round with a slim silver knife in his hand, Haroun was taken by surprise. 'No!' the Caliph smiled. He raised the blade against Haroun's throat. 'You are concealing things from me.'

'I am a true believer, O Prince. Only the angels and the prophets have ever known the Secret Name of Allah.'

'Then why, when you questioned the sages of Káf, did they grow pale at the very mention of it?'

'Because they knew that I was seeking a way to conquer death.'

'There is another way, then?'

'Indeed, O Prince.' Haroun paused suddenly, and his brow grew very dark, but then he winced as he felt the Caliph press the knife against his throat. 'For I have seen the proof of it myself,' he continued, 'in the accursed city of Lilatt-ah, and I know that it is the way of blackest necromancy.'

The Caliph smiled very bitterly. 'You razed Lilatt-ah, did you not, and made it one with the sands?'

Haroun nodded slowly.

'Then you were a fool,' the Caliph whispered, 'and worse, a traitor to your Prince.'

'And yet it was you, O Caliph, who ordered it destroyed.'

'Then you should have gazed into my soul and glimpsed there my secretmost desire, for did you not understand, O Haroun, that in truth I had desired the wisdom of that city for myself?'

Haroun stood motionless and did not reply to this, and

after a moment the Caliph smiled once again. 'Oh yes,' he nodded, 'you understand me well enough.' He drew the knife across the curve of Haroun's throat, so that a very thin line of blood rose from the welt. He touched the wound, then inspected his fingertip. 'I was a fool to spare you, I should have had you slain.' He tasted the blood. 'Yet reveal to me what you learned upon the Mountains of Káf, and it may be that I will keep you alive after all.'

There was a long silence.

'Think upon your oath to my father,' the Caliph pressed. 'You are sworn, O Haroun, to obey me in all things.'

But still Haroun paused. 'The secret,' he said at last, 'is forever buried, and cannot be restored into the light of this world. For the past is a darkness in which much should stay hidden, lest it appal and endanger the gaze of the now.'

'Yet still I would know what the secret is.'

For several long minutes, Haroun remained silent. Then he breathed in deeply. 'You are the Caliph,' he murmured, 'the Appointed One of Allah.' He turned back to the window. Beyond the gardens and the palace wall, beyond the mosques of the city and the silver of the Nile, he could see where the pyramids of Ghiza rose, like the sails of distant ships above a surf of silver haze. As Haroun gazed upon them, so he narrowed his eyes. 'When I spoke to the sages of Káf,' he said slowly, 'pressing them to tell me what the secrets of life and death might be, they shook their heads and asked me to state my native land. I did so. At once, they began to laugh. I asked them why. And then they answered me that I should not have wandered to all the ends of the earth, but stayed where I was born. For in Egypt, they told me, buried within its monstrous, immeasurable walls of stone, within its palaces and temples, within its tombs quarried out from the very bowels of the earth, mysteries of prodigious power had once been known, mysteries more terrible than human word could say, mysteries as ancient as the very sands themselves – for Egypt, they said, had been the birthplace of all magic.'

'And this magic . . .' – the Caliph licked his lips, his eyes bright like fire – 'had it taught how the secrets of the grave might be revealed?'

Haroun shrugged. 'The language of the Ancients is silent now,' he said, 'and there is no one who can read it.' Then he paused; he turned to the window and gazed again towards the distant pyramids. 'Yet in the Mountains of Káf,' he murmured softly, 'there is a tradition still preserved.'

'Tell it to me!'

'I heard it from a sage very learned in secret wisdom. It is damnable, and must be a horror to the ears of all believers.'

'Yet I would hear it,' proclaimed the Caliph, 'though it were Iblis himself who had spoken it!'

Haroun smiled faintly. 'It was, as I said, a learned sage of Káf. What he related to me, he had found in an infidel book – and this, O Prince, is how he told me the tale:

THE TALE TOLD BY THE SAGE OF THE
MOUNTAINS OF KAF

You should know, O Egyptian, that of all the many lands of this earth, yours is the most ancient kingdom by far. For it was there that the Jinn first fell to earth, having blazed through the sky more brightly than the stars. And many took the forms of strange cross-bred monsters, and appeared to men with the heads of dogs, and of birds and of cats, and of every kind of beast, so that the ignorant believed the Jinn to be gods. But there were some of the Jinn who were true believers, and who walked in the path of the love of Allah.

The greatest of all these bore the name of Osiris. He was the first king to rule over sacred Egypt, for until the time of the coming of the Jinn to that land, man had been as savage and wild as any beast; but Osiris taught his people the arts of how to live, so that the first cities began to rise upon the banks of the Nile, and the first monuments of stone, within which the mysteries of the stars were enshrined. Nor was there anything which Osiris could not teach, so that the period of his reign was later called the First Time – for it was then that true wisdom had first been opened up to man.

By the side of Osiris was his sister and his Queen, Isis, the fairest and most cunning of the Jinn, and his brother, Seth, who sheltered evil in his heart. For Seth was proud, and envious of Osiris, and wanted the throne of Egypt for himself; and so he conceived a plot to dispose of the King. He invited his brother to a banquet and then, when the festivities were reaching their height, he ordered gifts and treasures to be brought into the hall. The most splendid of all these was a chest, fashioned from the rarest cedars and gilded with patterns of wondrous beauty; and Seth promised it to the man who could fit in it the best. But he had prepared it beforehand, to ensure that it was his brother who would win the competition; and when Osiris lay down inside the chest, Seth gave the command for its lid to be brought out and hammered down with nails. Then he ordered the chest to be flung into the Nile, and so it was that it soon became the coffin of Osiris.

The body of the King, still secured within the cedar chest, was borne upon the currents of the Nile into the sea, where it was lost upon the vast expanse of the waters. But Isis, who was a magician of incomparable power, and who had read all the mysteries of the universe, did not despair when she learned the news of her husband's fate. Instead, she set out to discover where his body might be, and having wandered through every land to the very ends of the world, at length – for Allah is great and ever merciful – she met with success. The chest was still intact, and when she opened up the lid she found that the corpse of Osiris was perfectly preserved, and his body bathed in a beauteous odour, sweeter than the sweetest scent of a rose. She journeyed with the body of Osiris back to Egypt, and when she arrived there laid it carefully out, for it was her intention – great were her powers! – to perform a terrible and wondrous act of magic.

But Seth, who had been spying on his sister, learned of her intentions and was able to seize back the body of Osiris. Then, in the fury of his jealousy, he dismembered the corpse into fourteen parts and scattered them far and wide, for he hoped in this way that he would secure his throne at last. But Isis was still undaunted and, wandering the world a second time, she was able to find and gather the fragments of the corpse and piece them all together. It was then that she performed her act of fearful magic – for she had learned from the angels the Secret Name of Allah. Bending low across her husband's face, she whispered it into his parted lips; and as she did so, all the stars and the moon stood still and the heavens themselves seemed to shudder at the sound, for never before had the sacred word been spoken. And what that word might be, there is no one who can say – for there has never been a secret more terrible or deadly. Therefore, O Egyptian, beware of it! For to hear it, to speak it, is to risk destruction!

But Isis was the most cunning of the fire-bred Jinn, and when she had spoken her magic into the mouth of her husband's corpse, it began to breathe and to stir, and its life was restored. Then Isis mounted his body, and his sperm was mingled with the outflow of her blood, and from this union a tiny child was born. And in time this child became the new King of Egypt; for Allah, whose sight is never sleeping, rose him up to manhood and made his hand strong. Then there was terrible war, for Seth still claimed the royal throne, and he led an army of evil Jinn, all those who had refused to bow down before Allah. But it is related – for Allah knows all! – how their power was at last destroyed and overthrown, and Seth and his followers were banished to the deserts. And Seth became the Prince of all things dark – and he is that same one whom the Faithful in this present age name Iblis.

And you should know, O Egyptian, that his followers may still be found, haunting the evil places of the world, the deserts and the tombs of the long-dead Kings. Keep away from such ghools and their works, O Egyptian! For if they are disturbed, then they will be a horror and a wonder to you, for their prey is the lonely traveller and their food is mortal flesh. But Allah is merciful! Praise be to His name!

———————

And when Haroun al-Vakhel had finished this story, he bowed his head and lapsed into silence. But the Caliph al-Hakim, who had been listening with a rapt and motionless attention, seized him by the arms. 'O Master of wise words,' he exclaimed, 'this Tale of the Sage of the Mountains of Káf is indeed a remarkable one! But tell me – after the great Queen Isis had spoken the sacred word and brought her royal husband back to life, was there nowhere in Egypt where the word was written down?'

'O Prince,' Haroun replied, 'even if there had been, I have told you the warning I was given, that it would be a danger and a blasphemy to seek the secret out.'

'Even so, if it could be found, I would read it. For am I not the Appointed of Allah? And are there not stones left blank in my mosque, to receive the imprint of His holy name?'

But Haroun shook his head. 'It is true,' he answered, 'that the Sage of the Mountains of Káf told me of a strange and ancient tradition. For it is said that there were priests in Egypt who guarded the Secret Name, but that at length they grew proud and fell into evil. And so they built a temple to the Secret Name, and they worshipped it as a god – yes, and Isis and Osiris too, although there is only one God, and His name is Allah.'

The Caliph stood frozen a long while, gazing out at where his sister sat, the Princess Sitt al-Mulq. 'And this temple,' he whispered at last, 'where might it be found?'

'It was destroyed.'

The Caliph gazed at him in disbelief. 'By whom?'

'By the prophet Joseph, may peace be forever on his name. For when he rose to be the counsellor to Pharaoh – so I heard it in the Mountains of Káf – he taught the way of the one true God. And though the priests were his enemies, Allah was his guide. And so it was that the evil of the temple was destroyed – for all man's ambitions are nothing but dust. Allah alone is great!'

Still the Caliph remained by the window, perfectly frozen save for the faintest tremor which passed across his face. 'Yes,' he hissed at last, 'Allah alone is great.' He turned to Haroun; his cheeks appeared exceedingly pale, like the knuckles on a fist which is very tightly clenched.

But Haroun was nothing daunted and, seeing that the audience had come to an end, he bowed low before the Caliph, then turned away and left.

For a long while he did not see the Caliph again, nor did he pursue any further the mysteries of the past. As gold was said to gleam within the ancient pagans' tombs, so their learning too still seemed to beckon him onwards; yet both, Haroun feared, might be guarded by fearful enchantments. So it was that he sought to banish the very thought of them from his mind – for he dreaded to think otherwise where his fascination might not lead.

Yet it was his good fortune that he had little time to dwell on anything save his work amongst the sick, for his reputation was very great and his knowledge and his skills were always in demand. Nor did he ever refuse a patient's summons; for whenever one came, it was then that Haroun would recall his former life, the many men he had slain and the many towns he had burned. Through every quarter of Cairo he would move, from the splendid palaces and gardens of the rich to the hovels of the poor who dwelt amidst the cemeteries, or by the black midden pools beside the city gates and walls, and he would treat all who asked for him regardless of their poverty or wealth, as though they were a part of his own family. For although happy in all other things, and content with his life, Haroun was childless; and this caused him great grief.

But then it happened, one evening, that he had a strange dream. He imagined that a girl was whispering in his ear, yet when he turned around there was no one to be seen. But still the voice spoke to him, and it struck him dumb with wonder, as he thought how he had never heard anything more sweet, nor more alluring to the senses, for it seemed touched by the perfume of the gardens of Paradise. 'Very soon,' said this voice, 'you will be awoken from your sleep by a knocking at your door. It will be a Jew, in tears because his son has fallen sick in the night and appears very close to death. Go with him to his house. If you do so, you will not be much longer without a child!' And then the voice began to fade, and when Haroun woke up he could hear a knocking at his door.

All fell out as the voice had said, for Haroun was led by the Jew to his house, and to a room where his son lay very sick. The boy appeared deathly pale, and troubled by bad dreams, and Haroun was unable to wake him from his sleep. He frowned as he sought to treat the boy, for the sickness seemed very strange and, though he was wise in the arts of healing, he had never seen such symptoms before. He listened to the boy's heart, how it fluttered weakly, and then as he did so he suddenly froze, for he could see across the chest a thin, vivid scar. It was still bleeding, and the boy began suddenly to scratch at it and to moan.

Haroun called the boy's parents and pointed at the scar. 'Tell me,' he demanded, 'what is that?'

The parents gazed at it and at once grew pale. The mother

began to cry out until her sobs choked her, and the father bowed his head and muttered a prayer.

'What is it?' Haroun exclaimed. 'What has made you so afraid?'

The Jew turned to him. He was wringing his hands. 'Only a demon,' he muttered, 'could have made such a wound.'

'A demon?' Haroun shook his head. 'What men call demons are mostly what they cannot understand.'

'But this happened the night before to the daughter of our Rabbi; the same strange scar was found drawn across her chest. She went into a fever, just like our son, and by the afternoon,' – the Jew choked – 'the little girl was dead.' He choked again, then swallowed and sought to compose himself. 'According to our Rabbi,' he explained, 'it was most certainly a demon, for such a wound has ever been the mark of Lilith.'

'Lilith?'

'In our holy books,' the Jew stammered, 'it is told how she was the first wife of Adam in Paradise. But she grew greedy for the flesh of her own new-born – and so she was expelled to wander through the darkness of the night.'

Haroun stood frozen.

'How,' the Jew asked, 'can we keep her from my son?'

Slowly, Haroun turned to meet his eye. 'Lilith?' he murmured softly. 'No. It cannot be.'

'But I tell you, our Rabbi . . .' Then the Jew began to frown. 'But of course, you are a Muslim. Can it be, then, that you have never heard of Lilith? Yet in your books as well, are there not tales of the desert-haunting ghools?'

Haroun nodded very slowly. 'There are,' he murmured. But he said no more, for his mind was dark with memories and nightmares, and he seemed suddenly to see, risen before him, the glittering walls of Lilatt-ah again.

The Jew gazed at him, hope intermingled with despair. 'What then, O Master of knowledge, should we do?'

Haroun opened his mouth, to admit he did not know.

But at that very moment, from the street below there came a sudden knocking loud upon the door.

The Jew's wife left the room to see who the visitor could be. She returned with a man who appeared to be a merchant and who seemed, from the style of his dress, to be a Christian from the Empire of the Greeks. But though his robes were rich, he was clearly very ill, for his face was pale and he leaned upon a stick. When he saw the gathering all about him, however, his gaunt face was suddenly illumined by a smile. 'Praise be to God,' he exclaimed, 'this room is exactly how I saw it in my dream!' He looked from face to face. 'But which of you, pray tell me, is Haroun al-Vakhel?'

Haroun stepped forward. 'I am that man. But tell me in turn, please, how you know my name, for I am certain that I have never met with you before.'

'I was told by a strange voice in a vision to find you here. For you alone, it appears, possess the power to heal me.'

'Allah willing, I shall certainly do my best. But first you must tell me what your symptoms are.'

'Why,' the Christian exclaimed, pointing to where the Jewish boy lay muttering on his bed, 'the same as his!' And so saying, he parted his cloak to reveal a thin, oozing scar which ran across his chest. 'I can only thank God that I have reached you in time, for I have felt myself growing weaker from it with each successive day.'

But Haroun shook his head in perplexity. 'I am sorry, but I fear I cannot help you.'

'But my dream . . .'

'I do not have the cure.'

The Christian closed his eyes in disappointment and despair. 'But my dream . . .' he muttered again. 'I was told . . .' Then suddenly he laughed, and clapped his hands. 'Of course!' he exclaimed. 'I must show you the slave!'

'Slave?' frowned Haroun.

'Is it not true, you are still without a child?'

Haroun stared at him strangely, for he remembered what the voice in his own dream had said. 'What of it?' he asked.

But the Christian only smiled. 'You will find her, I think, beautiful and elegant beyond every description.' And so saying, he took Haroun by the arm and led him across to the window of the room. From there he pointed at a girl in the street and Haroun, as he inspected her, realised that the Christian had not been exaggerating. Never before had he seen such mortal beauty. The girl's figure was perfect, as slender as a reed, her breasts seemed like twin fruit of ivory, and her feet and hands were deliciously small. Her hair was the colour of deepest night, and hung in seven tresses far below her waist. Her cheeks were rosy, her lips bright red, and her teeth like delicate and lustrous pearls. Beneath her long, silken lashes her almond eyes were black, and their gleam seemed as bright as that of an angel. To Haroun, indeed, it appeared that the girl would put the very sun and stars from their orbits, and he shuddered suddenly, for he thought how he had only once seen such a beauteous face before, upon the statue of the goddess of the temple in Lilatt-ah. But then he gazed upon the slave again, and his fears were set to rest, for her stare seemed languid with a tender and captivating passion; and he knew himself dazzled and overwhelmed by love.

He turned to the Christian. 'Tell me, O Merchant, what is the price of that girl?'

But the Christian smiled. 'I have told you, she is yours.'

'But I cannot heal you.'

'So you say, and yet I am certain that you can. For would my dream have been true on all other counts, and untrue to me on only this one single matter?'

'Perhaps,' suggested Haroun, 'it would be best if you were first to tell me the story of your dream, and of how you came by this wondrous slave.'

'Certainly,' answered the Christian, 'if you are willing to hear it.' Then he eased himself down on to the floor and spoke as follows:

THE TALE TOLD BY THE
CHRISTIAN MERCHANT

You must know, my noble hosts, that I have always borne in mind the words of King Solomon, who said how the grave is better than poverty. For this reason I have travelled the world, selling and bartering my goods, and seeking out rare supplies of luxuries. But I do not travel simply to make a profit, for I have also, ever since I was a child, had a desire to visit far countries and discover strange and remarkable things. It was for this reason that I travelled to Egypt and journeyed down the Nile, for I had read much of its wonders in the books of my own people. More than anything I wished to see the ancient town of Thebes, which was once, long ago, the capital of this land. It shelters nothing now, however, beyond the jackals and the owls, and its great halls of stone are half-sunk beneath the sands. But a man may still gaze upon its splendours, ruined as they are, and wonder at the power which must once have served to raise them – and he may wonder as well at the wealth it must have owned.

Nor is that wealth wholly vanished even now. For there is a village on the opposite bank of the Nile – very small and wretched in appearance – where nevertheless, every once in a while, the villagers will produce strange and beautiful ornaments, made of gold or silver, and rich with precious stones. I fell into the habit of purchasing these treasures, for I realised that I could easily sell them for a profit, and so I soon became a regular visitor to Thebes. The villagers were reluctant to reveal the source of their discoveries, but at length, with the help of a bottle of wine, I was able to persuade one of them to betray the secret. It appeared there was a nearby valley where, in long-ago times, the ancients had chosen to bury their kings. These kings still lay there, deep within the rock, and all about them were piles of gold and jewels. But the valley was a dangerous place to visit, or so the villager maintained. It was haunted, he claimed, by ghools he named '*udar*'; and even as he said this, he began to grow pale.

Nor was he the only one to be in terror of these demons. That same evening as the sun began to set, I marked how all the villagers came in from the fields, and no one would willingly remain abroad. Around two I was woken by a far-off scream, and I imagined, when I peered out from my tent, that I saw in the distance the glitter of silver eyes. For all that, I did not wholly believe in the story of ghools until I was shown, the next morning, the corpse of a wretch who had fallen their victim, and whose scream I had evidently heard the night before. His chest had been sliced open and his flesh gnawed upon – but that was the very least of the horrors. For my guide pointed to a wound between the corpse's legs, and then tapped at its stomach, and as he did so the flesh split apart, and I saw, writhing within the guts, an infinite quantity of worms. For this, it seemed, was how the *udar* could be known: worms and maggots were borne upon their discharge.

This was a great wonder to me of course, and a great horror as well, but I have often discovered, in the course of my travels, how dangers will frame the most precious rewards. Gold, I had discovered, was not the only prize which the valley contained: I had seen for myself, in the markets of Cairo, the withered corpses of ancient kings, and I knew the price that such things might bring. '*Mummia*,' they are called, and it is believed – may Christ watch over and preserve my soul! – that their limbs, once melted and formed into a potion, may wondrously extend the span of mortal life. For should they be left in their tombs, these corpses will lie forever in unending silence, undisturbed by even the crawling of the worms, until the final Day of Judgement – and there are many here in Cairo who are eager to share in such a magic. But God and Christ His Son alone are great!

With such a rich supply of merchandise, therefore, I soon began to find myself blessed by great wealth. Yet at length, such was the demand that the supply in the village began to be exhausted, and the villagers, when I pressed them to search out more, claimed that the danger from the *udar* was become too great. I raised my price, but still they refused. They told me that the *udar* were now infesting all the tombs, and that it was becoming unsafe to search them even in the day.

At length, such was my sense of frustration that I resolved to visit the valley myself. I rode up the pathway which led towards its entrance, but alas, even before I had reached it, I was to pay the price for my greed and stupidity! I felt a sudden blow against the back of my head, and then the sky seemed to spin and I tumbled like a sack of coals from my horse. The next thing I knew, I could feel hands about my throat, and a stench of rottenness was thick all about me. A sudden sharp pain was slashed across my chest and I screamed, for I could feel damp lips sucking on the wound. Yet that was not the worst, for I was thinking of the corpse of the peasant I had seen, whose stomach had been bloated by burrowing, hungry worms; and as I did so, I screamed once again and consigned my soul to the love of Jesus Christ, for I was certain now that I was doomed to die. Upon this wave of terror my thoughts began to cloud.

It was then, however, even as I imagined that I was sinking into death, that I dreamed a strange dream. I saw before me the vision of a girl, standing in the shadows of a mighty temple. Then I heard a voice which told me to present her, O Haroun al-Vakhel, to you, so that by her you might at last have a child. And then I was granted a vision of this room where we are all standing together now, and I was told that in return for my gift of the girl to you, O Master, you would be able to heal me of my sickness. And when I awoke, it was to find that I was indeed exceedingly ill, pale and weak, with this wound across my chest. I ordered a litter to be made for me, and then I crossed the Nile, for I knew there was a temple of stupendous size situated on the eastern bank, very similar to the one which I had witnessed in my dream. And sure enough, as I walked through the ruins, I discovered at their furthermost point this girl you see here now. I pressed her to tell me from where she had come, and what her name might be, but she would not reply – nor has she spoken a word since that day. The only thing of which I am certain is that her face was the face of the girl in my dream. So, to be sure, it is a great mystery – but God alone can know everything!

At this the Christian fell silent, and Haroun shook his head in puzzlement. 'That is indeed,' he exclaimed, 'an extraordinary tale, but I still fail to see how I may heal you of your wound. Perhaps it would be best if you were to summon the girl so that I may discover if she is willing to say anything to me.'

The Christian did as Haroun had suggested, and the girl was brought up to the room. As she entered through the door Haroun felt his love for her blaze up again, for her body was as fair as the purest silver, and her eyes as profound as the fathoms of the ocean. But although she noticed his presence, she showed Haroun no veneration, nor spoke a single word, only flaring her delicate nostrils very slightly as though she had caught a scent upon the air. Then she stared at him more closely, and reached out to touch his cloak. Haroun unfastened it and passed it to her. She smelt it once again, then held it to the sun, and as she did so Haroun observed that the fabric was stained with several patches, black but touched by thin filaments of light. He frowned, wondering what the stains could be – and then suddenly he remembered, and raised a prayer of thanks to Allah.

For the cloak, he realised, was the oldest one he had, which he had worn on the day of the assault upon Lilatt-ah. He remembered the liquid which the priest had been heating in the very depths of the hellish temple, and how, when toppled, it had splashed and stained his cloak. 'Doubtless,' Haroun told himself, 'it was infected by some sorcery, but if it will serve to keep two people alive, then Allah in His wisdom will surely forgive me the sin.' And so saying, he tore away the patches from the fabric of his cloak and ordered them boiled, then shredded and made into a paste. When all was ready, he took the medicine and applied it to the wounds, which closed at once and began to heal. Both the Christian and the young boy felt their strength returning, and they fell upon their saviour with thanks and tears of joy.

But even as they were hailing him as the Prince of all Physicians, Haroun himself still felt puzzled and bemused. He glanced towards the slave girl, hoping that she might speak at last, but though she met his stare her ruby lips stayed closed. For the briefest moment, Haroun felt a shadow of unease pass across his thoughts, but then he looked at her again and felt his love for her renewed. 'Glory be to Allah,' he whispered to himself, 'who has the power to fashion such a creature. Something so lovely can only be good.'

Then he led her to his home with all due honour and attention. But the slave girl kept silent, and still said not a word.

Once Haroun had brought the slave girl back to his house, he sought to take care of her as well as he could. He went to a secret chest where he had kept all that remained of his former wealth, and then, going to the market, he hired servants, and bought clothes and delicious food and drink. The attendants bathed and adorned the girl, so that she was dressed in a way that was worthy of her beauty; and when Haroun saw her in her jewellery and fine clothes, and smelt the delicate perfume on her limbs and rounded breasts, he thought to himself how not even the Seven Heavens could rival her for splendour. Then he embraced her very tenderly and led her to a couch, where he ordered the servants to bring them the food. When they had done so, he dismissed them from his presence, and he fed the slave girl like a servant himself. But she, while she ate, kept her head bowed low, and still she kept silent nor even looked at Haroun.

And so it continued for the length of a year. To Haroun all this time seemed a single day, for he found himself ever more in love with the girl, nor had he ever known such passion before. Yet still he treated her with every tenderness, as though she were a blessing sent to him from Heaven, not to be touched and taken by force but cherished like a flame that might otherwise be snuffed out. She, though, remained as silent as ever through all these months; nor, when darkness fell, would she even stay beside Haroun, but would gaze from a window at the stars of the night, for it appeared that the sight of them could never weary her.

Then it happened one evening that Haroun discovered her standing on the roof of his house, staring across the city towards the western desert, where the moonlight fell silver on the ripples of the sand. So lovely did she seem, and yet so touched by regret, that Haroun thought his heart would break for love. 'O my heart's desire,' he cried, 'you are dearer to me than my very life! If you will never love me in return, then let me know, so that I may at least give up hope. Otherwise, my lady, speak to me, for I would surrender my very chance of Paradise for you!'

And when the girl heard this, she smiled suddenly and turned to Haroun, stroking his cheeks with her slender fingers, before kissing him softly. Then she led him to his room, and tended him gently as she made him lie down on his bed. There she did what no woman had ever done before, and laid herself upon him, but Haroun did not complain, nor seek to alter his position; for even as she ministered to him, he felt himself lost in a flame of rapture such as the Faithful are promised shall be theirs after death. And then, when all was done and she had anointed the length of his body with her kisses, she gazed into his face and smiled once again.

'O most kind and generous of men,' she said, 'may you be granted long life and your every wish.'

Haroun gazed up at her in wonder, for her voice was as enchanting as the beauty of her face, and yet he knew that he had heard it once before within his dream. 'O my heart's delight,' he asked her, 'tell me what you are, and where you come from, for you seem like a miracle sent to me from Heaven.'

'O my lord,' she answered, rising from his bed, 'I will tell you who I am. My name is Leila, and I am the princess of a strange and distant land.' She crossed to the window, where she pointed to the stars. 'Once I dwelt upon the breath of the air, for my people, you should know, rule the wide realm of the skies.'

'That is a great wonder!' exclaimed Haroun, as he crossed to join her and gazed up at the stars. 'But how is it possible for your people to live there without plunging to their deaths?'

'O my master,' she answered, 'we can live in the sky just as you can live on land. All things are possible to those who know how.'

'Truly,' Haroun mused, 'the greatness and power of Allah have no limits! But why did you not tell me this immediately? For you know how I have loved you, and yet for a year you did not speak.'

At this a single tear welled and hung upon her lashes. 'Forgive me,' she answered, brushing it away, 'but I am a slave and an exile in a foreign land.'

Haroun embraced her, and kissed her on the brow. 'You are not a slave, but the mistress of this house.'

She smiled as he said this, and reached up to kiss him. 'Do you think I would have stayed here a single hour,' she asked, 'if you had failed to care for me with such tenderness and love? And now, O best of men, you have been granted your reward, for you should know that since this evening I have been carrying your child.'

'O my lady, O my love,' cried Haroun in joy, 'let Allah be praised! For now I see how my dream spoke the truth, granting me a blessing which I had never thought to see.' But then he paused, and reached to take Leila by her hand. 'But how can I know, if you come from the stars, that you will not attempt to return there again?'

Leila smiled sadly. 'I have strayed so far from the realms of my own people that I doubt I will ever be able to return.'

'Then you will remain in my house, and live as my wife?'

She turned to meet his stare. For a moment Haroun felt a shiver of dread, for the blackness of Leila's eyes seemed suddenly very cold, inky like the night-time skies from which she came. 'Upon a single condition,' she whispered at last.

'To say it is to command me.'

Still the depths of her stare remained like ice, until her ruby lips curved into a slow and tender smile. 'That you continue to love me more than all the world.'

He laughed. 'That is an easy enough condition, then!'

But even as he said this, and reached to embrace her, she pressed herself against him and clasped him by his cheeks. 'Swear it,' she hissed. 'For I tell you again – should you ever love anything more than you love me, then at that same moment, O my husband, I will leave.'

So tightly she gripped him that Haroun felt a sudden spurt of blood from the gouging of her nails. For a moment the pain discomforted him, and he thought to himself what a mystery it was, that a girl so silent for the length of a year should now seem so violent and urgent in her passions. But then he gazed into her face again, and at once all his doubts and hesitations died away, and he raised a silent prayer of thanks for such a blessing. 'I swear it,' he whispered, 'I will always love you. For now' – he kissed her – 'for now, and evermore.'

So it was that Haroun lived with Leila, his beloved, in great contentment, and when nine months were past he became the father of a child, a little girl; and he gave to his daughter the name of Haidée. And from the first day of her life she was full of joy and grace, and Haroun, who had despaired of ever becoming a father, welcomed her just as a man lost in the desert, watching the vultures start to gather above his head, might welcome his first, unexpected glimpse of water – for there is nothing more precious than a blessing unforeseen.

So several years passed, and Haidée grew in beauty and charm, and she became ever more the jewel at the heart of Haroun's life. He thought that his happiness would be without end – for even as his joy in Haidée grew, so also did the pleasure that he took in his wife. Leila's freshness, unlike that of the rose, seemed immune to the tide and the passage of the seasons; so much so that at last Haroun, baffled by the mystery, asked her to explain her enduring bloom. But she smiled and shook her head, and would only answer, with a glance towards the stars, how there might be islands even in the ceaseless flow of time. When Haroun tried to press her, however, she grew silent and would say nothing more; and he noticed, from that time on, how she withdrew herself from him. Her stare grew colder too, and he would sometimes observe, as he sat with their child, that she would be watching him from a distance – her eyes half-hooded, but sparkling bright like jewels. At other times she would vanish altogether, and Haroun would find her at length as he had often done before, during the year when she had spoken not a word, standing upon a balcony and gazing out into the night.

Then it happened one evening, when Leila had been absent for a couple of days, that Haroun was called to his neighbour's house where a servant had fallen sick with an unknown disease. Haroun was not surprised to hear this, for Cairo at the time was vile with the stench and heat of summer. The southern winds were blowing sand through the streets, maddening the dogs and drying the filth into poisonous dust, and Haroun knew all too well how strange pestilences, bred upon the sleepless, burning air, could spread across the city with the deadliest of ease. But the moment he arrived at his neighbour's house and was shown where the invalid lay delirious and pale, Haroun knew that he had seen the illness once before. He knelt beside the servant and pulled back a sheet. Across the man's sweating chest there stretched a still-bleeding scar.

Haroun did his best to ease the wretch's suffering, but he knew that he had nothing which would serve as an antidote. He did not stay long, and when he returned home he sought out his wife. He found her in her private quarters, rocking a sleeping Haidée in her arms.

'What was the secret,' he asked her, 'of the potion I prepared on that first day when I met you?'

Leila met his stare unblinkingly. 'I do not know what you mean.'

'You know full well.' Haroun crossed to his wife. He felt his anger boiling up inside him, and he opened his mouth again to demand that she tell him the secret.

But Leila stilled his fury with a single smile. 'Tell me, O my dearest,' she asked, easing Haidée's head from her lap, 'do you not remember your oath?' She rose to her feet and clasped him tightly, so that he felt himself enfolded in the tresses of her hair. Then she reached up on her toes to whisper in his ear: 'Do you not love me more than all the world?'

She kissed him, and as she did so Haroun felt the final embers of his anger fade away, and he thought once again, as he met her parted lips, how he had no greater blessing and joy in his life. 'More than all the world,' he whispered. 'More than Paradise itself.' And so he pressed her no further; and all his fears and doubts were laid to rest upon her kisses. And that same night, his pleasure with his wife was very great.

But the next day, when he called upon his neighbour, it was to find that the servant's condition had grown worse. As Haroun bent down to inspect him he was shocked to discover, still damp upon the man's chest, a second violent scar.

Again Haroun sought to comfort the wretch as well as he was able, but he had little success; and so once more he returned in perturbation to his wife. As before, he found her with Haidée asleep upon her lap.

'Where were you,' he demanded, 'last night?'

She smiled up at him. 'Do you really need to be reminded, O my love?'

'But afterwards, I slept so deeply and so well that it was as though I had been drugged with mandragora. Where were you then? Asleep by my side – or abroad, O my Wife, upon the poisonous winds of the night?'

And again he felt his rage boiling up within him; but again Leila stilled it with a single smile, and she reached up to embrace him and fold him in her arms. And again, she kissed him and whispered in his ear, 'Do you not love me more than all the world?'

And again Haroun was silenced; and he said nothing more.

But the next day the same events occurred, save that this time, when Haroun called upon his neighbour, it was to discover the servant lying dead upon the floor; and indeed the corpse already seemed a skeleton, for its flesh had been picked away from its bones. And when Haroun saw this, he shuddered and offered up a prayer to Allah; and then he hurried from the house and returned to his wife.

He found her as he had done the past two days, sitting with Haidée asleep upon her lap. Haroun gazed at them in silence a moment, and as he did so, he could feel his dread start to fade before the bright flame of his love. But he clenched his fists tightly, then crossed to Leila and sat down by her side.

He gazed into her face, into the fathomless beauty of her black, silk-lashed eyes. 'What are you,' he whispered, 'what nature of thing?'

'Why,' she smiled back, 'your wife, O my love.'

But Haroun shook his head. 'Do not lie to me. You have said that you come from a kingdom in the skies, and I believed you' – he shrugged – 'for I have seen and heard many strange things in my life. But I believe you no longer.'

'Then what' – she smiled more faintly – 'do you think that I can be?'

Haroun shuddered, both with terror and with the force of his desire. 'I fear,' he whispered softly, 'that you are one of those Jinn who were flung down from Heaven, and who have never bowed their heads before Allah. And if that should truly be the case' – he glanced down at his daughter, and softly stroked her cheek – 'then I dread to think what your purposes may be.'

'No purpose,' Leila whispered back, 'save to love you, as I told you, until you cease to love me.'

Both gazed in silence at the other. Then at last Haroun moaned, and shook his head. 'How can I believe you?' he whispered. 'For Leila, O my beloved – how I long to believe!'

Her ruby smile faded. 'Let me give you this,' she murmured after a lengthy pause. So saying, she slipped a golden ring from her finger; she kissed it briefly, then passed it across to him.

Haroun inspected it in puzzlement. The ring was not plain but decorated with an image of the disk of the sun, beneath which were the outlines of two figures on their knees. 'What is this thing?' he asked.

'It possesses this magic, O my dearest,' Leila replied, 'that whosoever wears it shall always be guarded by the power of my love.'

Then she reached up to embrace him. Haroun sought to brush her aside and rise to his feet, but even though he struggled, his efforts were very faint. He felt her perfumed breath fall softly upon his cheek; and then he moaned, and sat back, and reached for her kiss.

Leila smiled once again. After a lengthy while, she broke from his lips and whispered in his ear, 'Do you not love me more than all the world?'

Haroun gazed for a moment upon the image on the ring. 'More than life itself,' he whispered at last. He slipped on the ring. 'Allah have mercy – more than life itself.'

From that time on, when people came to him with the news of a strange sickness, marked by an oozing scar upon the chest, Haroun would tell them that he could do nothing to help. Such news, that the famous physician was powerless to combat the mysterious disease, only added to the terror which it was beginning to inspire, for rumours, like the garbage on the wind, were gusting and swirling through the streets of the city. Some claimed that the sickness was not a sickness at all, but the mark of the anger of a terrible jinni who came upon the breezes, and whose lips brought death. Some claimed to have seen a black figure, shrouded behind a veil, by the beds of those who would then fall sick; some claimed to have seen the black veil fall and glimpsed, just for a moment, glittering eyes, deep and very lovely but deathly like poison. There was a Jew who had lately sickened and died, and his wife said that she had seen a figure upon his chest the very night he had fallen ill. 'Lilith,' she had wailed, 'Lilith is come!' Now the same cry had spread far beyond the Jewish quarter, and there was not a household in Cairo which had not learned to dread the nights.

Throughout the spell of this panic, however, Haroun still kept away from the sick, nor did he answer the appeals of those who sought him out. Instead, he kept himself immured with his wife and his daughter, playing with Haidée and reading books with her, and seeking to teach her all that he could, so that she would be instilled with his own sense of wonder at the world. And each evening, Leila would come to him and fold her arms about his neck, and then she would whisper in his ear, 'Do you not love me more than all the world?' And always he would answer, 'Yes'; and each night, after an ecstasy of pleasure, he would sink into deep and dreamless slumber.

Then it happened one evening, as Haroun was sitting with Haidée, that his servant announced a messenger arrived from the Caliph, and when Haroun looked up, he saw it was Masoud. 'You must come at once,' the blackamoor said. 'The Princess Sitt al-Mulq has fallen sick, and the Commander of the Faithful is frantic with despair.'

'What are the symptoms of the Princess's fever?'

'She is very pale, with terrible dreams – and across her breast is a bleeding scar.'

Haroun felt a tightening across his chest. 'I cannot help her.'

'The Caliph commands it.'

'Yet as I have said – I cannot help.'

The blackamoor glanced at Haidée. 'It is never wise,' he whispered, 'to refuse the Caliph's wishes. If you know what is best for you and for those you love' – he paused to bare his teeth in a hideous grin – 'then you will come with me at once.'

Haroun sat still a moment more, oppressed by dread and uncertainty, then kissed his daughter upon her brow and rose to accompany Masoud to the Palace. When he arrived there, he found the Caliph by the bedside of the Princess Sitt al-Mulq. A single glance was sufficient to confirm his worst fears, but nevertheless, although he knew it would serve little purpose, he did his best to ease the Princess's pain.

Despite his efforts, however, she continued to moan and the Caliph, watching her, suddenly thrust Haroun aside and clasped her tightly in his arms. 'Why do you not heal her?' he cried out, stroking the side of her breast with his fingers and gazing down in horror at the bleeding scar.

'I am helpless, O Prince.'

'You cannot be! You are the wisest physician in the whole of Cairo!'

'I can give her this potion, which may help her to sleep.'

'Do it,' the Caliph ordered. 'And the next day, come without fail, and bring with you a cure. Or else, O Physician . . .' – he drew his knife – 'or else . . .'

Haroun returned to his house with a heavy heart. Leila was nowhere to be seen, nor did she reappear all that long night. Haroun passed it instead in watch upon his daughter, and when Masoud arrived the next morning he gazed upon Haidée as though he might never see her face again. But Masoud grinned horribly and, crossing to the girl, picked her up and placed her on his shoulders. Haroun sought to protest, but Masoud shook his head. And so father and daughter went together to the Palace.

Once arrived in the Princess's sick-room, Haroun saw at once that her condition had worsened. A second scar had appeared across her breast, and she was waving her arms as though to ward away a phantom. The Caliph, sitting beside her, gazed up at Haroun with hatred in his eyes. 'Why has my sister not recovered?' he hissed. 'You swore she would be cured.'

'No, O Prince, I swore no such thing.'

The Caliph continued to stare at him raw-eyed. 'She shall be cured,' he whispered at last. Then he turned back to his sister, and began to hug her despairingly and kiss her on the lips. But even as he did so, she began to scream and beat at him with her arms, and Haroun rushed forward to attempt to calm her down. 'I must give her an opiate again,' he said, reaching into his bag.

The Caliph's eyes gleamed. 'Will it cure her?' he asked.

'It will help her to sleep, for she must have rest.'

The Caliph nodded distractedly. At the same moment, however, somewhere from the city there came the sudden howling of a dog; and immediately the Caliph screamed for his guards. 'You hear the noise of these animals?' he cried. 'Listen to them! They bark and howl while all the time my sister lies here sick – and still the curs howl! Well? Why do you stand here? Have you no love, no concern for your Caliph at all? *My sister needs rest!*'

The guards stared at him uncertainly. Then one of them bowed low, and they retreated in haste from the Princess's room. It was not long before Haroun heard the first yelpings of agony from the distant streets below, and he gazed up in horror and disbelief at the Caliph. But the Caliph himself was smiling with excitement as he stood upon the balcony, surveying the slaughter and shaking with mingled pleasure and rage. 'So shall all those be served,' he muttered to himself, 'who dare to think that my sister may not live!' He turned back to Haroun, and as he did so his eye was caught by Haidée, who sat huddled, confused and afraid, in the corner. The Caliph stood a moment as though transfixed by the sight, then crossed to the girl and crouched down beside her. As her eyes grew ever wider, he began to stroke her cheek.

'She is pretty, your daughter, very pretty,' he whispered. He gazed up at Haroun with a look of sudden venom. 'Yet my sister is lovelier – and you say she may not live? Does that seem fair to you, O Haroun?' His eyes blazed, and Haidée shrank back even further against the wall. 'She will die,' the Caliph muttered, rising to his feet. 'If my sister dies, then your daughter too will die!'

He glanced once more at where his sister lay, then swept from the room. Haidée, watching him depart, began suddenly to sob and Haroun, rushing across to her, rocked her in his arms. 'Do not worry, O my flower, O my lily, do not fear.' And so saying, he slipped off the ring which had been the gift from his wife and bound it to a string about Haidée's neck. 'There,' he whispered softly, 'now you are guarded by your mother's magic, and need never be afraid.'

But although he sought to smile, and comfort his daughter, he could feel nothing in his heart but a terrible sickness, and horror at the thought of what might now lie ahead.

That evening, once he had settled Haidée to sleep, Haroun ordered guards to be posted in the Princess's room. He stationed them not only by the doors but also by the windows, although the wall below them rose so steeply that it seemed impossible to ascend. Nevertheless, Haroun was insistent and, although he would not explain who or what it was he feared, he warned the guards not to close their eyes for a moment.

Then, when all had been readied, Haroun left the Palace, for he could not endure to pass the night within its walls. Sometimes, as he walked aimlessly through the streets, he would glance behind him at its distant silhouette and try to identify the Princess's room, although even as he did so he dreaded to imagine what it was that he might see, what figure or strange phantom framed upon its balcony. Seeking to banish all such thoughts from his mind, he dwelt instead upon the sights around him – but in the streets as well, there were horrors to behold.

Everywhere the dust wore a caking of blood. The corpses of dogs lay piled amidst the garbage and already, in the burning heat of night, a hideous stench was infecting the air. The streets, normally such a ferment of noise, seemed preternaturally quiet, and Haroun smiled with grim despair at the thought of how gratified the Caliph would be. But then, even as he imagined the whole of Cairo to have been silenced by the slaughter, he heard a soft, anguished whimpering and, looking round, he saw an injured dog struggling to rise upon its paws. With a great deal of effort, it finally succeeded and tottered, still whimpering, a few unsteady paces. It approached a couple of mangled bodies, and as it did so its whimperings grew ever more frantic. It began to lick their sodden fur and Haroun, drawing nearer, saw how tiny the corpses were. The dog, he supposed, must have been their mother, and even as he thought this the bitch began to howl. At once Haroun gathered her up into his arms, for he was afraid that the soldiers might still be abroad, but the bitch still howled and squirmed in his hold, trying to return to her murdered brood. Haroun sought to muffle her beneath his cloak, and as he hurried away the bitch subsided once again into a mournful whimpering. He began to stroke her, and whisper in her ear, and by the time he had arrived back at his house she was almost asleep. He tended to her wounds, then ordered his servants to ensure that she was given plenty of food and drink while he was away. Before he left her, he decided to name her Isis, because she had cared for her loved ones even after death.

He returned to the Palace at dawn-break, and hurried at once to where he had left Haidée asleep. She still lay there with eyes closed, her face the image of untroubled innocence, and as Haroun bent low beside her he made certain that the ring was still secure around her neck. Once he kissed her, very lightly on her brow, and he longed to pick her up and hold her in his arms, for he dreaded that he might never again have the chance. But he left her instead in the calm of her sleep and he continued to the room of the

Princess Sitt al-Mulq, praying that she too might have had a dreamless night. Even as he approached it, though, he could hear her wordless screaming; and he knew at once that some great horror had been inflicted in the night.

And so indeed it proved. The soldiers lay slumped around the Princess's bed, their eyes protruding with a look of inexpressible terror, and their throats cut so wide that their heads had been almost severed from their necks. The Princess herself was still alive but screaming horribly, her eyes tight closed, and though Haroun shook her, he could not wake her from her nightmare. She seemed very much paler, and horribly thin, and across her breasts was the line of a third oozing scar. Of her assailant, however, there was not a sign.

All that day, Haroun fought to save the Princess's life. At last, towards evening, he began to hope that he had kept her from the black gates of Death, although she remained very pale and still could not be woken from the horrors of her dreams. 'I can do no more,' he told the Caliph, who had been pacing the room behind him all day. 'As to what may happen in the darkness of the night' – Haroun shrugged and shook his head – 'Allah alone is all-seeing and all-great.'

'Then you must trust He hears your prayers,' the Caliph answered him curtly, 'if you wish your daughter to live.' And he turned, and left Haroun alone with the Princess. And Haroun, gazing from the window, saw that the sun was sinking into the western horizon, and night was already darkening the east.

He did not, though, order new soldiers to keep guard upon the room, but remained alone with the Princess himself. Sometimes he would rise from her side and cross to the balcony to survey the mighty labyrinth of Cairo spread below him, and he would imagine, standing where he was, that he could glimpse into the heart of every human soul it sheltered, and penetrate the mysteries of every narrow street; yet even as he thought so, he knew it was an illusion. And then he would raise his eyes from the city, and gaze upon the prickling silver of the stars; and he would dread to think what strange shadow he might suddenly see brushing past the moon, borne upon the winds.

Yet the hours passed and nothing came, and the darkness, slowly, began to fade. At the first light of dawn, high like an arrow, there rose a muezzin's cry and then another, and then cries without number, minaret answering minaret, and Haroun turned to the east and bowed down to pray. But even as he did so, he heard from behind him a sudden soft footfall, and turning, he saw a shimmering of brightness and then a ripple of gold bent low across the Princess.

'Leila?'

There was no answer.

Haroun rose to his feet. 'Leila?' He took a step forward, and as he did so the brightness shimmered and appeared to grow more distinct. He could see now, haloed by the gold, Leila's face and raven-black hair, and her bright ruby lips which were parted in a smile. 'O my Dearest,' she whispered. 'Do you not love me more than all the world?'

Haroun gazed at her in silence. She rose slowly, with the venomous beauty of a deadly snake, and as she did so he saw – which he had failed to notice since the first time he had met her – that she was the image of the idol in Lilatt-ah.

He tried to stagger backwards, but found he could not move. 'In the name of Allah,' he whispered, 'what hellish thing are you?'

'O my Husband,' she smiled at him sweetly, 'do you truly not love me more than all the world?'

'More than all the world,' he answered, 'save for only one thing.'

'And that is?' she whispered.

'Our daughter, Leila – our daughter, our child!'

She froze, and the smile began to vanish from her parted lips. 'And so it was,' she whispered, 'once before, long ago. Only one, O Haroun, have I ever loved like you – and he too betrayed me as you have done.' Her eyes suddenly clouded, and Haroun saw in them, to his astonishment, a loneliness as cold as the icy depths of space. Then she smiled again, and this time, upon her lips, he recognised mingled pity and contempt. 'As you have chosen,' she whispered, 'so must you pay. Farewell, O my Husband. Forever, farewell.' He felt her mouth brush his own, as his senses began to melt into a perfume of darkness.

The Caliph, arriving early that morning in the chamber of his sister, found her lying asleep, her expression very calm. Haroun was kneeling beside her and the Caliph assumed, for he had not been able to observe the physician's face, that all was well and a cure had been found. But then Haroun turned to confront him, and at the sight of his expression the Caliph was struck dumb with consternation. Never before had he seen a look of such despair – and at once he hurried forward to his sister's side.

He knelt down and seized her hand; but Haroun, watching him, shook his head wearily. 'Do not think you will wake her, O Prince, for she is lost in a sleep from which she cannot be roused.'

The Caliph's brows darkened. 'What do you mean? How can that be?'

'She is the victim of the spell of a most powerful jinni.'

'Can you not break it?'

'As I told you once before, O Commander of the Faithful, I have no knowledge of the magical arts.'

The Caliph smiled at him very coldly. 'Yet as you also told me once before, you do have the knowledge of how such arts might be invoked.'

Haroun shook his head impatiently. 'There is no time for this, O Prince.' He rose to his feet. 'I must leave here at once.'

'Not until you have given me your reason.'

'There is someone I must hunt down.'

The Caliph smiled coldly once again. 'But there is something else you must also find.'

At once Haroun froze. 'I do not understand.'

'Why' – the Caliph's smile broadened – 'the Secret Name of Allah.'

Haroun narrowed his eyes, but did not reply.

'If that were discovered,' the Caliph hissed with sudden force, 'if its syllables were pronounced, then would not the powers of the ancient jinn be mine?'

For a long while Haroun continued silent. 'You know, O Prince,' he murmured at last, 'that it would be a blasphemy and a danger to hunt the secret out.'

'Yet I command it.'

'And if I refuse?'

'You will not refuse me, O Haroun al-Vakhel.' The Caliph's grip tightened on the Princess's hand as he began to kiss it long and feverishly. 'For as I love my sister, so you love your child.' He laughed. 'But no matter – you have seen stakes above the gateways to this Palace before.'

Again, for a long while, Haroun did not reply. Then at last he breathed in deeply, and crossed to the balcony. 'You must swear to me,' he whispered, 'upon all that is holy, that you will protect my daughter for as long as I am away.'

'I swear it,' the Caliph replied, 'so long as you will swear to me now, upon your same daughter's life, that there will be nothing you will not attempt – nothing at all – to restore my sister from this spell and to keep her for ever preserved from death.'

Haroun paused. 'You cannot know what it is you ask.'

'Yet I ask it still.'

'You are truly prepared for the horrors I may uncover, horrors long buried these thousands of years?'

'For the power of the ancient Jinn, what would I not dare?' The Caliph crossed to Haroun's side and gripped him by the arm. Then he pointed towards the northernmost wall of the city, where two minarets could be seen rising high into the haze. 'The mosque,' he whispered, 'which I vowed to build is now complete – and yet not altogether, for there is a stone there still plain and unadorned. It waits to be inscribed with the Secret Name of Allah. Return with that secret! Return with it fast! For then, O my friend' – the Caliph paused, and smiled – 'I shall possess the wisdom and secret of all things. Why!' – he laughed suddenly – 'I shall be a god myself!'

A shadow passed across the face of Haroun, one of pain and foreboding, but still he bowed low in acceptance of the terms, then turned without a word and left the room. The Caliph listened to the echoes of the footsteps fading away, as he turned to gaze out across the city once again, and the minarets of the newly-completed mosque. 'Not long now,' he whispered. He crossed back to his sister and clasped her in his arms, kissing her lips and all across her face. Still she did not wake. The Caliph shuddered and grinned, and kissed her once again. 'All will be well!'

That same day, the Caliph rode from his palace to the Bab al-Futuh and passed into the marble courtyard of the mosque. He placed guards by the doorways to the two minarets, and ordered that no one but himself should ever be permitted to ascend them. Then he climbed one himself, until he paused midway up by a thick and heavy door, framed around its archway by unadorned blocks of stone. The Caliph reached up to touch the highest block, smoothing it reverently with the palm of his hand. It was on the same stone face, he had always trusted, that the Secret Name of Allah would one day be inscribed; and now, so it seemed, his faith would be fulfilled. Such good fortune, the Caliph thought, could not be an accident. He had always been the favourite of the stars and the heavens – surely such a favourite was ordained to be a god?

And from that time on, every evening he would ride to the mosque and climb the stairway of the minaret, and though the stone remained blank, yet still his dreams and ambitions ever grew in their scope. Rumours, as they did so, likewise began to grow, dark and turbulent, whispered in tones of horror, so that all of Cairo soon seemed dizzy with dread. In the minaret, it was claimed, a demon was kept; the mosque had been built with the blood and bones of children; the Caliph himself was none other than Iblis. All this was spoken, and increasingly believed, and reported back by the Caliph's spies. But the Caliph himself, when he heard it, only smiled; and still, every evening, for the course of one year, he rode from his palace to the Bab al-Futuh.

Then it happened one evening, as he passed through the gateway which led into the mosque, that he was greeted by a trembling captain from his guards. The captain fell to his knees and kissed the Caliph's feet. 'O supreme and happy Prince,' he gulped, 'some villain has entered your minaret, for I shortly arrived here to find my soldiers drugged, nor have I been able as yet to wake them up.'

But to the captain's surprise the Caliph only laughed, then reached into his saddle for a heavy purse of gold. 'Lead on,' he ordered as he tossed the purse into the captain's hand, and then, when the captain did so, laughed once again to see how the door to the minaret hung open. He climbed down from his horse and ordered a torch to be passed to him; then he hurried inside and began to climb the steps.

Midway up, by the heavy door, he raised his torch to inspect the stonework. Immediately, however, he frowned at what he saw. It was true that there was an inscription, freshly carved upon the stone above the arch; but it was not a name, nor even a word, but rather an image of the disk of the sun, and crouched underneath it were two kneeling figures. The Caliph shrank back in astonishment. 'What is this blasphemy?' he cried out aloud. Then at once he spun round, for he had heard from the darkness the sound of mocking laughter – and looking behind him, he caught the sudden glimmering of a face.

'Haroun al-Vakhel?' The Caliph swallowed. 'Haroun al-Vakhel?' He shouted now, trying to suppress a faint wave of panic. 'Haroun al-Vakhel, is that truly you?'

The pale face drew nearer, climbing the steps; and as it did so the Caliph saw that his supposition had been correct. Haroun paused before him and smiled, then slowly bowed his head. 'O Commander of the Faithful, you see I am returned.'

The Caliph observed Haroun closely. He appeared very weary, for he was not only pale but thin and hollow-cheeked, and his clothes were dusty and travel-stained. A dog was by his side and Haroun, as though almost unaware of what he was doing, stooped briefly to stroke the animal's head; and as he did so, so his expression seemed suddenly to lighten and ease. But then he gazed up once again; and the Caliph was filled with a sense of great wonder, for there appeared in the eyes of Haroun a strange and profound incandesence, which seemed to hint at the experience of unparalleled marvels. The Caliph turned again to glance at the image of the sun. 'Returned, I trust,' he asked, 'with your quest achieved?'

Again, Haroun smiled and bowed his head.

'What is the meaning' – the Caliph pointed – 'of this sun with its rays?'

'It will be a great wonder to you, O Prince, to learn of the mysteries I can now reveal.'

'I am desperate to hear of them.'

'Tomorrow, then, O Prince, return here to this tower, for at the moment I am weary from many trials and vicissitudes. Tell me, though, first, before you depart – how is my daughter?' He reached out to tug upon the Caliph's robe, and a strange look of craving seemed to pass across his face. 'Tell me, please, O mighty Prince – is she still alive and well?'

'She has been guarded, as we agreed, with the very closest of attention.' The Caliph frowned. 'But surely you will come with me back now to the Palace?'

'No.' Haroun climbed to the door and swung it open. 'I will stay here for now.'

'Why,' asked the Caliph suspiciously, 'what is your business?'

'Sleep. I must have sleep.'

'But my sister?'

'Your sister?'

'Will she recover? Will she live?'

A thin smile flickered across the lips of Haroun. 'Oh yes,' he whispered. 'As I promised . . . she will live.' He turned. 'Good-night, O Prince.' Then he passed through the doorway, his dog following him, into the darkness of the minaret beyond; and the Caliph stayed rapt a long while in wonder and thought. Then he left the mosque and returned to his Palace, and hurried to the sick-room of the Princess Sitt al-Mulq, where she had lain beneath a spell for many long months. But when he arrived it was to find that she was no longer there, nor had anyone seen her risen or removed. The Caliph, though, was nothing perturbed, for he knew that it was the proof of Haroun's new-found magic, the proof of the power of the Secret Name of Allah. And so he summoned Masoud and gave him instructions that the next day, in every mosque in every neighbourhood of Cairo, a new prayer was to be cried out from the minarets, proclaiming the divinity of the Caliph al-Hakim. And it was done as he had ordered; and the Faithful listened in shock and disbelief.

All that day, their murmurings of horror rose like the waves of the sea. But the Caliph only laughed when he heard the outcry, and commanded his soldiers to put the insurgents to the sword. That evening, as he rode towards the mosque by the northern gates, the whole of Cairo seemed lit by flames and the din of strife rose high into the heavens; but the Caliph knew that there was nothing now to fear. 'All shall be made plain,' he told himself, as he dismounted from his horse and began to climb the minaret. 'All shall be revealed.' And he hurried up the stairway with a brisk and eager step.

He found Haroun in a tiny square room at the minaret's summit, gazing through the window at the distant flames, slowly stroking his dog who lay stretched by his feet.

'Tell me, O Haroun,' the Caliph demanded straight away, 'what is the sound of the Secret Name of Allah, for you have promised to tell me and now the moment is arrived.'

The shadow of something unearthly flickered across the pallor of Haroun's haggard face. 'I must tell you first,' he murmured, 'how I came by the Secret, for otherwise, O Prince, you will fail to understand what its true power may be.'

'Then tell me,' said the Caliph, 'for I can bear to wait no longer.'

'It is a narrative which will stupefy you with the excess of its strangeness. Yet all that I tell you had been written for me many centuries before – for it is the mark of the hand of Destiny, that nothing it writes can ever be escaped. The ways of this world are infinite and strange, and both the past and the future may be bound by one Fate.'

'Tell me what you mean,' exclaimed the Caliph, 'for I am burning with curiosity to hear your account.'

'With the greatest pleasure, O mighty Prince. Listen, then, and you shall hear a full account of all I did, and saw, and learned.'

THE TALE TOLD BY HAROUN AL-VAKHEL

After I left you, on the morning when the Princess had been cast beneath the spell, I sought out the company of an old acquaintance of mine, a Christian merchant, who by great good fortune had just arrived in Cairo. It was this same merchant who had made me a gift of my wife many years before, after he had found her in the ruins of a mighty temple. What this temple might have been, and what secrets it might still preserve, seemed to me now a matter of great moment, and I was resolved to visit it as soon as I was able. The merchant, I knew, would prove an admirable guide, for he had travelled there often and was learned in the customs and the ways of the ancients. At first, it was true, he was unwilling to accompany me, for he told me that Thebes had grown an evil reputation as the haunt of ghools and desert-bred things. He was a man, though, with an insatiable thirst for adventure, and I did not find it hard to persuade him in the end. My only other companion was Isis, my dog, who despite my best efforts would not be left behind, but would always run after me as I sought to ride away.

For many days we travelled, O Prince, following the course of the wide-flowing Nile, and saw many wonders, built by the pagans in long-ago times. But always, when I expressed my astonishment, the merchant would smile and shake his head, and tell me to wait until my first sight of Thebes. Then he would describe to me the marvels of that ruined city, in terms so extravagant that he would make it sound the work more of giants than of mortal men. At the same time, however, he would also warn me of the darkness which had fallen on the place, of the demons which had risen from the tombs of the kings, the *udar*, whose discharge bore the poison of maggots and worms. Of course, I reminded myself, the merchant was a Greek, and it is a well-known fact that all Greeks are liars. Nevertheless, as we travelled ever further upstream, I began to observe how settlements were growing few and far between, and how some of the villages had been abandoned altogether. The irrigation canals seemed choked by dust and weeds, and where fields should have been the desert sands were spreading.

My heart had already grown dark, then, when at last the merchant pointed and cried out, 'Thebes!' I gazed into the distance and saw what appeared to be colossal trees, rising from the dunes, and forming a veritable forest of stone. As I drew nearer, I saw that the trees were in truth columns of stupefying thickness, ornamented with the carvings of strange talismans and demons, the symbols of a magic which no living man could read. Passing into the shadow of that monstrous temple, I grew certain that I had indeed arrived at the object of my quest, for I did not see how, unless by sorcery, such a place could ever have been raised. Much of it had clearly been buried by the sands; but of that vast expanse which still stretched unsubmerged above the dunes, even the blocks of rubble rose larger than I did on my horse. Built on to one of the columns I discovered a mosque, and I dismounted eagerly to offer up prayers. But the mosque had been long abandoned, and its puny brickwork was already decaying; and in truth it seemed, hunched in the shadow of the far vaster wreck, like a seabird landed briefly on the back of a mighty whale.

I longed to penetrate further into the darkness of the place, for it intrigued me to imagine what might lie within its heart, what secrets and marks of the priests' forgotten sorcery. But the sun was already sinking behind the mountains to the west, and the merchant was starting to grow uneasy. 'We must reach the village of the tomb-robbers,' he frowned, 'for it is not safe to be abroad in these parts after nightfall.' So saying, he spurred his horse forward and began to gallop towards the line of fields which stretched beyond the temple, and where we would find – or so I trusted – a boatman to ferry us to the far side of the Nile. But my expectations were disappointed, for the fields in truth proved to be stinking marshland; and of the settlements which must have once lined the eastern bank, there was nothing left but the few bare shells of houses. 'There must be a boat here somewhere,' the merchant muttered, 'for this was always a teeming stretch of the river.' But although we rode up and down, we could find nothing of use – and all the while the sky was growing redder to the west.

Then, just when we were both on the point of despair, we saw Isis tense and suddenly bark. She appeared frightened of something hidden in the reeds, for she was circling it and starting to growl, and when I dismounted she slunk by my side. I pushed my way through the reeds until I could see ahead of me a tiny boat, drifting in a stagnant pool of muddy water. I called back to the merchant to inform him of our good fortune, then waded out to retrieve the boat. Isis paddled beside me, but all the while she was growling deeply and sniffing the breeze; and I too, as I drew nearer to the boat, caught the sudden stench of something loathsome and sweet. Then I realised that there was an arm hanging over the edge of the prow, its hand still gripping the hilt of a sword. I reached out to pull upon the boat, the stench seemed to shimmer before my gaze and I discovered – may blessings and peace be evermore upon him! – the body of a young boy, his eyes bulging wide, but dead, quite dead.

When the merchant joined me, he gazed upon the corpse with pity and disgust. 'May Christ have mercy upon his soul!' he exclaimed. 'So it was before, when I was shown the corpse of the victim of the *udar*.' And so saying, he raised the lad's tunic, and I saw how the belly was bloated and purple. The merchant tapped it once with his staff, in the manner of someone testing a melon, and at once the skin of the belly, as though indeed over-ripe, parted and gave, and a sticky mess of worms slipped out through the gap. 'Dear God, dear God!' the merchant whispered, staring at the worms as they coiled by his feet. 'You see now, O my friend, that I exaggerated neither the wonders nor the horrors of this place.' Then he reached down and gently prised the sword from the young boy's hand. 'It were best, I think,' he muttered, as he handed it to me, 'that you keep this for yourself.'

'But I have sworn a great oath,' I answered him, 'that I shall never spill the blood of man again.'

The merchant, though, laughed, a ghastly, fearful sound. 'Then all is well,' he replied. 'For what makes you think that our foes might be men?'

I gazed down a moment more at the corpse of the boy, before nodding and slipping the sword into my belt. Together we swept the worms into the waters of the Nile, then bore the corpse of the boy from the boat on to the bank, where we dug a grave and raised up a pile of stones to mark the spot. Then, having made certain that our horses were safely secured, we returned to the boat and passed across the Nile. Even as we were drawing near to the western bank, I was careful to draw my sword, and as we clambered up the slope which rose from the river, I suddenly observed how Isis had grown tense and was poised like an arrow pulled back in a bow. At the same moment, from the twilight shadows ahead of us I heard a sudden scream, and then muffled shouting and a further scream. Isis leapt forward and I followed her as fast as I could, crying out a prayer to the Most High without whom there can never be either fortitude or hope. I could make out strange figures ahead of me now, three of them, and I saw that they were circling an old man whom they had trapped against the side of a crumbling wall. But the old man was holding a flaming brand, and he lunged forward with it suddenly, scattering points of light into the dark. I glimpsed two of his enemies illumined for a moment, and I could see how their limbs appeared horribly thin, like those of a water-skimming insect, yet with skulls remarkably distended and large. Then the light faded, and the figures were nothing but shadows again, and I saw them glide forward and wrestle the torch from the old man's hand.

At the same moment, Isis leapt upon them and I followed, swinging at them with my keen-edged sword. Two of the ghools fell before me and the third slipped away, melting into the darkness. I thought to pursue him but then, from behind me, I heard the ghools rising once again to their feet, although the wounds I had inflicted had appeared to be mortal. But then I recalled the city of Lilatt-ah, and the nature of the demons I had fought against there. The ghools before me were still nothing more than shadows; yet even so, when the first one attacked me, I sought to aim as well as I could for its heart. It staggered and crumpled, as though its two legs had suddenly snapped beneath it; and I saw how its companion at once disappeared.

I turned to the old man and seized his torch.

'You will not be able to kill it,' he cried out. 'They cannot be slain.'

But I shook my head. 'With the guidance of Allah,' I

answered him, 'all things are possible.' And so saying, I aimed again with the point of my sword, and as I felt it enter the ghool's chest and heart, so the demon buckled and writhed, and then fell still.

I knelt down beside it, to inspect the corpse. As I did so, I blinked and offered up a prayer, for never before had I seen a thing which filled me with such horror. In its outward form it appeared almost to be a mortal man, yet it was this very resemblance to the image which Allah granted Adam – may peace be upon him – which rendered the *udar* so monstrous to behold. Like its limbs, its body was very spindly, although both thighs and belly were strangely swollen; its eyes were slanted; the back of its skull was very domed, like a mosque, and extended back strangely from its pinched, narrow face. So might the faithless seem, I thought to myself, abandoned by the love of Allah after death.

I gazed up at the old man. 'From what strange darkness,' I asked him, 'have these hellish demons risen?'

'That would be a strange tale to tell,' the old man answered, glancing around him nervously. 'But let us first reach the safety of my village, for you have seen for yourself how the darkness is dangerous.' Yet even as he said this, he appeared reluctant to move, and I saw that his face appeared dark with misery.

At this point, the Christian merchant stepped forward. 'What then, O Headman, were you thinking of, to be abroad yourself at so late an hour?'

The old man's face lightened briefly at the sight of the merchant, and he greeted him warmly, but then the shadow of misery fell again across his face. 'I have been hunting my son,' he explained, 'who has been missing now these past three nights. How can I endure to return to my own hearth, when I cannot know where my poor son might be?'

The merchant caught my eye; then he stepped forward and took the old man by the arm. 'He is in the earth, O

Headman, at rest, eternal rest.' He explained how we had come across the body of the boy, and described how we had raised a heap of stones above his head. Then he sought to comfort the Headman as well as he could.

Once he had dried his tears, the Headman turned to me. 'It seems, then, O my guest, that I am doubly in your debt. Come with me now, and sit by my hearth, where I shall tell you it came that these *udar* were disturbed. Then, if you have any idea as to how they might be destroyed, I will listen to you with great attention, for I perceive that you are as wise in years as you are skilled with your sword.'

I bowed in acknowledgement of his generous offer, and together the three of us, with Isis by my heels, hurried through the darkness towards the fires of the village.

———————

But at this point in his tale, Haroun saw the approach of morning and fell silent.

'Why do you not continue?' the Caliph demanded.

'O Commander of the Faithful,' Haroun replied, 'I am still weary from my many adventures and would seek, with your permission, to spend the daylight hours in rest. If you would care to return here tomorrow evening, then I will continue my tale and relate to you what occurred to me in the village of the tomb-robbers.'

And so the Caliph departed from the room in the Mosque, and did not return until the following evening. And then, when he had sat down by the side of Haroun, he gave him orders to continue with his tale.

And Haroun said:

When we had arrived at the house of the Headman, a building of considerable magnificence for so mean and poor a village, he made us comfortable with food and drink, then related to us the story of how the *udar* had been disturbed.

'You should know,' he explained to me, 'how we have always, in this village, hunted the treasures which lie buried hereabouts, for the pagans, in the folly of their superstition, stored silver, and rubies and gold, and fine pearls, and statues of idols made from all precious metals, deep within the ground. Yet of these treasures very few now remain, for we are but one of many generations, and each one in turn has hunted out the hidden tombs. Even so, there are still riches to be found, especially in the valley which lies beyond the hills, and of all the treasure-seekers the most celebrated, the most unerring in his sense of where a hidden tomb might be uncovered, was my own great-grandfather, Mohammed Girigar.

'Here, then, is the story of his most splendid find. He was exploring the ravines of the valley one day when he discovered, by his feet, tiny chippings of stone. This excited him greatly, for such chippings are the infallible signs of a tomb. That very night he returned to the spot in great secrecy, bringing with him only his most trusted henchmen. He set them to labour, and it was not long before a work of jewellery was found, adorned with the image of a monstrous Jinni, such as the pagans were in the habit of worshipping as gods. If you wish to see what it looked like, here' – the Headman reached within his gown – 'inspect it yourself, for we have kept it in our family as a keepsake of that night.'

He handed it across to me. It was only small but lined with gold and very beautifully fashioned. 'You will see,' the Headman told me, 'that the jinni has the body of a ravening lion and the head of a woman.'

'There is such a monster,' I answered him, 'though male in sex, which lies on guard beside the Pyramids.'

The Headman nodded. 'Then you will understand the

excitement of my great-grandfather, for he knew that the image of such a creature could only presage hidden riches. He ordered his workmen to dig all the harder and soon, sure enough, they found a second wonder, an ancient corpse, with an expression of great horror still preserved upon its face and a hideous wound ripped out along its throat. This caused Mohammed's workmen to murmur amongst themselves, and threaten to lay down their picks, for they claimed that such a thing was the certain mark of sorcery. Mohammed, though, ordered the corpse to be buried once again, and then gave each workman an extra piece of gold, which proved more than sufficient to overcome their fears. At last, shortly before daybreak, the doorway to a tomb was uncovered, and when Mohammed inspected it he gave a cry of thanks to Allah, for he could see how the seal upon the join was unbroken, and he knew that beyond it there lay wealth beyond his dreams.

'And so indeed it proved, for once the door had been smashed open and Mohammed had forced a way along a passage filled with rubble, he suddenly heard the crashing of stones ahead of him into an open chamber and, calling for a torch, he caught the glint of gold. But as he leapt into the darkness, he was almost suffocated by a vast quantity of dust and a blast of loathsome air, so that Mohammed, experienced as he was in the exploration of tombs, shuddered and was almost persuaded to flee, for he had never smelt anything so vile and strange before. But then he thought again upon the glittering of gold, and so he stayed where he was and lifted up his torch.

'At once he stood frozen in wonder and dread. Everywhere there were treasures – piled up to the roof, reaching back into the shadows of the chamber – of a beauty and a splendour which lay beyond description. But it was not the sight of this wealth which had rendered

Mohammed motionless, but rather the presence in the chamber, seated upon a gilded throne and clutching a sceptre in his withered hand, of the body of a king. Or so at least Mohammed assumed it to be – yet in truth it appeared more like a demon than a man. It wore a gown embroidered with gold and precious stones, so that its limbs could not be seen, but the skull beneath its crown appeared hideously shaped and its brow was deathly like that of a phantom. Mohammed crept forward to inspect the corpse more closely, but then, as he reached out to touch the jewels upon the robe, the eyes of the withered king suddenly opened. Mohammed sought to shrink back – but he found himself motionless, caught within their glare, which blazed from between two narrow, almond-slanted slits. Long minutes passed; then haltingly, as though with an effort, the King spoke a few words in a harsh, unknown tongue. But Mohammed could not answer him, and the face of the King grew suddenly dark and he raised his sceptre with a strange, painful motion. He touched Mohammed with its tip upon the forehead – and it was at that point that my great-grandfather fainted from fear.

'When he awoke, he was alone. He clambered back out through the passageway, and found that the valley was deserted as well; for his men, imagining their master dead when he had not re-emerged, had fled the tomb entrance. It was clear that they had seen nothing of the King with the phantom brow, and so Mohammed chose not to make mention of his strange experience. Nevertheless, it appeared that the tomb still inspired a universal fear, for despite the gold he could now afford to pay, Mohammed found it hard to persuade anyone to enter the chamber and it was only with difficulty that he could clear it out at all. Some ornaments, it is said, were left scattered on the floor; nor has anyone sought to retrieve them since that day.

'For once the bulk of the treasures had been taken from the tomb, not even Mohammed was willing to return to it; and indeed, he kept away from the valley altogether. Instead he lived with his family as prudently as he could, spending the fortune which the Great Giver had sent to him, and being careful always to hand out alms to the poor. Yet it was noted, all the same, how his expression seemed haunted by some hidden dread, and how at night, when the shadows would flicker with the fire, he would start from them and shrink, as though afraid that they might shelter some darkness-bred demon. It was only on his death-bed, however, that he revealed the secret of what he had discovered in the tomb. Those who heard him, though, assumed he had grown mad, and certainly very few believed his tale of a King.

'But then, some years after my great-grandfather had been laid to rest in his grave, strange figures began to be glimpsed in the valley, phantoms risen, so it seemed, upon the coming of each twilight, haunting the burial-grounds of the pagan Kings. Some began to whisper of a race of ghools, bred, may Allah save us, from the darkness of the unclean practices of the ancients, while others recalled what my great-grandfather claimed to have seen – a Pharaoh, undead, and with the form of a ghool. A few still chose to scoff at the reports, and continue to search the valley for fresh tombs, but then it happened in due time that one of them failed to return. When the corpse was found at last, there could no longer be any room for doubt or dispute, for the mark of the *udar* is as certain as it is vile. And may Allah, whose grace and mercy are infinite, have mercy upon the soul of that poor man, and upon all those who have suffered a similar fate.'

At this point the Headman paused, and I saw the silver of tears line his eyes, and I knew that he was thinking on his murdered son. The merchant and I together sought to comfort him, but when he was recovered I pressed him further, for I was interested to know why, in view of the great danger, he and his neighbours had never thought to leave their village. But the Headman only frowned. 'Would you have us taste the bitter bread of exile,' he demanded, 'and abandon the earth where our forefathers lie?' And as he said this, he began to weep once again, and to mutter prayers and to tear at his white beard.

'Nevertheless,' I answered him, 'you must still leave, you and your women, and all your children, for I shall be leading every able-bodied man with me tomorrow into the valley, where I shall seek to extirpate the curse of the *udar*.'

The Headman gazed at me in horror. 'Would you seek to disturb a nest of hornets?' he cried. 'Such a course of action will surely send the *udar* swarming to destroy us!'

'Yes,' I answered him, 'but so will waiting here in your village, doing nothing, allowing your people to be picked off one by one. It is better to die with one's sword in one's hand than to endure such a fate. But do not think, O Headman, that our cause is without hope, for Allah is all-seeing and knows best what lies hidden. I have shown you already tonight what you said was impossible – how these ghools may be slain.'

But still the Headman gazed at me doubtfully. 'You must slay them all, then,' he muttered, 'while the sun is bright in the sky, for by the light of the moon they will surely overwhelm us.'

'That is why,' I answered him, 'I would have you leave this village – not far, but only to the temple on the far side of the river.'

'The temple?' The Headman seemed to shrink even more.

'Whatever its mysteries,' I answered, taking him by the arm, 'it will certainly be easier to defend than this place.'

And so saying, I led him from the house out to the very boundary of the village, from where we could glimpse in the shadows the burning of bright eyes.

'Is it not as I told you before?' the merchant muttered. 'Like a pack of hungry jackals they watch us – and they wait.'

'For how much longer, though,' I whispered, 'will they be willing to wait, when their power and their numbers are surely growing all the time?'

The Headman glanced up at me, then round at the village, before turning back to gaze at the darkness of the sands. 'Let it be done as you advise,' he nodded at length. 'And may Allah watch and guide you in everything you do.'

But at this point in his tale, Haroun saw the approach of morning and fell silent.

'Why do you not continue?' the Caliph demanded.

'O Prince of the Faithful,' Haroun replied, 'I am still weary from my many adventures. But if you would care to return here tomorrow evening, then I shall continue my tale, and relate to you what occurred to me in the valley of the *udar*.'

And so the Caliph did as Haroun suggested; and the following evening he returned to the mosque.

And Haroun said:

As soon as the first light of dawn had touched the sky to the east, everything was done as had been agreed the night before. The Headman led the women and the children and the infirm, and they crossed the Nile to where the great temple stood, and they sought to raise a fortification between the line of the pillars. The able-bodied men, however, I led myself, not towards the Nile but on the opposite route, along the path which wound towards the valley of the ghouls.

To enter this valley, O Prince, one must first pass between two mighty walls of rock, silent and heavy with clouds of white dust. Nothing grows there; only shoals of black pebbles intrude upon the gleam; high above the mounds of boulders and rubble, the cliffs appear formed as though from packed dust. It was in this same ravine that I had feared we might be ambushed by the ghouls – and yet we entered the valley without any alarm, and I offered up a prayer of thanks to the All-High. Even so, as I gazed about me at that haunted place of burning rock and sand, where no shade is to be found, no relief from the heat, still I felt a shadow perched upon my shoulder, gazing at my delight in all the sweet things of life; for I knew that I had come to where lean Death has his home. But then I thought upon Allah, and how He alone understands the purpose of our destiny, and I prayed to Him to keep me from the shadow of Death's wings.

That I might help myself in such a cause, I ordered the villagers to set to work at once, entering the opened tombs, for it was there that I thought the ghouls might be surprised. And so indeed it proved, for in many of the chambers, sheltered by the darkness, the *udar* could be found amidst the bodies of the dead, which would often lie piled in untidy heaps as high as the roof. And when I inspected these bodies, I was struck dumb with doubt and wonder, for I remembered at once where I had seen such bodies before – piled within the temple of Lilatt-ah, in the sanctuary where the idol of the demoness had stood.

For a long while I stood motionless, and it was fortunate indeed that there were others there beside me. It was fortunate also that the ghouls appeared confused by the sudden influx of our torches, and enfeebled by their brightness, for they would flutter their limbs rather as moths, when confronted by a lamp, will beat and flap their wings. It was an easy matter, then, to dispose of these creatures, weakened as they were and surprised by our intrusion – and yet the horrors of our business were very great indeed. For the blackness of the walls, the choking dust and the withered faces of the ancient dead, blank behind their wrappings but perfectly preserved, combined to unsettle us profoundly; and as the hours began to pass, so our fears grew all the more. Long before the twilight, we could observe how the strength of the *udar* was reviving, and so I ordered the villagers, while the sun was still high, to leave the valley and cross over the Nile.

I remained with a few of the bravest men, and together we sought out one particular tomb, for I wished to inspect, before the onset of darkness, the chamber from which the undead king had been released. I had been dreading to enter that place of darkest magic, yet the tomb itself proved to be wholly abandoned, with only a few scattered treasures still left upon the floor, just as the Headman had claimed that there would be. There was a coffin as well, placed against the wall, with a well-preserved corpse wrapped in linings inside. It did not appear ever to have been a ghool, yet the portrait on the coffin was clearly of an *udar*, and for a moment I stood puzzled by this mystery. But I did not have the time to consider it for long, and so I ordered the face on the coffin to be destroyed, along with certain talismans which I had found upon the walls, carved within oval circles, and which I assumed to have been the spells of the ancient sorcerers. There was also, half-filling the chamber, a structure somewhat like a giant tent but built of wood and covered with gold, and this I ordered to be broken apart and employed to block off the passageway. While this work was being carried out, I drew out from beneath my cloak the talisman which Mohammed Girigar had found, and which I had persuaded his great-grandson to hand over to me. I then buried it very deep, so that no one would ever uncover it again, and ordered the doorway of the tomb to be sealed. In this way, O Prince of the Faithful, I hoped that its memory would be eternally forgotten – and so indeed I hope to this day, for there are secrets which lie buried and should never be disturbed.

It was now nearing twilight and in the western sky, above the mountain peaks, a half-dozen hues, from pink to green and gold, were dying the horizon. Reluctantly, I ordered our retreat from the valley. Yet already in the shadows strange figures were gathering, and as we neared the ravine which led back to the plain, so large numbers began to rise up from the boulders, as ants will emerge when a rock is disturbed. I and all my men were mounted on horses, and were riding down the pathway with all the speed we could muster, yet as I saw the figures of the *udar* ahead of us, their spindly limbs jerking and their slanted eyes afire, I dreaded that we had lingered in the valley far too late. 'Faster!' I cried. 'Faster, for the love of Allah!' Then we were amongst them and I could feel their fingers, horribly thin and long, pulling upon me, seeking to drag me down – but my sword was bright, and its edge razor-keen. I knew that all those I had felled would rise once again, for I had struck none of the demons a wound through the heart; yet I only wished at that moment to force my way through their ranks. And so I did at last, breaking free into the burning white dust of the ravine, and when I glanced behind me it was to see that most of my companions had broken through as well. Two of them, however, were still surrounded by a horde of the *udar*, their horses bucking and whinnying with fear, and even as I watched one of them screamed and was plucked from his saddle, then vanished beneath a sudden surging of the enemy. I heard a hellish slithering, hissing sound; and then a second scream. 'Ride on,' I cried to the others, 'ride on to the Nile!' as I wheeled and galloped back towards the head of the ravine. It was black with the *udar* now, and even as I charged I saw the second villager submerged. At the same moment, however, as though their ranks were the waves of a mighty sea, the ghools appeared to surge and rise, and I feared that they would break and flood down the ravine. The sun, I saw, behind the western hills, was on the verge of setting; yet as the final red beam began to fade away, so all the ranks of the *udar* stood suddenly frozen. Then they began to part, and as the last light of day vanished, so I saw that they were turning to gaze into the darkness, at someone . . . something . . . approaching from the valley. I could not penetrate the shadows, but I had no wish to stay to see what it was. I delayed my flight no longer, and kept riding until I had reached the banks of the Nile.

We crossed without hindrance – and yet, gazing back into the darkness of the western bank, I dreaded to think what the night might now bring. The villagers had raised a wall between the pillars, and seemed to believe that they were safe behind it, but I could not put the darkness which I had sensed in the valley from my mind. In an effort to prepare for it further, I ordered all the wood that could be found to be gathered together and stacked in a line beyond our outer fortification. Then, when all had been completed, I retreated to the half-ruined mosque. Yet it was as though my prayers were weighted down, and Allah would not – or could not – hear them.

I rose from my knees at last, puzzled and afraid, and passed again into the stony night. I began to wander through the pillared hallways of the temple, and as I did so I felt a sudden chill of recognition. I gazed behind me, around me, ahead. The chill grew more icy. For I was certain now that, ruined though it was, I could make sense of the form of the hallways of the temple, the pattern which it formed and its seemingly infinite processional route – that once, years before, I had entered something similar.

I began to stumble across the sands, seeking the point which I knew would surely come, when the pillars came to an end and there was nothing instead but a tiny room, the innermost sanctuary, where in the temple of Lilatt-ah, the idol of a demoness had stood. I arrived at the point at last and discovered, to my relief, that there was nothing to be found save only rubble and sand. Yet even so, standing there, I felt my unease deepen, and again I knelt and sought to raise my thoughts in prayer. But at the same moment, from across the sands of the desert I heard the howling of a jackal, and at once I felt my mind clouded by a sickness, for it seemed that all the stone of the temple was melting, and that all its massive weight was become nothing but smoke. 'This is a great wonder,' I exclaimed to myself, 'may Allah protect me!' I rubbed my eyes; and when I opened them again, everything was as it had been before, and my sickness was gone. Yet I was certain now that the temple was surely damned; and rising to my feet, I sought out the merchant and asked him to show me the place where he had first discovered Leila, in accordance with the vision which he had been shown in his dream. He met my stare strangely; then led me through the temple, through the great halls of stone, to the very same place where I had just been kneeling, remembering the image of the idol of Lilatt-ah. 'Here,' the merchant said, pointing to the waste of dust and stone. 'I discovered her here.'

I knew then that that same night we were surely bound to die, for I could be certain now that the temple was not a place of refuge at all, but of sorcery and of terror and of long-buried evil. And even as I stood there, grim-faced, with the merchant, I heard distant cries of warning and I knew that the *udar* had surely crossed the Nile. As I returned through the temple to the barricades, I met with crowds of the villagers fleeing the other way; and indeed, it was all I could do not to run in blind panic myself, for I imagined that beyond my sight, seeping down from the hills upon clouds of star-touched dust, an evil was approaching – that same which I had sensed at dusk in the ravine.

Arrived at the barricades, I found my worst fears to be true. Massed before us, the *udar* stood in shadowy ranks, and I knew that the Nile had indeed been traversed. Turning to the villagers, I ordered all those who could not fight to join their fellows in retreat, while those few of us who remained, watching the hellish things gathering before us, prepared to consign ourselves to Allah's mercy. Then packs of the demons began to glide across the sands, and suddenly they were upon us, scaling our wall, their eyes burning fiercely in the prickling darkness, as we sought desperately not to succumb to their assaults. Still our strength held; yet I could sense it failing; and looking out I could see ever blacker, denser groups of shadows, a whole mighty army preparing to move. Then slowly it began to roll forward, wave after endless wave, crashing against our swords in a mighty cloud of dust, yet never passing them, so that I almost dared to hope that Allah might indeed be with us. But then at last it came, the moment I had been expecting, and dreading in my soul: screams and cries of terror, as dark figures climbed across the summit of our wall.

'Fire,' I shouted, 'bring me fire!' A burning torch was passed into my hand, and I leapt from the wall on to the sands beyond, where the line of wood had been carefully stacked, dry and ready to be consumed by our flames. And so indeed, praise be to Allah, it came to pass; and the ghools shrank back, appalled by the light, and I called out to the villagers to pursue them from the wall. Upon our assault the ghools turned and fled, and I observed, as the flames began to coil into the sky, how some of them were greasy with the corpses of our foe, and how the moon itself seemed stained a burn-ing red. Dimly through the smoke I saw the lines of the *udar* hesitate, then part. All across the battle scene, across the fields and the river, and the ruins of the temple, a silence fell, so that even the heavens seemed appalled by the moment.

I stood upon the wall. I pointed my sword towards the blood-red moon. '*Allahu akbar!*' I cried. 'Allah is most great!'

Nothing answered me.

But suddenly, as though the sands before me were living flesh, to crawl with dread, I sensed something stirring in the heavy air; and then Isis, beside me, threw her head back and howled.

I glanced round. My men, who moments before had been cheering with joy, now stood frozen and appalled, their arms dropped low; and then one, then two, and then the whole ragged line began suddenly to flee. I longed to join them; and indeed my own sword, in my own hand, had also dropped low. But I remained where I had been, upon the summit of the wall, and I turned again to gaze out beyond me.

The lines of the ghools still stood frozen and parted; but something was emerging from the gap they had formed. It was a figure, I realised, on a deathly white horse – and yet the horse was not so pale as its rider. His robes too were white, and rich with gleaming gold, and upon his head was a double crown – one white, the other red – such as I had seen, I realised, carved within the tombs of the Kings and upon the walls of the temple which stretched behind my back. Yet if ever he had been a Pharaoh of Egypt, he looked nothing like a mortal man any longer, for he seemed more hideous than the ugliest and most ghastly of the *udar*, and more ancient than the very dust and sand on which he rode. What nature of thing he might be – whether Afrit or Jinn, Phantom or Ghool – I could not imagine; but I knew he held a power far beyond my mortal scope. Even from where I was standing, I could see the ice within his stare; and I imagined, as I met it, that my soul was burning up.

The figure reined in his horse. He turned, and pulled upon something, and I saw that he had been holding a rope in his hands. A form stumbled forward and I recognised one of the villagers, captured no doubt upon the western bank. The poor wretch was still just alive, and as the King reached down to seize him by the throat, the man began to writhe, and kick, and scream out prayers.

The strength of the King, though, was something out of Hell. His grip tightened around his victim's throat, until at last there was a cracking and the poor man fell still. Peace and blessings be upon him.

Still holding the corpse in one hand, the King began with his other to rip it apart.

'No,' I cried out, 'no!'; but there was nothing I could do. I watched as the dead man's body was ripped to shreds, then smeared by the demon on the horse across his own, so that his limbs and chest were beslobbered with blood. Then at last the corpse was dropped back upon the sands, and the King leaned back and screamed out to the sky – a scream, Allah willing, such as I shall never hear again. Even the moon, I imagined, as though curdled by the sound, seemed to thicken and grow a more cruel and violent red.

But then I watched the moon no more. The King was riding forward. I jumped from the wall and fled.

———

But at this point, Haroun saw the approach of morning and broke off from his tale. 'O Prince of the Faithful,' he said, 'if you would care to return here tomorrow evening, then I shall relate to you what occurred within the temple of the sands.'

And so the Caliph did as Haroun suggested; and the following evening he returned to the mosque.

And Haroun said:

I feared, O Prince, as I stumbled through the stone-littered sands of the temple, that my time had surely come, for our line had broken, our wall had been breached and there was nothing now to hold back the army of the ghools. Dimly, through the crackling of the flames, I could hear a tumult of cries, terrible and inhuman, and the thunder of a million footsteps; but chiefly it was the hoofbeats of the King upon his horse I most dreaded to hear. Yet even as I listened for them, I realised the tumult was starting to fade, and I felt a sudden strange sickness, as I had done before when I had heard the crying of the jackal, and imagined that the stone of the temple was smoke. I glanced behind me. 'May Allah have mercy!' I cried, for again all the stone seemed nothing but smoke. The magical talismans which had been carved into the pillars by the ancient pagans, and the figures of the kings and beast-headed jinn, appeared suddenly lined with deep-burning fire, and as I walked on through the temple so the fire blazed all the more. But everything else was silent now, and the light of the moon was silver once again. 'What mystery is this?' I thought, for in all the vast wreck I seemed utterly alone, save only for Isis, who still walked by my side. Together we continued through the courtyards and halls, across the rubble and the heaped dunes of shadow-dyed sands, until at last ahead of me I saw where the pillars fell away, the same place where I had thought that the ancient shrine must once have been, if it had followed the pattern of the temple of Lilatt-ah. And immediately I stood frozen with wonder and doubt; for it was there also, I remembered, that the merchant had found my wife.

Very slowly, at last, I began to walk forward. Still there was silence, not a single sound, not the stirring of a palm tree nor the murmur of a breeze. But then again I felt the sickness, so that I staggered and closed my eyes, and when I opened them it was to discover that the light of the moon was blotted out. Instead it now appeared there was a roof above my head, very black and low, and ahead of me a brazier ablaze with soft incense. I could not see what might lie beyond the clouds of purple smoke, but I saw Isis grow tense as she gazed ahead, and then suddenly she growled.

I stroked her and sought to comfort her, as I whispered to her to be silent; but as I spoke her name, so I heard the sound of laughter rising from the smoke-obscured darkness ahead. For a moment I stood frozen again, for I knew, O Prince, whose laughter it had been, and I scarcely knew what I should next expect to see or hear. But then I continued forward, seeking to dispel the smoke with my arms; and as I walked down the hall, through the clouds, I saw Leila, my wife, upon a golden throne. Her skull had been shaven, and she wore a high blue crown, with a cobra made of gold rising up above her brow. Her robes were long and white, her necklaces broad and fashioned from rich jewels. Her face was very pale, her lips bright red, and her eyes thickly lined with the blackest kohl. She seemed more lovely than ever, but somehow very strange, so that I felt as though I had never truly seen her before. I could not, in those first few moments, explain such a feeling – yet it was sufficient to make me certain that she was a jinni as ancient as the temple

219

all around us — as ancient, indeed, as the very sands themselves.

As I stood before her, she rose to her feet. She took my
hands and laughed once again. 'Isis!' she exclaimed. 'You
have named your bitch — Isis! O my love' — she paused to
kiss me — 'you cannot know what a sacrilege that is.'

'There is much, it would seem, which I cannot know.'

'Cannot?' She raised an eyebrow. 'Yet you are here, are
you not?'

I stared at her in silence a long while. 'What will you tell
me, then?' I asked her at length.

'What do you wish to know?'

'The Secret Name of Allah. For otherwise, O my
Beloved, our daughter will be slain.'

Leila sat back on her throne, her smile impassive. 'What
would you be willing, O my Love, to pay for such a secret?'

'Whatever I must.'

Again she raised an eyebrow. 'Indeed?' She laughed.
'Indeed?'

'Provided that such a secret can indeed be revealed, there
is no price I would not pay.'

'There is a secret, most certainly. Once, long ago, it was
sheltered in this very place, where it was known as the Secret
of the Name of Amen. What its power could be, you have
already seen for yourself, in the valleys and the temples of
this ancient place. How can you doubt, then, that there is a
power abroad greater than man can understand? If you
would become the master and the lord of mortal things, if
you would venture into the Land of Darkness and learn of
the magic of the ancient jinn, if you would gain youth, and
wisdom, and immortality, then, yes, O my Husband — there
is indeed a secret, and a great one, to be learned.'

Silence, close and heavy, filled the perfume-scented hall.

'And the price?' I asked at length.

'Is something you may easily pay.'

'Tell me what it is.'

But Leila shook her head.

'How can I agree, then, to what I do not know?'

'But my Beloved, my Beloved – you have already agreed.'

I bowed my head in consternation and doubt. 'We all belong to Allah,' I thought, 'and must all return to Him at last.' And then I considered my daughter, how she was the sun and the moon and the stars of my life, and how there was nothing in all the world I would not dare to save her life. And then I considered further the wondrous magic of my wife, the manifold proofs which I had been granted of her powers, and the knowledge which she possessed of far-off worlds and distant times. And then in the end I considered my own desires, and how I had always longed to master the wisdom of the Ancients, and fought, in Allah's name, against the lure of that temptation. All this I considered as I gazed upon the beauty of my wife, and as I did so I felt my thoughts begin to melt and swim and fly, and I knew that I could fight against my own desires no more.

'O most powerful Jinni,' I said, 'for such I can no longer doubt that you are, tell me your secret and what I must do.'

But Leila shook her head. 'First,' she answered, 'I would tell you a tale.' And so saying, she indicated a throne of gold beside her own, and gestured to me that I should take my place upon it.

'What tale would you tell me?' I asked her as I sat down on the throne.

'The Tale of Pharaoh and the Temple of Amen.'

'I would be most eager to hear it, for it appears to promise many great wonders and surprises.'

Leila smiled. 'Nor are you wrong, O my Beloved. For until you have heard it, you will understand neither the secret of the powers I wish to grant you nor the price I shall demand in return – for you must learn, O my love, how all that is has already been, and, it may be, in time to come will exist once again.'

'Tell me, then, and let me learn everything.'

'As you wish it, so let it be.' And Leila smiled a moment more; and then she said:

The Turf Club,
20th Nov, 1922

My dear Lord Carnarvon,

I cannot, as I glance through this manuscript again, for-bear to recall my initial excitement, so overpowering that it almost caused me pain, upon realising the implications of this seemingly fantastical tale. I will confess that I had at first been dismayed by its ludicrous implausibilities, and con-sidered myself the victim of a monstrous hoax – yet still, through all the fantasy, I had begun to glimpse a faint residue of truth, as when, sifting through the wastes of rubble, one catches the outline of some artefact long buried in the dirt. A tomb had been found in the early Muslim period – that much was clear – and it had been found undisturbed, with all its treasures intact. What wonder, then, in that primitive and superstitious age, if the discovery of a Pharaoh in his full regalia of death should have come to breed legends of a curse, so that it came to be imagined that the King had not indeed been dead? One need not believe in the literal truth of Haroun al-Vakhel's tale, of course – that the Pharaoh had been seen risen upon his horse, riding with an army of demons against Karnak – to recognise the hints of a truth extraordinary enough.

For it was evident to me that the tomb described within the folk tale, point for point, was the same as that which Davis had found, and which he had persisted in ascribing to Queen Tyi. But I knew that Davis had been mistaken in his judgement – the pathologist had proved the skeleton to be that of a young man, a fact which the manuscript now appeared to corroborate. Who was it, then, who had been found in the tomb? Might not the tale I was reading give me some clue? And might not it offer me, in however garbled a form, clues as to mysteries more remarkable still – and even, perhaps, the existence of a still intact tomb?

All these questions seemed to pound upon the beating of my heart – as also, no doubt, they are presently pounding upon yours. I shall keep you no longer, then, from the tale the Jinni told – for when she promised a wondrous secret, she told nothing but the truth.

H.C.

THE TALE TOLD BY THE JINNI OF THE
TEMPLE OF THE SANDS

You must know, O Haroun, how in the depths of the ages and the antiquity of time, there was much which was known and now lies hidden, and many great wonders long forgotten, for the past is a desert filled with infinite buried things. Do not think that because you have never heard of a tale before, therefore it did not happen, for even in the lives of the Prophets there were deeds and events which were never recorded, and have long since been lost to the memory of this world.

By example, I might ask you what you truly know of Joseph, who was sold by his brothers into Egypt as a slave. You have read how he was purchased by a great man of the Court, and then falsely accused by the wife of his new master. You have read how he was flung into jail and then summoned by King Thoth-mes, Pharaoh of Egypt, to interpret the dreams which had been haunting his sleep. And you have read how Joseph explained the fat and the lean cattle, which King Thoth-mes had seen emerging from the waters of the Nile, as a warning sent by the will of the All-High – that the world would first enjoy the fruits of plenty, and then be reduced to bare bone by grim famine.

Everything happened just as Joseph had foretold, but since he had ordered granaries to be built, and filled them high with grain, the people of Egypt were able to be fed. And never had King Thoth-mes loved a man so much as Joseph, so that he raised him to be the Wazir over all his lands and gave him the title of 'the double of Pharaoh', which no foreigner had ever been granted before. Joseph ruled with great wisdom and care, so that all the people too – just like Pharaoh – came to love him, not only for having saved the land from famine but also for the kindness and generosity of his spirit. The priests alone hated him, seeing how he kept aloof from the worship of their idols – for in his heart Joseph never forgot that there was but a single God, self-created, eternal, omnipresent, whom he addressed in his own language by the sacred name of Yahweh. When the Egyptians learned of this, they named Joseph, as was their practice, after the name of his god, for they were pagans and had many strange customs and beliefs. Yahweh, in their own tongue, they pronounced as Yuya – and so Joseph too they addressed by the name of Yuya.

Now it happened that King Thoth-mes, although young, began to sicken, for his flesh appeared to wither and thin upon his bones. When this was reported, the High Priest came to see him, and for a night and a day the two were closeted together in the innermost sanctuary of the great temple of Amen. Who this god 'Amen' truly was, or what his appearance might be, was kept hidden from all but the highest of the priests, and yet he was said to possess a terrible magic too great to be inquired after, too powerful to be learned. 'Secret of transformations', he was named, and 'sparkling of appearances'; and yet in truth there was no one who had seen the god's true form, and people would fall down all at once for fear lest his true name be revealed. So terrible was it whispered to be that even Pharaoh would hesitate to cross the High Priest, who claimed alone amongst mortals to have learned it, and the understanding of the universe and its mysteries which it brought.

When their Pharaoh fell sick, then, the people had prayed that such knowledge might restore him – and to be sure, when he did emerge at last from the temple into daylight, the power of Amen's magic appeared immediately apparent, for King Thoth-mes seemed again in fullest health and even in his limbs looked whole and strong. Even so, for many days afterwards his mood appeared much troubled, and those of his courtiers who dared to meet his stare would sometimes catch the glimpse there of a wild and brooding terror, such as seemed to have chilled his innermost soul. At length King Thoth-mes sent for Joseph, and would not be parted from him, but asked him many questions about the god which he worshipped, whom Joseph had claimed was far greater than Amen. When the High Priest learned of this, he came to King Thoth-mes and sought to persuade him to banish Joseph from his presence; but King Thoth-mes refused and indeed, from that time on, he took Joseph ever more closely to his heart.

It was about this same time that the sister of King Thoth-mes, who shared both his bed and his throne as Great Queen, gave birth to a son. No one was happier for his master than Joseph; yet he fell to thinking, as he gazed upon the infant Prince, how he had neither son nor daughter whom he could call his own. He turned to the nurse, and asked her what the name of the young Prince was to be. She answered him, 'Amen-hetep' – which meant, in the language of the pagans, 'Amen-is-content'. Hearing the name of this mysterious god, the High Priest of whom was his deadliest enemy, Joseph fell into even deeper thought and he felt a great heaviness descend upon his heart. 'For I am a stranger in a foreign land,' he said to himself, 'and unless I have a family, there will be no one to whom I can pass on my name and teach the worship of the One and Only God.' And then he turned and left the Palace, and he rode his chariot across the sands until he came to a valley set amongst the hills, where the bodies of the Pharaohs were laid to rest in hidden tombs; and while he was there, he lay down in the shade and fell asleep.

The moment he did so he began to dream. He imagined that he saw the valley of the dead Pharaohs below him, just as he had done while lying there awake, save that from the doors of the hidden tombs a flow of blood was oozing, rising up through the sand and the rocks, and dying the whiteness of the dust a sticky red. 'This is a great horror!' exclaimed Joseph, 'but there is only one God, Whose will be ever done!' No sooner had he said this than he heard a strange rumbling, like that of the waves of a mighty flood, and then he watched as a deluge rolled through the valley, and when it had passed all the stains of blood were gone. And when Joseph awoke he was filled with great astonishment, for he wondered what the rolling of the waters might portend. Although he considered it a long while, the meaning was kept hidden from him – yet he was certain, all the same, that some great miracle had been foretold.

Then it happened, as he was returning from the desert to the Palace of Pharaoh, that he passed along the road which led into Thebes. This road was very heavy with all kinds of traffic, with merchants and caravans from all the corners of the world, for there was no city more splendid, nor richer, than Thebes. As Joseph drove in his chariot through the crowds, his eye was suddenly caught by a long train of slaves – Nubians, so it seemed, from the colour of their skin and their appearance – who had been made captive in the wars of Egypt to the south. Joseph gazed upon the chains which fettered the Nubians, and he listened to their cries of lamentation and grief; and as he did so he remembered how he too had once been a slave, loaded with chains, and sold into a strange and foreign land; and straightaway he was filled with a terrible pity. He reined in his chariot and approached the merchant at the head of the caravan, and he gave him a purse full of gold for the slaves. Then he ordered that the chains of the slaves be struck away and, sharing out a second purse of gold amongst them, he told them that they were free to depart. At once all the captives began to weep for joy as they fell at Joseph's feet, calling down the blessings of their gods upon his head; and then they rose, and began their journey back to their families and homes.

But one of the slaves still sat upon the road in the dust, a girl whose beauty put the fairest ebony to shame, and silent tears rolled silver down her face. Joseph crossed to her and sought to comfort her, trying to explain that she was free now to go. But the girl took his hand, and wet it with her tears, and she whispered how her parents and all her family had been slain, and her home and belongings burned down to the ground. Once again, Joseph felt a great upsurging of pity in his heart, and he drew her to her feet, and clasped her in his arms. As he held her, he felt his pity transformed into love, for he knew he had never seen such loveliness before; and he resolved that he would keep her, if she would have him, for his wife. So he led her from the dust of the road into his chariot, and drove her onwards to the Palace of Pharaoh, where he ordered her bathed and dressed in rich robes. And when he saw her adorned before him, he raised a cry of thanks and praise to the All-High, who had heard his prayers and thought to answer him; for Joseph never doubted that she was a gift sent from Heaven. He took her in his arms and brushed back her hair, as black and thick as the deepest night, and then he kissed her on her lips and asked her for her name. She answered his kiss softly; and then she whispered, 'Thua'.

That same day, Joseph led her into the presence of King Thoth-mes, to ask for the blessing of his master on the marriage. But King Thoth-mes, when he saw Thua before him, seemed suddenly to blanch, and to grip the two sides of his golden throne. Then he rose to his feet and took Joseph by the arm; but all the while, even as he led Joseph away, he could not tear his gaze from Thua's beauteous face. Only when they were alone together in a private room did King Thoth-mes turn back to Joseph, his expression still dark, and stamped with doubt.

'O Prince of Counsellors,' he exclaimed, 'I have had a dream which I must tell you, for you alone of all my servants have the wisdom to interpret it. I imagined that I was standing in the hills beyond the desert, above the valley where the tombs of my forefathers lie. As I watched, however, I saw that blood was rising up from the hidden entranceways, and all the dust in the valley was being stained by the flow.'

'This is a great wonder!' Joseph said. 'For just a few hours ago I fell asleep above the valley, and I dreamed the same thing myself. But tell me, O mighty King – did you not then see the blood washed away?'

King Thoth-mes gazed at him strangely. 'I did,' he nodded, 'by a mighty deluge. But did you not see from where the deluge flowed?'

'No,' answered Joseph, 'that was not in my dream.'

'But it was in mine; and I shall tell you what I saw. There was a Nubian girl by the entrance to the valley, and she was carrying a large jar of water in her arms. She tipped this jar, and spilt the water, and the water flowed from the jar without stop. And this was the cause of the deluge in the valley.'

For a long while Joseph stood, and did not answer. Then

at last he frowned and shook his head. 'O mighty King,' he said, 'how can I interpret your dream when you have not told me all?'

King Thoth-mes smiled slowly. 'Truly,' he answered, 'there is nothing which can escape you.'

'Please, O King, tell me what else it was you saw.'

Still the King smiled, but his expression grew very strange. 'The face of the girl in my dream,' he said at length, 'was the same as that girl's whom you have brought here to marry. Can you be surprised, then, that I was struck pale with wonder?'

'It may be,' said Joseph slowly, 'that you will not wish to hear the meaning of this dream.'

'Tell me nevertheless, without any fear.'

Joseph bowed. 'Very well,' he replied. 'You must know, O mighty King, that there is a curse upon your blood-line, stretching back I know not how far nor to what source. It must be that you too have the same curse within your veins.'

King Thoth-mes' face, once again, had become very pale, and his expression frozen. 'I have the blood of Osiris in my veins,' he said at last. 'I am the heir to that god who taught the arts of life to man, and revealed the wonders of the heavens and the stars. How can such a blood, then, such a heritage, be cursed?'

'That, I am afraid, your dream does not reveal.'

'Then how I am to judge what the curse might be?'

Joseph's expression, like his master's, was now very set. 'If you do not know, O Prince, then who am I to tell you?'

A shadow passed across King Thoth-mes' face, so that he seemed for a moment as fearful as before, when he had first re-emerged from the temple of Amen. 'This is folly,' he murmured at last.

'Indeed, O Prince?'

Still the King stood rapt in thought. 'Folly!' he repeated, clenching his fists. He shuddered suddenly. 'And yet if it were true – is there no hope at all?'

Joseph smiled. 'All things are possible to the will of the Most-High.'

'Then tell me, O my friend, what message of hope you can read in my dream, for I am filled with horror and a nameless dread.'

Joseph smiled again, and kissed Pharaoh's hand. 'You saw the flood which washed clean the tombs of your ancestors. What else could that mean, O Prince, save that the curse upon your blood-line will likewise be washed away?'

'But how?' he whispered. 'I beg you, tell me, how?'

'In your dream,' Joseph answered, 'it was Thua who washed the valley clean; it was from her jar that the water flowed. Similarly, I prophesy that it is from her womb that the saviour of your blood-line will come. All praise, then, to the Most-High, Who showed your dream to you, and Who at the same time cast Thua in my path to be my wife!'

But King Thoth-mes did not reply. Instead, he turned and crossed to where his gardens stretched away, filled with flowers of every colour, and sweet-smelling trees, and fountains as cooling as the snows upon the mountains, his best-beloved refuge from the burning heat of day. He stood there a long while, gazing out in silence, and Joseph, watching him, was filled with disquiet. 'O my dearest master,' he said at last, 'and my even dearer friend, will you not share with me this secret which oppresses you?'

King Thoth-mes turned slowly round, and Joseph saw what he had not observed previously – how thin his master's face had begun to seem again, as it had been before his entry into the temple of Amen, and how withered and taut the flesh across the skull. For a moment, indeed, he appeared barely like a mortal man at all; but then he smiled, and once more he wore the face which Joseph loved so well and knew. 'O Prince of Counsellors,' he whispered, 'give me your hand.'

Joseph did so, and for a long while King Thoth-mes held it; then he smiled once again. 'Marry Thua,' he whispered, 'and give birth to many sons. And let us pray that the meaning of what I dreamed is what you claim.'

———————

But at this point, Haroun saw the approach of morning and broke off from his tale. 'O Commander of the Faithful,' he said, 'if you would care to return here tomorrow evening, then I shall describe to you how the Queen bore a deathly portent, and how King Thoth-mes kept a mystery dark from Joseph.'

And so the Caliph did as Haroun suggested; and the following evening he returned to the mosque.

And Haroun said:

Joseph lived with Thua, his new wife, amidst great joy, and after a year she gave birth to a son, and Joseph gave him the name of Inen. He was loved not only by his parents but by King Thoth-mes as well, who ordered him brought to the Great Harim of the Palace so that he could be raised with his own son, the Crown Prince Amen-hetep, as though the same royal blood flowed in both of their veins. To Thua too, though she had been just a slave, he granted splendid honours, appointing her the Superior of the Harim and Chief Companion to his sister, the Great Queen. As for Joseph himself, that wise and happy man, King Thoth-mes hated to be parted from his company and whenever he was, it was observed how his spirits would begin to grow downcast and his temper shadowed by strange fantasies and fears.

Then it happened that Thua announced that she was pregnant once again, and some few days later the Queen announced the same. Joseph greeted the news with great joy, but King Thoth-mes, he saw, to his consternation, did not, and instead grew ever more nervous and withdrawn. Joseph sought to comfort his master, and distract him with his favourite pleasures, but still King Thoth-mes brooded, and as the months began to pass, so his moods grew ever worse, until at length he seemed as fearful as he had been long before, when he had first emerged from the temple of Amen; but what it was that he dreaded, he refused to discuss.

One evening, though, it happened that he and Joseph were walking through the gardens when they saw Thua and the Queen together by the lake, the marks of their pregnancies by now very plain. King Thoth-mes gazed upon their bellies in silence for a moment, then frowned, and shuddered, and took a step back. The Queen, made aware of his presence by the sound, at once rose to greet him, but as she did so King Thoth-mes frowned and flinched again. 'Keep away,' he whispered. The Queen gazed at him in perplexity. 'Keep away,' he whispered hoarsely once again. His face now was black with foreboding and revulsion, and for a moment it seemed, as his Queen stood before him, that he would raise his hand and strike her swollen belly. But with a visible effort he controlled himself and, turning violently, he hurried away. As he did so, it was not only the Queen who gazed after him in perplexity, for Joseph too, in all his years of service, could never recall his friend behaving so. He turned back to the Queen and Thua, to comfort them. At the same moment he glanced down at their swollen bellies once again, remembering King Thoth-mes' dream, how

Thua had been seen washing away the blood of the royal line; and he began to wonder all the more what it was that his master feared.

When the time came for Thua's confinement, however, Joseph observed how for a few days King Thoth-mes appeared almost happy. At length the news was brought to them that Thua had given birth to a second son, and Joseph praised the All-High and named the boy Ay. King Thoth-mes ordered the infant to be brought to him, and he stood for several minutes inspecting the child. 'What do you think?' he murmured at last, glancing up at Joseph. 'Is it this child, or your elder, or one yet to be born, who will purge my blood-line of the curse which you saw?'

Joseph bowed his head. 'I cannot answer that, O Prince, for there is only One Whose eye can penetrate all things.'

'So you say,' nodded King Thoth-mes. For a further moment, he inspected the child. 'And yet I wish I could glimpse the hidden pattern of the future. For in a very few weeks, my own child will be born.'

He said nothing more upon the matter, and Joseph wondered greatly at what his meaning could have been. He observed, though, in the following weeks, how the flesh upon King Thoth-mes' bones began to dry again, so that his whole appearance seemed ever more thin, save that at the same time his belly and his thighs were growing rounded. These marks of disease struck Joseph full of unease, for he had never heard of such symptoms and he knew himself powerless to suggest any cure. But King Thoth-mes, as when he had started to sicken once before, retreated to the sanctuary of the temple of Amen, and there he remained closeted deep within its blackness, even as the Queen went into her confinement. Only as the labour began to draw to its close did he re-emerge at last, and Joseph at once saw how the bloom of the King's health had been restored. But although in his appearance he seemed utterly recovered, his mood remained even more haunted than before, for it seemed that even as he listened to his Queen's distant shrieks, he dreaded the possible fruit of her childbirth. At length, when the screaming had finally faded and all sounded calm, Thua emerged, her cheeks streaked with tears, from the chamber in which she had been tending to the Queen in her labour. She wiped her face, then bowed low before Pharaoh. 'O mighty King,' she stammered, 'your child, your child . . .'

King Thoth-mes clenched his fists, as though grinding something small. 'What is it?' he whispered. 'What have you seen?'

Thua's brow creased for a moment with bemusement, and then she choked and shook her head. 'No,' she said, 'your child . . . your child was born dead.'

For a moment, it seemed to Joseph that the face of King Thoth-mes appeared to lighten with relief. 'And how did it look, in its appearance?' he asked.

'A girl,' Thua answered. 'She would have been a most beautiful girl.'

King Thoth-mes breathed in deeply, and his expression of relief could now no longer be mistaken, although he at once sought to conceal it and, hurrying to the chamber of his Queen, he sat with her a long while, seeking to comfort her in her grief. From that time on, however, for a few brief months, he seemed restored to his former good spirits, and Joseph recognised the man whom he had first learned to love. But then, just when he had begun to hope that all his fears had come to nothing, Thua announced that she was pregnant for a third time, and Joseph observed the shadow in King Thoth-mes' stare once again, and an expression almost of something like guilt – made all the worse, so it seemed, when he met

Joseph's eye. He began to dwell ever more upon his dream of the valley, and upon the meaning which Joseph had discovered within it. Whenever he did so, it appeared to Joseph, King Thoth-mes' flesh would hang drier and thinner upon his bones, and the marks of his disease grow more haggard in his face. Then his Queen revealed that she was pregnant once again; and the news cast Pharaoh deep into a black and icy fury.

Certainly, from that moment on his disease appeared ever more implacable, as though its grip were squeezing and moulding his bones and could no longer be loosened. In his moods too he no longer seemed himself, but rather the thing of strange and violent rages, such as Joseph had seen before in the garden, when he had almost raised his hand to strike his pregnant wife. His restraint, though, Joseph feared was now a thing of the past, for although the Queen never spoke of it, she was sometimes seen red-eyed and with the marks of bruises on her shoulders and arms. King Thoth-mes himself was more rarely seen by now, for he passed many days closeted within the temple of Amen. Yet even the mysteries of the god's sorcery, so it seemed, were losing their power to keep the sickness at bay; and it was whispered that a tomb was being readied in the valley beyond the Nile's western bank, where the dead had their realm. Not even Joseph though, the Great Double of the King, could be certain of this news; and so he came to fear that King Thoth-mes might indeed be dead.

A month passed, during which time he never once glimpsed his royal master, and then it happened that the hour of Thua's labour arrived. Joseph, infected by his memory of the Queen's last confinement, waited for the news from his wife's chamber with a nervous impatience, and a dread which he did not care to think upon too closely, for his dreams had recently been haunted by dark visions and omens. Dimly, from his wife's chamber he had heard the screams of childbirth all day; yet as evening began to deepen, they seemed to grow ever more desperate with pain. At last they reached a pitch, and then fell silent; and Joseph, listening to the murmurs of the palm trees in the breeze and to the far-off noise of the geese above the Nile, could not imagine that such sounds, at such a moment, could be real. His skin began to burn as though with a flush. Very distantly, he wondered why. The shadows were still dusty with the heat of the vanished day – yet he knew it was not the heat which was pricking his eyes.

A servant girl approached him and whispered the news. He followed her to his wife's chamber. Kneeling by Thua's side, he kissed her on her lips as though her eyes were closed only in sleep, as though her own kiss might suddenly meet with his. Then he did as his wife had once done to him, and dampened her hand with the flow of his tears. Only after a long while did he rise again, and leave the room behind. In the shadows of the passageway outside, the servant girl was waiting with a bundle in her arms. Wordlessly, she handed it across to him. As Joseph took it the bundle began to stir, and he smiled suddenly, gazing down and blinking through his tears. 'She has her mother's face,' he whispered, kissing the infant very softly on her brow. 'May the Almighty grant she be as beautiful and good.' And then he clasped his daughter tightly, and he gave her the name of Tyi.

That night, gathering together his sons Inen and Ay, he sought to comfort them as well as he could and then, while they slept, he sat in watch by their side. Only towards dawn, as the darkness of that death-haunted night began to fade, did Joseph leave his two sons and cross to a balcony, where he stood and gazed out towards the eastern horizon. He could see, peaceful in their fields, the distant cattle, and birds soaring high from their nests into song, while on the Nile the first rays of the sun were gleaming golden, heralding the beauty of the bright day yet to come. Joseph's heart was filled with a sudden sense of wonder, thinking upon the glories which the All-High had created; and then at once he remembered how his beloved wife was dead, and would never again see the risen sun. At the same moment he heard a footstep behind him, and turning round he saw the silhouette of Pharaoh.

'I had feared that you too might have died,' he said at last.

'Died?' King Thoth-mes' voice sounded distant, yet harsh. He laughed suddenly, and again the noise seemed dissonant and strange. 'But I have understood now,' he whispered, 'that I shall never truly die.'

Joseph shook his head. 'All men must die.' He turned away to gaze back at the sun. 'All women as well.'

'Yes.' King Thoth-mes stepped forward from the shadows into the light. 'I have heard the news.' He stood by Joseph's side and Joseph, turning again to gaze upon his face, saw how strangely the sickness had made it its own, for his eyes were like almonds now and his skull vast and domed. In his stare as well he appeared strangely altered, for there seemed barely a trace of mortality within it. Yet even as Joseph thought this, a flicker of something seemed to pass across King Thoth-mes' expression, and Joseph imagined for a moment that it might almost have been guilt.

'I have ordered,' said King Thoth-mes, 'a tomb to be made ready for Thua in the valley.'

'The valley?' Joseph stared at him in astonishment. 'But only Kings, O Pharaoh, are laid to rest in there.'

'Are you not my double? And was not Thua your wife?'

Still Joseph gazed at him in astonishment; then he bowed his head, and kissed King Thoth-mes' hand. But the King brushed him away, and turned instead to gaze towards the western hills. 'Your daughter,' he said at last, 'I was shown her by the maid. She is very lovely.'

'As her mother was.'

'Indeed.' King Thoth-mes forced a pallid smile. He half-turned, then tensed and looked again towards the hills. 'Do you think,' he murmured at length, 'that it is Tyi who is destined to wash the blood from the tombs?'

'I have told you before, O noble King, how there is only One Who can see what is to come.'

'The High Priest of Amen does not agree with you, O Yuya.'

'Yet what proofs has he given?'

'Of the powers of Amen? Many strange proofs.'

'I would be interested to learn of them.'

'Would you, O Yuya? Are you certain of that?' Still King Thoth-mes smiled, and yet the coldness seemed suddenly returned to his stare. 'I have glimpsed a very great darkness in the temple.'

Joseph gazed at him intrigued, not bothering now to conceal how urgent was his interest, for King Thoth-mes had never before chosen to speak on the matter. 'I would know,' he said slowly, 'what this darkness might be.'

'I cannot tell you.' King Thoth-mes paused. 'No – I cannot ever tell you that.'

'Why?'

'I have worshipped it, O Yuya. I have bowed down before it. I have been its supplicant and devotee.'

Joseph frowned. 'I do not understand. Why would a man such as you do such a thing?'

'Because it was the darkness which preserved me my mortal form, just as the High Priest of Amen had always told me that it would. Without it, I would have become the thing you see today' – he gestured to his face – 'long, long before.'

'But . . .' – Joseph swallowed – 'how, O mighty King? By what means did this darkness achieve such a thing?'

'You do not wish to know.' King Thoth-mes' smile twisted strangely as he shook his head. But then all at once his smile faded, and when he spoke again his voice was as harsh and distant as it had ever been. 'And yet in truth,' he proclaimed, as though to the dawn, 'I was a fool to fear the change. This form that I wear is no disfigurement. It is true I no longer wear the aspect of a mortal, but then such is the mark of my descent from a god. For I have been told by the High Priest of Amen, O Yuya, how Osiris too, when he came down from the stars and ruled over Egypt as its King in the First Time, looked just as I do now.'

Joseph gazed at King Thoth-mes in silence, at his distended face, his swollen skull and his strangely slanted eyes.

'What are you thinking?'

'I think . . .'

King Thoth-mes smiled bitterly. 'You do not need to conceal your disgust, O Yuya, for I can see it in your face. Yet for the sake of the friendship which we have known in our time, be honest with me – come – tell me what you think.'

'That Osiris was a demon, and that his blood was cursed indeed.'

King Thoth-mes' smile still lingered, frozen on his lips. 'How can you say so,' he exclaimed suddenly, 'when it was by his teaching that Egypt was founded, and mighty monuments built, and the sciences of the universe first revealed? What else could he have been but a mighty god?'

'He was a jinni, perhaps, who would not bow down before the only true God.'

'The only true God?' King Thoth-mes gazed at Joseph a moment, then suddenly laughed. 'You are a wise man, O Yuya, with the power to glimpse and interpret the future, and it may be that your god is a great god after all. And yet I tell you, your powers are nothing, nor your understanding, compared with those of the High Priest of the temple of Amen.'

'But the worship of Amen is that of darkness. Why, O King, you have told me so yourself!'

'Not of darkness alone. There are other mysteries too – O Yuya, such mysteries! – for it is the heir to a wisdom which has counted the stars and measured the earth, yes, and banished the realms of death. For beyond the tomb, I tell you, Osiris waits.'

Joseph laughed with a sudden, bitter contempt. 'You may believe what you wish, O King, but still – you will be dead.'

King Thoth-mes narrowed his eyes. For a moment Joseph sought to meet his stare, but its gleam was too bright, its depths too profound, in a way that he had never observed in it before. He shuddered and sought to turn, but the King, releasing the grip upon his arm, seized him by the chin and forced his face back round. Feeling the pressure of King Thoth-mes' fingers, Joseph grew suddenly aware of their strength – a strength so terrible that it seemed barely human at all.

He struggled in vain to shake himself loose. 'In the valley,' he exclaimed, summoning all his scorn, 'beyond the western hills, are the tombs not filled with the bodies of the dead, all of them your forefathers, all of them sharing in the blood of Osiris?'

King Thoth-mes answered him with scorn of his own. 'You may think what you wish.'

Joseph gazed at him in astonishment and a sudden fearful doubt. 'What are you saying?' He shook his head. 'I do not understand . . .'

'No, you do not, and I was a fool to think you might. What can you, a foreigner, a stranger, ever hope to know?

And yet if only, O Yuya, you were not so obdurate, so blind . . .'

Joseph frowned. 'If only, O Pharaoh, if only – then, what?'

'It may be that Thua would still be alive.'

Both men stood in silence a moment; then Joseph shook his head and sought to turn away, but King Thoth-mes, with the power which seemed to wait within his eyes, would not release him from the gleam of his stare. Joseph staggered; he could feel his sinews giving way; he did not wish to kneel, yet he could not help himself. Down he fell prostrate, and King Thoth-mes laughed at the spectacle.

'Can you doubt now,' he whispered, 'the greatness of my powers? And yet to prove indeed that they are what is claimed, and that the High Priests of Amen have told me the truth, I have been told to expect an infallible sign.'

'A sign?'

'A child,' said King Thoth-mes, 'born to my Queen.'

'But where is the wonder in that?'

'You will know,' King Thoth-mes answered, 'when the child is born.'

'How?'

King Thoth-mes stood in silence a long while. 'I had long dreaded it,' he whispered at last, 'for the sign will be a terrible and loathsome one. Now, though . . .' – he shrugged – 'I am no longer afraid. For I will know, when the child is born – a child, O Yuya, of hideous aspect – that my own entry to the Kingdom of Osiris is near!'

Joseph gazed up at the face of King Thoth-mes, his friend, and he thought suddenly that he no longer knew it at all, for it seemed to belong wholly to an alien thing. Despite himself he began to crawl backwards, but then, even as he turned to shrink away, shuddering with sudden panic and fear, he saw a deep gleam of pain within King Thoth-mes' stare and he knew that his friend was still a mortal after all. He sought to steady himself, to rise to his feet and take King Thoth-mes in his arms; but then, even as he prepared to do so, he started and froze.

Inen, his son, was standing in the doorway, his face very pale and his black eyes very wide. Joseph breathed in deeply, then crossed to him and picked him up in his arms. 'How long have you been here?' he demanded in concern. 'How much have you heard?'

Inen's eyes grew wider, but he did not reply.

King Thoth-mes smiled. 'What matter if he heard it all?' He tousled Inen's unruly black hair. 'What harm can it be for a child to hear the truth?'

'The truth?' Joseph whispered as he set his son down. 'The truth, O King? But Inen is only a child. How can I expect him to understand the truth, and not be damaged by all that he has heard, when there is the example of you, a grown man, before him?'

All the life seemed to bleed from King Thoth-mes' face. 'Be careful what you say,' he whispered, 'for all that you be my friend.'

'Yes,' answered Joseph, truly angry now, 'and it is because I am your friend that I must tell you, while you are still able to hear me and understand, what I think. Come to your senses! What need do you have for the sorcery of the priests, their mutterings of secrets and death-haunted mysteries, their promises of an eternity which they refuse to explain? Look about you, O King! See the Nile, lit blue by the rays of the sun, where we have sailed together so often on your barge, eating fish caught fresh from the sweet flowing waters, watching the swoop of brightly coloured birds, enjoying all the infinite beauties of your land. These delights, O great Pharaoh, I have known because of you.

There can be no magic, no sorcery, mightier than such pleasures – and that, O my friend . . . that is what is true.'

King Thoth-mes stood frozen a moment; then he reached for Joseph's hand, and he gripped it so tightly that Joseph could not be certain whether it was from an excess of anger or of love. 'I am the heir to Osiris – nor can I help it.'

'All I beg you, O Pharaoh, is to beware of the priests, for I dread their intentions and the lure of their sorcery.'

King Thoth-mes smiled. 'Yet they promise me immortality, and all the pleasures which you have listed, all of life's sweet delights, will then be mine for the passage of eternity.' He kissed Joseph once, then twice upon the cheeks. 'My only sorrow, O Yuya, is that neither you nor Thua will be there by my side.'

Then he turned brusquely, as though afraid to say more, and hurried away; and Joseph, watching King Thoth-mes leave, felt a strange weight settling on his heart. He sighed and bent down to pick Inen up. To his consternation, however, his son shrank away from him. 'What is it?' Joseph whispered. 'Inen, please come to me.'

But Inen did not answer, and his eyes appeared wide with hostility and doubt.

'Inen, please.' Joseph stretched out his arms, but still his son shrank back. He began to shake his head.

'Inen, what is it?'

'Is it true,' his son asked suddenly, 'the things that Pharaoh said?'

'What things?'

'That the priests might have kept my mother from death?'

'No.'

'And yet he forced you to your knees. I saw it, O my father. I saw you on your knees. So it must be that the priests spoke the truth after all.'

Joseph stood frozen a moment, uncertain what to say. 'Pharaoh did not mean to do it,' he whispered. 'For that brief moment, he was no longer himself.' Then he reached out once again, and this time Inen did not shrink away but allowed himself to be folded in his father's embrace. Joseph hugged him a long while, then kissed him on his brow and bore him back to where his brother still lay asleep. 'Do not fear,' Joseph whispered, kissing him once again, 'for there is One who will guard you, as He has always guarded me.' Then he rose, and turned and walked from the room, but as he reached the door he paused and turned again. He could see Inen still sitting against the wall perfectly motionless, his face deathly pale. Joseph smiled, trying to conjure a response from his son; but Inen would not answer and his eyes seemed very cold. Joseph sighed, and bowed his head. 'Only the All-High,' he thought to himself, 'can order the ways of this world. Yet I pray that He help me to comfort my son.' Then he left the room, vowing as he did so that he would return there that same day, when all his business of state had been completed, to console his two sons and to aid them in their grief.

Yet in the end he was to be gravely delayed. That afternoon, as had happened to Thua the evening before, the Queen was taken suddenly into her confinement, and when the news was brought to Joseph it was accompanied by an order to attend at once on Pharaoh. Joseph found him by the doorway which led into the Harim, gazing out beyond the Palace towards the flow of the Nile. 'I am doing as you advised,' King Thoth-mes said without glancing round, 'and imprinting the beauties of life upon my mind. See, the blueness of the sky and the greenness of the fields, and the grace of the birds soaring high before the sun! How can the world be evil when it contains such things of wonder?'

Joseph opened his mouth to answer, but then suddenly, from the depths of the Harim, there rose a scream, long and dreadful, before at last it fell away. Despite himself, remembering the same sound he had heard the night before, Joseph winced; and King Thoth-mes, as he turned round, saw him do so.

'The labour is many months early,' he whispered.

Joseph bowed his head. 'All may still be well.'

For a long while King Thoth-mes did not reply. 'I have been thinking much,' he said at last, 'of what you said to me this morning. Then, some hours back, I fell asleep, and I dreamed the dream once again which I described to you long before, the same which you had dreamed as you slept above the valley.'

From behind him, Joseph heard the sudden sound of feet running, and he half-turned to see who it was. But King Thoth-mes seized him by the arm and drew him very close. 'That first time,' he whispered, 'when I told you my dream . . .' – he swallowed – 'I did not tell you all.'

Joseph started. 'What, then, did you omit?'

King Thoth-mes swallowed again. The footsteps were drawing nearer, and it struck Joseph suddenly that his companion was afraid. 'Here,' said the King, drawing a scroll of papyrus from under his cloak and smuggling it into Joseph's hands, 'read this well.' Then he stepped backwards and Joseph, turning, saw that a stranger had entered the room, shaven-headed, and holding a staff on which was surmounted the talisman of Amen.

The priest bowed low.

'What news?' King Thoth-mes asked.

'The Queen,' the priest answered, 'your sister, O King . . .'

He left the rest unspoken and, turning, began to lead the way into the depths of the Harim. When he saw that Joseph was accompanying King Thoth-mes, however, he halted and attempted to forbid him access; but King Thoth-mes ordered him to be silent and continue on his way. The priest bowed again, with evident reluctance, but he did as he was commanded, and it was not long before the three of them had arrived by the place of the Queen's confinement. Joseph hesitated before entering, reluctant to intrude; but then he heard, from ahead of him, King Thoth-mes cry out, and at once he followed him into the chamber.

He too, gazing at the scene before him, could not restrain a gasp. 'May the All-High have mercy upon her,' he whispered, looking at the Queen, for she lay in a filthy pool of mingled blood and sweat, and a hideous gash had been torn across her belly. It seemed impossible to Joseph, gazing upon the wound, that the Queen could have survived it; but even as he thought this, she moaned very softly, and he saw a single tear well and then start to roll down her cheek. King Thoth-mes crossed to her and gently raised her in his arms, staining his white robes with his sister-Queen's blood; and Joseph, watching them together, remembered what the King had said to him earlier that day, that he was the heir to Osiris and could never die. Joseph felt a touch of something cold very deep inside him, at the horrible thought that such words might be the truth. And if they were, he wondered suddenly, then what of the infallible sign which the High Priest had promised, the marvel which would prove the truth of all his claims?

He looked again at the hideous wound to the Queen. 'The child,' he exclaimed urgently, 'where is the child?'

King Thoth-mes turned to glance at him, his face a mask of agony and foreboding. At the same moment, from the shadows, a man stepped forward, shaven-headed like his fellow but with a golden collar and a cloak of leopard-skin, and Joseph knew that these marked him as the High Priest of Amen. Despite himself, Joseph took a pace backwards, and the High Priest, observing this, smiled very faintly. Then he clapped his hands, and a servant girl came forward with a bundle in her arms. The High Priest took it from her, and as he did so Joseph saw that the bundle was stirring violently. The High Priest parted the cloth in which the infant had been swaddled, and for a moment – as he inspected it – Joseph imagined that his eyes betrayed a terrible void, more lonely than he had ever dreamed might exist. But then the thin smile returned and, plucking away the swaddling sheet, the High Priest held what had lain beneath it up to the light.

'No!' cried King Thoth-mes suddenly, gazing upon the infant – the thing – that was his child. Its skull was hideously distended and long, its belly swollen, its limbs very spindly: a loathsome parody of King Thoth-mes himself. Yet worst were its eyes, for they were burning bright and seemed more a demon's than a mortal child's; and then suddenly it began to hiss and spit, and reach out with its fingers, which were thin and hooked like an insect's claws. It appeared to be sniffing after something; and then Joseph realised that it was the blood of its own mother, spilled across the floor.

'No!' King Thoth-mes cried out again. He stumbled forward, and Joseph saw how palely the sweat gleamed on his brow. He tried to reach out for the creature in the High Priest's arms, but as he did so, he choked and began to clutch at his chest, as though the horror of what he had seen could be ripped out from his heart. But his heart would not be stilled; and Joseph, as he ran forward to take King Thoth-mes in his arms, could hear it thudding very fast and loud.

'The horror will kill him!' he cried. 'His heart will not endure it!'

'Then fetch physicians,' answered the High Priest. 'Go! I

will stay with Pharaoh, for it is you who knows where help can best be found.'

Joseph met his stare a moment in silent suspicion, then gazed down at King Thoth-mes and listened again to his heart. A second time, Joseph glanced up and met the High Priest's stare, and then he rose and hurried away, calling for attendants. By the time he had summoned sufficient servants, however, and returned to the chamber itself, King Thoth-mes was no longer there – nor the Queen, nor the High Priest, nor the hideous child. Of the blood as well, which had been smeared across the floor, there was now not a trace, and indeed, it was as though all the horrors which he had witnessed in the room had never been.

Still, though, long after he had dimissed all the attendants, Joseph lingered in the chamber, hoping that King Thoth-mes might perhaps reappear. All remained silent, however; and as the shadows of evening began to lengthen, so his sense of despair and dread grew the more. Then suddenly, just as he was on the verge of abandoning all hope and leaving, he heard footsteps from behind him and, turning round, saw the form of the High Priest.

The two men stood in silence for a moment, then the High Priest bowed his head. 'The falcon is flown to heaven,' he announced in a tone drained of emotion. 'The new falcon is arisen in his place.'

Joseph breathed in deeply. 'I am sorry . . .' he whispered, 'to hear such news . . . I am sorry.' He breathed in again, then he narrowed his eyes. 'Yet, so Pharaoh told me, it was your claim that he would never die.'

The High Priest's face remained utterly impassive. 'Do not, O Wazir, seek to intrude upon our mysteries – for have we ever trespassed upon your own affairs of state? King Thoth-mes is dead – King Amen-hetep is now the ruler over Egypt. He will need the guidance of a wise and loyal servant – and who else, O Yuya, can that be if not you? For you should know that it was the last wish of King Thoth-mes, spoken upon his dying breath, that you should be to his son what you had always been to him.'

Joseph remained silent a while; then he nodded shortly. 'In his death as in his life, I shall of course obey him.' He paused a moment more, meeting the High Priest's eye. 'Yet still I would like to know if he can truly be dead.'

For the first time that evening, a flicker of amusement touched the High Priest's lips. 'If there are mysteries which are hidden from all but the highest of my fellows, why then should I share them with you, when you do not even believe in our traditions and our gods?' He paused; and again, staring into his eyes, Joseph imagined that he caught the glimpse of an infinite loneliness. 'Do not pry,' the High Priest whispered suddenly, touching Joseph lightly upon the chest with his staff. 'For believe me – there are secrets it were better you should never come to learn.'

Then he bowed once again, and turned and left the room. Joseph did not seek to follow him. But later, when all three of his children lay before him asleep, he pulled out the papyrus which King Thoth-mes had smuggled to him and read it closely, the shadow of perturbation deepening all the while upon his face. When he had finished with it, he crossed to where Tyi, his infant daughter, lay, and for several minutes gazed down upon her tiny sleeping form, abandoned to his own thoughts. Then at length, he crossed to the balcony and slipped the papyrus under his cloak, gazing all the while at the distant western hills, beyond which lay the valley of the tombs of the Pharaohs.

It was from the same balcony, some seventy days after the death of King Thoth-mes, that Joseph watched the embalmed body being taken from the Palace, borne upon the shoulders of the worshippers of Amen, swathed beneath bandages and encased within gold. Joseph had not sought to join the procession, but even so, he stood a long while watching the passage of the torches as they flickered in a line across the western plain, winding through the night towards the tomb beyond the western hills, cut from the rock of the sacred valley. Only when all was darkness again did Joseph turn at last. He wandered slowly to the room where his daughter lay asleep and, picking her up, cradled her in his arms, inspecting the beauty of her face very closely. Then he stood a long while as before, lost in thought.

But at this point, Haroun saw the approach of morning and broke off from his tale. 'O Commander of the Faithful,' he said, 'if you would care to return here tomorrow evening, then I shall describe to you the fortunes of Joseph's daughter, Tyi.'

And so the Caliph did as Haroun suggested; and the following evening he returned to the mosque.

And Haroun said:

By the explicit order of the will of King Thoth-mes, Tyi was brought up as a royal princess, so that from her earliest days she lived in the Harim, in the splendour of its chambers and amidst its gardens filled with flowers. Yet she was fairer herself than the fairest flower in bloom; and since she was also the youngest of the children in the Palace, she did not find it hard to become the favourite of her nurses. Certainly she knew herself more admired than the Royal Queens and Princesses, for she was often told so by King Amen-hetep himself, who did not like his sisters save to pull upon their hair. But Tyi did not need Pharaoh to make her feel loved, for she already knew that her father loved her more than all the world. He rarely said as much; but she would often catch him watching her in silence and sometimes, when he hugged her, he would speak to her of her mother. Once he carried Tyi on his shoulders to a spot beyond the Palace, where trees lined the border of a tiny lake, and he told her that her mother had often loved to wander there. He never mentioned the fact again; but as Tyi grew older, so it became her father's favourite pastime to take her from the Harim and walk with her through the fields, to watch the ducks where they swam upon the lake or the pigeons flying brilliantly white against the sky. For Tyi, such excursions provided rare and fleeting glimpses of freedom; and so she too, like her father and her dead, unknown mother, fell in love with the lake, and with the views of the birds and of the hills towards the west.

This love grew all the more intense as Tyi's life in the Harim began to worsen. Her brothers, like her father, had always adored her, and it had pleased them – since it served to help them feel more like men – to spoil their younger sister horribly. In time, however, both Inen and Ay had left the Harim behind and entered the great world which stretched beyond its walls, so that Tyi, still a little girl, felt herself cruelly abandoned. She was bored with the gardens and the courtyards of the Harim; she did not love the company of the other girls about her; she wanted only to be with her brothers again. When either of them came to call upon her, then, she would ask them greedily for details of all the wonders of the world, and when they left she would be plunged deep into tantrums of resentment and frustration. But when she spoke of leaving the Harim herself, her companions, Pharaoh's sisters, would mock her and take their revenge for their brother's treatment of them by pulling Tyi's own hair. As she grew older and ever more beautiful, so the Princesses' hatred of their rival steadily increased, until at last Tyi was desperate with her passion to escape. But still her only tastes of freedom were her walks with her father – those, and the cherished visits from her brothers.

Both Ay and Inen, in their very different ways, were equally precious to her. Ay brought a taste of the wide-open deserts, for already, although he was barely fourteen years of age, he could hunt, and ride a chariot, and excel in all the arts of war as well as any man. Inen, the elder, was closer and more reserved, as though his silence protected some deep-buried secret, which he could barely endure to admit to himself. Yet his intelligence was piercing and ever restless: Tyi suspected that sometimes, when their father was away, he would spy on the priests of the Temple of Amen, and he could penetrate to their heart the workings of the Court. It especially pleased Tyi, enduring the torments inflicted upon her by Pharaoh's many sisters, to think that she knew more of their brother's doings even than the Queen; and so when Inen's visits began suddenly to diminish, Tyi grew upset and alarmed. Several months went by; and still in all that time, her elder brother never once came to call. One day, when Tyi was walking with her father through the fields beyond the Palace, she asked him where Inen had gone, and she watched as his expression, normally so calm, at once began to darken. But Tyi could not believe that her father might truly be angry, for she had never seen him lose his temper before; and so she asked him once again where her brother might have gone. Joseph paused in his walk, and stood frozen a moment. 'I dread to think,' he said at last, turning as he did so and raising his hand to silence any further questions from his daughter. 'He is the thing now of my deadliest enemies. I can do nothing for him. Do not, please, mention your brother's name again.' And so stern did he appear, and such was Tyi's respect for her father's wishes, that she restrained her curiosity for the whole of that evening and only succumbed to it on the following day, when she sent a messenger to hunt out Ay.

She had to wait for several days. The delay did not surprise her, for Ay, she knew, had grown to be King Amen-hetep's closest friend and the two of them were often abroad on their pleasures, leaving the tedious affairs of state far behind. Almost a week passed before Ay finally appeared, carrying the pelt of a lion on his back, and accompanied by King Amen-hetep who bore a second lion's head. Tyi immediately prostrated herself; for although the King had once been her playmate, she had not seen him now for almost a year, and she remembered how capable he had been of strange humours and rages. But at once he bent down and raised her by her hand, kissing it very lingeringly, so that she blushed and turned away. Ay, watching this, winked and laughed loudly, then gestured down at the corpses of the lions.

'You see,' he said, 'we have brought you some presents.'

Tyi gazed at the bodies, then wrinkled her nose. 'I would rather have live ones.'

King Amen-hetep shrugged and smiled. 'That can easily be arranged.' He glanced at Ay. 'For we are mighty hunters, are we not? Only just sixteen, and already there is no one in Egypt who can rival me.'

Ay nodded and smiled but Tyi, watching them together, doubted that the King could be the equal of her brother. Though still almost boys, they were both very large; whereas Ay, however, seemed carved from the hardest marble, King Amen-hetep's belly and limbs appeared far more soft. Nevertheless, Tyi kept her opinion to herself, for the King seemed determined to impress her with wild tales of his prowess, and he would pause every so often to fondle the lion's severed head. At one point, he dabbled his hands in the still sticky gore and sucked on each finger; then, just before leaving, he daubed Tyi's mouth red with another smear of blood. He began to lick his own lips extravagantly, and Ay promptly laughed; but Tyi, although she smiled, did not understand the joke. She was relieved when King Amen-hetep departed at last, and she could ask Ay what he might have heard of their elder brother. Ay frowned and shrugged his shoulders, for he knew nothing; but he promised her faithfully to find out all he could.

It was not Ay who called upon her in the following days, however, but King Amen-hetep, who kissed her hand as before and then suddenly, to her astonishment, seized her in his arms. The effort made him pant, but his fat lips were parted all the same in a hungry smile, and Tyi tensed as she felt them soft and damp against her own. With a sudden effort she wriggled from his grasp, but her assailant's smile only broadened all the more. 'It is fitting,' he wheezed, 'that I am such a mighty hunter − for I see you are not only beautiful but spirited as well. A pretty thing to chase!'

Tyi met his gaze with bare contempt. 'I would have hoped I was worthy of being something more than that.'

For a moment, King Amen-hetep's smile was frozen on his lips. 'You are indeed,' he whispered suddenly. He crossed to her, and as he did so his smile seemed to fade into a pout of half-regret. 'You are indeed,' he whispered again, taking her arm and leading her across to the balcony. 'For why else would I have brought you a gift so worthy of a queen?'

He gestured to the courtyard below where three black-maned lions, blood-streaked and covered in dust, lay slumped in a cage. King Amen-hetep beamed at Tyi with pride. 'I caught them myself, just myself and Ay.'

Tyi gazed at them in silence.

The King reached out to touch her on her arm. 'Why do you not thank me,' he whispered, 'for your gift?'

Tyi shrugged. 'I would rather have them free.' She glanced behind her at the Harim walls. 'Wild creatures should not be kept in cages.'

King Amen-hetep tensed, then nodded violently and clapped his plump, soft hands. 'And so it shall be done!' He took Tyi by the arm and led her down into the courtyard below, where she pressed her face closely against the bars of the cage. Despite the lions' wounds and evident exhaustion, their eyes were still agleam with a menacing dignity, and one of them, meeting Tyi's gaze, stirred and half-rose to sit on its haunches. It yawned very slowly, and the tails of all three began to beat to and fro.

Tyi was just thinking to herself that she had never before seen such beauty and power in living creatures, when a train of servants began to pull upon the cage and roll it across the courtyard. Tyi turned to the King, to ask him what his plans for the animals were, and he smiled and pointed towards a tiny metal gate, framed on one side by a high white wall and on the other by the highest portion of the Harim. Tyi frowned as she watched the metal gate being opened and the cage led inside. 'But those are the gardens of the Great Queen!' she exclaimed.

King Amen-hetep laughed. 'No longer,' he replied. He took Tyi by the arm again, and led her up to the Harim roof. Looking down, she could see the three lions, freed now from their cage, draped amongst the garden's rare and precious trees, and despite herself, she smiled and cried out with pleasure. Her suitor's own smile at once grew thicker. He raised her hand and kissed it once again. 'A gift worthy,' he murmured, 'as I said, of a Queen.'

Then he turned and left, and Tyi, watching him go, felt a

thrill of ambition and sudden hope, all the sweeter for having risen so unforeseen. She lay an hour, watching her lions, before descending back into the coolness of the Harim, and the gardens appointed to the women who dwelt there, for she felt a strong desire herself to sit by fountains and flowers. But when she arrived there, she saw to her annoyance that someone had already taken her favourite spot; and as she drew nearer, she realised that it was Pharaoh's eldest sister, the Great Queen herself.

Tyi froze and would have walked away, save that the Queen had observed her and called out her name. Nervously, Tyi approached her and knelt before her feet.

'Do not wonder,' the Queen said at last, 'that I am forced to sit in your garden, Harim-girl. My own, as you will know, has been closed to me.'

Tyi bowed her head, but did not reply. Suddenly, the Queen kicked her and sent her sprawling backwards. 'What did Pharaoh say?' the Queen hissed. 'What did he promise you?'

Tyi blinked back her tears of indignation. Now she could see that there were more of King Amen-hetep's sisters gathered behind the Queen, their faces all as frozen with hatred as their elder's. The sight filled Tyi with fury herself and she rose to her feet, drawing herself up to her full height. 'He told me,' she announced, 'that I would be Great Queen.'

To her pleasure, from the circle of the Princesses, she could hear whispers and gasps. But the Great Queen herself only shook her head and laughed. 'That is what he told you?' she exclaimed. 'Then it means he is intending to make you his whore.'

'You may think that if you please,' Tyi laughed, 'yet it is plain he loves even my lions more than he loves you.'

At once all the blood seemed to drain from the Great

Queen's face, but as she rose to her feet she appeared almost strangely, icily calm. 'You will never be more than his concubine,' she whispered, reaching out to touch the side of Tyi's face. 'For – do you not know, my child? – only a Princess may become Pharaoh's Queen.'

'I have been raised as a Princess.'

Again, the Great Queen laughed. 'Hear her!' she exclaimed. Then at once the smile faded away from her lips, and she seized Tyi's chin and jerked her head backwards. 'You lack the royal blood,' she spat. 'Therefore you are nothing. Why!' – she laughed even more, but hysterically now – 'you are not even Egyptian – and yet you think to be our Queen? Look at this hair!' She pulled upon it violently. 'See how it crinkles, how ugly it is! See this skin!' She tore away the tunic to expose Tyi's breasts. 'It is black like pitchest night!' She reached behind her, and Tyi saw that one of her sisters had handed her a whip. 'It were better for you,' the Great Queen whispered, 'if you truly wish to serve as the concubine of Pharaoh, that we flayed your skin from your flesh, so that you might then appear less of a Nubian.' And so saying, she tore Tyi's clothing fully from her body, then began to swing down the whip upon her back. Desperately Tyi sought to rise to her feet, but she was seized by the Princesses and pinned to the ground, and the blows did not stop until the Great Queen was exhausted. She tossed the whip aside and gave Tyi a final, parting kick; then she turned with all her sisters, and Tyi was left alone.

The nurses came to her some time later, nervously, afraid of being glimpsed by the Princesses, and they bore her to a bed which they had prepared for her in her chamber. Tyi did not even speak to thank them, but lay in silence gazing at the wall. Only with the coming of night, when everyone else in the Harim was asleep, did she rise at last and cross to the balcony, to gaze in the direction of her favourite lake; but a wall blocked her view, and so she soon turned away. Very carefully she treated her wounds; then she dressed and adorned herself with all the skill that she could muster. For hours she sat in the light of the moon, braiding her hair, until at last dawn rose and she laid her mirror down.

As she did so, she saw behind her the silhouette of a man. 'Who is that?' she cried out, alarmed; then she smiled with mingled astonishment and relief. 'Inen! Is it you? But what are you doing here?'

'Why, what do you think? I have missed my little sister.'

'But it is forbidden at this hour,' she whispered in sudden panic.

'No.' He shook his head. 'Nothing is forbidden to me any more.' And so saying he stepped forward, and Tyi saw that his head had been shaven bald and around his neck there now hung the symbol of Amen. He fingered it and smiled. 'With this I have the power of a hundred Pharaohs.'

Tyi gazed at him, appalled. 'But . . . no . . . how could you?' She shook her head. 'Our father . . .'

'Was afraid to seize the chance which I have taken.'

'What chance? O my brother, what are you talking about?'

'Our father knew – for I once heard him told – of the mysteries hidden within the temple of Amen. He was afraid, though, to pull back the veil which concealed them. But I, as you can see' – he touched his shaven scalp – 'have not been such a coward. And, O my sister, O my sister – what mysteries they are!'

Tyi gazed at him wide-eyed. 'Why,' she whispered eagerly, 'what have you found?'

'You think I would tell you that?'

'Why not?'

Inen smiled. 'Because they are secrets which come from

before the dawn of time, written within the sacred books of instruction, guarded by only a handful of priests, and revealing the wonders of the very gods themselves – all good reasons not to tell you a thing.'

Tyi turned and sniffed, to disguise her disappointment. 'Why mention them at all, then?'

'To impress you, no other reason.' Inen smiled again, then reached out to take his sister in his arms. As he did so, however, she flinched and shrank away, and Inen looked down in surprise. 'What is it?' he asked; and then he saw the marks of the whip across her arms.

Tyi would not tell him what had happened at first, and instead tried to rise and run away, but then suddenly, with heaving, panting sobs, the whole story flooded out. Inen listened in silence, then drew out a tiny flask from his belt. 'It may be,' he whispered, cradling Tyi in his arms, 'that I can show you something at least of my powers.' And so saying, he reached for a piece of cloth and dampened it with a liquid, thick and black, which he poured from the flask. He applied it to the wounds upon his sister's arms, and at once she felt the pain fade, and when she looked the scars were gone. 'O Inen,' she cried, 'that is sorcery indeed! What secrets, what magic, could achieve such a wonder?'

But Inen only smiled and raised a finger to his mouth, then unfastened her robes and inspected the wounds upon her back. Again, he applied the liquid to the welts, and again Tyi felt the pain immediately fade away. 'And the scars,' she asked him, 'are the scars all gone as well?'

'There is not a single marking left.'

Tyi nodded with a fierce satisfaction, and at once reached down for her robes and her finery. Inen frowned, though, as he watched her dress herself again. 'Would you gild the dawn?' he muttered. 'You are already quite beautiful enough for such an hour.'

But Tyi shook her head. 'Pharaoh,' she whispered. 'I must – I will – have Pharaoh.'

Inen's frown deepened. 'But did you not hear what the Great Queen said? Only a Princess of the blood may marry him.'

'That was a lie, surely?'

'No.' He rose to his feet, to take his sister in his arms. 'No, it was not.'

'By whose determining?'

'By the determining of the ancient wisdom of Amen.'

Tyi gazed at her brother a moment in disbelief, then shook her head wildly. 'I cannot believe you!'

'And yet – I am sorry – it is the infallible truth.'

'Infallible?'

'As it has been since the time of the very first Pharaoh.'

Tyi raised her hand-mirror and adjusted a tress. 'Then we shall see,' she said. She pursed her lips, and coloured them again. 'For an unchanging custom may still be brought to change.' And then she turned and hurried from the chamber, nor would she stop to hear Inen's cries of protest. Instead she climbed to the highest roof of the Harim, and she sat there a long while, gazing down at her lions where they lay amidst the early-morning cool of the trees. In due course, it happened that King Amen-hetep emerged into the court-yard below and, glancing upwards, he saw where Tyi sat, and he felt his desire rise up in him again, for he thought he had never seen such beauty before – not in the stars, nor in the sun, nor in any of the works of the heavens or the earth. So he paused in his business and climbed at once to Tyi, and he took her in his arms and sought to kiss her. But Tyi turned away, and would not meet his lips until he had promised her faithfully that she would be his Great Queen. Then she kissed him very softly, and at once broke away and ran down the steps. And King Amen-hetep was left alone.

The following morning, when he emerged into the courtyard, he looked up again and saw Tyi in all her beauty, and again he felt overwhelmed by his love for her, and by an uncontrollable desire. As before, however, having climbed to the roof and sought to take her in his arms, Tyi would not meet his lips, but instead looked away and reminded him of his promise.

King Amen-hetep shuddered with desire. 'I am the Lord of the Two Lands!' he cried out in sudden fury. 'I can do with you what I please!'

'Yet I would rather hurl myself from this roof,' Tyi answered, 'than serve as your whore.'

'You cannot be my Queen.'

'Why not?'

'It is forbidden by the priests of the temple of Amen.'

'And yet you said it yourself, you are the Lord of the Two Lands – or is the High Priest of Amen the true King of Egypt?'

King Amen-hetep clenched his fists. 'Very well,' he nodded curtly. 'It shall all be arranged.' And so saying, he reached out to seize her again, but again she stepped away. 'It must be proclaimed in every corner of the land,' she insisted, 'so that there can be no doubt.' And then she kissed him lightly, and turned and skipped away.

The next morning, so sleepless had King Amen-hetep's night been that he rose before dawn, and seated himself in Tyi's favourite spot, on the roof above the Harim, overlooking the garden. When Tyi emerged there, King Amen-hetep thought again that she was lovelier than the sun, even as it rose from the east behind her head, lighting her hair with a halo of gold. He felt a chill of fire flicker up and down his spine, like the breath of a goddess, as Tyi smiled at him and then lowered her black eyes in mockery.

'Do not be coy with me,' he bellowed, rising to his feet.

At once he felt the breath of the goddess in his stomach, and he almost groaned with the agony. 'O Tyi, O Tyi . . .' He paused, for he had never before sought to put words to his love, never before having known what love might be. He stood, feeling stupid, as Tyi began to laugh; then he lumbered forward suddenly and seized her slim wrist. He sought to smother her with his bulk, pin her to the roof, but as before she wriggled and slithered from his grasp.

This time, when she met his stare, she did not look down. 'Have you done as you promised?' she asked him. 'Am I to be your Queen?'

King Amen-hetep breathed in deeply.

'Am I to be your Queen?'

The King breathed in again. 'You do not understand.'

'Oh yes.' Tyi hissed the words violently as she began to back away. 'I understand all too well.'

'No.' King Amen-hetep gestured helplessly. 'There is nothing I can do – not without a sign of permission from the gods.' He watched the glittering of contempt in Tyi's eyes, and felt his cheeks start to burn, as though the goddess had begun suddenly to breathe on them with fire. At the same moment all his rage and frustration boiled up inside him, and he could no longer bear not to have Tyi in his arms. 'It is no matter,' he cried, lunging forward again and seizing her by the hair. 'I am Pharaoh still, and may do as I please.'

She screamed, and twisted as hard as she could, but King Amen-hetep seized her arms and she could not escape. Then she felt him reaching for her legs and she at once fell backwards, away from his grip, so that she stood on the edge of the roof above the garden. When she glanced down at the courtyard she saw there was a crowd of people gathered there, gazing up at Pharaoh and herself, summoned no doubt by the sound of her cries. Then she turned round further, to look down into the garden. She could see the topmost leaves of the tallest trees, a long way below her. By a fountain, a lion was inspecting her lazily.

Ponderously, King Amen-hetep lunged forward once more and seized her by her ankle.

'Shall I be your Queen?' Tyi cried out.

But King Amen-hetep was shuddering now, so that all his flesh was quivering and rolling, and he did not seem to hear her. He began to pull on her leg, reaching upwards with his hands again, and Tyi closed her eyes, feeling the Harim roof beneath her – how solid it was, how firm the stonework. Then she squirmed and twisted backwards – and suddenly she could no longer feel the Harim roof at all. Dimly she heard Pharaoh bellow with mingled horror and frustration, but the sound was already fading, lost upon the air as it rushed past her ears, and Tyi smiled, just for a moment, to think that she was free. Then she felt herself bounce against the side of something rough, and smelt the aroma of rare, precious leaves, and she knew that she must have hit the branch of some tree. But it seemed barely to break her fall, for she could still hear the whistling of air in her ears, and then all at once she smelt the perfume of flowers, and the dampness of soil, and then she cried out, as she felt her skull seem to melt.

The agony was a searing explosion of red light. Yet although the impact seemed to have crumpled her whole body, for she could feel her limbs twisted in peculiar ways, one single thought still remained with her, an island preserved above the tempest of her pain: 'I am alive.' The idea baffled her; and yet it was true. 'I am alive.'

For a long while she did not attempt to move, merely felt the heat of the sun against her face, smelt the leaves of the acacia and tamarisk trees, heard the songs of the birds amidst the bushes of the garden. How many hours passed she could not tell, since she never once opened her eyes; but at length she could sense that the evening was approaching, for she could no longer feel the sun against her cheeks. But she was still, to her surprise, as warm as before, so that she imagined that something might be lying down beside her, until at last she stirred and found that something was.

She sat up at once. The pain, though great, was not unbearable – and yet she was certain she had felt her skull cave in. She reached up to touch her head. There seemed no trace of a wound. How was it possible? Why was she not dead? She opened her eyes. Two lions lay stretched out on either side of her, while the third lay half-curled in a ball by her feet. Tyi almost laughed, watching the lions start to stir, to think that she had survived her fall only to be eaten by wild beasts – but then the lions began to nuzzle her and to lick her wounds, as though she were not a girl at all but a lion like themselves. Their tongues felt very coarse against her battered limbs, but even as they licked her she felt the pain begin to fade. At last she felt able to rise to her feet, and the lions at once began to stretch playfully and roll upon their backs, and when Tyi stooped to tickle them they curled against her legs. Even when she began to walk towards the garden gates, they continued to play, padding around her like overgrown kittens. She paused by the gates, then unlocked the bolt and set the lions free. But they continued to follow her as she crossed the deserted courtyard and beyond the Harim, into a quarter of the Palace where she had never been before. Yet she remembered the descriptions of its layout which Ay had once given her, and so she knew where Pharaoh was most likely to be found. She passed through one archway, and then a second, where a couple of guards attempted to stop her. But then they looked her in the face, and then glanced down at the lions, and they stammered something and stepped aside in fear.

Beyond the archway there stretched further gardens. At first sight they appeared empty, but then, when Tyi stood still, she could hear the sound of two distant voices engaged, so it seemed, in a heated conversation. She began to walk towards them, her lions still padding silently behind her, until, by a pool lit a rippled silver by the moon, she paused, and listened to the voices again.

She could recognise her father's now. It was very low, and seemed tense with a barely controlled anger. 'I tell you,' she heard him say, 'she cannot be dead. It is impossible. Therefore I ask you again, O Pharaoh, where did she fall from? Where can she be found? I must go to her.'

'She is dead.' King Amen-hetep paused. 'I saw it. And so it has been, O Yuya, all this day, that I have been unable to go to her and gaze upon her face. It is strange.' He paused again. 'It has not been my habit to shrink from seeing death.'

'If you look in her face, I promise you, you will find she is still very much alive. For Tyi has been guarded by mystery since the day of her birth.' And with such certainty did her father say this, and with such impatience, that Tyi suddenly wondered with a chill shock what it was her father knew. 'I say again, O Pharaoh – my daughter is alive.'

But King Amen-hetep laughed wildly. 'If only she were!'

'Yes? And what then?'

'Why, then I would have my blessing from the gods! Then I could have her as my Queen after all!'

Listening, Tyi smiled slowly to herself, then glanced down for the first time at her reflection in the pool. Her face and limbs appeared cruelly battered, and her long hair was matted and tangled with blood. But with her lions ranged about her, she appeared almost like a goddess, and the moon upon the water crowned her head with silver.

She smiled again, then turned and continued along the

path. As she approached them, both her father and King Amen-hetep fell silent. Her father's face appeared frozen, almost appalled, but then suddenly he smiled and took her in his arms. She winced, and laughed, and then winced again, breaking free from his hold, so that she found herself staring into King Amen-hetep's eyes, which were wide with disbelief. 'But . . . no . . .' he stammered, 'I saw you . . . you were dead . . .'

'Did you not demand,' Tyi answered him, 'a sign from the gods?'

'Yes.' King Amen-hetep swallowed, then nodded violently. 'Yes – yes I did.'

He reached for her and Tyi, despite the pain from her wounds, allowed herself to be clasped, allowed her lips to be kissed, allowed herself to smile with the pleasure of her conquest; for she knew, as she watched him and met his stare, that she had won. And so indeed it proved, for her new status was proclaimed that same evening through the Palace, and all who saw her wondered to find her still alive, so that it was rumoured that she was indeed a true heiress of the gods. Amidst the general consternation and the fever of gossip, no one paused to wonder at her blood-line, and to think that she was not a sister of Pharaoh; for it was repeated only how she had been brought back from the dead to be Great Queen.

But Tyi, even in the first thrill and excitement of her triumph, did not forget that there was still one final obstacle to cross. Nor was she surprised, the following morning, as she walked through the Palace surveying her new domain, to be informed by a servant that a priest of Amen wished to see her. She turned and saw, waiting for her by the entrance to the gardens, her brother Inen, his expression very grim. He waited for her to join him, then they walked together alone through the trees.

'I believe,' said Inen at last, bringing out something from under his cloak, 'that you will be requiring this.'

He handed her a flask, and Tyi smiled as she inspected the black, sticky liquid, then dabbed a touch upon a scar across her arm. She stared in fascination as the wound began to fade. 'It is truly,' she whispered, 'the most extraordinary magic.'

'Yes.' Inen frowned. 'And dangerous as well, for those who do not understand with what it is that they are dealing.'

Tyi looked up in surprise. Her brother's face was even grimmer and more set than before. 'What do you mean?' she asked. 'Are you going to try to forbid my marriage to Pharaoh?'

'I cannot. The gods have spoken. They have brought you back from the very jaws of death, and so have marked you out as a worthy Queen.'

Tyi smiled. 'Then it seems that the gods have changed their minds.'

'Yes.' His frown deepened, and he looked away.

Tyi hurried to keep abreast with him as he continued to stride ahead. 'Inen,' she asked, reaching out to touch his hand, 'what is it? What do you know?'

He glanced at her impatiently, then suddenly his face seemed to crumple and he seized her hand. 'I wish . . .' he whispered. He shook his head, then kissed her fingertips. 'I wish,' he said again, 'I wish that things were different.'

'What things?'

'That you were not . . . that . . . no.' He smiled, and shook his head. 'You know it is forbidden for me to tell you what is hidden.'

Tyi paused, then looked up at him through half-lowered lashes. 'Did it surprise you to learn that I had not been killed by my fall?'

'Enormously.'

'Yet it did not surprise our father.'

'Indeed?' His frown returned. 'Indeed.'

'Can you imagine a reason?'

Inen paused a moment, then shrugged and shook his head. 'I cannot talk to you any longer,' he said, 'for I am afraid what I may otherwise give away.' He turned, but Tyi called out to him and he stopped, as though despite himself, and glanced round once again. 'I am your brother,' he said, 'and I love you very greatly – but even more I am a priest of Amen.'

'But does Amen see fit to bless me in my marriage?'

'Oh, indeed.' He bowed. 'Indeed, O Great Queen.'

Then he turned once more and hurried on, and Tyi did not attempt to halt him again. Even as she watched him depart, though, she felt troubled for a moment at the thought of his strange words and the note of warning they had appeared to convey. But then she laughed and shook her head, and began to skip along the path. 'Why should I be afraid?' she cried out aloud. 'As Inen said himself – am I not the Great Queen? There is nothing in all the world which is not mine now to command!'

Beyond the gardens she paused in a courtyard, for there were sculptors at work upon the brickwork of the gate. Tyi glanced up at the words they were carving, and as she did so she clapped her hands, before hurrying on her way into the Palace itself. Behind her, the workmen were finishing their work. 'Tyi,' they had carved, 'the Heiress, Greatly Favoured. Tyi, Mistress of All Countries, Lady of Delight, who Fills the Palace with Love. Tyi, Mistress of Upper and Lower Egypt, Queen of the Two Lands.'

But at this point, Haroun saw the approach of morning and broke off from his tale. 'O Commander of the Faithful,' he said, 'if you would care to return here tomorrow evening, then I shall describe to you the fortunes of Pharaoh and Queen Tyi.'

And so the Caliph did as Haroun suggested; and the following evening he returned to the mosque.

And Haroun said:

Tyi did not take long, nor require much encouragement, to discover how delightful a Great Queen's life could be. All that she had dreamed of from within the high Harim walls, all the manifold wonders of her imagination, now stood revealed as but the palest shadow of the truth, for the reality of the magnificence of Pharaoh's court, its inexhaustible pleasures, beauties and wealth, seemed to lie beyond dreams. To be the mistress of such a world appeared to Tyi a glimpse of Paradise; for there too, she supposed, would be found luxuries beyond compare – gold and silver, incense and perfumes, sweet-smelling woods and chairs built from ivory, the rarest of meats and the choicest of wines. Not a day went by when there was not a cruise upon the Nile, a hunting party out across the sands or festivities held within the cool of the gardens; and not an evening without a banquet at which Tyi would preside, the companion of her husband, the very greatest of Great Queens.

For Tyi, having left the Harim behind, was determined that she would never now return behind its walls. She had seen for herself how easily a Queen could be deposed and sometimes, when the mood took her, she would stand behind the screen which her husband always used when he wished to inspect his Harim unseen. It amused Tyi to watch her rival, the former Great Queen, sitting with her sisters – just a Harim-woman now; yet the sight also offered a terrible warning, for Tyi knew that, until she had given her husband a son, her position would never be wholly secure. In truth though, for all King Amen-hetep's power, she soon learned to despise him, for she saw that he was lazy and loved only his pleasures, and so she made herself adept at providing him with those, confident that it needed no greater skill to rule him. As Tyi began to twist him round and round her finger, so King Amen-hetep grew ever more besotted until at last it was he who was frantic to please her. Watching how she loved to walk beside the lake, the scene of her happiest childhood hours, he enlarged the lake and built a palace on its shores, richer and more splendid than any palace seen before. Upon the waters by its walls a golden barge was moored; and it was upon this same barge that Queen Tyi would be rowed, across the artificial lake or along the flow of the Nile, dressed in jewellery bright with precious stones, and surrounded by her lions, seated on her throne. To the crowds gathered along the shore, eagerly awaiting her scattered munificence, she appeared a vision drawn from the tales of the gods – and indeed, she had always been spoken of in whispered terms of awe. For people knew how she had survived her fall from the Harim, they wondered at the lions always padding at her heel, and they marked how King Amen-hetep, in the massive sculptures of himself, had his wife portrayed on an identical scale. All these were strange and unheard-of wonders; and so it was no surprise that, as the years began to pass, men started to think of her as a great and fearsome god – greater even, it was whispered, than Pharaoh himself.

But Tyi, brought up in the Harim far away from the world and sometimes still an innocent despite her best attempts, remained ignorant of the effect which she had had upon her subjects. It was her father who finally brought it to her attention. He found her one morning, seated upon the terrace which looked out across the lake, very near to the spot where they had always been accustomed to sit. He stood above her in silence a moment. 'I have been hearing strange things of you,' he said at last, dropping a bracelet into her lap.

Tyi picked it up and inspected it closely. There was a plaque lined with gold and crafted from cornelian. It portrayed a goddess with wings and the body of a lion, and the head of a queen which Tyi at once knew was herself. She clapped her hands with delight. 'But it is exquisite!' she exclaimed.

'No,' said her father. 'No, it is not.'

Tyi looked up in surprise. His tone had seemed angry, yet her father had never been angry with her before. 'I do not see the harm.'

'Look at it more closely.' Her father snatched it from her hand. 'Can you not see? You have been portrayed as a deadly thing, hungry for prey. People dread you, O my daughter, even as they love you and worship you, for it is said that you are the goddess of the wild beasts of the sand.'

'Is that my fault?' asked Tyi with a lazy shrug. She reached down to stroke the head of one of her lions, asleep by her side. 'I cannot help what people want to believe.'

'You must disavow it at once.'

'Disavow it?'

'You must proclaim to the people that you cannot be a god, for there is only one true God in Whose hands are all things.'

Tyi sat in silence a long while until at last, failing to meet her father's eyes, she lowered her own and looked away. Joseph sighed and crossed to the steps where the lake waters were gently lapping, a shimmering blue against the marble of the stone.

'I cannot surrender this,' Tyi whispered softly as she gestured to where her golden barge lay moored. 'Not all this.'

'You would not need to.'

'It is easy for you to say that. You are a man. You do not face the risk of being returned to the Harim.'

Joseph smiled at her ruefully, but still he shook his head. 'You may be certain, O my child, that your destiny is a great one, for it was revealed years before, in a dream which was sent by the will of the All-High.' And so saying, Joseph crossed to her and took her by the hand, raising her up to hold her in his arms; and he told her King Thoth-mes' dream of the valley of the tombs, and of its meaning that the curse in the royal blood-line would one day be cleansed.

But when he had finished, Tyi frowned and shook her head. 'If it was my mother whom King Thoth-mes saw holding the jar of water, then how can you be so certain when you speak of my destiny? You might just as well speak of Inen's or of Ay's.'

At once, as she looked up into her father's face, she saw a grey look of pain; and she remembered how she had seen such an expression only one time before, when she had shown herself to him for the first time on the evening after her fall. 'What is it?' she whispered. 'Please – you are frightening me now.'

She could barely breathe, so tight was her father's embrace. 'You will always love me, I trust,' he whispered at last.

'But . . . yes . . . yes, of course . . . why would I not?'

'I . . .' Her father breathed in deeply. 'I did not tell you everything when I told you King Thoth-mes' dream. There was something else – something which the King could never bring himself to say, but wrote upon papyrus on the same day that he died.'

'What?'

'You may read it for yourself.'

Tyi took the papyrus which her father handed her. She

read it very fast, then slowly once again. 'I . . . I do not understand.'

Joseph smiled bitterly. 'Why, is the meaning not as clear as the sunlight of day? In his dream, even as he watched your mother pouring water from the jar, King Thoth-mes saw himself taking her and filling her with his seed. Certainly, he did not require me to interpret such a vision.'

'How . . . how do you mean?'

Joseph's smile grew tighter. 'When I read the papyrus which King Thoth-mes had given me, I approached your mother's servant, who confirmed for me that once, some nine months before, the King had given her a potion and ordered her to give it to her mistress that same evening. I have no doubt that the potion served to plunge your mother into sleep; nor do I doubt what King Thoth-mes' business with her must have been upon that night. I know his dream had been weighing sorely on his mind. He must have thought it a sacred command, sent to him by his gods, to do what he did behind the back of me, his friend.'

'No.' Tyi shook her head. 'No. For, surely . . . is it not possible . . .' She swallowed, then looked away. 'How can you be certain?'

'I was not – not for a long while – not until I saw you alive despite your fall from the Harim roof. Then I knew that . . . that the blood in your veins could not be mine.' He smiled at her sadly and stood frozen a moment, then folded her tightly in his arms once again. 'You will always be my daughter,' he whispered. 'My youngest, dearest child.'

Tyi felt the tears wet against the side of her cheek, and she kissed his own gently, then wiped the tears away with her hair. 'O my father . . .' she whispered.

He looked at her, and despite his sadness he smiled.

'The marks of this blood-line – you said they were a curse?'

'So I fear.'

'What might this curse be?'

He shrugged very faintly. 'I cannot say. All I do know is . . .' – he paused a moment, swallowing, then looking down at the bracelet, at the portrait on its plaque – 'you must stay true to the will of the All-High. Look upon that. Look upon it closely.' He pressed the bracelet back into his daughter's hand. 'Be warned by what you see, and guard yourself well.'

Tyi gazed at her portrait a long while in silence. 'I remember,' she said at last, 'on the evening of the announcement that I was to be the Great Queen, Inen came to me and said how he wished that things were different. I have often wondered what he meant by that, what he might have known.'

Joseph frowned coldly and turned away. 'A great many things, no doubt.'

'It is seven years now since I saw him last.'

'And in that time he will doubtless have learned even more, for he is very high now, I hear, in the favour of the temple.'

'Do you think he would tell me any secrets he might know?'

'If he was willing to trample upon the love of his father, and turn to the worship of sorcery and idols, then do you think he would betray his precious secrets to you?'

'It may be.' Tyi smiled, then fastened the bracelet round her wrist. 'For remember, I am not only his sister, I am also his Queen.'

And so it was that same evening, when she lay by King Amen-hetep's side, that she repeated everything which she had learned that afternoon, and her husband listened in great confusion and wonder. Seeing this, Tyi determined to press her advantage, and so she demanded that the High Priest be summoned straight away, to reveal to them both all the secrets which he knew. King Amen-hetep, however, grew pale and shook his head, for he dreaded, he confessed, to cross the High Priest of Amen, since the powers of his sorcery lay beyond all mortal scope. But Tyi did not despair, having long grown used to her husband's terror of the god, and so she worked hard all that night to alter his resolve. Such were her skills, and her arts of persuasion, that in the end she succeeded; and the next morning, together, they proceeded to the temple.

Tyi marked, as they passed through the outer court, with its clanging of gongs, its chanting of prayers, its cries of terror from the sacrificial animals, how her husband-brother had once again grown pale, but she refused to meet his eye and continued along the route. Beyond the second court were two enormous doors, and Tyi gestured to the servants to have them flung apart. As they were swung open, she saw beyond them a vast and flickering darkness, and she felt in her own heart, to her surprise, a touch of fear. 'O great Pharaoh, O great Queen,' an unseen voice rang out, 'you are about to pass from the realm of man into that of mystery, and of the star-dwelling gods. Cross the boundary of the secret realm!'

For the first time since entering the temple, Tyi allowed herself to meet her husband's eye, but then she turned again and did as the voice had commanded. Passing through the doors, she saw a priest waiting for them, and it took her a moment to recognise Inen, her brother. It was not, though, that he had changed – rather that, despite the passage of seven summers, he had not changed at all. His face was unlined, his body still firm, and he seemed younger, Tyi thought, than she did herself. 'But Inen,' she whispered, 'you are my elder. How can this be?'

Inen did not answer her, however, nor even meet her eye, but turned instead and led the way towards a further gate. It opened ahead of him, and Tyi saw that beyond it there waited another further gate. On and on they led, the roofs of each room becoming ever lower, and the darkness deeper and lit by fewer candles, so that the talismans carved upon the walls could not be read. It seemed to Tyi that the shadows were mocking her ignorance, and she felt her anger flare and ordered Inen to stop.

He turned, impassive.

'What is the secret of this place,' she demanded, 'and of the royal blood-line which I share with great Pharaoh?'

'It is not yet the time for you, O my sister, to find out.'

'I am the Queen!' Tyi cried. 'I may find out what I wish!'

'No.' Inen's voice was suddenly brusque and very firm. 'Pharaoh may come' – he bowed very low – 'for he is ready now to glimpse the mysteries of Amen, and to learn what it means to be descended from the gods. But you, O my sister – you must still wait.' And so saying, he turned and walked a few paces on, then rapped upon two doors which were small and set deep in the furthermost wall. They opened with a strange sound, gliding apart without the aid of human hand, and Tyi gazed at them in wonder, for she knew that she was in the presence of a terrible sorcery.

Inen beckoned to King Amen-hetep. He glanced once more at Tyi, his eyes bulging from his head; then he passed very slowly into the darkness beyond. Tyi moved to follow him and brush Inen aside, but he blocked her path, and even as he did so the doors behind him glided shut again. 'I am sorry,' he whispered, 'but you must have patience, O my sweet, much loved sister. For why else would we have permitted you to enter so far into this temple, unless to give you a foretaste of the secrets which will come?'

Tyi breathed in deeply, and did not meet his eye, but gazed upon the doors barring her way. They seemed made of a strange metal, very bright and smooth, and inscribed with markings in an unknown language. She frowned, trying to make sense of them, then shuddered, for she realised that she had never seen their like before – that for all she knew, they might indeed have come from a world of strange gods. 'Our father . . .' she whispered, glancing at Inen, '*our father* – he was right. This is a hellish place.'

She turned and began to hurry back towards the daylight. Inen, though, ran after her and seized her by the arm. 'Trust me,' he whispered, 'I beg you, please!'

'Then tell me what the secret of this place is, for I fear it terribly.'

'I cannot.' Inen glanced about him, then lowered his voice still more. 'But I swear it, O my sister, that the time will come when you will understand.' He glanced round hurriedly again, then kissed her hand. 'Everything that I am doing – O Tyi, it is all for you.'

Then he turned again and vanished back into the shadows, so that Tyi was left alone to return towards the light. All that day, in great perplexity, she pondered her brother's words and awaited her husband's return with impatience, confident that he at least would be able to keep back nothing from her. But when he finally reappeared he would say not a word, although his face appeared expressive of a terrible shock, and all that night he muttered and moaned in his sleep. The next morning, Tyi pressed him on the secret once again; but again he resisted her most enticing persuasions. 'It is forbidden,' he whispered, the colour draining from his cheeks, as he seemed to drift at the same time into unbidden thoughts. He began to extend his fingers, then to stretch his limbs, as though he had never properly been aware of them before. Tyi gazed at him, alarmed, and sought to take him in her arms, but he shuddered horribly and brushed her away. Then suddenly, as though waking from a nightmare, he stared at her in confusion and reached after her once more;

and as he did so, he caught sight of the bracelet on her wrist. 'What is this?' he asked, inspecting the image; and then he threw back his head, and began to laugh.

'What is it?' Tyi demanded.

Still Pharaoh laughed.

'What is it?' she screamed, in a wild fury now. 'You cannot keep what you know from me any longer!'

At once Pharaoh's laughter died upon his lips. 'I can,' he whispered. 'I can, and I do. For indeed, it fills me with such horror that I can scarcely bear to think of it, still less put it into words.' Then he brushed her away again, and would say nothing more; and Tyi flushed, and felt a panic start to surge up within her. She listened to Pharaoh's footsteps as they echoed into silence, then touched the bracelet with its image on her wrist, recalling that it had been her intention and solemn vow to hurl the thing away. She inspected it closely, frowning, then turned to see where her three lions lay. Tyi crossed to them and stroked their thick, black manes, as was her habit whenever she found herself angry or distressed. Then, sitting down beside them, she inspected the portrait closely once again. She knew already that she would not dispose of it. For what other piece of evidence, what other clue did she possess, in her quest to discover the nature of her blood? There was only the memory of King Amen-hetep laughing, laughing wildly as at a hidden joke, at the image of herself as a ravening lion; and yet however hard she tried, Tyi could not see the joke.

———————

But at this point, Haroun saw the approach of morning and broke off from his tale. 'O Commander of the Faithful,' he said, 'if you would care to return here tomorrow evening, then I shall describe to you the anxieties and the discoveries of Queen Tyi.'

And so the Caliph did as Haroun suggested; and the following evening he returned to the mosque.

And Haroun said:

In the weeks that followed, and then the months and then the years, Tyi came to treasure the bracelet which her father had first brought her as though it were a charm, a pledge that the temple's secrets would indeed one day be hers. That her husband already knew them was something that she never ceased to resent, nor to fret over; for it seemed to her that, since their visit to the temple, she had lost her power to rule him, and she was constantly afraid that it might slip utterly away. Certainly King Amen-hetep was often in the temple of Amen, and his silence as to what he did there was as total as before. But all the same, Tyi had noticed a subtle change in his manner which was always most pronounced when he came back from the temple, for his laziness then seemed banished and his appetites renewed, and it was sometimes all that she could do to keep pace with his demands. At other times, he would journey for days into the desert, and would not return until vast numbers of animals had been slain, so that their carcasses could be dragged back in triumph through the dust, and the evidence of the slaughter piled before the Palace. Tyi would survey the fly-blown corpses with disgust, then reach for her lions as they fretted at her feet, and seek to calm both her restless animals and herself, hugging them tightly and stroking their manes. Sometimes, in an effort to purge the stench from her nostrils, she would order her barge to sail across the lake, and watch the bright-plumed birds as they rose against the sky, and breathe in the scent of lilies on the breeze. Such pleasures grew ever more precious to her, the more threatened they came to seem; for with each day that King Amen-hetep spent abroad upon the hunt, away from her presence and her influence, so the higher the walls of the Harim seemed to rise, and the darker their shadow seemed to fall across Tyi's thoughts.

It was when King Amen-hetep announced his intention to journey to war, to ride with his troops against the far-off Asian tribes, that she could be certain that her influence was under mortal threat at last. Only a son now, she thought, would renew it once again, and so her yearning for one grew ever more desperate and urgent. But King Amen-hetep, excited by the prospect of war, scarcely visited her bed before his departure from Thebes – and Tyi knew, even as she watched him riding away, that she was not with his child. It would be a long wait, she feared, before he came to her again, and indeed the weeks began to drag and then to lengthen into months. Sometimes a letter would be brought in which Pharaoh would describe in high excitement an annihilation of his foes, how he was a 'raging fire', a 'fierce-eyed lion'; but there was little hint, amidst the boasts, that he was missing Tyi at all.

It was with trepidation, then, and a certain grim resolve, that she heard the news at last of Pharaoh's imminent return. It was brought to her by Ay, already Egypt's most celebrated general, who had been sent ahead to Thebes in command of the advance guard, to escort the treasures plundered in the wars. And yet in truth, so Ay revealed, there had barely been any wars, for there had barely been any enemies strong enough to fight – and so King Amen-hetep had contented himself with the pillaging of towns, and the occasional massacre, whenever he found himself growing too bored. Indeed, so Ay reported, he had appeared uninterested in anything much at all save for the capture of prisoners, of which there were now many hundreds loaded down with chains, and being brought in the train of the army back to Thebes.

'And me?' Tyi dared to ask her brother at last. 'Did he never mention or seem interested in me?'

Ay smiled at her, then shrugged and took her by the hands. 'You must get him a son.'

She cried out in frustration. 'As if you need to tell me that!'

'Why,' Ay frowned, 'there is not a problem, I trust?'

'How can I know?' Tyi swallowed very deeply, but suddenly she could no longer keep back her tears. Ay reached out for her and she buried her face against her brother's barrel-chest, sobbing uncontrollably, until at last her anger and her passion had been spent and she sat again dully, the tears drying on her cheeks.

Ay scratched his head. 'You should pay a call upon my wife, the Lady Tiya.'

Tyi frowned. 'Why?'

'She is wise in many arts.'

'Arts? What do you mean?'

'The sacred arts. For you know that the Lady Tiya is the High Priestess of Isis.'

'What of it?'

'Isis is a goddess of powerful magic.'

Tyi stared at him in disbelief. 'Magic?' she repeated. Then she frowned and shook her head. 'Not you as well, O my brother! What will our father say?'

Ay shrugged. 'Why does he need to know?'

'No.' Tyi shook her head. 'No, I cannot.'

Ay shrugged again. 'Very well – as you please. But should you change your mind . . . I know that my Lady will be eager to help you. Decide soon, though, O my sister. Pharaoh should be here by tomorrow night.'

He kissed Tyi briefly and then strode away, leaving her alone. All that day and evening, Ay's words gnawed at her thoughts. She had been determined at first not to betray her father's trust, to stay faithful to the worship of the One and Only God; but then, as she walked by the side of her lake, she realised again how beautiful and precious it was, and felt that to lose her throne would be a form of death. She glanced down at her reflection. It shocked her to see how much her beauty had faded, for her face had grown thin, and her legs and arms too. 'I am almost a dry, old woman,' she thought.

Upon a sudden impulse, she called for a cloak and swathed herself beneath its folds; then she walked to the Harim and stood behind its screen, watching the women in the garden below her. There were many, she saw, who wore wigs in the Nubian style, fashioned in imitation of herself, the Great Queen; and one of them, she realised with a sudden shock, was her long-deposed rival, the former Great Queen, who had once pulled her hair and mocked it for its ugliness. Tyi smiled; but the sweetness of her triumph seemed strangely bitter all the same. The taste of it resolved her: she hurried back into the night.

Even so, as she approached her brother's house, it was with a sense of trepidation. Ay had not lied to her: strange things were indeed spoken of the Lady Tiya's powers, for it was claimed that, like Isis, the goddess whom she served, she was 'Great of Magic', and could read the meaning of the stars. Tyi paused uncertainly by the entrance to the house, but the Lady Tiya, it seemed, had been expecting her arrival, for she appeared suddenly in the doorway without announcement. She took her guest by the hand with a silent smile and led her out into the cool of the garden, walled and secluded from any prying eye. Even so, Tyi still looked about her, nervous and unsure. 'My father,' she whispered, 'he must never find out.'

Tiya smiled and shook her head, and then gazed up at the stars. 'Does he not say how his god formed the heavens and the stars?'

Tyi bowed her head. 'He does.'

'Then where is the fault if we read the patterns there enshrined?'

Despite herself, Tyi raised her gaze towards the sky. 'You can understand what they say?'

Tiya nodded very gently. 'It is said, in our deepest mysteries, how the Lady Isis had the knowledge of every secret contained within the stars, for it was she who had gained the wisdom of the secret name of Amen and all the magic which it bore.'

'And what can you read, then, in the heavens tonight?'

Tiya smiled, then whispered urgently in her companion's ear. 'Tomorrow! When Pharaoh returns – it must be tomorrow!'

Tyi breathed in with relief. 'And that is all I have to do? Sleep with him tomorrow?'

'You will certainly then be granted a child, for I have read the patterns of the stars of your birth and there can be no mistaking them. Yet there is still one problem. They promise you a girl.'

'No.' Tyi felt her spirits plunging back into despair. 'No, no, I must have a son!'

Tiya raised her hand. 'All is not lost.'

'What must I do?'

'When I read the pattern of your stars, I read my own one as well. I am promised a son if I sleep with my husband tomorrow. Twin destinies, then – but different ends. They must be mingled, intermixed – somehow exchanged . . .'

'You think that can be done?'

'It may be – by the most secret magic of the goddess which I serve.' So saying, Tiya reached for a box by her feet and, picking it up, laid it carefully on her lap. 'What you are about to see,' she whispered, 'is a glimpse of a wonder which very few have seen, for it is the true form of She Who

Dwelt Beyond the Stars, the Lady of the Place of the Beginning of Time. Do not betray my trust then, O Queen, for I take a great risk in revealing this mystery to you.'

'I swear by the God of my father,' Tyi answered, 'that I shall never breathe a word.'

Tiya removed the lid, to reveal two tiny figurines.

'What are they?' Tyi exclaimed, picking one up and studying it closely, for she had never before seen an image so unsettling. It was of a woman, garbed in the crown and regalia of the Lady Isis, but with long, thin legs and a swollen belly, a narrow face and a swollen skull. Tyi shivered with revulsion, then glanced up at Tiya. 'Why do you portray your goddess in this way?'

'Because this is how she looked when she first came from the stars, she and Osiris and their brother Seth. It is a memory which has been guarded in the temples since the First Time, when the gods taught the arts of living to mankind.'

'And what of these portraits? Do they too possess the power of sorcery?'

'So we must trust,' Tiya smiled. 'For it is written, in the most secret and ancient of our texts, how man was first formed by mixing blood and clay, and brought to life by the power of Isis, when she spoke the magic of the Secret Name of Amen. Therefore' – she reached by her side for a golden knife – 'we must trust that such magic is not wholly dead. Give me your wrist, O mighty Queen.'

Tyi did as she was commanded, and, with a nick of the blade, a thin cut was drawn. Tiya positioned it so that the blood fell upon one of the figurines, then cut her own wrist and spilt her blood across the second. The strangely domed skulls were spattered with red spots, and then the clay began to drink it, sucking on it deep. Tiya reached down and held the figurines up to the moon. 'Blood of blood,' she whispered, 'dust of dust,' and then she threw the figurines hard against the ground. They shattered at once into tiny fragments and Tiya mingled the debris with the tip of her toe, round and round, until it was no longer possible to tell the two of them apart. When all was done, she scooped up the dust, and tossed it away so that it was caught upon the breeze. 'O Lady Isis,' she whispered, 'hear your servant's prayers.' Then she turned back to Tyi; she smiled and took her hands, squeezing them tightly. 'Now you know what you must do.' She smiled again. 'Tomorrow night, O Queen. It must be tomorrow night!'

Tyi prepared for it the next day with her deepest skill and care. She bathed a long while, then ordered her limbs to be anointed and perfumed. Watching as it was done, she thought again how strangely thin her legs and arms had become, but she did her best to put them from her mind. When her body had been prepared to her satisfaction, she ordered her most beautiful gown and most precious jewels to be brought to her and, having been adorned in them, commanded her favourite maid to style her hair. As the girl set to work, Tyi sat with a mirror inspecting her face. Again, as with her limbs, she felt appalled to gaze upon it, to see how narrow and high-boned her features had become. 'Like the statues,' Tyi thought suddenly, 'the figurines of Isis'; and at once she felt the shadow of a strange thought fall across her mind. 'No,' she told herself, 'no, it is not possible'; yet still the memory of the figurines remained before her eyes. Then suddenly she heard her maid breathe in deeply and, turning round, caught an expression of wonder and disgust upon her face. 'What is it?' Tyi demanded. 'Tell me. Do not fear.'

The girl shuddered. 'O my mistress,' she whispered, 'I am sorry, very sorry . . .'

'Tell me – please.'

'Your skull,' the girl whispered. 'Your skull – your skull . . .'

Tyi raised her mirror and bent her head forward, then at once dropped the mirror so that it shattered on the floor. At the same moment she rose to her feet, abandoning her toilet, and screaming for a litter to the temple of Amen. Arriving there, she found the gates of the inner courtyard closed, but as she had done before, Tyi ordered them flung open and passed at once into the darkness beyond. Door after door she similarly commanded to be opened, so that she penetrated ever deeper into the temple, until at last she came to the place where she had reached once before, there to find that the doors of metal could not be forced. Tyi began to strike upon them, crying out loudly for her brother, until at last they glided open and Inen emerged.

Tyi lifted off her wig and pointed to her skull. 'See, O my brother!' she hissed. 'See how it is swollen! Do not hide from me any longer what I am becoming, for I have glimpsed the hidden image of the gods from the First Time. No more secrets, then, no more silence! It is time you told me all!'

Inen stood motionless a moment, then kissed her suddenly on her cheeks. 'You are right,' he whispered. 'The time has come indeed.'

He turned and passed back between the open doors, and Tyi – following him through – found herself walking down a long, thin room, very dark and swathed in smoke. Along its side ran a channel such as she had in her own chamber, leading to her bath; and indeed, as she peered through the clouds of incense, she saw a circular pool, empty of water, into which the channel seemed to lead. Beyond the pool there stood the single silhouette of a man, and beyond the man a mighty altar. Otherwise the chamber was empty, and Tyi wondered what secret it could possibly contain.

'Wait here,' Inen ordered as they reached the pool. Tyi did as her brother had commanded, then watched him continue round the pool's edge and approach the man on its opposite side. He began to whisper in his ear, sometimes turning and pointing back at Tyi, and she was able to observe, peering through the incense-clouds, that the man was shaven-headed and dressed like her brother; and she knew that he could only be the High Priest of Amen. Studying his face, she began to understand why King Amen-hetep should have dreaded him so much, for there seemed something barely mortal about him, something predatory and cold, as though he were one of those cobras which she had occasionally discovered, coiled within the shade of the Palace walls. Thinking this, and recalling the ageless appearance of such serpents, Tyi suddenly knew what it was she found so strange in the High Priest: it was not that he was lined, or withered, or stooped, for in truth, in his looks he was as youthful as Inen – yet still, for all that, Tyi felt certain that he was fantastically old. As he began to round the pool and approach her, she could not restrain a shudder; and the High Priest, observing this, bared his teeth in a smile which seemed both mocking and cruel.

Yet as he approached her, he reached out and touched her on her arm in a gesture of reassurance. 'It is no wonder you are afraid,' he said softly, 'for I can well imagine how unsettling it must be to discover the meaning of your descent from the gods.'

'The meaning?'

The High Priest tightened his grip upon her arm and led her across to the wall beyond the channel. There were portraits upon it, carved into the stone – thin-limbed, round-bellied, with giant, swollen skulls. 'Isis?' Tyi whispered, pointing at one whose regalia she remembered from the evening before.

The High Priest nodded. 'And here . . .' – he pointed – 'Osiris – and Seth. The gods of the First Time. The gods who made man.'

'And Amen?' Tyi whispered.

The High Priest frowned. 'Why, what of him?'

'Is this not his temple?'

'True.' He breathed in deeply. 'Yes, very true.'

'Then are there no portraits of him here to be seen?'

'No.' The High Priest spoke the word with unexpected force. 'For he is the god who is within here but can never be glimpsed, whose name is the source of the power of this world.'

'And what is that power?'

'It is the power with which the gods fashioned man out of mud. It is the power of the blood which they have within their veins. And it is the power, therefore, O Queen' – he looked her up and down – 'which exists within you and your veins as well.'

As he said this, his stare seemed so glittering and eager that Tyi, despite herself, took a step back. She reached up to touch the back of her skull. 'How shall I recognise this power within me, then?'

'In many ways,' the High Priest smiled, 'for you and your line have been blessed above all mortals.'

'Tell me,' Tyi whispered. 'Tell me what I am.'

The High Priest glanced at Inen, and smiled once again. 'After the gods had fashioned man and brought him to life by the power of Amen's name, they slept with the fairest of their new creations – and their children, O Queen, were the first of your kind. The gods have long since left Egypt and returned to the heavens, but their descendants still sit upon the Throne of the Two Lands. And I' – he gestured to Inen – 'we – the priests who guard the mysteries of the gods – are the heirs to those who first guarded the blood-line, and who have handed down the secret from the very dawn of time.'

Tyi gazed between the two of them, back and forth. 'That, then,' she whispered, 'was the reason you would not permit me at first to be Great Queen?'

The High Priest nodded. 'The purity of the blood-line must always be preserved.'

'But then,' Inen smiled, 'when you fell from the Harim roof, we knew that you possessed the sacred blood after all. For it is the quality of those who own it, O my sister, that they can survive what to others would be certain death.'

'And yet . . .' – Tyi frowned and narrowed her eyes – 'when you had first discovered what I was, on the evening when Pharaoh proclaimed me Great Queen, you came to me, did you not, O my brother, and told me how you wished that things had been different? Did you not, O Inen? Tell me – did you not?'

Inen glanced at the High Priest, then took his sister's hands. 'It is true,' he whispered, 'that the power of Amen which courses within you is a thing of the heavens and the far-away stars, and therefore not of this world at all. Do not be surprised, then, if in its outward appearance it should sometimes seem a thing of horror to men.'

'How do you mean?' Tyi whispered, her voice hoarse now with suspicion.

Inen glanced at the High Priest again, then past him towards the portraits of the gods upon the wall. 'Do you wonder,' he asked Tyi, 'that we keep the truth of their appearance veiled from mortal eyes, and portray them instead as being like their worshippers? So also, O my sister, we must do now with you.'

'What, you do not mean . . . it is not possible . . . that I will end up as loathsome to look at as these gods?'

'Unless – precautions – are taken, yes, you will.'

'"Precautions"?' Tyi whispered. 'What . . . "precautions"?'

Inen turned to the High Priest, who stood motionless a while and then slowly nodded his head. Tyi observed how her brother glanced down at the channel, then back towards a side-door from which the channel led. 'Come,' he said softly, taking her by the hand. He escorted her towards the empty pool and then ordered her, very calmly, to remove her jewellery and to undress.

'Before you?' Tyi gazed at him in horror. 'I shall never do that!'

'And yet you must. Do not fear – I shall not watch.'

'I cannot.'

'Very well.' Inen shrugged. 'Then you know what you will become.'

Tyi closed her eyes. When she opened them again, Inen met them for a moment, then turned and looked away. Tyi breathed in deeply before reluctantly doing as he had ordered her.

'I am ready,' she said at last.

'Enter the bath,' Inen said, still looking away.

Tyi did so, her shoulders hunched and her arms across her breasts. The stones felt sticky and damp beneath her feet. She did not dare to look down, to see what might be there. 'O Inen,' she whispered, 'I am afraid, so afraid.'

'As well you might be,' said Inen softly. 'For what happens now is a thing of wondrous horror.'

'Why,' she stammered, 'what might it be?'

'It is the way of the divine that it must feed upon the mortal, as a hungry plant must draw upon water. Within you, O my sister, the mortal is growing dry. You must prepare then, like a plant, to be watered anew.'

'No!' Tyi cried out. She could hear from the darkness sudden muffled sounds, strange and indistinct; and, turning round, she saw that the High Priest had gone. At the same moment, she observed a flood of liquid coursing down the channel, moving very thickly, and then it started to splash down upon her where she stood in the bath. 'No!' she cried out again, then screamed, as she gazed up at the liquid and realised what it was. She began to scrabble despairingly at the side of the bath, trying to escape, but even as she sought to pull herself up she saw Inen crouched above her, shaking his head.

'I cannot endure it!' she screamed.

'And yet,' Inen whispered, 'O my beloved sister, you must.'

'No,' she sobbed, 'no . . .' When she looked up again, though, she saw that Inen was now holding a mirror in his hands. She gazed at her own reflection, streaked and damp with blood; and she gasped in amazement, seeing that her cheeks were already growing fuller, and her limbs were no longer so thin upon the bones. 'What sorcery is this?' she whispered. 'Is it my imagination, or do I see my lost beauty restored?'

'Yes, O my sister,' Inen smiled. 'That same for which Pharaoh made you his Queen.'

Tyi stared at him dumbly.

'Wash yourself,' he whispered. 'You know you must do it. You know you have no choice.'

She stood frozen a moment more, gazing up into her brother's eyes; and then she knelt and bowed her head, as more blood splashed from the channel down upon her. She reached with her hands to soap her belly and breasts, and as she did so she felt a golden warmth as sweet as a rush of love, tingling and spreading very deep into her bones. She moaned softly. All sense of time, all sense of space, seemed dissolved upon the pleasure. She barely felt the stream of warm blood start to cease, and then be replaced by a flow of clean and cleansing water. Only as Inen helped her to emerge from the bath, and to dress her in her scattered jewellery and robes, did the pleasure of the trance at last begin to fade. For a moment she smiled, gazing at her reflection in the mirror he was holding; and then she remembered. She staggered backwards, turned round and ran.

In the chamber beyond the magic doors of iron, she saw the High Priest standing by the side-wall, barely illumined in the faint wash of the candles. He smiled at her, then vanished into the shadows. Tyi ran on and, as she did so, heard footsteps behind her echoing upon the stone, drawing nearer. She glanced round, and saw Inen. Stumbling on, she knew that she would be caught, but still she continued, for she did not want him to think that she was his willing accomplice. Then at last she felt his hand reaching out to touch her arm, and then she was stopped and pushed against the wall.

'Let me go!' she screamed.

'There was no choice,' Inen hissed.

Tyi shook her head wildly.

'You knew,' Inen repeated, 'that there was no choice, not if you wished to avoid the Harim. So do not blame me, O Tyi, for it was all as you desired.'

'The blood, though,' she whispered, 'the blood, it was warm. How many of Pharaoh's prisoners, O my brother – these captives he has brought back with him here to Thebes – had to be slain so that my beauty could be restored?'

Inen smiled grimly. 'You will soon learn to forget such considerations.'

'Never.'

'Oh, but you will.'

Tyi gazed at him with hate, then twisted suddenly and broke from his grip. She began to run again.

'Wait!'

Despite herself, she froze. Such had been the note of agony, such the longing of Inen's tone, that she could not help herself. She turned again. Inen gazed at her a moment in silence, then drew near to her once more and whispered in her ear. 'I have already told you,' he whispered, 'how everything I do here is for you.' He breathed in deeply, then glanced about him. 'And in token of that promise . . .' – he reached within his cloak – 'I give you this.'

It was a bottle, which Tyi took.

'Please,' Inen whispered, 'you must keep it hidden. Do not tell a soul. It is forbidden for me to give it to such as you.'

'What is it?' Tyi asked.

'You have had it before, when I came to you and applied it to the wounds of your whipping, and then again to the bruises of your fall.'

'What should I do with it now?'

Inen smiled. 'If you would keep your beauty,' he whispered, 'then drink it with your wine.'

He kissed her fleetingly, brushing her lips, then turned and walked away, back into the temple. Tyi watched him go. She touched the bottle which she had concealed beneath the folds of her gown, and despite herself, as she did so, felt a flickering of joy and fierce excitement.

That night, when King Amen-hetep returned, Tyi was ready to welcome him. The sight of her beauty, restored to a loveliness which he had almost but never quite forgotten, dizzied him utterly. All duly happened as had been read in the stars by Lady Tiya. Nine months later, Tyi gave birth to a son.

––––––––

But at this point, Haroun saw the approach of morning and broke off from his tale. 'O Commander of the Faithful,' he said, 'if you would care to return here tomorrow evening, then I shall describe to you the adventures of Queen Tyi's son, Prince Amen-hetep.'

And so the Caliph did as Haroun suggested; and the following evening he returned to the mosque.

And Haroun said:

Prince Amen-hetep's earliest memory was of being kissed by his mother, but the second was of being licked by the tongues of her three lions. He had not known at the time that they were lions, of course; that only came later, when he had learned to understand his nurse's shrieks and her repeated insistence that lions liked to eat small children. The Prince was not a little startled by this warning, for until that time he had rather assumed that they were creatures like himself; and certainly the lions, who continued to groom him, appeared to believe that the Prince was just like them. Nor him alone, for they also tended his dearest comrade, Kiya, the daughter of the Prince's Uncle Ay, who had been born (so his mother said) on the very day that he had, and whom the Prince therefore assumed had been created just for him. Wherever they went to play, there the lions would pad about them, growling lazily at anyone who dared to draw near; and at night when they slept together, the lions would lie in a tangled ring about the children's bed – a circle of fur, and manes, and twitching tails, guardian spirits such as none of the nurses dared disturb.

It was not surprising then that it was soon widely claimed, by those who saw the two children abroad, that they were protected by a strange and dangerous magic, and had been marked out by fate for miraculous things. In their faces there was a beauty such as it was said inspired the nightingales to sing, and in their limbs a radiance which rendered many afraid, for it seemed bright like the sun or the stare of a god. Some people, meeting with the Prince as he clung to a lion's mane, riding on the beast's back as though it were a horse, or with Kiya as she ran with the creatures by the lake, imagined indeed that they were glimpsing gods, and grew perturbed when later they discovered the truth. A few complained to the Keeper of the Harim that it was not proper for a girl of Kiya's age to run about so freely; and the Keeper, who agreed, ordered her to remain henceforth within the Harim, along with the Prince's younger sisters.

But the Prince, when he learned this, was plunged into the depths of wretchedness, and was discovered by his mother, Queen Tyi, in floods of tears. She raised him in her arms and kissed him tenderly, wiping away his tears with her hair; but when she had learned the cause of his sorrow, she smiled strangely to herself and promised her son that Kiya would soon be released. And so it proved, that very same day; nor was Kiya ever kept within the Harim walls again.

Indeed, from that time on, it seemed to the Prince that there was nothing which his mother could not achieve. Even the passage of the years seemed her slave, for unlike every other woman she appeared not to age, and her beauty remained in perpetual spring; but when the Prince asked her why, she would smile and touch her lips. Then it happened that one of the lions, who were by now all very old, fell sick so that even Pharaoh's best physician, a man of great skill, despaired of its life. But Tyi, when the news was brought to her, came to the sick-bed where the dying lion lay, and as she knelt by its side it whimpered softly and lifted its head, trying to lick the hand of its mistress, but in vain. The Prince watched wonderingly as a single tear welled in his mother's eye; and then she reached within her gown and drew out a flask. Within it there was a liquid, very sticky and black, and his mother poured it out between the lion's unresisting jaws.

A minute passed – and the lion yawned. It stretched very slowly, then lumbered to its feet. Another yawn, and then suddenly it began to run, round and round, as though chasing the breeze, as though it were a cub and had never been sick at all.

Yet there were some griefs, the Prince was soon to learn, which not even his mother could ease away. Some years later, when he and Kiya were out upon the sands, one of the lions disappeared and could not be found until at last, after several days and nights of search, its corpse was discovered half-eaten by the birds. Its two companions approached it, and sniffed at its flanks; then they seemed to sigh, and slumped down, one on either side. The Prince sent a message at once to his mother, but although she hurried she arrived too late, for the lions were already dead, a tangled bundle with their fellow as they had so often been in life. Tyi ordered them buried; but even as the grave was dug, the Prince and Kiya clung to the lions' sides, ears pressed to their hearts, as though in disbelief that there was nothing any longer to be heard. 'Can you not bring them back?' the Prince asked his mother, gazing at her despairingly as the bodies were laid within their graves. 'Bring them back, as you did before.'

But his mother shook her head. 'It is the way of the world. All things must die.'

'Must I die?'

She gazed at her son strangely. 'You are the descendant of a god,' she said at last. 'That makes you different.'

The Prince considered this a moment. 'Then why can I not bring the lions back to life?'

His mother continued to stare at him a moment longer, a brittle smile now upon her lips, but then she turned to glance out at the burning red sands and her face grew suddenly as blank as the desert. 'Because the gods,' she murmured, 'do not bring life but, to those who are not of their kind, only death.' She turned back to face her son. 'I tell you,' she whispered, clasping him in her arms, 'that the time will come when you, even you, will not only witness but bring death yourself – for that, as I have said, is the way of the world.' Then she kissed him on the ruffled tangle of his hair, and on his lips, but did not talk to him again during all their journey back to the Palace.

Her words, though, remained with the Prince. He was afraid to share them with Kiya, who stayed silent and puffy-eyed upon her bed all that morning, as though his presence were reminding her of the beasts no longer there; and when he tried to rouse her she turned and curled up, staring at the wall. The Prince left her and sat for a while by the fountains, then rose and ran down to the side of the lake. He knew it was the habit of his grandfather Yuya, at such an hour, to take a walk along the path; and sure enough, hurrying to the lakeside, the Prince saw the familiar, much-loved figure of his grandfather ahead of him. Running to join him, he took the old man's hand and they continued together, neither saying a word. At length, arriving by a spring beneath the shelter of a tree, Joseph halted and smiled, and sat himself down. 'When she was a girl,' he told the Prince, suddenly breaking the silence, 'this was always your mother's favourite place.'

The Prince nodded dumbly and sat down close by his grandfather's side, clutching him tightly.

'Tell me,' said Joseph at last, feeling his grandson start to shake, 'what is it, O my grandson, that is weighing on your heart?'

Still the Prince sat hugging him until at last, without looking up, he repeated what his mother had told him that morning.

Joseph sighed, so that it suddenly seemed to the Prince,

watching his grandfather, that he was far more frail and old than he had ever realised. 'Your mother,' he said at last, 'did not always think the power which rules this world to be so cruel.'

'But what do you think?'

'What have I always taught you? That there is only one God, and His rule is good.'

'Yes.' The Prince considered this. 'So one of you must be wrong.'

Joseph shook his head smilingly and then rose to his feet, crossing out of the shade. 'See the beauty of the sun!' he exclaimed, pointing with his stick. 'How blazing it is, how wondrous, how great! It burns high above every land of this earth, so that there is no one who could ever hope to approach it – and yet the power of its rays are here all about us! For by what other means do animals exist – all the wild and beautiful creatures of this world, the birds which fly up in song into the sky, and the fish in the river and the lakes, skimming silver? And yet the sun is but the image of the One and Only God – and so I say to you, O my grandson, yes, His works are good.'

The Prince thought of the lions, buried beneath the sands. 'Then why must there be death?'

'Only He Who sees all things can know all things as well.' Joseph smiled, and half-cradled his grandson in his arms. 'Do not think, though,' he whispered, 'that death itself cannot be a blessing and relief.'

'How do you mean?'

But Joseph did not answer and the Prince gazed upwards in trepidation into his grandfather's face, thinking of how the lions had looked when they were dead. 'How do you mean?' he whispered again.

'I remember,' said Joseph at last, 'speaking to your grandfather, my friend, King Thoth-mes, of how a world so beautiful and various as this, so filled with pleasures and wonders and joys, should give us the strength to face death with bright hope. Yes, O my grandson' – he paused – 'I must die very soon, for I am old and weary, and my time is drawing near. Yet how can I doubt that all is for the best, when everywhere are the proofs of the goodness of the Creator, Who is brighter, more burning, more brilliant than the sun?' He kissed his grandson lightly on his brow, then raised up his stick towards the sky. 'When I am gone,' he whispered, 'look upon the sun, and remember what I have said. Live in truth, O my grandson, and let that be your motto – for you are called, I dare believe, to a high and wondrous purpose. Live in truth – which is to say, blessed by the warmth and the light and the power of the All-High.'

And so saying, Joseph raised his eyes to gaze into the sun and the Prince did the same, and then they bowed their heads, for they could not endure the brightness; and the Prince vowed to himself that he would do as his grandfather had instructed. From that time on, it became his practice to walk with the old man as his helper every day, and he saw for himself, what Joseph would point out to him wherever they went, how infinite were the beauties and wonders of creation, all brought into being by the rays of the sun, and the All-Mighty who dwelt beyond the brightness of its disk.

Then it happened that Joseph grew very ill, and he could no longer rise and walk abroad with his grandson, and then one day he fell asleep and he never woke again. When the news was reported, there was great grief and wailing throughout the Palace, and all of Egypt, for there had never been a servant of Pharaoh so beloved as Joseph. A great line of mourners followed his body to his tomb, to see him laid to rest within the valley's stony depths, reunited at last for all time with his lost wife. But the Prince, as he watched the stone being lowered to seal the entrance to the tomb, thought of the birds as they rose above the rushes of the lake, and of the trees which had always sheltered his grandfather's favourite spot; and he could no longer endure to remain in the valley. Instead he turned and ran, stumbling through its barren, lifeless rocks, ignoring all the cries and appeals of his mother, until at last he reached the paths where he had walked with his grandfather; and he thought again upon all which Joseph had taught.

So it was that from that time on he ignored the worship of every other god, and continued to roam with Kiya far and wide, admiring all the splendours illumined by the sun, wondering at all the living things, the animals and plants, from the giant hippopotamus to the tiniest petals on a flower, given life by the golden touch of its rays. He wondered at the fields with their clusters of wild poppies, their herds of patient cattle coated in softest, lushest mud. He wondered at the marshes, where the birds would flock as thick as the bullrushes, and snakes with fabulous patterns and flask-nosed crocodiles would lurk. He even wondered at the burning red sands, which all his countrymen detested and dreaded, for the memory of his lions still remained precious to him, and he knew it was in the desert that they had dwelt while they were free. For even in the desert, the sun provided life; and wherever there was life, there the young Prince would walk.

Yet it soon happened, such was the length of time he began to spend abroad, that his absences were brought to the attention of his father. King Amen-hetep straightaway sent for the Prince and was astonished, on seeing his son before him, to realise that he was on the verge of becoming a man, for his strength now seemed almost the equal of his beauty, which had always, since his earliest years, been wonderfully great. King Amen-hetep observed this with a strange sense of resentment, such as he did not at first altogether understand; and although he ordered his son to remain by his side, to see if he might not overcome his unease, he discovered instead that it was growing all the more. He did not care to have the Prince see him at his pleasures; he could not endure the sense of his son's eye on his wine-cup, or on his fingers as he licked them clean of a sauce. Above all he could not endure to see his son with Queen Tyi; for the sight, in a strange way, would make him feel foolish, and conscious of his belly, and of how he was growing old.

But then it happened that King Amen-hetep was struck by an idea. He had long resented the burdens of kingship, which had begun to oppress him more and more since Joseph's death, and so he resolved that his son should learn the duties of a Pharaoh, while he himself was left alone to the enjoyment of his court. So it was that the Prince was straightaway named regent, and to be sure he soon proved himself the finest kind of ruler, since he cared for the lives and fortunes of his subjects, he did not build colossal temples to himself, and he did not indulge in glamorous and pointless wars. Instead he travelled up and down the length of his country, always patient with the sufferings of the poor and the oppressed, always angered by the exposure of cruelties and bloodshed – always seeking, in short, to do as he had vowed, both to himself and to Joseph . . . to live in truth.

And then in time it happened that the Prince decided he would marry, for he desired to have Kiya by his side as his Queen; but the news, to his astonishment, met with a flat interdiction. Stirring himself from his couch, King Amen-hetep ordered his son to attend him in his throne room, where he instructed the Prince instead to marry his sister – a command which the Prince indignantly refused. King Amen-hetep was at once thrown into a stupendous fury; but although he screamed, and grew red and began to shake, so that all the vast folds of his flesh began to quiver, the Prince would not give way.

'Do as I command!' King Amen-hetep screamed.

'I shall not,' replied the Prince.

'I forbid you to marry Kiya!'

'Of course, you may do so for now.' The Prince smiled grimly. 'But the time will come, O my Father, when I am Pharaoh myself.' And then he bowed, and turned and walked quietly away; and King Amen-hetep could only splutter. But Inen, who had been standing behind a pillar of the throne room, turned to his companion, the High Priest of Amen, and whispered something urgently into his ear; and the frowns upon the faces of both men grew deeper.

The following day, while the Prince was sitting with Kiya in the garden, he was approached by his mother, who embraced her niece fondly and then asked if she would leave her alone with her son. Kiya glanced towards the Prince, but then rose and slipped away. Tyi straightaway took her son by his arm, and begged him in a low, urgent voice to marry his eldest sister, so that he could then make her his Great Queen. She did not command him, as her husband had done, nor lose her temper; yet the Prince's response, though polite, was the same. Still his mother pressed him, but he shook his head and laughed. 'I am astonished,' he exclaimed, 'that you of all people should be asking me not to make Kiya my Great Queen. Why, you were not even Pharaoh's cousin, yet you persuaded him to depose his sister in your favour.'

Tyi lowered her gaze. 'That was different,' she replied.

'How?'

Tyi shrugged helplessly. 'It was the will of the gods.'

'Then maybe it is the will of the One God – the God of your own father, do not forget – that I should marry Kiya and make her my Queen.'

Tyi shrugged helplessly again, and then she turned towards the colonnade and beckoned with a graceful gesture of her arm. The Prince watched as a priest emerged from the shadows and then, raising his hand to shade his gaze from the sun, he recognised the man as his uncle, Inen. He turned back to his mother. 'If you cannot persuade me,' he asked her, 'then why do you think he will have any greater success?'

'Because he is a man of great wisdom, who knows many secrets and sees many wondrous things.'

'But I doubt he can see as far as my grandfather did.'

The Prince watched as his mother flinched and bit her lip. Then she reached out, almost gingerly, to touch him on his forearm and kiss him on his brow. 'Would I ask you to do anything, O my beloved son,' she whispered, 'if it were not for your own good? So go with him. Listen to what he says. For it is all – I say it again – for your future good.'

The Prince frowned at her doubtfully, but then he shrugged and bowed his head, and did as she requested. He went with his uncle, who led him from the Palace and into the very depths of the temple, as far as the magical door of gliding metal, and then beyond it into the chamber with the round, empty pool. Once there, Inen pointed to the carvings on the walls, the secret portraits of Osiris and the gods, and then revealed to the Prince how his own blood was divine, descended through countless ages from the stars. 'And yet you,' he said with a sudden dry anger as arid and burning as a desert wind, 'would presume to spoil a blood-line which has flowed since the very dawn of time? Why, it is as criminal as to seek to dam the Milky Way or the sacred waters of the life-giving Nile!'

'No,' answered the Prince, 'for they are both the gifts of the One Who Dwells On High.'

'The blood-line is the gift of the great god Osiris.'

'No,' the Prince repeated, 'for there can be only one God.'

Inen smiled very thinly. 'You will not think that, O Prince, when the moment of your death arrives and you discover that in truth you will never die at all.'

'All men must die.'

Inen's smile only broadened. 'Not those of the royal blood, the blood of Osiris – the blood, O Prince, which flows within your veins.'

But the Prince laughed contemptuously. 'I have seen the tombs in which my forefathers have been laid.'

'Yet such tombs are merely the portals to the eternity of Osiris. You as well, O Prince, whether you desire it or not, will be taken there by virtue of your royal descent.'

The Prince stared at him closely a moment; then he shook his head. 'I believe neither in Osiris, nor in anything you say.'

'But the time will come when you must.'

'I do not think so.'

'But I tell you, the time will come all the same, for your blood is your fate and cannot be denied.'

'How do you mean?'

Inen did not reply; but as the Prince watched his uncle's stare, he saw that it seemed to flicker to the pool by his side, before darting back to size him up and down.

'I have had enough of this,' said the Prince with sudden impatience, and he turned to walk back through the metal doors. But his uncle pursued him and seized him by the arm. 'It were better for you,' Inen whispered, 'yes, and the Lady Kiya too, if you abandoned her now, before you ever have a child.'

'Why?' asked the Prince, feeling suddenly nervous. His question seemed to him like a fragile jar, flung from a roof and dropping through silence – and yet, though he waited, there came no impact.

At last his uncle cleared his throat. 'She is not already carrying your child, I hope?'

The Prince did not answer but, even as he sought to keep his face impassive, he knew that his uncle had read his silence.

'I had hoped,' said Inen at length, 'that it would not come to this. It is possible, of course, since the child will have your blood, that it will grow to be an order of being like yourself. More likely, however . . .' – he met the Prince's eye – 'your child will be dead before it can ever be born.'

'How can you know that? Why should it be?'

'It is, as I have said, the nature of your blood. Your child must share in it, or – I am sorry – be stillborn.' He reached out to touch his nephew's shoulder. 'And so you see,' he whispered, 'what your mother said was true – I have had nothing but your own best interests at heart.'

For a moment, the Prince stood frozen rigid; but then he shook away his uncle's hand and, turning, began to run through the many chambers of the temple, towards the distant gold of the light of the day, towards the light of the sun. Nor, for the next half-year, did he once return to the temple or speak with his uncle, ignoring his mother's most earnest pleadings but instead devoting all his time to Kiya, caring for her and his unborn child. Yet still, despite all his attentions, some weeks before the birth was finally due she was rushed into her confinement, and the child was born tiny, frail-limbed and dead. For the next week, neither the Prince nor Kiya left their chamber but remained closeted away in the privacy of their grief; and when at last the Prince emerged back into the light of the sun, his face appeared strangely harrowed and thinned.

From that moment on, he made public his devotion to the One God of Yuya – yet Joseph was dead, and he had no guide save himself. But he remembered what his grandfather had said to him, standing beneath the shade of the trees and pointing to the sun; and so the Prince gave to the All-High the Egyptian name of 'Aten', which in the language of the pagans meant 'the sun'. It was in the name of the Aten that he continued to reign, seeking to do so – as he had always done before – for the benefit of all, so that the poor, the oppressed and the powerless might approach him, just as easily as any of the great men of the Court. And so it was that one day a Nubian came to see him; very old, and covered in dust, he had travelled the whole vast distance of the Nile, from his own tiny village all the way to mighty Thebes, to ask the Prince to release his son, who had been captured and made a prisoner in King Amen-hetep's wars; and the Prince did so at once, and released all the Nubian's fellows too. Then a Syrian came, as old and wretched as the Nubian had been; and his request was the same, and the Prince's answer the same also. Then a Libyan came with a similar request; and again the Prince ordered the prisoners released. He asked that all of them give praise and thanks to the Aten, and he taught them that men were all the same beneath the sun.

But when the news was brought to him, King Amen-hetep was roused a second time from his debaucheries, and came to his son in a greater fury than before, demanding to know by what right the prisoners had been freed, when it was by his express command that they had first been brought to Thebes. Then he laughed suddenly. 'For what purpose, O my son, you will soon find out yourself.'

But the Prince shook his head and merely repeated what he had said to the liberated captives, how all were equally blessed by the sun.

At this, though, King Amen-hetep laughed bitterly once again. 'Men are not equal,' he snarled, jabbing with his finger, 'for there are those who are mortal and there are those of us who are gods. The stronger must ever feed upon the weaker, the greater upon the lesser, blood upon blood, for this world is nothing but a pattern of destruction – and it is time that you learnt to take your place within its order.'

So saying, he seized the Prince by his arm, and ordered his chariot and weapons prepared, and he led his huntsmen out into the desert, with Ay, the Prince's uncle, the Master of Chariots, at their head. A stately tent was erected for them in the shade of a cliff, filled with cushions, and gold plates, and splendid rugs; and King Amen-hetep lolled there for a day, being plied with food and wines. Then at last Ay came to him and spoke into his ear, at which the King grunted with satisfaction, and heaved himself to his feet. With the aid of two servants, he stepped into his chariot, then ordered his son to ride his own alongside. Upon the brow of a ridge, King Amen-hetep reined in his horses and the Prince, looking down, saw a flock of bleating goats. They were pawing the sands and milling frantically against a high fence made of net; and when the Prince turned to look for the cause of their terror, he saw three black-maned lions crouched low against the sands. One of these suddenly bounded forward, crushing a goat beneath its weight, and then the other two – padding forward likewise with hungry, bared-teeth snarls – similarly pounced and seized their prey beneath their paws. King Amen-hetep laughed contentedly, watching as the dull sands were stained a deeper red. He leaned from his chariot and dug the Prince in the ribs. 'And there you have it, O my son – the way of this world!'

The Prince did not answer him; for he was remembering how his mother had once said the same thing, and promised him that one day he would be the bearer of death himself. King Amen-hetep, misinterpreting his son's silence, chuckled once again, then shook out his reins and urged his chariot forward. By the fence of netting, he reined it in again while Ay, with his vast strength, bent and strung his bow. King Amen-hetep took it and drew an arrow, then aimed, and with a mighty wheeze, let the arrow go. It grazed the flank of one of the lions, who spat and snarled; then, its side streaked with red, came running forward towards the chariot. Suddenly it leapt, but could only hit the netting, and as it struggled in confusion to release itself, King Amen-hetep aimed and shot from his bow once again. Leaving the lion still struggling feebly against its bonds, he then rolled his chariot around the circuit of the fence, aiming at the infuriated lions trapped within it, until all three had been injured and made frenzied with their pain. Only then did King Amen-hetep return to his son, and hand him his bow and a quiver full of arrows.

'Finish it,' he ordered.

The Prince gazed down at the bow.

'Finish it!' King Amen-hetep bellowed, as the thick folds of his flesh began to shudder once again, and the sweat to dampen the lank strands of his hair.

The Prince dropped the arrows and the bow upon the sand.

King Amen-hetep goggled in disbelief. 'Coward!' he screamed.

The syllables echoed around and out from the cliffs, fading out into the silence of the desert. The Prince observed that all the huntsmen were perfectly motionless, and that Ay, his uncle, would not meet his eye.

'Coward!' shrieked King Amen-hetep again, tottering forward now as though to choke his son, but the Prince nimbly avoided him and jumped on to the sand. He drew out his knife and cut a hole through the fence, then approached the lion which was still tangled in the nets and being almost throttled by its attempts to save itself. As he walked across the sands, so the other two lions, arrow-gashed and foam-streaked, came bounding towards him; but the Prince turned, and met their flaming eyes, so that the lions paused in puzzlement, then slowly dropped back. The Prince continued towards the lion entangled in the netting, and freed the animal from its bonds; then he drew out the arrows embedded in its flank, while stroking its mane, so that the lion half-rolled and closed its eyes with pleasure. Then, when he had done the same with the animal's fellows, the Prince returned to the hole which he had cut into the netting and held it apart. The three lions slipped gracefully through it and paused a moment, their tails twitching, gazing up at King Amen-hetep as he sweated in his chariot; and then they tossed their manes and bounded away.

Watching them escape, the Prince approached his own chariot. As he did so, Ay stepped forward and picked up the bow and scattered arrows. He handed them across, his face perfectly motionless, but with a hint of something like amusement in his eyes; and the Prince, receiving them, passed them in turn to the King. But in King Amen-hetep's stare there was no amusement at all, as he reached out slowly to touch the face of his son. 'Your cheeks are growing hollow,' he whispered. 'You must be careful' – his fat lips flickered at last into the faintest of smiles – 'or your beauty will fade.' Then he turned and shook out his chariot reins, and bellowed a command to return to the Palace; nor did he speak to the Prince again all that journey, save to order him, as they rode at length into Thebes, to continue onwards to the temple of Amen.

Arriving together in the temple's mighty forecourt, King Amen-hetep reached out again for the face of his son, then pushed down his head so that he could feel the back of his skull. 'Yes,' King Amen-hetep whispered, 'yes, the time has come. For I tell you again, O my son, you cannot – you will not – escape what you are, but must accept, as I have done, that this world is built on blood.' Then he laughed, as though in triumph, and yet his face, so the Prince thought, seemed almost frantic with his eagerness. The Prince allowed himself to be taken and dragged by the arm; yet never, he thought suddenly, had he felt less afraid of his father, and less in awe of those secrets at which his parents had always been hinting. Even the very temple, so magnificent and vast, seemed somehow – in comparison with his previous sense of it – strangely reduced and unimpressive: for there appeared to be fewer priests and less commotion in the courtyards, and within the inner sanctuaries many of the riches and idols had been removed. Glancing at a plinth where before a statue must have stood, the Prince thought to himself how easily a god might be toppled from its place; and then, as he passed through the magic iron doors, how easily a custom, however ancient, might be changed.

And so he continued to think, even as the terrible secret was revealed to him, and the hideous purpose of the sacred bath. 'I will not do it,' said the Prince, gazing down into the empty pool. 'I will never do it.'

'But you must!' his father cried, anguish and despair intermingled with his rage. 'Or see what you must become!' He gestured towards the portraits of the gods upon the walls. 'How can you endure to become a thing like that!'

'Yet what choice do I have?' answered the Prince. 'For it is either that or become, like you, a murderer and a shedder of innocent blood. I will not be the cause of all your captives' deaths.' He met his father's stare a moment more, then turned and left the empty bath behind. Nor did he choose to visit it again but accepted, as the months and then the years began to pass, the strangeness which was moulding his form more and more. Not hiding it, he chose instead to have it proclaimed, the very mark of his ambition and intent to live in truth.

But it was noticed how from that moment on King Amen-hetep could no longer endure to be beside his son, nor even bring himself to gaze upon his face. And so he hid himself away with his pleasures and his drink, and the Prince was left to rule Egypt alone.

———————

But at this point, Haroun saw the approach of morning and broke off from his tale. 'O Commander of the Faithful,' he said, 'if you would care to return here tomorrow evening, then I shall describe to you how certain dreadful secrets were uncovered.'

And so the Caliph did as Haroun suggested; and the following evening he returned to the mosque.

And Haroun said:

Tyi had never forgotten the agonies of giving birth to the Prince, but she could tell, as she felt a sudden excruciating pain rip through her guts, that the coming birth would be infinitely worse. In the faintest of lulls, she cursed herself again . . . and the error commited some nine months before, when she had failed to resist her husband's drunken demands, and condemned herself to bearing a second child. The pain wrenched deep through her stomach again. Tyi imagined that tiny monsters were squatting all across her, pulling on her breasts, reaching deep beyond her thighs, parting the flesh and gristle of her belly, and hissing amongst themselves at the sight of what they found. Tyi could not actually see what the monsters were like, but she could feel that they were thin-limbed, and slippery to the touch, and she vaguely imagined that their skulls were very large.

Again there came the faintest lull in the pain, and Tyi

found herself held in someone's arms. She looked up. It was Kiya. 'Wha . . .' she muttered feebly, 'why . . .?'

'I heard your cries,' Kiya answered. 'I was finding it hard to sleep.'

Tyi clutched at her own belly, then gazed up at her niece's in sympathy; it was already starting to swell. No wonder, Tyi thought, that Kiya seemed so nervous. How terrible it must be to witness a foretaste of your own coming agony, and to know that it would all be in vain, for nothing . . .

The pain returned, and with it the monsters, still hissing as they dipped their fingers deep into her flesh. But then suddenly she tasted something bitter in her mouth, and swallowing, felt the pain and the monsters fade away. She opened her eyes again, wide in bemusement. Kiya was holding a flask of black liquid. 'But . . . how?' Tyi whispered, gazing at the flask. 'I thought . . . it is a deadly secret . . . Where did you find it?'

'It was your brother,' Kiya answered, 'Inen, the Priest. He remembered how cruel my pain had been before. He told me the potion was a magic charm.' She inspected it herself. 'Is it not working?'

'Yes,' Tyi nodded feebly. 'Yes.' She smiled. 'Yes.'

'You will not . . .' Kiya glanced down nervously at the bottle in her hand. 'The Prince . . . you must not tell him I have been using it. He must never know.'

'No.' Tyi smiled again; then she felt the pain return, but gentler now like a lapping wave, and she surrendered to it as though it were to sleep, for it seemed like darkness. Dimly, she felt herself being carried to her quarters, laid upon cushions, tended to by servants; and she could feel her thighs growing damp with warm blood. Then gradually, upon the flood of strange nightmares, the waves of pain began to deepen once again and she became aware of a loathsome, unnatural stench, rising, so it seemed, from the depths of her stomach. Tyi moaned, and tried to lift her head. Vaguely she could see streaks of yellow matter oozing amidst the blood as it spread across the cushions; and then she screamed and twisted uncontrollably, for the pain had stabbed anew, but now a million times worse, as though some hideous clawed thing were scratching at her womb. Desperately, she raised her head again and imagined she saw her husband, his features numbed by anguish and despair, watching as someone, his back turned to her, cut with a knife through her quivering belly. Tyi gasped and moaned again, and struggled to fight against the eddies of delirium. She imagined she saw, being yanked through the incision, what appeared to be a tiny, curled human creature, and yet something was wrong, horribly wrong, for it was glistening and sticky with the putrid yellow matter, and its limbs, as they stirred, appeared preternaturally thin. Was it her husband she heard scream – or was it herself? Tyi could not tell; for all was growing black. Faintly, she felt her mouth being opened, and a thick familiar taste flowing bitter down her throat; and then, with relief, she surrendered to the blackness.

When she woke again, the pain was almost gone and her belly felt purged. She opened her eyes. The room seemed empty; but then she realised that someone was with her after all, for her hand was being held.

'O my beloved sister.'

'Inen?' she murmured. She turned to face him, then frowned as she saw how tight-lipped and drawn he appeared. 'What is it?' she asked.

'Your husband,' he whispered, 'great Pharaoh – he is dead.'

'Dead?' Tyi looked away. 'But . . . no . . . I remember . . .' – she gazed round suddenly, wildly – 'my child!'

Inen tightened his grip upon his sister's hand. 'There is much,' he whispered gently, 'I have to reveal.'

'Where is my child?'

'Dead as well – and yet, O Tyi, it was never a child.'

Tyi gazed at him wild-eyed; then she shook her head.

'Listen to me.' Inen stroked Tyi's cheek gently. 'It was a monster, a . . . monster. I ordered it cut out early from your womb – for, had I not, then the birth would surely have caused your own death.'

'But . . .' – still Tyi gazed at him in disbelief – 'how could you have known?'

'Have I not always told you how there are many secrets within the sacred books of Amen, those which the priests have always guarded in his temple, speaking of the nature of the descendants of the gods? One of them warns of what has happened now to you – of how the Queen will grow infected by the emission of the King, for the time must come, with the passage of the years, when monsters, not children, will be grown from his seed. Monsters, I say – and yet, in truth, they are the very image of the star-born gods, and of all that is more than mortal within you. Even so' – Inen paused – 'when the moment arrives – when a monster emerges from the womb of a Queen – then it heralds the moment of the death of Pharaoh.'

'What' – Tyi shook her head – 'and so it has proved?'

'Try to clear your mind of it,' Inen answered softly, squeezing her hand before rising to his feet. But Tyi, despite her pain, struggled in vain to reach after him. 'And me?' she asked, slumping back into her cushions. 'This birth of a monster – what does it mean for me?'

Inen's face, for a moment, appeared cold and still, but then suddenly he smiled and bent down to kiss her. 'Do not fear,' he whispered, 'for there is a secret I must reveal to you very soon, more strange and wonderful than you could ever believe.'

'And this secret,' Tyi pressed him, 'what might it be?'

But Inen only smiled again. 'Do not say "this secret". Say rather . . . "this gift".' Then he slipped her a flask, stoppered and full, before turning and leaving his sister alone. She longed to rise and pursue him, but the pain from the wound to her stomach was too great; nor did it heal for several days, despite her consumption of the contents of the flask.

During the period of her recovery she was visited several times by her son, newly proclaimed King Amen-hetep the Fourth, his withered throat adorned with the necklace of Pharaoh and his swollen skull surmounted by the Double Crown of Egypt. From him she was careful to keep the flask of potion hidden; but to Kiya, the first time that they were alone, Tyi revealed her supply, for she had long been eager to share the secret, which to her had always been a hard one to keep. Kiya smiled back guiltily but acknowledged, when Tyi pressed her upon the matter, that she was suffering none of the customary pain of her pregnancies. 'And yet,' she whispered, her look of guilt returning, 'so miraculous do the powers of this potion seem to be, that I dread to imagine from what sorcery it might proceed.' Tyi as well, watching her wound now healing by the hour, had been wondering the same; and at length, when she found that she could rise up from her bed, she resolved that Inen should put off telling her no longer.

She found him in the secret chamber of the temple, praying to the altar beyond the empty pool. Within the sanctuary, everything was just as she remembered it; yet throughout the larger chambers and courtyards beyond it, silence had reigned and the floors had been empty of worshippers and priests. 'What has happened?' Tyi demanded, as Inen came to join her. 'How is it that the temple has grown so deserted?'

Inen glanced back at once to where the altar stood. 'We

have looked to the stars,' he said slowly, turning back round, 'and seen disaster written there, abomination.'

'Abomination?'

'Of the gods, and the sanctuaries, and their most sacred mysteries.'

'Then what is being done? Where has everyone gone?'

Again Inen gazed back at the altar and beyond. 'It was not to be risked,' he murmured at last, 'that the wealth of knowledge contained within this place, the riches preserved from the very dawn of time, be seized and destroyed by impious hands.'

Tyi narrowed her eyes. '"Impious hands", O my brother? Who can you mean?'

Inen met her stare for a moment, but he did not answer her. Instead he gestured towards the chambers beyond the magical doors. 'There is a place, set far within the desert, to which the sacred treasures of Amen are being taken. They will remain there until the period of danger has passed. Very shortly, I too will be leaving for the desert, when my business in Thebes has been brought to a close.' He paused, then reached for Tyi's hand and raised it to his lips. 'You as well,' he whispered, 'if you wish, may come with me.'

'Leave Thebes?' Tyi exclaimed in astonishment. 'Leave my palace, my son?'

Inen smiled thinly. 'I spoke to you before of a . . . gift . . . within my power. If you choose to come with me, then that gift will be yours.'

'But I do not even know what such a gift might be.'

Inen's smile still flickered, and then he nodded. 'Very well. Please – wait here.' Turning, he passed back beyond the empty pool, into the darkness which stretched beyond the altar to Amen; and Tyi listening, imagined that she heard the opening of a door. There was a silence of several minutes, then Inen returned with something in his hands. It appeared

318

withered and black; and then, as Tyi was able to see it better, she realised that it was a segment of a human arm.

At once she shrank back but Inen, seeing her response, laughed bitterly and reached out to seize her. 'What,' he sneered, 'do you dare to parade your scruples like this, when you have been bathing these long years in human blood?'

'I had no choice.'

'Your son, King Amen-hetep, would not agree.'

'Yet you know the time will come when even he will change his mind.'

'Indeed? When he grows too hideous for mortal eye to bear? While you, O my sister — you will have remained as beauteous and youthful as ever. But as a result of what?' Inen laughed once again. 'Not your baths alone!'

Tyi gazed at him in slowly dawning horror. 'The potions,' she whispered, 'from what were they formed?'

Mockingly, Inen raised the fragment of the arm. 'Why, from this,' he smiled.

'No,' Tyi shuddered. 'It is not possible . . . But . . . how?'

'By means of the mystery which was learned by Isis, the mystery of the sacred name of Amen. What that is I may never tell you, for the wisdom of a god is a terrible thing — and yet its effect, its power, you shall see now for yourself.' So saying, he pulled again upon his sister's arm and led her out beyond the magical doors, where he crouched down on his haunches with the piece of flesh held out before him. From the shadows Tyi heard a sudden skittering, and then a cat emerged cautiously, its delicate nostrils flared. Inen scooped it up and clasped it in his arms, feeding strips of the meat into its jaws until at last the cat had had its fill. Inen glanced at his sister, and for a moment he smiled; then suddenly he swung the cat and smashed its skull against the wall.

Tyi screamed. She rushed forward but Inen, seizing her,

held her back. 'See.' He pointed to the cat and Tyi, staring down at it, saw that its head was nothing but a pulp of blood and bone. Yet even as she broke free and bent down beside it, she saw that its body was stirring and struggling to rise, and her horror grew intermingled with disbelief. 'How can this be?'

Inen smiled again, even as he brought his foot down upon the animal's back. There was the sound of delicate bones being snapped but the cat, for all the horror of its injuries, still writhed and twisted about on its paws. 'Kill it,' Tyi sobbed, 'in the name of pity, please, kill it, *now*!'

Inen gestured with his arms. 'Is it not a wonder?' he asked.

'*Kill it!*' Tyi screamed.

'Very well,' Inen sighed. 'Yet there is only one way.' From beneath his cloak he drew out a dagger, then seized the cat and pressed it down against the floor. 'The heart,' he whispered, aiming with his knife, 'it must be pierced.' He drove the point down hard. The cat tensed, then twitched, and then at last grew still. Inen smiled at his sister. 'As I promised you,' he nodded, 'a miracle and a wonder.'

Tyi breathed in deeply, one hand on her heart, the other clasped across her mouth. 'Never,' she whispered, 'have I seen such a horror.'

'And yet the cat, as you saw, would soon have grown whole.'

Tyi shook her head. 'How is it possible?' she whispered.

'All things,' Inen answered, 'are possible to the gods.' He paused, waiting for his sister to reply, then seized her impatiently. 'Well?' he pressed her. 'What do you say? For it is not everyone, O my sister, who is offered immortality.'

Tyi glanced down at the bloodied mess by Inen's feet. 'I . . .' She swallowed. 'I need time . . . to think . . . to consider . . .' she replied.

Inen's face hardened. 'Not long.'

'But I must have time.'

'Within seventy days your husband will be laid to rest, and within seventy days after that I must have your decision, for it cannot be delayed any longer. In the meantime, O my sister – do not betray what I have shown you here today.' He paused, and glanced back into the inner sanctuary. 'For knowledge can sometimes be a dangerous privilege.'

'Then why have you told me? Why have you risked the secret?'

'Can you truly not tell?' Inen gazed at her almost in disappointment; then he reached for her again and clasped her very tightly. 'I shall be living,' he whispered, 'for all eternity. Do you think I can face that, if it must be without you?' He kissed her suddenly upon her brow, then released her, and turned and walked back towards the doors. 'One hundred and forty days!' he cried out as the doors glided shut. Tyi was left alone.

That afternoon, returning to the Palace, the sun seemed brighter, the light more vivid, the colours richer and more imbued with life than Tyi had ever seen them – yet their beauty served only to deepen her disquiet. The cool of twilight brought her no relief, nor the profounder stillness of night – and so at length, discovering that she could not sleep, Tyi rose from her bed. She called for a cloak, then walked through the gardens towards the side of the lake. The way was not difficult to follow, for it was lit by the moon, and she could remember, as she drew nearer to her father's favourite spot, every twist, every turn, from the days of her childhood. Yet as she approached it, she saw that someone was already there, standing beneath the trees; and she could just distinguish his domed skull against the stars, his withered body, his narrowed arms, the ruined beauty of King Amen-hetep, her son. 'Not here,' Tyi thought, 'not now, not with him.' Instead she turned back to the Palace, and called for a horse, then rode up the path which led towards the hills. By the ravine which marked the entrance to the valley of the dead, she found no guards, which surprised her but seemed also, such was her mood, a relief. Passing between the cliffs, she dismounted from her horse and led it as far as her parents' tomb. Having tethered it, she then knelt down in prayer, to ask her father for his comfort and aid.

Yet she had known, even before arriving at his tomb, what her father would have said – and therefore, as well, what it was she had to do. When at last she rose again, she felt resolved. Head bowed, she stood a moment more before the hidden entrance to the tomb, then returned to her horse to unfasten its reins. Suddenly, though, even as she was loosening the knots, she heard the murmuring of a far-off voice and looking up, caught a glimpse of faint, distant lights. Immediately she felt a chill of horror, for she knew, at such an hour and in such a place, that they could mean only one thing. Nevertheless, concerned to make certain, she hurried quietly back up the hill and when she reached a ridge of boulders peered out from behind them. Ahead of her, far up the valley, she could make out flickering torches and a body of men, some ten or twelve, gathered by a tomb – and then she heard, very faint, the chink of picks against stone.

The noise was at once lost beneath the pounding of Tyi's heart. She could not be certain what horrified her more: the threat of danger to herself, or revulsion at the sacrilege. She glanced down at the packed dirt beneath her feet, below which she knew her parents both lay. 'Let them be kept safe,' she whispered. 'O All-mighty and All-seeing One, let them never be disturbed.' Then, her heart racing ever faster, she crept slowly back down the hill and, untethering her horse, climbed into her saddle. She sat frozen a moment, gathering her courage, for she suspected that the robbers must have murdered the guards, and she knew that they would surely have posted sentries of their own. Then all at once, she spurred her horse on and galloped down the track as fast as she could, not concerned now to be quiet but only to escape the confines of the valley. By the narrow ravine which led out from the hills, she heard a muffled cry and saw two figures running out from the shadows towards her. One reached out and seized hold of her cloak, but Tyi loosened the fastening, and it slipped from her shoulders. She galloped on, out through the ravine and on down the road, towards the lights of the Palace twinkling on the Nile. Half-way towards them, however, Tyi saw a company of horsemen, and she cried out with relief when she recognised the shaven heads of priests. As she hailed them they all grew pale, reining in their horses, and preparing to kneel and bow down upon the road. Tyi, though, raised her hand and ordered them not to delay but to continue towards the valley, so as to surprise the robbers. At the news of what she had seen, the priests grew even paler and their eyes seemed to bulge with indignation and alarm. 'Desecration in the valley?' their leader exclaimed. 'That is a horror and an evil barely to be believed. Your brother, O great Queen, our new High Priest, will be shocked indeed when he learns of this.'

Watching the priest continue towards the valley with his men, Tyi did not doubt what he had said, for it was the responsibility of the High Priest to keep the valley secure, and she suspected that when the news was brought to Inen, it would confirm him in his dread of a looming time of sacrilege. Yet she did not search him out to confirm this supposition, nor even meet with him or glimpse him by chance, and she wondered if he – as she had begun to do – was avoiding those places where the other might be found. Only on the day of her dead husband's interment, when the body was transported from the temple to his tomb, did Tyi at last set eyes upon her brother again – yet never once did he choose to meet her stare. He walked instead at the very head of the procession, far apart from the new Pharaoh and the royal mourners, who followed in the rear of the mighty train of treasures, riding by the side of the coffin on its bier. By the time Tyi arrived at last before the tomb, the treasures had already been borne into the darkness of the rock and only the giant coffin of gold remained outside. As Inen led chants and prayers to Osiris, it was raised from the bier and placed beside the doorway, where it was then levered upright by two masked priests – one dressed as Isis, the other as Seth. Both, as they did so, raised a sudden chant of mourning, and Inen at last turned to face the royal party.

Still, though, he avoided his sister's eye but gazed instead, very coldly, at King Amen-hetep. 'O Osiris!' he cried out in a ringing voice. 'Your descendant comes, your kinsman, who is flesh of your flesh, blood of your blood! Hail to you, Lord of Brightness, Great Teacher of Mankind, Ruler of the Stars! You who were slain, and placed within a wooden chest, and dismembered by your brother into fourteen parts, guard great Pharaoh, who comes here now in death, that he too may never rot but live with you for ever, O Master of both the Living and the Dead!' Then for a moment Inen paused, yet Tyi saw that he continued to gaze coldly at her son, King Amen-hetep, before turning at last to face the coffin again, the staff of his office raised in his hand. Gently he brought it down upon the image of the dead Pharaoh, which had been crafted with wonderful skill upon the coffin. Inen touched it lightly upon the left breast. 'Guide Pharaoh's heart through the season of night.' He raised the staff once more, then again brought it down, this time upon the lips of the image's head. 'Open Pharaoh's mouth. Give him his breath. Preserve in him for ever the life eternal.'

Inen stood a moment more with his head bowed low, then he raised both his arms and renewed a sombre chant. The other priests joined him as the coffin was lifted and borne into the tomb. Still the priests chanted, as the bearers re-emerged from the darkness at last, and all was made ready for the final sealing of the tomb. The stone blocks were lowered; the bricks carefully mortared; a great mound of rubble piled against the doorway, until at last it was as though there had never been a tomb there at all.

Inen turned back to King Amen-hetep and bowed very low. 'O mighty descendant of the star-dwelling gods, your father is now at one with Osiris. The ritual of thanksgiving must therefore be proclaimed. Will you, as is the custom, lead our sacred rites?'

But King Amen-hetep shook his head. 'You know,' he answered shortly, 'that I have no belief in your gods. If I came here at all, it was merely to make certain that my father was indeed safely sealed.'

Inen's lips tightened almost imperceptibly, but otherwise he betrayed not a flicker of emotion. 'I trust then, O King, that you are now content.'

'Indeed,' King Amen-hetep nodded. 'Yet not everything, I fear, even now may be secure. There have been reports, O my uncle, dark rumours, of the actions of thieves abroad in the night.' He paused a moment, narrowing his eyes. 'Guard well against them. I would not have my father, in his sleep of death, disturbed.'

Again, Inen bowed low. 'Nothing shall disturb him,' he answered, 'in his sleep of eternal life.'

A smile flickered faintly on King Amen-hetep's swollen lips. 'I am glad to hear it,' he nodded. He glanced once more towards the hidden tomb, then turned and walked back to his waiting chariot. His courtiers and attendants followed in his train, and of all the royal party only Tyi remained where she had been. Inen was still standing as though rooted to the spot, gazing at the rubble concealing the doorway; but then at last he raised his head, and this time he did meet his sister's eyes. Tyi could not interpret what she saw within his stare, whether it was an appeal, or a warning, or something even more – the hint of a secret as yet unrevealed. She almost brought herself to cross to him, but then Inen turned again to speak to the priests, and Tyi knew that the moment had not yet arrived. 'Within another seventy days,' she thought to herself as she crossed back to her chariot. 'Then let us speak and, if needs be, part for ever.'

Yet when the seventieth day after the burial arrived, there was not a sign of Inen, nor even a message; and when Tyi, in perplexity, went to the temple, she could find no trace of her brother even there. The seventy-first day passed, and then the seventy-second, until at length ten days had gone by without contact, before a message marked as secret finally arrived for her.

However, it proved to be not from her brother, but from her son, ordering her to meet him upon the road to the hills, and when she rode there she found him with a body of his guards. King Amen-hetep kissed her warmly, then turned to the captain. 'Tell the Queen,' he ordered, 'the mystery you have found.'

The captain bowed his head. 'You must know, O mighty Queen,' he said, pointing to the valley, 'that I have been appointed to guard the royal tombs.'

Tyi frowned in puzzlement. 'Is it not the duty of the priests to guard the tombs?'

'A duty,' answered King Amen-hetep, 'which lately they have been neglecting, for in the past few weeks there have been ever more tombs broken into. I therefore decided' – he gestured to the captain – 'to appoint some men of my own to the valley.'

'And did you inform the priests of this decision?'

King Amen-hetep smiled grimly. 'I did not.'

'I see.' Tyi nodded slowly. 'Then tell me,' she asked the captain, 'what it was that you found?'

'Some ten days ago,' answered the captain, 'I was patrolling with my men when we heard – by the tomb of your husband, O great Queen – the sound of footsteps scrabbling over stone. We at once descended to inspect the entranceway and discovered, as we had feared, that it had been broken open. Inside we found five men despoiling the coffin, and so we seized them and then sealed up the tomb as best we could. The robbers we treated as the law proscribes, by removing their noses and cropping their ears, then impaling their bodies upon stakes beside the tomb. All this was done, as I said, ten days before.'

'Then where is the mystery?'

The captain glanced nervously at King Amen-hetep, then back at Tyi. 'Four of the robbers, as you might have expected, have long since expired. But the fifth, O mighty Queen . . .' – the captain swallowed – 'is still alive.'

'No.' Tyi breathed in deeply. She could feel a grip like ice growing tight about her heart. 'How is that possible?'

'I had thought, O my mother,' said King Amen-hetep softly, 'that you might be the one to answer that for me.' From beneath his cloak he drew out a bottle, half-filled with black liquid. 'I discovered that Kiya has been drinking this. She had been given it by Inen. She said that he had been giving you the very same drink, to preserve your beauty in the face of the passing years.'

Tyi gazed at the bottle guiltily, yet still spoke with defiance. 'It is not a sin,' she said at length, 'to wish to retain one's beauty and one's youth.'

King Amen-hetep laughed bitterly, concealing the bottle beneath his cloak once again. 'We should journey at once to my father's tomb,' he said with sudden brusqueness. 'It would be interesting to discover what other spells the High Priest of Amen might possess.'

'Why, you surely do not think . . .'

But King Amen-hetep raised his hand. 'Tell me,' he asked, turning to the captain, 'did you not say, in your report upon the wretch, how the point of the stake has extended through the skull?'

The captain bowed. 'I did, O mighty King.'

King Amen-hetep turned back to his mother. 'Very well, then. Let us go, and see what we shall see.'

Yet in truth, even as they rode along the lonely track and long before the thief upon his stake could be seen, his screams of agony could easily be heard, and as she listened to them, Tyi knew they were her brother's. Drawing nearer to the tomb, she saw five contorted bodies blackened by blood and the pitiless sun, four of them lifeless but one still twisting as he shrieked out violent curses, disfiguring even more his already ruined face. As Tyi approached him, however, with her son by her side, the wretch fell silent; then all at once, unexpectedly, he started to laugh.

'Why?' Tyi cried up at him with sudden fury. 'O Inen, tell me why?'

But still he laughed, and would not reply, and to all his sister's and nephew's questioning he would only splutter in mingled mockery and pain. 'Bring him down,' King Amen-hetep ordered, turning to the captain. 'I cannot endure the sight of such suffering. And you' – he nodded towards the other guards – 'open the tomb again. You said that you had found them' – he gestured to the bodies on the stakes – 'attempting to despoil the coffin of Pharaoh, my father. I want to know what it was that they were hunting.'

The guards bowed, and at once set about following their orders. While the majority laboured to reopen the tomb, Tyi watched as her brother on his stake was gently lowered. She saw that the captain had not exaggerated, for the point had indeed emerged through Inen's skull, and as the guards sought to pull his body from the stake, she could endure to watch no more but had to turn away. When she glanced back at last, she saw her brother twisting and spitting blood upon the sands, freed of the stake but with his hideous injuries still oozing and wide, and he continued to laugh even as he screamed. Only when King Amen-hetep bent down beside him, and forced the bottle with its potion into his mouth, did he fall silent at last; and even when the potion had been drunk and the bottle tossed aside, he remained in silence, raising not a moan. King Amen-hetep sought to press him, but he seemed barely to hear; and Tyi saw that his eyes were very wide, and fixed on her.

Then there came a sudden slithering of pebbles, and panting gasps, as the guards emerged from the entrance to the tomb. They were carrying a chest the size of a man, and Tyi saw that the seals upon its side had been broken. 'This was what they wanted,' reported one of the guards as the chest was laid down carefully. 'It lay within the innermost of the Pharaoh's coffins. When we found it, the lid had been only half set back in place.'

King Amen-hetep glanced down at Inen, who began suddenly to laugh – not wildly as before but with an insolent menace. Tyi marked how the blood had drained from her son's face, and for a moment she thought that he would strike his uncle; but then he turned back to the chest and nodded to the guard. A heave, and the lid was pulled away. King Amen-hetep gazed down, then at once looked away. However, as Tyi stepped forward to see what lay inside, he joined her again in inspecting the contents, and the two of them, for a long while, stood together in silence.

'Fourteen pieces,' said King Amen-hetep at last. He

turned back to Inen. 'You have sawn him, like Osiris, into fourteen pieces. But why?' He seized Inen; he shook him. 'Why?'

Inen did not reply, but Tyi could already feel the answer deep within her stomach. 'Look,' she said, pointing, 'the flesh beneath the wrappings – how it seems to stir – how it seems still alive!' She reached for the head and raised it to the sun.

Even beneath the blackened swathes of linen wrapping, a very faint flickering could be seen from the eyelids, and when Tyi pulled the wrappings away from the mouth she saw how the shrivelled tongue still seemed to move. She gazed at it dumbly and then passed it to her son, who shuddered with mingled revulsion and disbelief.

'Truly,' he exclaimed, 'never have I seen such a horror before, nor anything stranger nor full of darkest mystery!' Reverently he laid the head within the chest, then turned, still shaking, to stare back down at Inen. 'What is the nature and the meaning of this sorcery,' he demanded, 'this evil so loathsome that I dread to learn your answer?'

Inen smiled but still did not reply. It reminded Tyi, watching him, of how he had smiled at her before, standing in the shadows of the temple of Amen, listening to the mewling of the mutilated cat.

'I can tell you,' she said slowly, stepping forward.

'No!' For the first time since being brought down from the stake, Inen spoke. 'No!' he cried out again. 'No, you must not!'

'Why not?'

'The secret must remain ours.'

'No.'

'But surely . . .' Inen gazed at his sister in disbelief. 'You will not . . . not turn down the offer I have made? Come!' He rose suddenly to his feet and sought to take her by the arm. 'We must leave now, leave here, the moment has come!'

But Tyi shrank away from him, shuddering violently. 'Never!' she cried out. 'I would rather die than leave with you!'

Inen froze. 'Rather die?' he whispered. All the emotion, all the life seemed to bleed from his face. Then suddenly he laughed, as he had laughed before, with a mockery compounded of bitterness and rage. 'But you will never die,' he whispered. 'Not you, nor him' – he gestured to her son – 'nor any of your blood-line, you will never die! See!' – he reached for the severed head of Tyi's husband – 'Witness the fate you have chosen for yourself!'

'So it is true' – King Amen-hetep gazed down at the segments of his father's body – 'he is still alive indeed?'

'Were he to be sliced into an infinite number of particles, were his blood to be mingled with the waters of the world, were his bones to be crushed and ground into a dust, even so – the essence of his life would remain.'

Tyi gazed at her son with undisguised fear, yet King Amen-hetep's expression remained perfectly calm. 'How can that be possible?' he asked.

'By the will of the gods.'

'I do not believe you.'

'Yet even so, it is the truth.'

'How?'

'It was ordained and achieved by the Lady Isis, most cunning of the immortals, mistress of the secret wisdom of the stars, who bred from Osiris a line of deathless kings. What magic such kings might then possess, what qualities of sorcery were flowing through their blood, was suggested by the actions of the goddess herself, when she ordered her husband to be sealed within a chest and his body dismembered into fourteen parts.'

'No,' Tyi cried out, 'no, no, that was Seth!'

Inen laughed. 'So it is taught. But do you truly think that we who guard the wisdom of the gods would betray our deepest and most ageless mysteries, and reveal them to the ignorant prying of the masses? No, for were the truth to be wholly understood, then all would be immortals, for all would eat the flesh of the line of living gods, preserved and dismembered as the rituals have taught us.' He gazed down again at the corpse within the chest. 'Food for the gods, formed from the gods.'

King Amen-hetep gazed at him impassively, then stared down into the chest. 'And all my forefathers,' he asked softly, 'you have served in this same way?'

'As I said,' answered Inen, 'the ritual demands it, that the bodies be preserved within the coffins for seventy days, and then dismembered into fourteen parts.'

'So that was why you broke into my father's tomb. Yet why have you been disrupting the other Pharaohs' tombs?'

'To remove the bodies and replace them, so that no one would ever know they had been taken. Yet now it matters little, for they have all – save this one – been safely transported.'

'To where?'

'To an older temple, far within the desert, which marks the place where the gods first arrived from the stars. Do not ask me for its location, for I shall never reveal it, nor will you ever discover it for yourself.'

'Yet why do you need so desperately to flee there?'

'Because, O great Pharaoh, we feared what you might do. You may take it' – he inclined his head – 'as a compliment. Yet do not think' – he paused, to gaze again into the chest – 'that we shall never return, for in time you will grow to be a withered, ancient thing, a breeder of monsters like your own father here. Until that moment, as the rituals demand, we must leave you to rule upon the throne of your fore-fathers – and yet in the end,' he smiled, 'do not doubt that I shall feed upon you. Yes' – he glanced at Tyi – 'and upon your living flesh as well.'

'Yet still,' said Tyi slowly, 'you are not immortal after all.'

Inen breathed in deeply as though suddenly winded, and gazed at her silently through narrowing eyes.

Tyi smiled; she turned to her son. 'Pierce his heart. Then you will see him die.'

For a long time no one spoke. 'Is this true?' said King Amen-hetep to Inen at last.

Inen met his stare; then he looked away.

King Amen-hetep smiled crookedly and, shielding his eyes, raised his gaze up to the sun. 'I am sworn,' he murmured, 'not to slay any living creature.' He glanced back at Inen. 'Not even you.'

Tyi gazed at her son in disbelief. 'You will set him free?'

'Cruel, to live for ever with a face marked like his.' King Amen-hetep gazed at his uncle's noseless face, at the still bleeding wounds where the ears had been, then turned back to Tyi. 'Even crueller, O my mother, to live for ever with-out love – to live for ever without you.'

Inen bowed low, and seemed almost to spit with con-tempt. 'Yet not so cruel, O Pharaoh, as to live with the knowledge of what must happen to you.'

King Amen-hetep gazed again into the brightness of the sun. 'All things, we must trust, are possible to the All-High.'

'It may be. And yet the solution lies before you already, in this chest.' Inen reached for a portion of the withered arm. 'Eat it,' he whispered, brandishing it slowly before both Pharaoh and Tyi. 'It is not too late. You may both yet be saved. It does not need your god in the sun to help you now.'

Tyi gazed at the flesh with a sudden desperate longing, and Inen smiled as he interpreted the gleam within her eyes.

She turned to her son. Even he, she realised, seemed filled with an eager, wavering doubt; then, as she watched him, he reached out for the morsel of flesh. 'And yet . . .' he whispered suddenly. He stared up at the sun. 'If we eat this, what a curse we may prove to be to man. Dangerous enough, even as we are – yet how much more so if we never wither or decline. No!' He placed the portion of flesh back in the chest. 'Take it away! We cannot endure the temptation of its presence here.' He paused, then gazed down at the severed portions of his father. 'See how he proves what he always said – that the world is nothing but a pattern of destruction. And yet I vow – I pray – that all shall be reversed.'

So saying, he turned and walked away, leaving Tyi for a moment standing rooted by the chest. Her eyes met Inen's; then she too turned and left. Neither looked behind as they rode down the path, but continued on their way until they came into the temple. Once arrived there, they passed into the innermost sanctuary and then beyond, past the pool and into the darkness. Set far back in the wall there was a tiny door, and beyond the door one further, final room. A statue stood there with the crown and robes of Isis, and a form that Tyi could recognise by glancing at her son; and yet, in truth, the statue seemed barely to have a mortal form at all, so hideous, so deformed the sculptor had made it, more loathsome than anything that Tyi had ever seen.

'No wonder,' King Amen-hetep whispered, 'that they kept it hidden in this place of darkness. For it is dangerous for mortals to endure such a sight.' He paused a moment – then heaved at the statue, which toppled and shattered into fragments on the floor. King Amen-hetep trampled the pieces into dust beneath his feet.

It was later that day that Kiya gave birth. The child was a boy, and it was not stillborn. He was given the name of Smenkh-ka-Re.

It was also on that same day, when King Amen-hetep lay down to rest, that he saw in his dreams a burning image of the sun.

———————

But at this point, Haroun saw the approach of morning and broke off from his tale. 'O Commander of the Faithful,' he said, 'if you would care to return here tomorrow evening, then I shall describe to you the nature and the fruit of King Amen-hetep's dreams.'

And so the Caliph did as Haroun suggested; and the following evening he returned to the mosque.

And Haroun said:

———————

Every night the dream would be the same, a vision of a blazing, infinite sun, of a brightness impossible for mortal eye to bear; yet King Amen-hetep found that, as the months began to pass, so the brilliance of the light grew easier to endure. He would imagine that he was starting to see, almost imperceptibly through the wheeling golden rays, the outline of something else, something other than the sun. 'O Divine Lord of all,' he would cry out in his dream, 'mighty living Aten, grant me the strength to glimpse what is veiled'; and then he would stare into the very heart of the sun. But the brightness would fade, the dream melt away; and King Amen-hetep would wake alone in his bed, as the dawning of the true sun filled his room with morning light.

How he would long then, in the bitterness of his disappointment, for Kiya, his Queen, to be again by his side. He knew, though, that he could not permit it – had not permitted it, indeed, since that afternoon when he had first learned the full truth about his state. What other hope did he have, after all, of destroying the curse, of damming the ages-old flow of tainted blood, save by being the last of his long line to bear it? Already he had a son; and when he gazed upon Smenkh-ka-Re, suckling at Kiya's breast, or lying asleep, he would dread to think that even such a child, so lovely to behold, and so innocent, might bear poison in his veins. Sometimes King Amen-hetep would seek to put the terror from his mind; yet he knew, in the end, that he could not afford to do so, for it was that terror alone now which served to keep his will alive. Without it, he knew he would have slept with Kiya each and every night, for his desire seemed to grow the more his body came to change, flickering and scorching through his limbs like a desert fire – urging him, taunting him to put the flames out.

So it was that he came to hate the very sight of Kiya, as the reminder of a happiness forever lost; and he banished her from his presence, and lived with her no more. And so it was that he grew to hate all his favourite pleasures – the calm of the lake where he had once sat with his grandfather, the walks through the fields to see the blooming of the flowers, the voyages along the stately curving of the Nile, where the wealth and the beauties of life lay spread before him – all that he had ever valued and most adored; for everything now seemed as though turned into dust. Desperate were King Amen-hetep's prayers to the Aten – but ever looming the temple of Amen still rose. For all that he had toppled the idol in its heart, King Amen-hetep feared to touch that vast edifice of stone – in dread, perhaps, though he would not admit as much, that the power of the Aten was indeed an illusion, that nothing could succeed against the ancient, deathly gods. As though it were a veil of sands upon the winds, scalding the fields and the cooling lakes, the temple's shadow spread wide and dark across Thebes, so that King Amen-hetep imagined it even in his soul.

Yet still there were his dreams; and in those the blaze of the sun remained undimmed, and with it, perhaps, a token of the power of the Aten. So at least King Amen-hetep prayed, for as time slipped by so the glimpse of some vision beyond the blazing sun, seeming to grow stronger with each succeeding night, tantalised the dreamer with a gnawing sense of hope. He began to distinguish, still faintly, a crescent of cliffs framing what appeared to be a dusty plain of sand. Soon, as the vision grew clearer, he saw that a river was flowing by the plain, very wide, with a fringe of reeds along its bank, and he knew when he awoke that such a river could only be the Nile. In great excitement he summoned his uncle, Ay, and described to him the vision of the scene from his dream, then ordered that men be sent along the Nile, to the reaches of both Upper and Lower Egypt, to see if such a place might indeed be discovered. Impatiently King Amen-hetep waited, for still, every night, the scene grew clearer in his dreams, and he was certain that it could only be a message from the heavens, filled with a strange and terrible promise. Then it happened at last that a messenger returned and, having bowed low before King Amen-hetep, looked up at him with joy. 'O happy King,' he cried, 'for many days I did as you commanded, and followed the river as it flows out to the sea. I saw how, all along the eastern bank, the cliffs rose up sheer and inhospitable, and I despaired of discovering the scene you had described. But then it happened at last that the cliffs curved away, and I saw a plain in the shape of a circle cut in two, and marshes fringing the river bank.' And King Amen-hetep, hearing this, raised up a prayer of exultation; then he left that same day upon his barge down the Nile, until at length he arrived at the place found by his servant, and he knew, as he gazed at it, that it was the place from his dreams.

He stepped ashore and ordered his tent erected, and

when he fell asleep that night, he dreamed once again. He imagined that he saw the cliffs and the plain still before him, but transformed into a scene of wondrous beauty, for now there rose a city filled with gleaming towers and walls, bird-thronged gardens and fish-stocked pools, palaces and houses of unparalleled splendour, and above all of them a temple open to the sun. Gazing at the vision, King Amen-hetep felt a sense of rapture so bright that it seemed to blaze within his heart, and the very streets, he could see now, were filling up with light. 'Some great wonder,' he thought, 'is presaged by all this,' as the pleasure in his heart still soared and grew more bright, and the city seemed to shimmer and rise to meet his joy. It was then that he awoke; yet like the distant echoing of music, the pleasure still remained, though faint and deep within his heart, and as he felt it, he knew what it was he had to do.

Returning to Thebes, he summoned his Court and described to them the vision of the city in his dream. 'That same city,' he proclaimed, 'we must now attempt to build, for I am certain that, if we succeed, some great blessing will be afforded by the grace of the All-High.' These words were greeted with wondrous acclammation, and the news was spread throughout all Egypt and beyond, so that the world's finest craftsmen and architects and artists, eager with a passion to fulfill Pharaoh's dream, gathered at the site of the crescent plain, and a city was raised up from the sands into the sky. When all was completed, the news was brought to King Amen-hetep; and he prepared in great hope to embark for the place. First, though, he journeyed to the temple of Amen, and he ordered the roof to be torn down from its walls, so that the light of the sun could purge its rooms of mystery and melt, so he trusted, the darkness of its secrets. 'Let the weeds grow across its floors,' he proclaimed, 'and let its pillars be haunted by jackals and owls.' And then, to illustrate how the past was henceforth to be abandoned, he announced that his name was no longer Amen-hetep but instead Akh-en-Aten – which meant, in his language, 'the glory of the sun'.

So it was that when he landed on the crescent plain, his heart was already filled to overflowing with hope; but when he first saw the city conjured up upon the sands, he cried out in rapture and approbation, for it seemed the very image of the city from his dream. Remembering the brightness which he had also witnessed then, and the emotions of joy which had seemed to presage some great wonder, King Akh-en-Aten stepped into his chariot and drove towards the city; and as he neared it so he prayed for a miracle, a sign. Then all at once, borne upon the breeze, he caught the perfume of an infinite number of sweet flowers, and he saw, when he gazed about him at the city, how lotuses were suddenly blooming on its pools, shady arbours were sprouting lushly by its walls, and fragrant-leaved trees were bending low above its buildings and its roads. From their boughs rose the songs of brightly coloured birds, in a chorus louder than any which King Akh-en-Aten had ever heard before, and he gazed about him in astonishment, for it seemed that every beauty of the living earth was emerging there to greet him, risen up all at once from the dust.

Then at the same moment, from amongst the crowds which had gathered by the roadside, there came a sudden murmuring, and then gasps of astonishment, and King Akh-en-Aten saw that they had turned to gaze into the distance. He shook out his reins and rode his chariot on, and as he arrived by the gateway to the city so a messenger, panting and covered in dust, came stumbling forward to kneel down in the road. 'O mighty Pharaoh,' he cried out, 'a blessing and a wonder is drawing near to greet you! Upon the road which leads into the far side of the city, a litter is approaching, veiled, so it seems, with golden light. Behind it is a train of every kind of beast, lions and leopards, and gambolling panthers, deer of a slender and marvellous grace, spotted cattle and gleaming white bullocks, all perfectly tamed, as though by the beauty of that peerless Princess, fairer than anything, fairer than life, who rides in splendour high upon the litter – for in truth, O happy King, she seems to put the very sun to shame!'

'Not the sun,' answered King Akh-en-Aten, suddenly shuddering, 'do not say the sun – for there is only One who may do that.' But even as he spoke he turned to stare ahead, and his words were suddenly frozen on his tongue, for now he could see, borne high upon a throne of gold, the Princess, and at once he was filled with a brightness of rapture, such as he only ever remembered feeling in his dream. Numbly he stepped down on to the road to receive her. Drawing near, the princess ordered her litter lowered with a gesture of her hand, and stepped down likewise; and then she stepped forward into the light of the sun.

King Akh-en-Aten realised now that the messenger had not been exaggerating. Never before had he seen such mortal beauty. The Princess's figure was perfect, as slender as a reed, her breasts seemed like twin fruit of ivory and her feet and hands were deliciously small. Her hair was the colour of deepest night, and hung in seven tresses far below her waist. Her cheeks were rosy, her lips bright red and her teeth like delicate and lustrous pearls. Beneath her long, silken lashes her almond eyes were black, and their gleam seemed as bright as that of an angel. King Akh-en-Aten watched as she angled her head upon her neck, which was long and slender and bejewelled with gold, and lowered her painted eyelids to hood her gleaming eyes, as though with fascination at her first sight of him. King Akh-en-Aten longed to speak to her, to say anything at all, but he found that her presence had struck him utterly dumb, for he could only think that the messenger had spoken less than the truth. The Princess was indeed more lovely than the sun, and more lovely than the moon, and more lovely than all the infinite number of stars, for indeed it was as though their fire had been stolen from the heavens, and their radiance enshrined within the beauty of her form; and as he stared at her, the King felt that he too was being somehow enveloped by the light. And when he met her gaze, he found it languid with a tender and captivating passion; and he knew himself dazzled and overwhelmed by love.

Almost without an awareness of what he was doing, he brushed the softness of her lips with his own. He took her slim hand and led her towards the Palace; and all the crowds who were watching shouted out in wonder, giving to the Princess the name of Nefer-titi, which in their own language meant, 'She Who Comes in Beauty.' And King Akh-en-Aten, barely conscious of anything save the presence of the Princess, nevertheless heard the cries of this name; and when at length they had left all the crowds far behind and stood alone together within the gardens of the Palace, he turned to his companion and, discovering his tongue, he too addressed her as Nefer-titi.

She smiled at this, and gently stroked his cheeks. As she did so, King Akh-en-Aten felt himself once again consumed by soft flames, and as she reached out to kiss him he broke away, for he was desperately attempting to stay true to his resolve — yet he sensed how that too was being burned up by the flames. He met her lips and felt his body melt, so that he lost all sense of time, all knowledge of place. Then King Akh-en-Aten felt the Princess's lips break from his own; and he stared at her, blinking, as though trying to wake up from a dream.

'Who are you?' he whispered softly. 'What is your name?'

She smiled at him again. 'Let me be known,' she answered, 'by the name which you have called me, for in truth, before this time I have borne many names.'

'Why,' King Akh-en-Aten frowned, 'how can that be?' He took a step backwards, suddenly fearful. 'Where are you from?'

'From the Kingdom of the Stars,' Nefer-titi replied, reaching out to take the King Akh-en-Aten by the hand, even as he tensed and sought to step back once again. 'Do not be astonished,' she whispered, feeling his resistance melt upon her touch, 'for you should know, O mighty King, that there are as many worlds within the sky as there are grains of sand within the desert, and many orders of beings other than man – and yet all have been formed by the single hand.'

Still King Akh-en-Aten gazed at her with doubt upon his brow. 'You have come, then,' he asked, 'by the will of the Aten?'

'Do you think,' she answered softly, 'that your prayers have gone unheard?'

'My prayers?' King Akh-en-Aten narrowed his eyes, then he suddenly laughed. 'But I asked that the poison in my blood be purged away. I asked that I be able to love, and father children and know that I will not then wreak an evil on the world. I asked in short' – he shrugged with bitterness – 'that I be like other men. How can you possibly answer those prayers?'

'Why,' Nefer-titi answered him, 'is your faith indeed so faint?'

The King gazed at her with sudden astonishment and doubt, daring to wonder, just for a moment, what it might mean if her words could be true. 'I wish . . .' he muttered, 'I wish I could believe.'

'Why,' frowned Nefer-titi, 'what do you doubt?'

'You say that you come from a Kingdom in the stars, and that you are a servant of the Aten, come in answer to my prayers. Yet how can I be certain you are not a demon in disguise, arrived here to tempt me?'

Nefer-titi smiled, then gestured out towards the city spread around them. 'Did you not see,' she asked, 'how the very flowers and trees rose to hail my arrival, and how the beasts of the deserts and the fields were in my train? Do you think that my powers could achieve such wonders and not also, O Pharaoh, grant you the gifts of life?'

King Akh-en-Aten gazed at her with longing and a terrible, burning desire. 'Then it is true?' he whispered. 'You are indeed that blessing for which I have prayed to the All-High?' A moment more he stood frozen; then he surrendered to his desire and Nefer-titi's embrace. 'What must I do?' he whispered. 'What must I do?'

'Love me with all your heart.'

'And that is all?'

The Princess gazed at him deeply. 'Do you think that we too, who once dwelt in the stars but now dwell here on earth, may not also know what it means to be alone?'

The King met her gaze with wonder; but its depths now seemed immeasurable, and the loneliness he glimpsed there was immeasurable as well, icy and silent like the vast depths of the heavens; and he felt himself chilled, merely to glimpse it. Slowly Nefer-titi lowered her lashes, as though the depths were tears to be blinked away, and then she seized him fiercely, squeezing his hands in her own and almost biting his lips with her kisses. Breaking away once again, she pointed through the leaves of the garden to the sky. 'Swear it upon the sun,' she whispered, 'whose sacred rays give life and light to all the world. Swear to me, O Pharaoh, that you will love me more than all this world.'

343

'I swear it willingly,' King Akh-en-Aten answered.

'Then I grant you,' she whispered slowly, 'those gifts of life you desire. But be warned, for I swear this in turn to you – should you ever love anything more than you love me, then at that same moment, O my husband, I will leave you for ever.'

King Akh-en-Aten gazed at her in silence, a frown upon his brow, and then he smiled and shook his head, and kissed her once again. 'We shall never be parted.' He kissed her once more, gently, on her brow, then turned and left her, and summoned his jeweller, whom he ordered to craft two twin rings of gold. That same evening he brought them to Nefer-titi and showed her the design, which portrayed the disk of the sun with two worshippers beneath. He slipped one on to her finger, and one on to his own. 'Wear that ring,' he ordered, 'and be certain of my love.'

The next day Nefer-titi was proclaimed as Pharaoh's Queen; and high upon the cliffs, in a ring about the town, her image was sculpted with King Akh-en-Aten's, so that all who came might bear witness to her beauty, and know that it was she who was the guardian of the realm; and by her image were carved salutes, couched in royal terms: 'The Heiress, Great of Favour, Lady of Graciousness, Worthy of Love, Mistress of Upper and Lower Egypt, Great Wife of the King, whom he loves, Lady of the Two Lands, She who is the most beautiful of the Beauties of the Aten, Nefer-titi, may she live for ever!'

But at this point, Haroun saw the approach of morning and broke off from his tale. 'O Commander of the Faithful,' he said, 'if you would care to return here tomorrow evening, then I shall describe to you the fruit of King Akh-en-Aten's love for his Queen.'

And so the Caliph did as Haroun suggested; and the following evening he returned to the mosque.

And Haroun said:

As she had promised she would do, the Queen brought great joy to King Akh-en-Aten, and the blessings of plenty and peace to all his lands. In the fields the crops grew plentiful and rich; upon the Nile the ships were loaded with good things; within the house of every person there was contentment and health, and upon every table in the land a weight of wondrous foods – almonds and nuts, pastries and chickens, sweetmeats and rare fruits, and well-buttered lambs. But most blessed of all, and most filled with joy, was the new city built upon the crescent plain, for there Nature herself seemed at peace with man, so that the beauties of both dwelt together side by side. By its streets could be found every bright-petalled flower, every sweet-smelling plant, every shade-granting tree; and within its gardens and its pools every wondrous kind of animal, every living thing of beauty granted breath by the sun. Nor did the wonders in the city made by man – all the works subtly crafted from metal, wood or stone – pale in comparison; for they were rich in splendour, and loveliness, and comfort. The walls were covered with hangings of rose silk, the floors were spread with brightly patterned rugs, and the cooling marble was interlaced with gold; in every hall was a fountain, and in every garden a pool. Never before had so marvellous a city been upraised; and people named it, in astonishment, 'the Dwelling of the Sun'.

Yet there was no one happier in all that happy city, no one more joyous than King Akh-en-Aten himself. What he had always most desired was now his at last, for the Queen bore him children – sisters for Smenkh-ka-Re, twin daughters at first, then a third and then a fourth. Carefully nursed upon their mother's own milk, they grew up blessed by the love of their father, for it was Pharaoh's greatest pleasure to sit with his family in the shade of his garden, by the side of his Queen. At such moments he would gaze up at the sun and raise a heartfelt cry of thanks, then turn to his Queen and whisper in her ear, 'Truly, there has never been a man so blessed as me!' She would smile at this, and make no reply, save to stroke his cheek and kiss him softly. Then one day he turned to her and whispered in her ear, gazing at his children, 'Truly, they are more precious to me than all of this wide world!' Again the Queen smiled; but this time she did not kiss him and, as she lowered her eyes, so she veiled the glint of something strange.

It was the very next day that King Akh-en-Aten was visited by his mother, who reported how her three lions had all fallen ill. These beasts had been found in the trees of her garden, draped upon the boughs and perfectly tame, upon the day of the arrival of Queen Nefer-titi. Where they had come from was a mystery; but Queen Tyi, enraptured, had adopted them straightaway. King Akh-en-Aten too, in memory of his childhood, had come to love them deeply, and so the news of their sickness filled him with distress. He ordered his physicians to tend to the lions, but in vain, for the next day they seemed even more ill, and dangerously weak as though emptied of their blood. Then the next day they could barely raise their heads up from the ground, and Tyi came to her son and spoke to him in private. She claimed to have seen, at the darkest hour of night, while gazing from the window of her chamber, the figure of a woman gliding through the shadows, unearthly and strange like a breath of gold upon the breeze. Tyi had found herself utterly frozen, even as she watched the woman lie beside the lions, petting them, and then draining them, each in turn, of their blood. 'And when she had finished her meal,' Tyi continued, 'she raised up her head, and I glimpsed her face, and I saw, O my son – I saw it was the Queen!'

King Akh-en-Aten gazed at her in astonishment, and then in anger, as he realised that his mother was speaking in earnest. 'Why are you telling me this lie?' he cried out bitterly.

'I tell you,' she answered, 'it is not a lie, but the truth.'

'How can it be?' King Akh-en-Aten exclaimed. 'You know full well, it was only upon the Queen's arrival in this city that the lions appeared at all. How can she be guilty of their sickness, when everywhere, like the sun, she grants the blessings of life? Look upon yourself, O mother!' He seized a mirror, and raised it to her face. 'You no longer bathe in blood, yet your face has stayed the same. You no longer drink your potions, yet you seem unwithered by your years. How can that have been achieved, save by the powers of the Queen?'

Tyi stared at the reflection of herself within the glass. 'I do not know,' she answered, finally lowering her gaze. 'And yet . . .' – she shrugged despairingly – 'I can be certain of what I saw.'

But the King, in a rage, refused to listen to his mother any more, and the next day, when she brought him the news of the lions' deaths, he could barely bring himself to show regret. His mother gazed at him with bitter reproach. 'When you were young,' she said, 'you would have suffered a terrible grief over this.'

But King Akh-en-Aten shook his head. 'All is changed,' he replied. 'Not even the keenest grief can pierce my heart now. Whatever I lose, still I have my Queen, who is more precious to me than all this wide world.' And so saying he turned and left his mother behind, and searched out his Queen, and held her fast in his arms. She smiled at him, and this time she did meet his kiss; and all was calm for the following year.

But then it happened that Ay came to him, to say that his wife – Kiya's mother, the Lady Tiya – had fallen sick. King Akh-en-Aten ordered his finest physician to her side; but again, as with the lions, every effort seemed in vain, for as each day passed so the Lady Tiya grew weaker and more pale, as though she were being drained of all her blood. Then Ay came to his nephew and spoke to him in private, and said how he had seen a shadow bending low across his wife, drinking from wounds to the Lady Tiya's chest; and that when this shadow had raised its head, he had seemed to recognise the face of the Queen. King Akh-en-Aten was immediately thrown into a rage, and accused his uncle of having drunken dreams; but Ay answered him, in a towering fury of his own, by saying that the wounds could still be seen across the Lady Tiya's breasts.

But the King refused to listen any more, and the next day, when Ay brought him the news of the Lady Tiya's death, his sorrow seemed strangely distanced and dulled. Ay frowned, his honest face furrowed in puzzlement. 'When you were young,' he said, 'you would have suffered a terrible grief over this.'

But King Akh-en-Aten shook his head. 'All is changed,' he replied. 'Not even the keenest grief can pierce my heart now. Whatever I lose, still I have my Queen, who is more precious to me than all this wide world.' And so saying, he turned and left his uncle behind, and searched out his Queen and held her fast in his arms. She smiled at him, and met his kiss; and all was calm for the following year.

But then it happened that Kiya, whom King Akh-en-Aten – with the encouragement of the Queen – had banished to the Royal Harim, came to him with the news that his youngest daughter was sick. The King gazed at Kiya

348

with doubt and suspicion, for since the coming of Nefer-titi, he had not been able to endure the sight of his former Queen; but then he agreed to accompany her to his daughter's bed. The little girl was shivering, very pale and weak; and when Kiya lifted the coverlet from her chest, King Akh-en-Aten saw there were delicate scars in a pattern across her chest. 'My father,' Kiya whispered, 'when my mother, the Lady Tiya, fell sick, discovered the same strange marks upon her. I know that he told you of them, and what he suspected the cause of them to be. So when I heard of your daughter's sickness, I resolved that I would come to you myself.'

Still King Akh-en-Aten gazed down at his softly moaning child and did not choose to meet with Kiya's eye. 'See that she wants for nothing,' he said at last. He stooped and kissed his daughter on her brow, feeling how her skin seemed to prickle and burn, and then he turned and left her to seek out the Queen. But when he found her he discovered that all his questions were silenced, and he could do nothing but melt into the softness of her kisses. He said nothing to her of their daughter's sickness; and the next day it was reported how their child had died in the night.

Once again, it was Kiya who brought King Akh-en-Aten the news. She reached out nervously to touch him on the arm; but he flinched, and stepped violently away from her, and still he refused to look into her eyes but ordered her to go. She remained though, frozen and numbed, where she stood. 'Your daughter is dead,' she told him once again. She waited for his reply, but still there came no answer. 'When you were young,' she continued at last, 'you would have suffered a terrible grief over this.'

But King Akh-en-Aten shook his head. 'All is changed,' he replied. 'Not even the keenest grief can pierce my heart now. Whatever I lose, still I have my Queen, who is more precious to me than all this wide world.' But when Kiya had left him, he raised his eyes up to the sun and felt a great wave of sorrow, intermingled with doubt. 'So this is death,' he thought to himself, 'for which I have prayed so hard and so long. Yet now that I have it – yes, and all my children too – it fills me with horror, and its shadow seems to shade even the rays of the sun.' Then he ordered a tomb to be prepared for his daughter, and he buried her there, he and his Queen together; and as he did so it struck him how he too would one day now pass away, and so he ordered a tomb to be prepared for himself, high in a ravine which lay beyond the plain. Upon its walls he commanded images of the Aten to be painted, its rays bestowing blessings of comfort and light; but upon one of the walls he ordered that the funeral of his daughter be represented – her body laid out in state, with himself and all his family prostrated by their mourning, bowing before her as though it were to Death.

And then it happened that Kiya came to King Akh-en-Aten once again, with the news that another of his daughters had fallen sick, and that she too had strange scars running up and down her chest. Now at last the King did raise his eyes to meet Kiya's; and he felt soaring up within him, what he had long sought to repress, doubts and imaginings too terrible to utter. Yet Kiya, not needing to hear them spoken, took him by his arm and led him to his daughter, so that he could see for himself the evidence of the wounds. Then she led him into a neighbouring room, for the shadows of evening were starting to lengthen, and the two of them sat there concealed behind a curtain. Dusk grew into night, the long hours passed, and still the sick girl lay undisturbed. But then at last, upon the distant howling of a jackal, King Akh-en-Aten felt a sudden gale blowing through the room, so that the curtain before him was ripped down from its hangings and he saw, bending low across his daughter's bed, a shadow which was formed, so it seemed, from streaks of flowing gold. This shadow was drinking from his daughter's chest; and yet the King found that he could neither move nor speak. Then at last, when his daughter lay bled utterly white, the shadow shimmered to its feet and turned to meet his eye. Still, for a second more King Akh-en-Aten sat frozen in silence; and then he cried out in wordless fury and disbelief.

The Queen smiled at him. Her cheeks seemed flushed, her lips very red. She glided across to him, and reached out to touch his cheek. 'O my beloved,' she whispered, 'do you not love me more than all the world?'

For a moment, such seemed the weight of pain upon his chest that King Akh-en-Aten discovered that again he could neither move nor speak. 'Love you?' he whispered at last. He gazed down at the corpse of his second daughter. 'Love you?' he repeated. Suddenly, he laughed.

But the smile upon the Queen's lips had at once begun to fade. 'So you have chosen,' she whispered; and King Akh-en-Aten glimpsed in her eyes that terrifying loneliness which he had seen once before – as deep and eternal, so it seemed, as the skies. She raised her hand before him and, with a single graceful movement, she drew the ring from her finger, then turned and flung it from the room into the night. Upon the same gesture, she too seemed to rise and fade away, melting upon the darkness, so that only her voice still lingered in the air. 'Farewell, O my Husband. Forever, farewell.' Then that too seemed to fade into the darkness of the night, and all in the room was silence once again.

King Akh-en-Aten turned to Kiya. 'How I have wronged you,' he whispered. He met her lips. 'And how I have missed you, O my love. For it was as though a mist had been cast across my eyes.' He kissed her again. So urgently did he seize her, so tightly did he grip her, that she stumbled and half-sobbed, and sought to break away. 'Your daughter . . .'

she cried out; but the King silenced her, crushing her lips beneath his own. He could feel the whipping of the flames through his limbs once again, the scorching fire such as he had not experienced since the coming of Queen Nefer-titi; and his desire seemed so violent that it felt like a pain. Kiya stumbled again as he began to thrust against her, and he fell with her this time – down upon the bed, down upon the body of his daughter; but still he felt the fire. He closed his eyes . . . the flames were reaching upwards and with a shriek, he imagined them beating against the sky; then he opened his eyes and saw his dead daughter's face.

When he gazed down at Kiya, her eyes seemed like glass and her face, like his daughter's, appeared bled utterly white. 'What have I done?' he whispered. 'I felt . . . I felt . . .' His voice trailed away. He struggled to think of some words of regret. But then, even as he opened his mouth to speak them, he heard from far-off a second shriek – so piercing, so shrill with disgust and despair that both he and Kiya were utterly frozen by it; and then the scream rose again.

King Akh-en-Aten ran from the room to discover what the source of the horror might be. 'No! No, no, no!' The cries, he realised now, were coming from the quarters of his mother, Queen Tyi, and even as he ran towards them he heard her voice start to choke and become submerged beneath sobbing. There was a sudden crash, like that of a pot being smashed, and then a second, and when the King entered his mother's room he saw her, with her back to him, her shoulders heaving, hurling her jewels and pots of paint upon the floor. 'Mother!' he cried out. At once she froze. 'What is it?' he demanded. Still she did not move. He crossed to her, reached out to touch her shoulder; and as he did so he saw how withered it appeared, knotted and twisted like the wood of desert scrub. Slowly she turned to face him; and the King, as he gazed at her, could not repress a shudder.

All her youth had vanished, for she seemed as dry and shrivelled as an ancient monkey, and yet that was not the worst, for the taint of her blood had now claimed her utterly, and she appeared more like the statue which King Akh-en-Aten had destroyed, the loathsome image of Isis in the temple, than the mortal woman whom she had seemed the day before. Then suddenly the King felt an even deeper sense of horror, for he understood that the magic of his Queen's protecting hand – which he had imagined had redeemed him for ever from his blood – was now removed, and that everything was plunged back to its former state. And then he thought of Kiya, and of how he had done what he had always sworn he would never do – he had fertilised her womb with the poison of his seed. He realised that he was praying that the child would be stillborn.

But this did not come to pass. A son was born, and he was named Tut-ankh-Aten, which meant in the ancient language, 'the Living Image of the Sun'. And so King Akh-en-Aten trusted he would be, for as yet there was no sign that his blood might be cursed, nor any mark of change upon Smenkh-ka-Re. 'It may be, then,' the King thought to himself, 'that I am still the last of my tainted line'; but in his heart he dreaded that all his prayers would be in vain, and that the power of Amen would triumph in the end. Already, in the city where before he had dwelt in such joy, the sands were skimming in from the plain, choking the flowers, clogging the pools, giving to the winds a lash of fiery dust. Then the Nile failed to rise and the crops began to die, so that all the former plenty was soon reduced to bone; while from far-off frontiers there came rumours of war.

Still King Akh-en-Aten prayed; but even as he did so, it seemed to him that the rays of the sun had grown pitiless and cruel, shrivelling the corn, scorching the fleshless bodies of the cattle, poisoning his city with heat, and stench, and dust.

Plague began to spread through the dying streets; and when it reached the Palace, it bore Kiya from King Akh-en-Aten's arms, swept her away into that darkness where he feared he would never now follow. And so he mourned her for herself, for her beauty and her kindness, and her great love for him which had survived all his cruelty; but even more he mourned for himself. For with Kiya gone, so his past also seemed to have fled, and his memory of it to be like a pool turned into mud.

Once he had laid Kiya's body to rest, King Akh-en-Aten wandered out into the desert alone; and eventually arrived at his own, half-finished, tomb. Within the furthermost corner of its deepest chamber, a portrait of the vanished Queen Nefer-titi had been painted, so vivid and so perfect that it seemed almost alive, and the King, inspecting it alone by the light of his torch, imagined for a moment that it was stepping out from the rock. 'O mighty Queen,' he cried out, 'help me, help me, please!' No answer came, though – for in truth nothing had ever moved. All remained as it had been before.

That afternoon, returned to his Palace, King Akh-en-Aten knew what it was that he had to do. Summoning Ay to him, he ordered that Smenkh-ka-Re be crowned as Pharaoh, and that his own death be proclaimed throughout the Two Lands.

'But what will you do?' asked Ay in consternation.

'Journey the world,' the King answered. 'Nor shall I rest until I have found Nefer-titi once again, for she alone can spare me – and, maybe, my sons – from our doom.' And so saying, he took his uncle by the arm and led him across to a courtyard in the Palace, where Tut-ankh-Aten was being taught to ride a chariot by his brother, both of them laughing and shouting at the other. 'Guard them well,' King Akh-en-Aten whispered. He turned back to his uncle. 'For there is no one else into whose hands I dare to trust them.'

Ay nodded deeply, and then the two men embraced. A moment more King Akh-en-Aten gazed at his sons, but he did not approach them, turning hurriedly away instead. 'Let them think that I am truly dead,' he told Ay, 'so that they may never suspect what their own fates may be.' Only to his mother did King Akh-en-Aten bid farewell; but she seemed barely to hear what he said, muttering instead without meaning to herself, hunched upon a couch and gazing at nothing. King Akh-en-Aten kissed her lovingly upon her brow, then turned back to Ay. 'Guard her well too,' he murmured, 'for I know that she is as precious to you as she has always been to me'; and then he turned and left, and set out into the world, no longer as a King but as a common man.

For many years he wandered, through far-distant lands beyond the Great Green Sea, across mountains which reached up to brush against the sky, and past cities of unimaginable splendour and strangeness. In all of these, Akh-en-Aten would ask if anyone had heard of his lost Queen. Some men, when he described to them her beauty and her powers, would grow pale and accuse him of seeking a god. Some, though, would lead him into their temples, and show him statues of a goddess which did indeed seem like his Queen, save that the colour of her skin and her dress were not the same; and these would vary in turn with every city, so that she seemed to possess a thousand and one different forms. But still, of the Queen herself Akh-en-Aten could find not a trace; and the longer he searched, the more he despaired, for it seemed to him, at length, that he had searched the whole world. So it was, at last, after twelve long years that he found himself drawing back to Egypt; and his heart grew black, for he knew that he had failed.

Even so, as he finally crossed the border into his native land, his spirits lightened at the thought of meeting with those he loved once again. Carefully wrapping a scarf about his head, so that his face and skull were concealed beneath it, he approached a frontier guard. 'How is Pharaoh's health,' he asked him, 'and that of his brother?'

The guard stared at him strangely. 'Pharaoh's brother?' he frowned. 'King Ay has no brother, not so far as I am aware.'

'King Ay?' Akh-en-Aten gazed at the guard in horror and surprise. 'But what of King Smenkh-ka-Re?'

The guard laughed shortly. 'You have indeed been abroad a long while, my friend. King Smenkh-ka-Re has been dead now these past ten years.'

'And what of his brother? What of Tut-ankh-Aten?'

Again the guard stared at him strangely. 'King Tut-ankh-*Amen*,' he said, with emphasis, 'died some hundred days ago. There is no one who would name themselves "Aten" now.' His eyes narrowed even further with sudden suspicion, and he reached up without warning to pull the scarf from Akh-en-Aten's head. But Akh-en-Aten pushed him away and, urging on his camel, galloped past him and on down the road. No one pursued him; yet so grim had his talk with the frontier guard been, and so laden did he find himself with dark forebodings, that Akh-en-Aten dreaded to remain upon the public road; and so he turned and left it, and passed into the desert. He knew there was no one who would follow him there, and so indeed it proved, for there seemed nothing else living in all those burning wastes. Yet sometimes, even so, he would meet with trains of nomads who would be able to direct him across the seemingly featureless sands. Nearer and nearer Akh-en-Aten drew to his goal; and then at last he saw ahead of him a mighty quarry, its rocks gleaming white with veins of bright pink; and he knew that he was but a day's journey from the Dwelling of the Sun.

He resolved to travel on, for all that it was growing late, but even as he approached the quarry the winds began to rise, and a stinging veil of sand to blow against his face. Desperately he struggled to continue on his path, but the winds were soon shrieking as though in violent agony, and the sands seemed almost an impenetrable wall. Swept backwards upon the gusts, Akh-en-Aten wheeled his camel round and, dismounting, sought sanctuary in the massive gulf of the quarry. Yet however deep inside it he retreated, however high the cliffs rose above him, still the sands whirled and burned against his face, and not even in the narrowest ravine could he escape them. Despairingly he gazed back at the swirling darkness, and then ahead at what appeared to be a cliff at the end of the ravine. Even as he stared at it, however, it vanished from his view, blotted out by a black cloud of dust. Akh-en-Aten shivered. As the dust swirled upwards, it seemed to form, just for a moment, the figure of a woman with arms outstretched, her hair blowing wild, and then it was gone and he could see the cliff again. He stumbled towards it. Again, though, it seemed to vanish, and Akh-en-Aten imagined that he saw the woman a second time, still formed of black dust but now also streaked with gold, and he cried out almost without thinking, 'O my Queen!' There was no answer. Akh-en-Aten rubbed his eyes. He could still see the flecks of gold, flowing into crimson, dying the currents of the blackness on the winds, and he imagined at the same moment that he heard a whispering of his name. 'O my Queen!' he cried out again. 'Answer me, I beg you! Show yourself to me!' But the winds, as though in mockery, began to shriek even louder. All was black again now, for the gold and the crimson seemed utterly lost. Akh-en-Aten moaned in confusion. He felt that he was dissolving upon the storm, that the gales were blowing from within his skull, that he was made of nothing but swirling dust himself. 'What must I do?' he screamed. He moaned again, and closed his eyes. 'What must I do?'

'I told you long before what it was you had to do.'

Upon her voice, at once everything had plunged and grown silent.

Akh-en-Aten opened his eyes.

She was standing before the cliff. All was perfectly, unnaturally still, as though frozen within a moment outside the flow of time. In the sky, a narrow strip between the edges of the ravine, the stars blazed distantly.

'And I did it,' he answered. 'I loved you.' He took a step towards her. 'But I could not do it at the expense of everything else I ever loved.'

'Yet that was what you promised me.'

'Then I did not understand what it was you were demanding.'

'So much, at least' – she laughed contemptuously – 'was evident.'

'What are you,' Akh-en-Aten asked slowly, 'to have set so cruel and impossible a requirement? I had thought you were good. I had thought you brought life.'

'And so I did.'

'Yet you also brought death.'

She laughed once again, but with less bitterness now, and she seemed suddenly to flicker as she reached out for his hand. 'It is the way of things, O my husband, that I shall always offer both.'

'Why?' Akh-en-Aten frowned. 'I do not understand.'

'Why should you?' she answered. 'You are not from the stars.'

'Is it so different, then, in the realm of the heavens?'

'Indeed,' she laughed, 'for it is a realm of infinite power, where things may be achieved impossible to recount, and marvels of a kind which you have witnessed for yourself and yet still will never understand, for you are intermingled with the dust of this world.' She seemed to flicker again suddenly and to rise, partaking of the blaze of the tapestry of stars. 'I am spirit and flesh, dissolution and control, life and, yes . . .' – she paused – 'death as well. Within the realm of the Heavens, this would seem no wonder – yet on this world it is a mystery which no one can endure.'

'Why, then,' asked Akh-en-Aten, narrowing his eyes yet determined to continue meeting with her gaze, 'do you not return to the stars?'

'I cannot,' she answered shortly; and in her stare, for just a fleeting moment, there seemed to stretch again the expanse of an icy loneliness. 'I have said,' she murmured, 'that my powers are infinite – and yet in truth they are not, for I cannot escape from this narrow world, this place of exile to which long ago I plunged from the Heavens and which now, I dread, will serve me as my prison for all time.'

But Akh-en-Aten frowned and shook his head. 'All things are possible by the will of the All-High. If you fell then so also you may be raised. If you were exiled, then so also you may be summoned back to your home. Do not despair, O my Queen. Walk in the paths of goodness, and much may be achieved.'

But the Queen laughed at these words with a deathly bitterness. 'There was one once,' she answered, 'who did try to walk along the paths which you advise – one of my fellows, for when I fell to this world I did not come alone. It was he who first taught the arts of living to men, who sought to raise them from their brutish state and reveal to them the wonders of the universe of things. Everywhere, all across the world, he travelled – and yet his true home, the realm which he most loved, was this of Egypt.'

'Then I know his name,' said Akh-en-Aten, speaking very quietly. 'His name was Osiris.' He swallowed, his horror intermingled with awe. 'And I know now that you,' he

continued, 'should be truly named Isis, and that it was you –
you and Seth – who caused Osiris to be slain.'

'So it was.' The Queen bowed her head. 'And yet . . .' –
she raised her eyes to gaze at him again – 'it was not done in
the sense which the High Priest doubtless told you.'

'Then in what sense?'

Still she gazed at him, and it seemed to Akh-en-Aten that
she did so now almost with pity. 'O my husband . . .' she
murmured at last. She reached out gently to pull the scarf
from his head, then to stroke the distended curve of his
skull. 'As I told you,' she whispered, 'he sought to do good,
the first King of this land, for his heart was filled with
the love of all things – and yet soon he was betrayed by the
nature of this world, for it is not like the Heavens but ages
and grows old, hurrying without break towards decrepi-
tude. The King sought others to love – but in vain! – for
whatever is loved upon this world must fade and die. And so
at last he declined, and grew sapped by despair and came to
loathe his own nature, for he longed himself to die. He
came to me, the wisest of his fellows, as I was also the dearest to him, and asked me to achieve an impossible miracle –
to dissolve him into mortality.'

Akh-en-Aten gazed at her in wonder. 'And did you
achieve it,' he whispered, 'this impossible desire?'

She smiled very thinly. 'In a manner of speaking,' she
replied.

'Then it was true what the priests always claimed, that you
had the mastery of the magic of the Secret Name of Amen?'

Her smile grew broader. 'Anything may be called magic,'
she answered, 'which one cannot understand.'

'Very well.' Akh-en-Aten frowned. 'What, then, did you
do?'

'Can you not guess?' She raised her other hand and
clasped both his cheeks. 'Can you truly not guess?' She

kissed him softly, as she had kissed him long before, on the first time of their meeting in the Dwelling of the Sun. 'Osiris was dissolved,' she whispered, 'into the line of Egypt's kings. It might be said, therefore, O Pharaoh – he was dissolved into you.'

'No.' Akh-en-Aten shrank back. 'No. But I . . . No.'

'Yes.' She smiled, and kissed him once again.

'How is it possible?'

'You share in his essence. What he was, his nature, helps to form what you are now. You demonstrate in your very being the miracle I achieved.'

'And yet, in truth,' said Akh-en-Aten slowly, 'the miracle – it failed.'

The Queen froze a moment, then arched an eyebrow. 'Indeed?'

'We age, that is true – yet still we never die. It was not a prize, then, that you granted your fellow but a curse, a cruel and hideous curse. What a fall, O my Queen – to have been a creature as great and mighty as yourself, and then to be transformed into a pitiful creature like me, a creature like all those Kings who came before me, who are nothing now but the playthings and the secret food of priests.'

The Queen smiled. 'It was what he desired. For the fate you have described . . . is it not, after all, a form of extinction?'

'And yet you loved him.'

'Loved?' Her smile grew more cold. 'You think I was a fool like him, to repeat his mistakes?' She shook her head. 'I have never truly loved. I have seen what it may bring.'

'And yet he was not mortal. He was a being like yourself.'

'What of it?'

'I know that you loved him.'

She smiled again. 'How?'

Akh-en-Aten gazed at her in silence a moment. 'Why did

you come to me?' he asked her at last. 'Why, of all my line, did you come to seek me out?'

'You dared to penetrate my sanctuary and shatter my statue.' She shrugged. 'I was – I confess it – diverted . . . intrigued.'

'And yet it was also – I am certain – something more than that.'

'Oh?' She smiled. 'Indeed?'

'I dare to believe – in my ambitions, in my hopes – that you caught an echo of the ambitions and hopes of someone else.'

The smile remained frozen a long while on her lips. 'That is indeed,' she murmured at last, 'a great presumption.'

'And yet is it not true?'

The Queen turned from him. She seemed to quicken once again upon the distant flickering of the stars, and for a moment Akh-en-Aten dreaded that she would melt and disappear into their light. Yet she turned again at last, and fixed him with her stare. 'Tell me, then,' she whispered, 'what it is you want from me.'

'I want . . .' – Akh-en-Aten paused – 'what you failed to give before.'

She reached out with her hands again and cupped his face. 'Mortality?' she whispered, the word melting into a kiss.

Akh-en-Aten broke away from her lips to answer her question. 'Mortality,' he echoed. 'I want the peace of death.'

She laughed. 'A small desire.'

'Yet is it possible?'

'For those of your line to know death, after all?' She paused. 'It may be.'

'How?'

'Only an immortal may consume an immortal. Only the deathless may give to the deathless true death.'

Akh-en-Aten gazed at her in a fury of hope and frustration. 'What do you mean? You are speaking in riddles.'

She smiled at him. 'It would require a great sacrifice from one of your line.'

'Sacrifice?'

'You, O my husband.' She kissed him once again. 'If I have indeed caught an echo of your great ancestor from within you, if your ambitions are indeed not merely presumptions – then I know you will be willing to sacrifice yourself.'

He gazed at her in horror but also, still, some hope. 'What, then,' he whispered, 'would this sacrifice mean?'

The Queen parted her lips again in a smile. Akh-en-Aten did not this time seek to break from her kiss; and, even as he felt her lips upon his own, he seemed to hear the sound of her voice from deep within his mind. 'It will teach you,' he heard her whisper, 'how in love there must be hatred, and how in life there must be death. It will teach you what my fellow never understood. It will teach you, in short, what it means to be alone – not just now, not for a while, but for the eternity of time.' She paused; and he felt himself melting all the more into her kiss. 'Such would be the sacrifice. Such would be your fate.'

Dimly, from afar, he could feel himself fading. Dimly, from afar, one last time he heard her voice.

'Do you accept, then, such an offer?'

He knew he did not have to answer her, knew she understood. Darkness was rising thick upon her kiss, so that even the stars now seemed blotted out. Darkness seemed the breath that was blotting out his thoughts. Darkness seemed the world, seemed the universe itself.

———————

But at this point, Haroun saw the approach of morning and broke off from his tale. 'O Commander of the Faithful,' he said, 'if you would care to return here tomorrow evening, then I shall describe to you the price which Akh-en-Aten found that he had paid.'

And so the Caliph did as Haroun suggested; and the following evening he returned to the mosque.

And Haroun said:

It happened one morning that King Ay rode out to hunt. He was by now an old man, and had seen two of his great-nephews rule as kings and pass away. There was no one in all the royal court who could bend and string his bow so well, or rival his skill in the pursuit of wild beasts. Furiously that day he rode his chariot, and thrillingly he felt his blood starting to course through his limbs, so that he almost imagined himself young once again. He laughed in exultancy and ordered his charioteer to step down, taking up the reins and controlling them himself. It soon happened that all his party were left far behind, but still Ay rode onwards, and if he stopped, it was only to pull back an arrow on his string. Many were the beasts that fell before his skill, and in the end the greatest, the deadliest of them all – a giant lion, black and wild-maned, who would have killed King Ay in turn had the King's aim not been good.

The beast's death made certain, he reined in his horses. Stepping down from his chariot, he crossed the sands to inspect his prize. As he did so, he heard his horses suddenly whinny as though with fear. King Ay glanced back at them, then around him, and slowly drew out his sword. He could see nothing, but even so for a moment he stood frozen with his sword aimed at the air. Then, slowly again, he bent down beside the lion and drew out his arrows from the dead beast's flank. He gazed at it in silence, at the stillness of its death; then suddenly he heard his horses neigh wildly again and he felt, across his back, the falling of a shadow.

He twisted round, raising his sword, and saw before him a figure shrouded in dark robes. As he gazed up, King Ay shuddered with a terrible, unaccountable fear, and he felt his fingers grow numb and his sword fall from his hand. 'Who are you?' he whispered.

The figure did not answer.

'Who are you?' King Ay whispered a second time; but suddenly, as he gazed upon the figure's distended skull, visible even through the swathes of his scarves, he knew, barely believing it, who the stranger was. 'Pharaoh.' The word seemed to hang and burn in the air as King Ay stumbled forward, falling to his knees. 'You have returned!'

'Do not draw near me.' The voice had been barely above a whisper and with a note that seemed hauntingly, musically strange, like that of silver pieces being blown on by a wind. Still though, King Ay recognised it and, despite himself, stumbled forward again.

'*Do not draw near me.*'

'Why?' King Ay gazed up at his nephew baffled and uncertain. 'What will you do?'

'What I cannot control in myself.' And so saying Akh-en-Aten shuddered and seemed to clench his fists, as though fighting some desperate, monstrous urge, borne to him upon the very scent of his uncle. 'No more of this,' he hissed. He shuddered again, and half-closed his eyes. 'I would have you tell me what you did to my sons.'

King Ay frowned. 'To your sons? But . . . I did nothing.'

'Then how did they die?'

King Ay's frown deepened and he rose slowly to his feet. 'Of those frailties to which we are all of us the heirs. Smenkh-ka-Re, within a few months of your departure, grew sick of a fever. All that could be done we sought to do – but alas, it was in vain. So great was the surprise that there had not even been a tomb prepared for him, and so my sister gave him hers, which had been built for her in Thebes. He was buried within the shrine she had prepared for her own death, with every honour, O my nephew – every honour, I swear it.'

Akh-en-Aten nodded shortly. 'And Tut-ankh-Aten?' he asked.

'Tut-ankh . . .' King Ay swallowed in sudden confusion. 'He . . . sat upon the throne for ten years, growing to man-hood, a handsome, much-loved King. But then he also, like his brother, died of fever. No mystery, O my Nephew, no mystery at all. Such things must happen, for we are all of us mortal, even Pharaohs, O my Nephew, even the greatest of Kings.'

Akh-en-Aten smiled very thinly. 'And yet I tell you, O my Uncle, that if Tut-ankh-Aten is truly dead, then it is a wonder that the earth has not been shadowed by the news, that the Nile has not dried up, that the ocean has not swayed, and that the land itself has not been turned upside down. *If* he is truly dead – for you cannot know what it was that ended with him.' Akh-en-Aten paused a moment, and then he shook his head. 'And yet he died of a fever – and that was all?'

King Ay shrugged helplessly. 'He was laid to rest with every splendour, I promise you.'

Immediately, Akh-en-Aten tensed and narrowed his eyes. 'Where?'

'In the valley beyond Thebes.'

'Thebes.' Akh-en-Aten almost spat out the word. 'Why not in a tomb beside Kiya, his mother, in the cliffs above the city of the Dwelling of the Sun?'

Again King Ay swallowed and stammered in confusion, but Akh-en-Aten, in a sudden surge of fury, raised his hand. 'I have seen it for myself,' he cried. 'Abandoned to those weeds which will grow amidst the sands, to the serpents and the jackals, and the mournful-sounding owls. Why, O my Uncle? How could you have permitted my great work to be destroyed?'

'Did you not order me,' King Ay answered, 'to obey your sons' commands?'

'Yes, but I cannot believe they would have wanted you to destroy their father's cause.'

'You may well be right – yet all the same, when they spoke, they did so as Kings.'

'Inen.' Akh-en-Aten whispered the name very softly. 'Inen. Has he returned?'

King Ay paused, then nodded. 'He is once again the High Priest.'

'Then it was he,' Akh-en-Aten whispered, almost to himself, 'who must have ruled my sons. And it was he, it may be, who delivered them to their tombs.' He turned, glided across the sands and seemed to melt into the haze.

'Wait!' King Ay shouted out.

Akh-en-Aten did not pause.

'Wait,' King Ay cried again, 'there is something I must tell you!'

But only an echo answered his cry. Where before the figure of Akh-en-Aten had been, there was nothing but the shimmering of dust in the air. King Ay stumbled to his feet and ran across the sands. Still he could see nothing. He gazed about him, then frowned and shook his head. 'May peace be with him,' King Ay muttered. He shivered, despite the burning heat. 'For I fear he greatly needs it.' He glanced about him once again, then crossed back to his chariot. He could see his courtiers now approaching in a heavy cloud of dust. As they joined him they fell and knelt down in the sand, then gazed in wonder at the body of the lion. King Ay accepted their cries of praise without comment; nor during all the ride back to the Palace in Thebes, did he say a further word. But the servants marked the strangeness of the expression on his face; and they whispered that their King must have witnessed something wondrous.

And it happened, even as King Ay was riding back to Thebes, that his brother Inen also found himself shadowed by strange emotions. He had entered the innermost sanctuary of the temple, where silence – deep silence, the silence of stone and of a close, heavy darkness – had at last been restored. Inen raised his candle. Although the room was small, still the darkness remained in dense, deep-brooding pools, only thinly lined by the faint wash of his flame. Here, Inen thought to himself, is true mystery – and where there is mystery, there must be terror as well. He stepped forward; raised his candle; gazed at the statue against the furthermost wall. He had had to piece its fragments together himself, for no one else could have been permitted to gaze upon its form, and since he lacked any skills his work had been clumsy. Even so, barely recognisable as it was, the aspect of the statue served to fill him with dread – as must all things, he reflected, which touch upon the gods.

Inen thought, suddenly, that he heard something from behind him. He spun round, raising his candle, even though he knew he would see nothing there. He smiled to himself ruefully. Ever since his exile from Thebes, his imaginings had seemed feverish, uncertain, not his own at all. He had hoped that his return might have served to ease such fears. He raised his hands to where his ears once had been. Much had been lost. He touched the noseless scar which ran up his face. Much that would never, for all his efforts, be restored. He turned again to face the shattered statue. Such vandalism, he thought. Such sacrilege, such ruin! He cursed beneath his breath the criminal who had wreaked it.

Then suddenly, even as he spoke his nephew's name, he heard a noise like a footstep, and this time he was certain that he had not imagined the sound. 'Who is that?' he shouted, raising his candle. 'Who dares to enter this most secret, holy place?'

Silence still answered him but he could see now, as though it were itself composed of the darkness, a silhouette yet more black than all the shadows around it. Its limbs seemed thin, its belly distended, its skull – like the statue's behind him – very swollen. 'Who is that?' Inen cried out again. He had attempted in his voice to preserve a tone of authority, but as he spoke, fear made it suddenly crack. The figure took a single pace forward and, with a sweep of its hand, removed the swathe of cloth which had been wound about its face. Inen shrank back with a horror he no longer sought to disguise. He could see now who the stranger was, for despite the darkness his skin seemed to gleam very palely, as though lit from within by a burning white light. In his eyes as well there was an astonishing brightness, and Inen knew, without asking, that his visitor had been marked by a wondrous and deathly change.

Despite himself, he took a step forward, but the figure raised its hand. '*Do not draw near me.*'

'Why?' Inen clenched his fists in fear and rage. 'What will you do?'

'What I cannot control in myself.'

'And what might that be?'

The shadow of a smile seemed to flicker on Akh-en-Aten's lips. 'You are not,' he said softly, 'the only guardian of mystery. But tell me' – he gazed about him, at the stone above his head – 'how is it that this roof has been restored, and that statue' – he pointed – 'erected once again? When last I saw this place, it had been abandoned to the weeds.'

'It is the temple to your god, O Criminal, which has been toppled and abandoned now.' Inen clenched his fists again, no longer with terror though, but in a sudden flush of

triumph. 'Your works and your statues have been flung into
the dirt, and your very name defaced wherever it was found.
In times to come it will be forgotten that one such as you
has ever even been – you and your city, your god, and your
sons.'

'My sons . . .' Akh-en-Aten spoke the words so harshly,
and with such an icy force, that Inen felt all his terror suddenly return. 'My sons . . .' Akh-en-Aten narrowed his eyes.
'Is it true what Ay told me, that they both died of fever?'

'So it was reported.'

'They were both unmarked, untainted by the curse of my
blood?'

'So it was reported,' Inen answered once again.

'But was it true? I have to know. Tell me, was it true?'

Inen swallowed. Despite himself, he met with Akh-en-
Aten's eyes. Drawn into their brightness, he imagined
himself suddenly stabbed upon their glare and he moaned
with surprise. 'It was true,' he muttered, 'yes, it was true . . .'
Desperately he sought to break free his stare, yet still he
found himself trapped, so that he imagined he was drowning
beneath a rolling wave of fear.

'It was true, it was true . . .' he muttered once again.

Akh-en-Aten's eyes seemed to flicker and blaze all the
more. 'I wish I could believe you,' he murmured at last.

'Why can you not?' Inen almost screamed now, so great
was his fear, so desperate his longing to be released from his
nephew's burning stare. 'Do you think that if they had
indeed borne the marks of the sacred blood, I would have
wanted to see them buried before either had in turn fathered
sons? What value did the magic of their flesh have to me,
compared with the need to perpetuate their line? Within the
temple of the sands, far and safe from here, there is magic
flesh enough, rows and rows of bodies bound by funeral
wrappings – but upon the throne of Egypt there will sit no

370

more heirs of Osiris.' He swallowed. His every thought still seemed illumined by the blaze of his nephew's eyes. 'Unless Tyi fathers sons. Unless Tyi fathers sons and perpetuates the line . . .'

'Yes,' Akh-en-Aten murmured. At last he closed his eyes. 'I had forgotten. Only she remains.'

'Why?' Inen had sought to suppress any note of alarm; but he knew, as he heard his own voice rise and tremble, that he had failed. 'What will you do with her?'

'What business is that of yours?'

'She is my sister.'

Akh-en-Aten laughed in contempt. 'She is your only chance, you mean, to perpetuate the line. Why else would you care for her?'

'She was . . . she is . . .' Inen swallowed, his gaze once again drawn into his nephew's stare. 'I have never loved anything,' he whispered at last, 'save only her.'

Akh-en-Aten laughed again bitterly. 'And so you showed your love by snaking back here to Thebes and attempting, no doubt, to persuade her to share the horror of an eternity with you – to consume the flesh of her own flesh, to become cannibal as you had done.'

Inen gazed at him in surprise; then he smiled very thinly. 'I brought none of the magic flesh with me,' he answered.

'Then why did you return?'

'I have told you – I hoped to find that Tut-ankh-Amen was the true heir to your blood. But in vain.' His thin smile broadened. 'For he was already in his tomb.'

Akh-en-Aten started with an ill-concealed astonishment. 'Yet that was barely seventy days ago.'

'Indeed.'

'You had not returned before that?'

'No.'

'Then . . .' Akh-en-Aten frowned, and the blaze in his

eyes seemed suddenly transformed into a blankness just as deathly and grim. 'Then . . . who was it abandoned my city and my god? Who was it persuaded my son to change his name? Who was it' – he gestured with his arm at the darkness all about him – 'ordered this place of monstrosities rebuilt?'

'You did not know?'

'Who?' Akh-en-Aten's face seemed etched again with a burning look of pain. 'Who was it?'

Inen's laughter was as thin as his smile. 'Your mother,' he spat. 'Your mother, O Pharaoh, my sister, Queen Tyi! All was done by her!'

'I do not believe you.'

'And yet it is the truth.'

'It cannot be.'

'Look into my thoughts. You know there is nothing I can hide from you.'

Akh-en-Aten stood shrouded in silence a moment. 'Then I am resolved.' He said this slowly, as though he were surprised. The gleam in his face was growing icy once again. 'I am resolved.' He turned. 'It must be done at once.'

'Wait!'

Akh-en-Aten did not pause but Inen, stumbling forward, ran after him and reached out to pull upon his robes. 'Wait!' But Akh-en-Aten was already turning round, his face so hideously contorted that Inen, gazing upon him, could barely credit the transformation, for his nephew's cheeks were growing hectic and his eyes aflame, and his mouth was wide in a trembling snarl. 'Get away,' he moaned, 'get away from me now!', even as he reached down with his hands for Inen's throat and Inen, twisting desperately, barely succeeded in escaping. Scrabbling backwards, he gazed at his nephew in disbelief. 'What has happened?' he whispered. 'What have you become?'

Akh-en-Aten breathed in deeply and with evident care, as though too sharp an intake might undam once again the mighty flood of his desire. He smiled horribly. 'Have you not always taught, O my uncle, how the Lady Isis had the power of the secret name of Amen, and could achieve with it whatever magic she so pleased?'

'Yes,' answered Inen. 'That is what we teach, for she is titled "Great of Magic".'

'Then you should know that what she gives she may also take away.'

'How do you mean?'

'That the immortality of the line of Osiris is no more. That those who share in it at last may be granted their repose. That there is no life so eternal that I may not choose to end it.'

'You?'

'Me. For have you not understood?' Again he smiled horribly. 'I am become Death myself.'

'No,' Inen stammered, 'no, I do not understand.'

'I am hungry for life – and what is Death, in the end, if not such a hunger?'

'Then you . . .' Inen recalled the snarl of desperation he had seen on his nephew's face, the burning, quivering gaze of desire. 'You were hungry for me? Hungry for my . . .?'

'Taste.' Akh-en-Aten spoke the word softly; and yet to Inen, the sound seemed to spill throughout the darkness. 'And so it is, O my Uncle, that you should keep far from me. As before, so now, I would have you live for ever – for there can be no more terrible nor more truly deathly fate. Yet draw near me, and all the same I will drain you of your life, for it is sweet and golden, and precious to me, and I will no longer fight against the lure which it extends. All life is a temptation to me now, but yours, O my Uncle – yours especially so.'

As he said this, his eyes seemed to open upon a darkness that was infinite; and Inen, gazing upon it, sought to break his stare away, lest he be lost within anything so eternal and cold. 'Why?' he whispered softly. 'Why should mine be so precious to you?'

The darkness in Akh-en-Aten's eyes seemed to cloud. 'I am Death,' he said again. 'I am not permitted what for mortals is the dearest prize of all – the love of family . . . of a mother, a brother, a sister, a child . . .'

'Of a mother?' Inen whispered.

'Of course.' Akh-en-Aten smiled. 'For even more than you, Tyi is life of my life – and she, for that reason, will taste the sweetest of all.' His smile faded, and for a moment he stood frozen; then it seemed to Inen that he started to flicker, as though he were made of the darkness which lined the wash of the candle flame. 'Leave me well alone,' he whispered. 'Depart Thebes today. For should I ever meet with you again, then I swear it – you will die.' His final word lingered as an echo in the air, sounding again and again through Inen's mind; yet the figure of his nephew seemed already disappeared. Inen stepped forward. 'Die,' he heard, 'die'; yet there was no one there with him. There was no trace, no other sound of Akh-en-Aten at all.

Quickly Inen gathered his possessions together, then hurried from the temple almost at a run. The single word, strangely echoing, still sounded through his head. He would leave, he decided, that very afternoon. Leave across the deserts. Leave, if it had to be, regrettably, alone. Before departing, however, he sought out his sister, pacing through her quarters and visiting her every favoured haunt and spot, desperate for her son not to have found his mother first. Inen rehearsed what he would say: 'Come with me,' he muttered, 'come with me, let us live with each other and be happy for all time.' Suddenly the thought that he might not find her, that her son might kill her after all, struck him as a horror too great to be borne; and he remembered, as though understanding them for the first time, the words with which his nephew had sentenced him to life. 'There can be no more terrible, nor more truly deathly fate.' 'No,' Inen thought to himself, 'no – not if my sister, not if Tyi can be found.'

But it happened, even as Inen was searching through the Palace, that she was already riding with great speed towards the Valley. For King Ay, upon his return to Thebes, had at once sought his sister out and given her the tidings of her son's return; but Tyi, to the King's surprise, had displayed no joy but only dread. 'You were certain,' she had pressed him, 'certain it was my son?'; and her mood, as King Ay had nodded, had only darkened all the more. She had risen at once and scuttled from the room, and when King Ay had sought to follow her, she had screamed at him in fury to leave her well alone. So the King had not seen her give orders to the captain of his guards, nor witnessed the gathering in the forecourt of some twenty men, mounted on horses and laden with picks. Nor had he seen her leave the Palace, leading her party along the road towards the Valley; for it was now growing dark, and the sun was near to setting.

Tyi herself rode well apart from her horsemen, for she could not endure to be stared at by those whose limbs were not like hers, whose bellies were not swollen, and whose skulls were not hideously distended and vast. It had been her habit now for years to swathe herself in black, so that even her eyes were concealed beneath a veil; yet even so, it discomforted her to be abroad upon a public road, and away from the protecting walls of her quarters. Nevertheless, she had no difficulty in outpacing the men behind her: for the more that the stamp of her blood seemed upon her, so the greater she found that her strength had become.

As she passed between the cliffs which led into the Valley, the last light of the sun disappeared behind the hills. Tyi reined in her horse and glanced behind her. The guards had stopped as well and were busy lighting torches. Tyi smiled. She had no need of flames to illumine her path, since for many years now she had seen better in the dark than in the fullest light of day. She called out impatiently to her men to follow her, then wheeled her horse round and continued along the path. There was not far now to go. She studied the contours of the rocks ahead, and made out her twin destinations with ease. To her left the hurriedly prepared tomb of Smenkh-ka-Re; to her right that of her younger grandson, Tut-ankh-Amen. There was nothing to indicate where either tomb lay, yet Tyi had chosen the spots herself with great care, and she knew exactly where the work of excavation would have to begin. Only the choice of the first tomb to open made her pause; then she smiled and nodded, and turned to the left. 'Let he who has lain longest be recovered first.' She clambered up the rocks; then stood above the doorway to the tomb of Smenkh-ka-Re.

Tyi bent down, scooping up pebbles and dust, then allowing them to slip through her long, curling fingers. She glanced down at her hand, withered and claw-like as it was, with a disgust which she had never quite learned to master, then turned impatiently to look for her men. But all was dark, and of the torches which they had been lighting there was now not a trace. In a fury of disbelief, Tyi cried out to the guards to join her – but only the echo of her own voice replied. She stood motionless, listening to the sound fade away into the night; and then suddenly she shuddered, and knew that she was not alone after all.

She turned and gasped, an exclamation of mingled horror, and fury, and dread. 'You!' she whispered. He was standing above her on a flat ledge of rock; his face bare and his head uncovered. The marks of his blood, she saw, seemed touched by some other, even stranger stamp.

'Draw near to me,' he smiled, holding out his arms. 'For do you not wish, O my Mother, after so long, to embrace me?'

'Ay told me . . .' she stammered, '. . . said you had returned.'

'And so you rode out here to the valley of the tombs?'

She laughed bitterly. 'Why should I not?'

'It is an accursed place.'

'Then it is all the more fitting a place for me.' She fumbled suddenly with the veil across her face, pulling it away and turning back to face her son. 'See!' she cried out, 'how ugly I have grown! I, who was once so beautiful and desired, am become a thing of horror, and people shrink and look away should they ever see my face!' She swallowed, trying to choke back her sobs, then her misery was consumed by a scorching blast of rage. 'I must keep to my rooms, I must never walk abroad, I must shroud my face and limbs beneath veils and scarves and robes. It is worse, O my Son, than any Harim – yet as I escaped the latter, so also I shall escape this prison of disgust.'

'How?' he whispered.

'You may join me,' she told him suddenly. 'Yes,' she nodded with a furious violence, 'yes, yes, you must.'

'What must I do?'

'Why,' she answered, 'rule with me as King. For as I am immortal now, so soon I shall cease to wither and grow old, and who then would there be who could stand in my way?'

Akh-en-Aten shook his head slowly. 'How will you cease to wither and grow old?'

But Tyi ignored him and spoke on wildly, almost as though she were arguing with herself. 'It had been my intention,' she muttered, 'to wait until Ay's death, for I loved him, I loved him . . . But why should I wait?' She laughed even as she also began to sob again, her fingers twitching as they plucked at her robes, tearing them away to reveal the withered, distended limbs beneath. 'When I am King,' she choked, 'when I sit upon the throne, there will be no one who will dare to look away from me again. And I shall be loved. And I shall be loved. And all shall be as it was before.'

But Akh-en-Aten shook his head very slowly once again. 'How,' he repeated, 'will you cease to grow old?'

She gazed up at him, startled, then gestured with her arms. 'Here, beneath the sands, there waits a wondrous prize!'

'No,' said Akh-en-Aten gently. He half-raised his hand as though to reach out for her, even though he still stood high upon the ledge. 'The bodies of the Kings have been removed, O my Mother. Removed and replaced. Do you not remember? Inen told us so.'

'Then he lied.' Tyi bent down suddenly, scrabbling with her hands and scratching at the pebbles piled upon the rocks. 'He lied!' She laughed again, gazing up and beckoning to her son, only to find that he was already coming, descending from the ledge, walking with a measured step down the face of the slope. Some four paces from her he tensed, then stopped once again; and Tyi saw suddenly that his eyes seemed like bright points of fire.

She gazed down at the dust in her hands, then scattered it and slowly rose to her feet again. She had been ready to tell him, she realised suddenly, ready to betray her most precious secret; but now, gazing upon his face, there seemed the hint of such a danger that it froze her dumb with shock. How pinched his cheeks appeared, how parted his lips, how mobile, and restless, and hungry his stare! 'What is it?' she whispered, rediscovering her voice. 'O my Son, tell me what has happened to you, for I have never seen such a strange look in anyone before.'

Akh-en-Aten breathed in deeply. He did not reply.

Enraptured and appalled, Tyi still gazed into his eyes. She thought of the tomb below her. It would have been so easy, she thought in a sudden fury of regret, to unplaster the stonework, and to dismember the body of the still-living King – laid out as it had been upon the floor of the tomb, while the corpse of another had been placed within the shrine. Neither Ay nor the priests had ever discovered the subterfuge, and those servants who had accomplished it she had then ordered slain – so as to be certain that the body would still be easy to retrieve. And as with Smenkh-ka-Re, so also with Tut-ankh-Amen: it would be a simple matter for both bodies to be seized and born secretly away.

Desperately, Tyi broke from the gleam of her son's eyes. She gazed about her again, searching for any sign of torches, for any hint that her men might not all have fled. But darkness was everywhere; and once again Tyi felt a surge of frustration and rage. To be so near, she thought, to the long-awaited prize, to be so near – and now for her son, of all men, to have arrived . . .

She glanced once again very briefly at her feet. 'It may be,' she said slowly, 'that there is still magic flesh to be found beneath the rocks.'

'No,' whispered Akh-en-Aten, as gently as before. 'All, O my Mother, all, all is gone, and of the magic line of Osiris – only you remain.'

'Yet it may be we should look.' She gazed at him eagerly. 'Yes – you and I.'

He did not answer for a long while, but Tyi saw that his eyes blazed as brightly as before, and at last he shook his head. 'Why,' he asked her, 'have you forgotten the All-High, the God of your father – the God of your son?'

'Has He not forgotten me?'

'He forgets nothing.'

'Then look upon me!'

'I do.' Akh-en-Aten nodded, parting his lips. 'I do.'

Both stood in silence a moment; then Akh-en-Aten smiled, so sadly and yet with such a radiance of love that it seemed to Tyi, gazing upon him, that the marks of the curse upon his face were no more, and that she was gazing again upon the small boy she remembered – her beloved son, her beauteous child. He held out his arms as he had done before, and this time, enraptured, she stepped forward to meet them. She felt him hold her; felt the softest touch of his lips upon her brow; and then suddenly she gasped, for she felt his fingers on her throat.

'What will you do?' she whispered, briefly attempting to escape from his hold; and then she could speak no more, for her neck seemed muffled by a warm tide of moistness, and she felt all her strength draining softly away. She sought to twist and observe her son's face, but in vain, for it was buried deep within the wound which he had gashed across her neck. Her head lolled back; for the briefest moment, in the sky she saw the blaze of the stars; and then they faded, and their light was utterly extinguished. 'Can this be death?' Tyi wondered in astonishment; and she moaned, both with fear and exultation. She thought briefly of the tomb and its contents below her, and she wanted to speak, to warn her son of the secret. But already the darkness she had glimpsed within the sky was rolling down upon her, and as it had extinguished the stars so it bore across her thoughts. She barely felt the touch of the sand upon her back as gently, very gently, she was laid on the ground; and she barely felt her son's final parting kiss upon her brow. Yet she knew what he had done; and her last thought, her last feeling, was remembrance of her son.

Yet Akh-en-Aten knew nothing of that; and when at last he was certain that his mother was dead, and that the curse of her immortality had indeed been banished by his thirst, he could not endure to gaze upon her face again. He dug a trench, very rough and ready, and buried the corpse as rapidly as he could; then he rose, and departed, and left the Valley behind. And where he went, and what he became, there is no man who can say; and that is the Tale of Pharaoh and the Temple of Amen, and as I have told you it, so it truly occurred.

————————

And when Leila had concluded her tale, she fell silent and smiled to behold my astonishment and wonder. 'By the holy name of Allah,' I exclaimed, my eyes as wide as the fullest moon, 'this Tale of Pharaoh and the Temple of Amen which you have related to me is indeed a remarkable and a terrible one! Much which was dark now stands illumined, and much which was secret now stands revealed. Yet I could almost wish, O Mighty Jinni, that I had never listened to your tale, for I dread now to learn what it is you wish to grant me.'

But Leila smiled and reached out to stroke my cheek. 'How can you doubt that, O my Beloved?' she whispered. 'For did you not, as Akh-en-Aten did, overthrow my sacred statue? And did you not, as Akh-en-Aten did, keep me as your wife? And did you not, as Akh-en-Aten did, break your solemn vow, and yet seek me out again once I had melted from your embrace, as I had promised I would do? You know what I gave him, and the price which he paid. Dare you, O my Husband' – she smiled – 'pay the same?'

'May Allah have mercy upon me, I cannot!' And even as I said this, O Prince, I was thinking of Haidée, my daughter, and imagining what it might mean never to be with her again, never to watch her grow into womanhood, lest I be drawn to slay her and feed upon her flesh. For in all this wide world, with its many riches and beauties and wonders, still there is nothing more precious to me than my child – my only, sweetest, beloved child. As Allah is great, I thought to myself, never shall I throw such a peerless joy away! But then suddenly, O Caliph, I remembered your threat, how Haidée's life would be forfeit should I fail to meet with your command, and return without the mastery of the powers of life and death. And all at once I imagined that I saw before me, as though conjured up by the sorcery of the shrine, a vision of my daughter slain upon your word. So vivid she appeared that I cried out in sorrow and rose up from my seat, for I longed to take and cradle her in my arms. But the vision at once began to melt and change before me, and I imagined that, where before my daughter had been, I saw an image of the sleeper released from his tomb, that man who once, I knew, had been a Pharaoh of Egypt and had borne the name of Smenkh-ka-Re, but was now the monstrous father of an army of the *udar*. I saw him raise his bloodied mace in triumph; and all at once I saw the vision start to change, and there stretched before me a view of Cairo, Mother of the World, fairest of fair cities and jewel amongst jewels. Everywhere, though, appeared silent and still; and then I marked how in the streets, and the markets and the mosques, bodies lay piled to be the food of flies and dogs, and corpses were bobbing upon the waters of the Nile. And then I understood, O Caliph, that all the world might be in peril, for the danger unleashed from the tomb would surely spread, unless something were done, some marvel achieved; and then I thought to myself how Allah alone can see all things for the best. I rubbed my eyes and the visions faded, and I turned back to Leila, and she took me by the hands. And although I said nothing, I felt her presence in my thoughts; and I did not break away when her lips touched my own. And at once, like a sweet and wondrous sleep, I felt a darkness; and the darkness filled me, and I saw nothing more.

When I awoke I found I was alone save for Isis, my dog, who lay sleeping by my feet; and I imagined, for a moment, that I had passed through nothing but a dream. But then I arose; and I realised that I was changed, and I saw all about me the marks of Leila's power. The temple, it was true, was as ruined as before, its bare abandoned pillars half-sunk beneath the sands; but all about them, piled against the giant blocks of stone, were the bodies of the *udar*, the ghools bred from the tomb, and of all that vast number, the army I had seen, massed before the wall which I had built across the temple, not one remained alive. In wonder I passed through the ruins of the temple, and beyond their shadow, gathered by the Nile I saw the villagers bowed low in praise of the All-High. Then, as I approached them, they all turned and rose to greet me, proclaiming me a magician of unparalleled power; but even as they thanked me, I saw that their wonder seemed touched by something almost like fear, and I wondered if the mark of my transformation were very plain.

But no one spoke of it to me, and I in turn revealed nothing to them. Only to the Headman, as I walked with him alone through the valley of the tombs, did I repeat the story which I had learned the night before; and I ordered him to remember and guard the secret well. Then, when all had been told, I showed him, painted upon the walls of the opened tombs, the figure of Osiris, the god who could not die. 'Wherever his image is discovered,' I commanded, 'let an image of the sun be laid at his feet, in memory of that man who had sought to purge the valley of its evil. And let no further tombs be searched for or disturbed, not now nor in any of the ages yet to come, for one still remains here where the evil is preserved.'

But I told him nothing of the evil which flowed within my blood; and although I knew myself an afrit now, and could feel my hellish hunger, I fought hard against it all the while I spent at Thebes. And when I left and continued on my way, still I had not surrendered to it; and my only companion was Isis, my dog.

Then at length, as I followed the Nile down-river, I came to a plain encircled by cliffs, where there seemed nothing to be found save for dust-piled mounds; and yet I wondered, all the same, what more there might be hidden. Approaching a band of nomads encamped upon the plain, I asked them to guide me to any pagan tombs. They led me at once to a wild and steep ravine where a tomb, half-built yet very extensive, could be entered, and upon the darkest wall of its darkest chamber there was a painting of a Queen – and I knew her at once, for it seemed to be my wife. I could be certain then that her story had been true, and in my horror I painted an image of King Akh-en-Aten's sun upon her wall. I was filled, as I did so, with a strong sense of wonder, to think that all which had befallen me had befallen him as well, and so I determined to visit the quarries in the desert, to discover the place where he had met, like me, his wife, and been granted the same deathly gift which she had granted me. The nomads led me there and I discovered the place – and as I had done before, I carved an image of the sun. And when I told the nomads that the place had been cursed, they bowed their heads and nodded, as though they had always sensed as much.

But I told them nothing of the evil which flowed within my blood; and although I knew myself an afrit, and could feel my hellish hunger, I fought hard against it all the while I spent with them. And when I left and continued on my way, still I had not surrendered to it; and my only companion was Isis, my dog.

I returned to the plain and passed across the river, and found there a village, very straggling and mean. I thought to myself in wonder, gazing at the wasteland on the opposite bank where once a mighty city had been raised up to the stars, how there is nothing which endures save Allah's love alone. And so I told the villagers – who had seen my look of wonder, and were filled with consternation at the thought of what I might be – something of the story which I had heard from the jinni; and then I continued on my way towards Cairo, and this mosque. And so it was, O Prince, that I arrived here at last.

And before I sat down in this chamber with you, I had told no one of the evil which flows within my blood; and although I know myself an afrit, and can feel my hellish hunger, I have fought hard against it all the while I have been here. And still I have not surrendered to it; and my only companion has been Isis, my dog.

And all has been, O mighty Prince, as I have related it to you; and that is the tale of what I saw and heard, and how I grew to be this thing which you see before you now.

And when Haroun had finished his tale, the Caliph gazed at him in astonishment, but also in fear, and he shrank back at once and leapt to his feet. 'In Allah's name,' he exclaimed, 'this tale of yours, O Haroun, is a very wonder of wonders, and yet I dread the meaning of your words and the look of hunger in your eye!'

But Haroun only smiled. 'Have no fear,' he replied, 'for I swore long ago to your father, O mighty Prince, that I would never raise my hand against you. Yet I would have you remember an oath of your own, that Haidée, my daughter, in turn shall not die.'

'Do you have the power, then,' the Caliph asked, his

composure restored, 'to heal my sister, the Princess Sitt al-Mulq?'

Haroun bowed his head. 'I have the power to release her from the threat of death.'

'Then your daughter will be spared.'

'You must grant her a palace, and servants, and wealth; for I, as you know, may no longer protect her.'

'All,' the Caliph nodded, 'shall be done as you request.'

'Then let it be achieved by tomorrow evening, and I shall return you your sister, the Princess Sitt al-Mulq, upraised from her sleep. Do you agree to my terms, then, O Commander of the Faithful?'

'I hear, and I agree.'

'Then may Allah be praised.' Haroun bowed once again, and kissed the Caliph's hand. 'Let us meet upon the road across the Mukattam Hills – for it were best, since we will be invoking dark and wondrous powers, that we do it far from mortal eye. Until tomorrow, then, O Prince.' And so saying, even as the Caliph gazed upon him, he seemed to melt like mist upon the morning air; and the Caliph was left alone in the chamber of the tower.

He descended the stairs in a mood of great consternation and excitement, and straightaway ordered that everything be done as he had promised. And so it was that Haidée was dressed in beauteous robes, and escorted by a train of a hundred servants, and taken to a palace rich with marble and gold, where a cup of fruit stood upon every table, and a plate piled with jewels upon every stool. And then, when all had been done and the hour of the evening prayers had arrived, the Caliph summoned his servant, Masoud, and the two of them left for the Mukattam Hills.

As they neared the plateau which led on to Hulwan, the Caliph paused and turned back to gaze at Cairo, and beyond. Bright were the hearth-flames which twinkled across his city, and purple gleamed the deserts where the sun had lately set, yet these were as nothing compared with the light of the stars, for they blazed all above him, a myriad points of silver, and the Caliph thought, as he gazed at them, of the Kingdom of the Jinn. And then he felt rise up within him, as though it were the stars which had served to torch it, a furnace of impatience such as he had never felt before; and he gazed all about him, and then he cried out Haroun's name.

Silence was the only answer.

'O Haroun,' the Caliph shouted out again, 'the moment has come for you to display your mastery over the powers of life and death!'

Still no answer came.

'O Haroun,' the Caliph shouted for a third time, 'give to me what I am promised, or I shall order your daughter slain!'

As his words echoed across the desert hills, the Caliph saw that Masoud had begun to quail. His teeth were chattering, and his eyes were staring wide, and he slowly raised his arm to point behind the Caliph, who spun round at once, and saw, standing upon the very crest of the plateau, silhouetted against the stars, the figure of Haroun. Yet his face, for all the shadow, seemed strangely illumined, a flickering, deathly silver; and the Caliph thought, as he gazed upon it, that he had never seen a look of such ravening hunger in his life, for it seemed to pinch Haroun's cheeks and hollow out his eyes, so that the Caliph imagined that their depths might drain the very stars. For a long minute he stood there frozen; then at last he breathed in deeply and ordered Masoud to follow him. But Masoud would not be moved, and so the Caliph cursed him and set off alone. The ascent was harder than he had imagined it would be, for the path was steep and rocky underfoot, and it took him a while to reach the crest of the plateau. But when he did so at last, it was to find that he was standing there alone, and though he gazed all about him there was not a trace of Haroun.

The Caliph could feel a great terror now, very soft and sickly, rising from his stomach and mottling his throat. He tried to call out Haroun's name again, but he found that his voice was no longer his own, and so he started to slip and slide back down the hill, and at last he found his voice and he cried out for Masoud. A shadow rose ahead of him, and the Caliph exclaimed in relief, 'Masoud, Masoud, we must leave here at once!' But then the shadow turned and the Caliph saw it was Haroun, the look of hunger utterly banished from his face. 'Welcome, O Caliph!' he called out with a bow. 'The moment has come when all must be fulfilled!'

'Masoud?' the Caliph whispered. 'Where is Masoud?'

Haroun smiled. He gestured to something bunched up by his feet. It appeared to be nothing but a pile of shredded rags; but when he knelt by it, the Caliph found it was the blackamoor, his flesh picked clean in strips from his bones. The Caliph rose again slowly. 'You swore . . .' he whispered, 'you swore you would not slay me.'

'Nor shall I,' answered Haroun, 'for all has been done, and will be done, just as I vowed.'

'My sister . . .' The Caliph licked his lips. 'Where then is my sister? You vowed she would be well.'

'I vowed,' Haroun answered, 'that I would seek to keep her forever preserved from death.'

'What then have you done with her?' the Caliph cried.

'Why,' Haroun answered, 'did you imagine that an afrit lacks the power to make of a mortal his own kind?'

'I . . .' The Caliph swallowed. 'I do not understand . . .'

Haroun smiled but did not answer, and gestured with his arm; and the Caliph saw, emerging from the darkness of the road, a glimmer of silver, flickering and ghostly, like the flesh of Haroun. And then suddenly he did understand; and he screamed and sought to flee. But already his limbs had frozen, so that he could do nothing to escape the gaze of his sister, burning bright with need and hunger as it was. Instead, the Caliph stood waiting for her like a block of stone; and his sister embraced him; and still he did not move.

Haroun, though, had not lingered to watch, but had already set off along the road, even as the Princess had taken the Caliph in her arms. And where he went, and what he became, it is not related and cannot be known. For only Allah in His wisdom can see all things, and with Him alone lies the knowledge of the future and the past. Praise then be to Allah, and blessings on His name, for His mercy and His wisdom and His power must guide us all!

Interpolation, inserted within the sheets of the manuscript given to Lord Carnarvon

The Turf Club,
20th Nov, 1922

My dear Lord Carnarvon,

  Time indeed, it appears, will wait for no man, and it so happens, even as I finish skimming through this tale again, that I am told that my cab is come to take me to the station. What, though, I now wonder, will you make of it yourself? Is it just my folly to have glimpsed what I have done – beneath all the many layers of fantasy and myth, the accretions of millennia of superstition, can it be, truly be, that a tomb of gold lies hidden? Within a week, maybe less, we shall know for certain. Come soon then, dear Lord Carnarvon. Hot and harsh the Valley may be, yet the very thought of it fills me with a wonderful energy! I am sure you too, when you behold it, will find all your strength and fitness returned.

  I shall await you and Lady Evelyn with all the patience I can muster.

H.C.

The
TALE
of the
OPENED
TOMB

*A*s the train hissed and steamed to a shuddering halt, Howard Carter, standing upon the platform of Luxor Station, braced back his shoulders as though standing to attention. He was fully aware that every eye was fixed upon him, for such was the interest in the news of his discovery that even the Governor of the province was in attendance, drawn by the rumours of mystery and gold. Carter, however, impervious to all the stares, stood with his own gaze fixed firmly ahead as the door of the first-class carriage swung open. A young woman stepped out, and then turned to take the arm of a much older man who descended – not without difficulty, for his leg was somewhat lame – and stood a moment blinking in the sun. He was tall and slight, and fastidiously dressed, as though for Pall Mall rather than any excavation, yet in his face could be glimpsed, so Carter imagined, a great strength of will and a fondness for adventure.

He stepped forward, the Governor of the province by his side.

The Earl of Carnarvon, still shielding his eyes, suddenly saw the two men, and at once his frown was lightened by a smile. 'Carter!' He took his colleague's hand and shook it vigorously, and then in turn, as he was introduced, the hand of the beaming Governor. Once greetings had been exchanged, he gestured to the young woman who stood by his side. 'And may I present to you my daughter, Your Excellency, Lady Evelyn Herbert.' Again the Governor beamed; and again there was a profuse exchange of salutations. As they proceeded, Lord Carnarvon turned back to Carter. 'I trust you will not take it amiss,' he whispered with an apologetic sloping of his shoulders, 'but I could not possibly come without her, for my daughter, as you will know, has long followed your work with the keenest sense of interest. Also' – he lowered his voice still further and winked – 'she insisted she come so she could continue to fuss at me.'

Carter bowed. 'It is always a pleasure, of course, to meet with Lady Evelyn.'

Overhearing this, she extended her hand and, as Carter kissed it, she smiled at him in a conspiratorial manner so that, glancing between her and her father, he could not restrain a sudden frown of concern. He waited with impatience now for the ceremonial of the Governor's greeting to be concluded, and when all had been brought to a finish at last, he turned hurriedly and began to push a way through the crowds, out from the station to the waiting motor-car beyond. Lord Carnarvon and Lady Evelyn both followed in his wake, and as they waited for their luggage to be brought, Lord Carnarvon paused next to Carter and took him by the arm.

'We have both read your document,' he whispered, 'Lady Evelyn and I.'

Carter knew that his concern must again have been immediately apparent, for Lord Carnarvon smiled nervously and raised his hands. 'Please, please, my dear Carter, you have nothing to fear! My daughter, I can assure you, is the very soul of discretion. And upon my word' – he smiled with his customary diffidence – 'one can quite see why you wanted to keep the matter quiet.'

Carter glanced round at the porters, who by now had finished loading up the car. 'Come,' he muttered, opening the door for Lady Evelyn, 'you must both be tired. Let us get you to your rooms.' He waited until she had eased herself down, then walked round the car to sit next to Lord Carnarvon, as the engine was coaxed into spluttering life. 'So then,' he whispered, 'you say you have read all my papers? And what did you think? A queer business, is it not?'

Lady Evelyn smiled across at him. '"Queer", Mr Carter, is barely sufficient an adjective.'

'What in the world might lie behind it?' Lord Carnarvon asked.

'Something very . . . well . . .' – Carter shrugged – 'queer.'

'You truly believe, then, that the tomb *is* that of Tut-ankh-Amen?'

'I have found no proof as yet upon the stonework itself, yet the evidence of the manuscript seems to suggest as much, at least.'

Lady Evelyn leaned forward, her eyes sparkling brightly. 'The manuscript claimed that he had been buried with every splendour!'

'So he would have been,' Carter nodded, 'for such was the immemorial custom of the Pharaohs.'

'My goodness! Then what do you think we might find?'

Carter shrugged again. 'More than treasure, more than gold, I hope for anything – inscriptions, papyri, whatever – which might serve to shed light upon Tut-ankh-Amen's reign. You have read your stuff. You both know how he was heir to the most extraordinary episode in history. What would I not give to know more about that!'

'We have your manuscript,' said Lord Carnarvon softly.

Carter snorted. 'That has no value whatsoever without corroboration.'

'Then we must pray that the tomb has not been plundered.'

Carter smiled thinly. 'One must always, I am afraid, be prepared for that chance.'

But Lady Evelyn shook her head. 'Yet surely it cannot have been robbed,' she said brightly, 'or else the monster inside it would have escaped.'

'Monster?'

'Yes, yes, the ghoul – King Tut himself!'

'I see that you are as droll as ever, Lady Evelyn.'

'You do not think, then . . .?'

'What,' Carter scoffed, 'that there is a demon, a curse?'

'You truly do not think so?'

He laughed curtly. 'Indeed, Lady Evelyn, I must apologise, for so unaccustomed am I to the company of ladies, as you yourself will know, that I can scarcely tell whether you intend to pull my leg. The tale is a compound of superstitions and fantastical romance, for all its undoubted underlay of historical truth. Each age must reinterpret the past in its own light. Our light, fortunately, is that of reason and documented fact. That, after all, is why I am so eager to know what Tut-ankh-Amen's tomb contains.'

With such decisiveness did he pronounce this, and with such a grim-set expression, that it served almost to extinguish Lady Evelyn's smile; but then faintly, after a pause, it flickered once again. 'Even so,' she murmured, 'there must be something strange within the tomb – and I for one, I will confess it, cannot wait to find out what!'

Carter did not reply but sat in silence, almost stony-faced, as their motor-car pulled up by the Winter Palace Hotel. All three passengers then descended from their seats, but still Carter remained silent, even as they entered the lobby. Lord Carnarvon turned to his colleague, to shake him by the hand. 'Just spruce ourselves up a bit,' he said, gesturing to the stairway. 'Dust of travel, and all that. Then we'll join you in the Valley and inspect our tomb.'

Carter nodded.

'Well . . .' Lord Carnarvon pointed to the stairway again. 'Jolly good! See you in a while.'

Carter nodded a second time, but still he did not leave and then suddenly he reached out for Lord Carnarvon's hand again. 'I say,' he blurted out, 'I really am most terribly grateful.'

'My dear fellow!' exclaimed Lord Carnarvon in some confusion. 'It is I who should be grateful. Why, I would rather see inside that tomb than win the Derby.' He shook Carter's hand once again, then turned and hurriedly climbed the stairs. Lady Evelyn, however, as though waiting for her father to be out of earshot, still lingered in the hall by Carter's side.

'You know this is the most thrilling adventure imaginable for him,' she said at last.

'I meant what I said. Without him all my work would have been for nothing.'

'Yes.' She lowered her gaze. 'Yes, yes, I know.'

Carter tensed. 'What is it, Lady Evelyn? You have something more to say?'

'He is not well,' she blurted out suddenly. 'Yes, yes, he will tell you that he is as fit as a fiddle, but it is not true. He has been really jolly ill. So please, Mr Carter . . .'

'He should rest, then. Take it easy. After he has seen the tomb, of course.'

'Yes.' Lady Evelyn smiled. 'Yes. That would be best.' She squeezed Carter's hand, then turned slowly and began to climb the stairs.

'Lady Evelyn!'

She paused.

'We are drawing very near the finishing post. Your father would not want to miss it for the world.'

'Of course not.' She smiled. 'How could you think I don't understand that?'

Carter bowed his head and turned, then paused once again. 'Oh,' he added, 'there is one other thing.'

Lady Evelyn arched an elegant eyebrow.

'The steps to the entrance of the tomb – I am reliably informed that they will be cleared by tomorrow afternoon.'

Howard Carter crouched by the doorway on the bottom step, sifting through the rubbish which still obscured the base of the entranceway. He picked up a shard of pottery and held it to the light; then he placed it on a pile of similar shards which he had stacked carefully behind him.

'Carter! I say! What have you found?'

He glanced up, then smiled and rose to his feet. 'Lord Carnarvon, Lady Evelyn. Please – come down.'

As they both did so, he stooped and picked up a couple of the shards. 'See,' he said as they stood beside him, 'you can trace the cartouches stamped upon the clay. "Smenkh-ka-Re".' He read out the hieroglyph. 'And here' – he pointed – '"Akh-en-Aten".'

Lord Carnarvon took the fragment with a reverent care. 'So this proves that the tomb must date from that period, do you think?'

'Almost certainly. But I suspect . . .' – Carter crouched down once again – 'that we will very soon know precisely whose it is.'

'How?' asked Lady Evelyn.

Carter scraped some rubble away from the door. 'There are some cartouches here as well,' he explained, 'carved into the stone. I have been awaiting your arrival before exposing them fully.'

'Well,' said Lady Evelyn sunnily, 'here we are!'

Carter glanced up at Lord Carnarvon, who slowly nodded his head.

'Very well,' whispered Carter. 'Let us see whose tomb this is. Discover if all our conjectures are correct.'

Again, with great care, he brushed away the dust. For several minutes he worked in silence, and neither Lord Carnarvon nor Lady Evelyn spoke a single word. Then suddenly they heard Carter inhale very deeply; and they saw how he bowed his head and rocked back on his heels.

'What is it?' inquired Lady Evelyn impatiently. 'What have you found?'

'Here,' said Carter, pointing to the outline of a cartouche. 'Can you make it out?'

Lord Carnarvon crouched down. He dabbed at his brow, which was sheeny with sweat. 'What does it say?'

'It is a title,' answered Carter. '"He-who-is-the-very-manifestation-of-Amen, the-Beloved-of-Osiris".' He looked up. 'The title of King Tut-ankh-Amen.'

The following morning, after the seals had been carefully photographed, the doorway was opened, and the great stone blocks removed. Beyond there stretched the rubble which Carter had observed three weeks before, piled to the roof of a sloping passageway. How far into the rock the passageway descended, and to what it might lead, it was impossible to tell.

Under the watchful supervision of Ahmed Girigar, the work of clearance was immediately begun. It was soon discovered that there were numerous artefacts intermingled with the rubble – potsherds, vases, alabaster jars, some of them stamped with the cartouches of Pharaohs, Akh-en-Aten, Smenkh-ka-Re or Tut-ankh-Amen. Despite Lord Carnarvon's growing impatience, Carter insisted that even the tiniest fragment be preserved, sifted from the rubble and brought to him at once. He did not betray what he imagined he might find; but Lord Carnarvon observed, as his colleague laid each fragment aside, that he did so with a visible exhalation of relief.

Slowly, then, the work proceeded, and as evening fell it had still not been completed. There was no sign as yet of a funerary chamber, nor even of a door.

It was reached in the middle of the following afternoon. Carter emerged from the passageway, waving his arms, before plunging back into the darkness with Ahmed Girigar. By the time Lord Carnarvon and Lady Evelyn had joined them, the outline of the doorway could easily be distinguished, and Carter pointed with evident relief to the seals. 'You see?' he asked. 'They have not been broken. Whatever was buried in there' – he gestured – 'still remains.'

'Well?' asked Lord Carnarvon. 'Shall we take a look?'

Carter glanced at Ahmed, then shook his head. 'The remaining debris is still to be sifted. Let us hurry nothing. We must at all times – *at all times* – conduct ourselves according to the principles of scientific investigation.' Yet even as he said this his own impatience was evident on his face, and as he spoke to Ahmed he smiled with a sudden wryness, as though in an effort to ease his own tension. 'For God's sake,' he instructed, 'make it fast. I cannot endure to wait for much longer.'

Ahmed met this order in silence for a moment; then he turned to the workmen and, clapping his hands, cried out to them in Arabic. The work was continued at a redoubled pace and at last – at long last, as it seemed to the spectators – the debris was removed and the whole door stood revealed. Ahmed turned back to Carter. 'Now, sir,' he whispered. His stare was very glassy, his lips strangely pinched. 'The moment has arrived.'

With trembling hands, Carter made a breach in the upper left-hand corner of the door. Only darkness could be made out. When a test was made with an iron rod, nothing could be felt save open space. 'A candle,' ordered Carter, 'give me a candle, for there may be foul gases!' A candle was lit and passed into his hand, and then, when the tests had been successfully completed, Carter sought to widen the breach a little more. His hands were shaking very badly by now, and it was all he could do to keep hold of the candle; yet he would not for his life hand it to anyone else. With a scattering of rubble, the widening was complete. Carter inserted the candle and at last, long last, he peered through the gap.

Even as he did so, he remembered the document from the Mosque of al-Hakim and the tale of what had been found in the tomb of Smenkh-ka-Re; but he sought to banish the memory from his mind. He did not know what he was hoping to discover but certainly, he thought to himself with a slight measure of self-contempt, it was not a Pharaoh waiting on a throne. He narrowed his eyes. He could make out nothing at all at first, for the hot air escaping from the chamber was causing the candle flame to flicker; but then gradually, as his eyes grew accustomed to the light, details of the room beyond emerged from the mist. Carter gazed in blank amazement; he felt his grip upon the candle beginning to grow numb. He sought to speak, but could say nothing at all.

'What is it?' inquired Lord Carnarvon anxiously as he reached up to place a hand on Carter's shoulder. 'Can you see anything?'

'Yes,' whispered Carter hoarsely. 'Wonderful things.' But he found he could add nothing more; and for a moment, although he knew that he had to pull back his head and widen the hole so that all could see, he could not endure to tear away his gaze. Still he feasted upon the marvels of the chamber, upon a vision of strange animals, statues and gold . . . everywhere, everywhere, the glint of gold.

It had been, Carter reflected later that night, the day of days, the most wonderful that he had ever lived through, and certainly one whose like he would never see again. He pulled out the chair from his desk and sat down, stretched with the pleasure of a myriad images and emotions. Never, he thought, had he known such a feeling of awe as when that hole had been opened and the chamber revealed. Millennia had passed since the last human feet had moved across it, and yet, as he noted the signs of recent life about him – the half-filled bowl of mortar for the door, the blackened lamp, the fingermark upon the freshly painted surface, the farewell garland dropped upon the threshold – he had felt as though it might have been but yesterday. The very air he had breathed, unchanged throughout the centuries, had been breathed by those who had laid the mummy to its rest. Time itself, in the face of such details, had seemed annihilated.

Then, following the awe, had flooded other sensations: the exhilaration of discovery, the fever of suspense, the almost overmastering impulse to break down seals and lift the lids of boxes, the strained expectancy – why not, Carter thought, confess it to himself? – of the treasure-seeker. And what treasures, to be sure, had been revealed within that room! The effect had been bewildering, overwhelming, for it had been packed with wondrous objects, piled one upon another in seemingly endless profusion: exquisitely painted and inlaid caskets; alabaster vases; strange black shrines; bouquets of flowers; beautifully carved chairs; a confused jumble of overturned chariots; and gold, gold, always gold. Three great gilt couches especially had attracted Carter's wonder, for their sides had been carved in the form of animals, curiously attenuated in body, as they had had to be to serve their purpose, but with heads of a startling realism. Carter smiled at the memory and closed his eyes, as the image of one of the heads, that of a lion, rose before his mind. Such beasts, so fierce, so strong, so magnificent, he reflected with sorrow, would never again be found in the Egyptian deserts; for they were dead, hunted to extinction, forever gone. Yet the head of the couch had been carved long before, when the lions, like the Pharaohs, had still ruled in Egypt; and Carter recalled how suddenly, as he had been gazing in wonder at its form – the brilliant surface picked out by the torch-beam, the profile throwing grotesquely distorted shadows on to the wall – it had seemed to come alive!

Carter opened his eyes suddenly. Was it only his imagination, he wondered, or had he – at the very moment when he had been remembering how the lion's head had appeared to move – heard a noise from the verandah outside? He rose to his feet and gazed out into the darkness of the night. There appeared to be nothing, and it was to be sure exceedingly late – it seemed unlikely that anyone would be abroad at such an hour. He returned to his chair and slumped back into it; yet even as he did so, almost despite himself he glanced towards the statue of Tut-ankh-Amen on his desk. Two such figures had been found within the tomb, portraits carved in black of the King, but life-sized and with headdresses sheeted in gold. They had been placed opposite each other like sentinels, and in their hands had been maces; upon each of their foreheads there had risen the protective sacred cobra. Carter wondered what they guarded. So far only the antechamber of the tomb had been revealed. What else might there not be waiting to be found? Treasures still more wonderful, Carter trusted – treasures beyond compare. No papyri had been uncovered yet: no documents or records from the time of the buried King. Without them, he thought, his manuscript would be worthless as a historical record, and his great find would somehow seem incomplete. But the corroboration was surely waiting somewhere. It had to be, Carter thought – surely it did?

He gazed again upon the cobra on the head-dress of his statue. '*Wadjyt*,' he whispered softly to himself. He felt he understood its purpose more clearly now. *Wadjyt* – guardian of the wisdom of the waiting Pharaoh's tomb.

Then suddenly Carter heard a noise again, and this time he could be certain of it, for it had come not from his verandah, but from outside his study door. There was a knock and Carter, rising and crossing to open the door, discovered Ahmed Girigar. 'Ah,' he nodded, feeling almost foolish, 'so it's you.' He gestured with his arm. 'Please, will you not come in?'

'I am very sorry, sir,' Ahmed whispered, moving into the study, 'to come here so late . . .'

'It is no matter. I have only just returned from Lord Carnarvon.'

'He must be, I think, a very happy man.'

'We all are, Ahmed, are we not?'

But Ahmed did not reply, and his glance strayed towards the figure of the Pharaoh upon the desk. 'When, sir,' he asked at last, his voice an even lower whisper than before, 'will you open up the tomb?'

'The tomb has been opened.'

'No.'

Carter frowned. 'How do you mean?'

'The figures of the King which we found within the chamber – is it not true, sir, that they are the guardians of a further doorway?'

Carter stroked his moustache. He did not reply.

'Please, sir,' whispered Ahmed, his tone now one of urgency, almost of desperation, 'is it not true? For in the wall against which they stand – I have seen it for myself – there is the mortared outline of a further doorway. Must not something, then, be waiting beyond it? Is that not where the King will be found?'

Carter paused again. 'Beyond any shadow of a doubt,' he acknowledged at last.

'Then I must ask you again, sir – when do you intend to open up the door?'

'It will be done in due course – when all has been pre-pared.'

'No, sir!' Ahmed shook his head violently. 'It must be done now! It must be done this very night!'

Carter gazed at him in astonishment. 'That is out of the question,' he replied. 'We shall have to clear the antechamber first.'

'We cannot, sir, risk an opening of that doorway, not when all the eyes of the world will be upon it.'

'It is I who am the head of this excavation, I would remind you.'

'I have not forgotten it, sir. And yet I would remind you in turn, with very great respect, that you would never have discovered the tomb, nor even thought to look for it, if you had not been shown the secret of the Mosque of al-Hakim.'

Carter bowed his head almost imperceptibly.

'You know, sir, why the secret was revealed to you.'

'Yes,' Carter answered, a degree of heat returning to his voice. 'It was because you knew that in the end the tomb would be discovered, and you were afraid that it might be found by a man like Mr Davis. You wanted an archaeologist, did you not, Ahmed? You wanted a man of science? Well' – he paused – 'that is what you have.'

'Not only a man of science, sir.'

'Indeed?'

'A man, as well, who knows and loves this land.'

'I know it – and love it – well enough, I think.'

'Then do not despise its secrets. Do not believe it to be barren of what you may not understand.'

Carter breathed in deeply and half turned away. 'You know I do not.'

Ahmed bowed, but did not reply.

'And yet . . .' Carter smiled mirthlessly. 'You cannot expect me to believe there is a demon in that tomb.'

Still Ahmed stood, head bowed, in silence.

Carter sighed again. 'It is too late tonight, at any rate,' he said, turning again and crossing to his desk where he picked up the figure of Tut-ankh-Amen. 'I cannot enter the chamber without telling Lord Carnarvon, and he is resting at present, for he is very tired.'

'No!' Ahmed gazed at him, startled. 'No, sir, you cannot do that.'

Carter frowned. 'Why ever not?'

'Would you risk his life?'

'Risk his life?' Carter smiled. 'His reputation, perhaps, along with mine as an excavator – but nothing worse than that.'

'I beg you, sir . . .'

'No.' Carter raised his hand. 'So far I have gone, Ahmed – but no further. If we are to enter the tomb tomorrow night, then I cannot do it without informing Lord Carnarvon. He is my patron – and more, he is also my friend.'

Ahmed gazed at the figure of Tut-ankh-Amen. 'Then you must tell him,' he whispered, 'of the danger he may face. And may Allah guide him, and guide you, and guide us all.' He bowed. 'Good night, sir.'

Carter was left alone again. He stood motionless a while,

lost in thought, a phrase unbidden running through his mind. At length, as he crossed to his desk and placed back the statue, he muttered it to himself: '"Death on swift wings will come, to whosoever toucheth the tomb of the Pharaoh"'. He half-laughed, and shook his head. 'Nonsense,' he whispered. 'Arrant nonsense.' He glanced again at the statue on his desk. 'All sane people should dismiss such ideas with contempt.'

Even as he said this to himself he felt resolved. Yes, he nodded, he would indeed tell Lord Carnarvon. If it had to be done, then it were best to do it soon, and his patron, certainly, would not want to miss out on the fun. And at once Carter felt a thrill of renewed excitement, a golden flood of anticipation at the thought of penetrating, the very next night, the innermost sanctum of the treasure-filled tomb – of finding, in all its magnificent panoply of death, the funerary shrine of a Pharaoh of Egypt.

Carter had chosen to make the opening at the very base of the doorway. 'It will then be an easy matter,' he had explained, 'to conceal it, so that no one need ever know or suspect what we have done.' Even so, his mood of unease had been palpable, and when at length the opening had been knocked through the masonry he glanced up at the guardian figures of the Pharaoh, one on either side of him, as though in silent apology.

He reached for a torch, then shone it through the hole he had made. An astonishing sight was revealed to him, for there – within a yard of the doorway, and stretching as far as he could see – stood what appeared to be a solid wall of gold, inlaid with panels of a brilliant blue faience. 'We have him!' Carter whispered in exultation. 'Tut-ankh-Amen!' He pointed to the gold. 'There can be no doubt at all now that this is the sepulchral chamber, for within this shrine' – he pointed to the gold – 'we will discover in its very heart the coffin of the Pharaoh.' He glanced back at Ahmed, and permitted himself a smile. 'Not much chance of anything escaping from that. I think we are secure from any demon for a while.'

'No, no,' said Lady Evelyn breezily, 'you are forgetting the Tale. It is not Pharaoh buried in the coffin, but a substitute, for Queen Tyi wished to be able to remove the true corpse without any bother.' She smiled at Ahmed. 'Is that not correct? The ghoul might still be in there, at perfect liberty and waiting to pounce?'

She bared her teeth to display imaginary fangs, but Carter interrupted before Ahmed could reply. 'Let us forget this talk of demons!' he exclaimed impatiently. 'There are wonders enough concealed beyond this door. Why, it is the very Holy of Holies of archaeological science!' He glanced round at his companions. 'Who will be the first to enter such a shrine?'

No one replied, until at length Lord Carnarvon shuffled and cleared his throat. 'You, Carter. This is your find.'

But Carter shook his head. 'I have already told you, we would not be here had it not been for you.' He paused, then handed across the electric torch. 'You must be the first.'

Lord Carnarvon crouched down by the opening and peered through it, his emotions very visible as he gazed at the wall of gold. He glanced back once, then seemed visibly to brace himself before wriggling, head-first, through the gap in the wall. The light of his torch bounced and played upon the gold and then, when he had passed through and stood up, seemed to vanish. 'Hello?' Carter called out. 'What can you see?'

'You are right!' came the answer, sounding muffled. 'It is indeed the very Holy of Holies!'

Carter gestured to Lady Evelyn that she should follow her father through the opening; and then, having ordered Ahmed likewise through the hole, he finally passed into the inner room himself. The moment he climbed back to his feet, he realised that his initial supposition had been perfectly correct, for he was indeed confronted by a funerary shrine so enormous that it almost filled the entire area of the chamber, with only a space of some two feet between itself and the walls. He could see, turning to his left, that Ahmed and Lady Evelyn were inching along the gap, and so he turned to his right to see what might lie there. Once again, as he stepped into the stillness of more than thirty centuries, he felt a sense of profoundest wonder and awe, distilled from the secrets and shadows of the past, so that the very tread of his foot, the slightest noise, seemed a desecration.

When he glanced behind him, both Lady Evelyn and Ahmed appeared to have rounded the corner of the shrine. 'Hello?' he whispered. Nobody answered him. He flashed his torch the other way, at the corner of the shrine towards which he had been advancing. 'Hello?' he called out again, but there was still no reply. Very slowly, he began to slide forward once again. Suddenly, though, as he approached the corner of the chamber, he heard from ahead of him a soft, gasping moan, and then the muffled crashing of something upon the floor. At the same moment, the torch in Carter's hand failed and the entire chamber was cast into darkness.

He heard a squeal of mingled panic and excitement from Lady Evelyn.

'It is all right,' he called out, 'please, all is well!' He wondered, though, whether it truly was. All had fallen silent again. He strained with his ears; the tomb now seemed as silent as it had been for millennia. Nervously, Carter took a further step forward and, feeling with his hands, turned the corner of the wall. Still inching onwards with the utmost care, he felt the wall suddenly vanish from his touch, and at the very same moment all the torch beams blazed back into life.

Carter could see now that he was standing by a doorway, not sealed as the others had been but opening on to a further chamber, smaller than the others and with a much lower roof. A single glance sufficed to tell him that he had before him the most beautiful treasures of all, for the chamber was filled with emblems of the underworld, a figure of a jackal, statues of the gods, so lovely that they made him gasp with wonder and admiration. There still seemed no trace of papyri, though, nor any inscriptions on the walls of the room, and he flashed round the beam of his torch in a sudden surge of desperation. He gasped a second time – but now with consternation for he saw, rising dazedly from the floor, the figure of Lord Carnarvon, his face as white as dust.

'Good Lord!' exclaimed Carter, stepping forward to take him by the arm. 'Did you have a fall?'

'Went out like a light,' said Lord Carnarvon, wincing as he dabbed at a cut on his cheek. 'Terribly sorry. Bit of a shock.'

'What happened, do you think?'

Lord Carnarvon frowned, and shook his head. 'Really not sure.' He glanced around him at the piled treasures. 'All got a bit much, I suppose. Sense of the tremendous past and all that. You know what I mean. Black cloud, sudden mist of darkness. Strange, really.' He gazed about him again. 'Very strange.'

'Pups!' Lady Evelyn emerged in the open doorway. 'Are you hurt?'

'No worry,' he smiled, 'no need for concern.'

'You have cut yourself.'

'Just a little scratch.'

'We should leave.' She reached for her father's hand but

then suddenly froze, conscious for the first time of the splendours of the chamber. 'I say,' she whispered at last, turning to Carter, 'I have never known anything as exciting as tonight. I think it will prove the *Great Moment* of my life.' She gazed once more at the figure of the jackal; then tugged upon her father's arm. 'Come on, Pups,' she whispered, 'you are still looking groggy. Your glands have gone up like cricket balls. Time to get out.'

She turned to Carter again and kissed him, so quickly that he did not have any time to step back; then she slipped out between the shrine and the wall, past Ahmed who stood waiting as Lord Carnarvon likewise stepped past. 'What happened, sir?' he asked urgently, once he was alone in the chamber with Carter.

'He was . . .' – Carter paused, then shrugged – 'overwhelmed.'

'He saw nothing? Heard nothing?'

Carter shook his head. 'Why would he, Ahmed? There is nothing here.'

But Ahmed swallowed, and gazed into the shadows. 'How do we know? We have not yet fully looked.'

Carter grunted, and swung the beam of his torch about the room. The shadows danced, but in the pools of darkness all else remained still.

'We should search, sir,' said Ahmed. 'We should make doubly sure.'

'No.' Carter spoke with sudden firmness. 'We have done more than enough even as it is.'

'Please, sir . . .'

'No.' Carter took Ahmed's arm. 'We must leave here at once.' He gestured to Ahmed that he should continue towards the exit from the chamber. Reluctantly Ahmed did as he was ordered and Carter, following him, ensured he could not turn back. 'The temptation to disturb or even to remove certain objects,' Carter said as he followed Ahmed through the opening, 'would have proved far too great, had we stayed within that chamber.' And even as he said so he glanced behind him once again, longing to return to the tiny room, to see if some papyri might not be there after all – but he tensed and clenched his fists, and forced himself on. 'No, no,' he muttered, 'let the hole be sealed at once. Safer that way, safer by far.'

'Safer, sir?' Ahmed glanced at Lord Carnarvon who sat, still pale, against the furthest wall; but once he realised that Carter would not reply, he began the work of plastering up the tell-tale gap.

When all had been completed, Carter carefully arranged a basket to conceal the work, before leading his party back up the steps. Feeling the cool night air against his face, Lord Carnarvon breathed it in deeply, and Carter saw the colour begin at once to return to his patron's face. 'Do you feel better now?' he asked.

Lord Carnarvon nodded. 'So sorry,' he muttered. 'Embarrassing, really. Very poor display.' Then he paused and absent-mindedly rubbed at his cheek, smearing blood upon his finger which he delicately sucked. 'But I say!' he exclaimed suddenly, a contented smile upon his face. 'The Holy of Holies! Wasn't it just the most marvellous thing?'

The next morning Carter arrived very early at the site, for he had been finding it hard to sleep. Early though he was, however, he was not the first; for as he approached the tomb he found Ahmed waiting for him, uneasy-eyed, his face bled of colour. 'Please, sir,' he whispered, 'come and see.' He led Carter down the steps, through the doorway and into the tomb; and once they had slipped through the second doorway into the antechamber, he pointed towards the third –

that same one through which they had passed the night before. Carter gazed at it in surprise, for the basket he had placed across the hole had been tossed aside, and the mortaring lay scattered in a pile across the floor.

'Someone else has broken in!' he exclaimed. 'Who would dare do such a thing?'

'No, sir,' answered Ahmed, as he pointed to the rubble. 'Someone – something – has broken out.'

Carter gazed at the debris in silence a moment; then he shook his head violently. 'Your work last night – it was clearly too hurried. It must have caved in.'

'But, sir . . .'

'No buts. Finish it again, and this time do it properly. And for the love of God' – he glanced towards the steps – '*do it fast!* There will be others coming soon, and no one must know. *No one must find out!*'

With a secret smile Carter removed the last stones of Ahmed's brickwork, thereby effacing the proof of their clandestine entry several weeks before. It was all he could do not to turn to Lord Carnarvon, who had been sitting, he knew, amidst the other guests with a smile like that of a naughty schoolboy upon his face, clearly nervous at the thought that their stunt might be suspected. However, as he passed back the final brick, Carter did not catch his friend and patron's eye but turned instead to face all the rows of gathered guests, seated upon their chairs in the antechamber. These men, Carter thought suddenly, who had come here for the official opening of the doorway, formed the very cream of Egypt's archaeological community; yet upon all their faces were expressions of the utmost stupefaction, such as any untutored layman would betray. The same expression, Carter suspected, could be glimpsed upon his own face, even though he knew what lay beyond the doorway, even though he had passed inside it before.

He was the first to enter the newly opened room and then, once he had completed his own inspection and returned into the antechamber, he was followed by Lord Carnarvon. Neither man uttered a word as they passed each other; yet Carter, gazing upon his friend, saw that his brow was beaded with white drops of sweat and his lips half-parted in a foolish smile. He seemed in the grip of some profound emotion and Carter, who had never seen him in such a state before, felt a sudden surge of worry, almost of fear. As Lord Carnarvon finally emerged through the doorway from the funerary chamber, Carter studied him closely. He had a dazed, bewildered look in his eyes, and as he met Carter's stare he threw up his hands before him, an unconscious gesture of impotence to describe what he felt. Nevertheless, crossing to the wall where Carter stood, he seemed eager to speak, to try to put his emotions into words after all. 'The damnedest thing,' he whispered, 'the damnedest thing. The strangest feeling of desecration. Not of the rest of the Pharaoh, don't you know, but of the flow of time itself, if that makes any sense at all. Do you know what I mean, Carter? The feeling that we have somehow knocked the boundaries away?'

'Boundaries?' Carter frowned. 'Boundaries of what?'

'Oh, how can I put it?' Lord Carnarvon threw his hands up once again. 'Those that should exist, I suppose, between the deep past and ourselves.'

Carter's frown deepened, but he did not reply.

'Not making much sense, I suppose,' shrugged Lord Carnarvon apologetically. 'But I do feel – yes, I truly do feel it – that we have mixed the currents of the past with the present, with the now. And so – I cannot help but wonder . . .'

Carter raised an eyebrow. 'Yes?'

'Well – don't you know – whether it was wise.'

'Why would it not be? We are archaeologists, after all. Introducing the past into the present is what we aim to do.'

'Oh, I don't know.' Lord Carnarvon shrugged once again. 'You must think me foolish. But even so, I cannot help but wonder . . . Carter – my dear Carter,' he suddenly hissed, 'was it wise?'

A bright shaft of sunlight fell across the room, illuminating motes of slow-dancing dust, and causing Lord Carnarvon's mirror to sparkle. He paused in his shaving, blinded for a moment by the gleam, then carefully angled his mirror round a fraction, to keep the glass from the early morning sun. As he gazed at his own reflection, however, he found that he barely knew himself. The face that met his own was lost in shadows, so that it seemed to him that it might be anyone's at all. The shadows, he imagined, were billowing upwards, rising from the depths of he knew not what.

Suddenly he winced, roused from his reverie by a sharp pain. He raised a finger, and angled the mirror again to inspect a cut to his face. It was the same, he realised, that he had suffered several weeks before, when he had fallen unconscious in the tomb of Tut-ankh-Amen. The scar had never properly healed – and now, once again, he had opened it up.

A drop of blood splashed on to the porcelain of the basin. Lord Carnarvon turned on the tap and the water, as he swirled it, was stained a pinkish red, before it emptied and drained away.

He was brought back in a cab, muttering strangely and making no sense. Lady Evelyn, who had already been warned of his relapse, was waiting for him on the hotel steps. 'Oh, Pups,' she whispered as he was helped out from the cab. She took his arm and guided him up the steps. 'What were you thinking of, you silly man?'

Lord Carnarvon gazed at his daughter as though startled to observe her. 'The mosque,' he whispered. 'Went to see the mosque.'

'Mosque?'

'To see if it was true.'

Lady Evelyn paused, as she looked at the swollen glands on his neck. 'I should never have allowed you to come to Cairo,' she said at last, 'not while I knew that you were feeling so seedy.'

'Eve.' He clutched at her suddenly, as though to stop himself from tumbling back down the steps.

'Yes, Pups?'

'There was no one there.'

'Where?'

'In the mosque. In the summit of the minaret.'

Lady Evelyn shrugged. 'I do not see why there would have been.'

'But do you not see?' he whispered. 'How can I know now if any of it were true?'

'Please, Pups . . .'

'No . . .' He reached up with his hand to touch his swollen glands. 'How can I be certain . . . what this is . . . what it means?'

'Pups.' Lady Evelyn reached up to kiss her father on his cheek. Feeling how his skin was burning hot, she took care not to display her concern or her shock. 'There is no cause for worry,' she whispered, 'but only so long as you do what your doctors say. You know, if you do not, that you will grow ever more rotten – and where, dearest Pups, is the mystery in that?'

She squeezed his arm, then continued to lead him up the steps towards the lobby. He swallowed and attempted to add something more, but his words, as he babbled them, no longer made sense.

Carter tore open the telegram as soon as it was delivered. He read it greedily, then cursed, and his face grew blank.

'Bad news?' asked his colleague as casually as he could. 'Nothing serious, I hope?'

Carter stood in silence a moment more, then unfolded the sheet of paper again. 'It is from Lady Evelyn,' he muttered, handing it across. 'Lord Carnarvon is sick, and she is very alarmed. I must leave for Cairo at once.'

'Dear, oh dear. Bit of a nuisance, you having to go just when we were really getting ahead with our work. Let's hope the old man gets well soon.'

'Yes.' Carter nodded slowly. He gazed about him at the empty antechamber, then through the gap in the wall to the golden shrine beyond. 'I had been hoping to be able to take him some good news.'

'Oh?'

Carter stroked his moustache. 'Been hoping to find some papyri, don't you know? Records, personal writings, stuff of that kind. But it seems certain now there's nothing. Not a single scrap.'

His colleague laughed. 'Dammit, Carter, but you're greedy. Isn't what you have found enough to keep you going?'

'To keep me going, yes. But it is still not enough.'

'What did you want, then?'

'Oh, to know what really happened. To find the truth — to understand.'

Carter's colleague paused a moment, then shrugged. 'It all happened so horribly long ago.'

'Yes. And there is the problem. I had thought, if I made this discovery, if I brought the artefacts to light, then the . . . I don't know . . . the . . . the inner life of the Ancients might be brought to life as well. That sounds foolish, I suppose. But then, after all, what has always been my inspiration? Why, the idea that they lived and thought and felt like us. But we don't know that. In fact, we can't be sure at all. Standing here, even in this tomb – what *do* we know? So little. So little. We are utterly removed.'

His colleague clapped him on the back. 'Come on, old man, don't you realise this find has made you more famous than any archaeologist who's lived? It won't do at all for you to show yourself so glum.'

'No,' Carter sighed. 'And yet I cannot help it.' He glanced round again at the shrine of the King, sweeping his torch across the gap in the wall. 'The mystery still eludes us. The shadows move, but the dark is never quite dispersed.'

He lapsed into silence and bowed his head, then glanced down at the telegram crumpled in his hand. He smoothed it out and read it through again. 'I had better be heading off for Cairo immediately.'

His colleague nodded. 'Let's hope the old man gets well soon.'

'Let us hope so indeed,' Carter smiled grimly. 'Or we will be hearing all sorts of nonsense about how this tomb has brought bad luck.'

In Cairo, in the Continental Hotel, a sick man, early in the morning, breathed his last.

At the same moment, across the city, all the lights flickered and then at once went out. A darkness veiled Cairo, as heavy as that of an unopened tomb.

At the same moment, in the Valley of the Kings, a guard by the tomb of Tut-ankh-Amen was disturbed. In the rocks above his head he heard a sudden noise, and as he rose from his chair he saw a scattering of dust, descending in a rivulet of dislodged pebbles. When he went, however, to investigate the cause, he could find nothing, nor hear anything save a gusting of the wind.

DRAMATIS PERSONAE

The historical record

AKH-EN-ATEN: The son of Amen-hetep III, after whom he was originally named, he reigned alongside his father for a number of years, although there are some historians who dispute whether there was in fact a co-regency at all. In the fifth year of his exclusive reign he changed his name and ordered the construction of a new capital in Middle Egypt, on the site now known as El-Amarna. It was from this city that he promulgated the exclusive worship of the sun disk, the 'Aten', a policy which resulted in unparalleled cultural and economic turbulence throughout Egypt and her empire. After Akh-en-Aten's death, his name was excised from every public monument, so that all memory of him and his revolution was lost. Only the excavations of the nineteenth century revealed that he had ever been.

Inevitably there remain massive gaps in the historical record, and accounts of his character and reign vary wildly. Modern historians have tended not to be charitable in their interpretations; for Flinders Petrie, however, Akh-en-Aten stood out as indisputably 'the most original thinker that ever lived in Egypt, and one of the great idealists of the world'.

AMEN-HETEP III: Titled 'The Magnificent' by subsequent generations, his long reign marked the apogee of Egypt's opulence and wealth. Judging by reliefs from the end of his reign, he suffered from appalling obesity.

AY: Although the relationship has not been absolutely proved, he was most probably the brother of Queen Tyi, and therefore the uncle of Akh-en-Aten. Under the reign of Tut-ankh-Amen he rose to the position of Vizier, and is portrayed on the wall of his great-nephew's tomb administering the final rites to the dead king's mummy. Ay was by then ruling as Pharaoh himself, but he was an old man and his reign was short. He was succeeded in turn by Horem-heb, a general in the army who was unrelated to the royal house. It was during Horem-heb's reign that the names of Akh-en-Aten, Smenkh-ka-Re, Tut-ankh-Amen and Ay were all excised from the royal records.

GEORGE HERBERT, 5TH EARL OF CARNARVON: Enormously rich as a result of both his inheritance and his marriage into the Rothschild family, he was a keen sportsman whose twin obsessions were horses and automobiles. Almost crippled in a motoring accident in Germany in 1901, he took to visiting Egypt for the purposes of recuperation, and it was while there that his fascination with archaeology grew. Having been introduced to Howard Carter by Gaston Maspero, the head of the *Service des Antiquités*, he proceeded to fund Carter's excavations for fifteen years, finally being rewarded with the discovery of Tut-ankh-Amen's tomb. He died some months after its opening, most probably of a shaving cut which had grown infected.

HOWARD CARTER: 'The great Egyptologist', as he was described in his obituary in *The Times*, his discovery of Tut-ankh-Amen's tomb was the most extraordinary achievement in the history of archaeology. Carter had never had any formal training, however, and his great find was the culmination of many years' hard work.

First sent to Egypt at the age of seventeen, he worked as a draughtsman upon the tombs of Beni Hasan and the ruins of El-Amarna, and then the funerary temple of Queen Hat-shep-shut at Thebes. In 1899 he was appointed the Inspector General of Upper Egypt, in which capacity he cleared many tombs and installed the first electric lights in the Valley of the Kings. In 1903 he resigned from his post, following a dispute with French tourists at Saqqara, and subsisted for the next four years as an antiquities dealer and occasional guide. It was only his meeting with Lord Carnarvon which rescued him from penury, and enabled him to continue his archaeological excavations.

Following the discovery of Tut-ankh-Amen's tomb, he was to devote the remaining years of his life to analysing its contents, and squabbling with the Egyptian authorities. He never married. He died in 1939.

THEODORE DAVIS: A rich and elderly American lawyer, whose excavations in the Valley of the Kings resulted in the discovery or clearance of over twenty tombs. His reports on the tombs are marked chiefly by their errors and omissions. He finished his excavations in 1914, commenting, 'I fear the Valley of the Tombs is now exhausted.' He died some months afterwards.

AHMED GIRIGAR: Carter's long-serving foreman, he supervised the work in the Valley of the Kings both before and after the discovery of Tut-ankh-Amen's tomb.

BI-AMR ALLAH AL-HAKIM: Infamous in Egyptian history as 'the Muslim Caligula', al-Hakim was the son of the Caliph al-Aziz, and is represented in histories of the period as having been almost fabulously psychotic and sacrilegious. It has generally been assumed that he was slain by one of his many enemies – possibly even, it has been claimed, by the Princess Sitt al-Mulq herself, whom he had supposedly wished to marry. In Coptic legend, however, it is said that he was visited on the Mukattam Hills by a vision of Christ, after which he retired to a monastery, while to the Druze he is a messiah, and to the Ismailis a saint. The Ismailis, indeed, have recently restored his crumbling mosque, so that of its former aura of evil and decay nothing now remains.

LADY EVELYN HERBERT: Lord Carnarvon's daughter, she was his constant companion upon his Egyptological adventures, and tended him on his death bed. It was also claimed that she was 'very thick' with Carter. She married and became Lady Beauchamp in 1923.

INEN: The brother of Queen Tyi, he held the official position of 'Second of the Four Prophets of Amen'. The details of his career are otherwise obscure.

KIYA: Secondary Queen of Akh-en-Aten, she is titled in inscriptions as 'The Royal Favourite Kiya'. She appears to have had a prominence at Court that contradicted her ostensibly junior status, and it is evident that she must have been much loved by Akh-en-Aten himself.

MASOUD: The fabled Nubian manservant of the Caliph al-Hakim. His appetite for sodomy was feared by every corrupt shopkeeper in Cairo.

NEFER-TITI: The Great Queen of Akh-en-Aten, her parentage and origins remain obscure. Even more than Queen

Tyi, she appears to have wielded unusual power, and is regularly portrayed as the equal of her husband, officiating alongside him in religious ceremonies, and sometimes even smiting foreign enemies. Her ultimate fate is uncertain, and her tomb, if it exists, has never been found.

PERCY E. NEWBERRY: Leader of the Egypt Exploration Fund expedition to record the tombs at Beni Hasan (1891–2). Despite his disappointment at not discovering Akh-en-Aten's tomb, and his feud with Blackden and Fraser, he did not abandon his chosen career, instead becoming Professor of Egyptology at the University of Liverpool. In the years following the discovery of Tut-ankh-Amen's tomb, he grew to be one of Carter's closest friends and supporters.

WILLIAM FLINDERS PETRIE: The founder of professional Egyptology, his techniques of excavation were far in advance of those of his contemporaries, concentrating as they did on the preservation of every fragment of evidence. His report on his work at El-Amarna, published in 1894, is a classic of archaeological scholarship.

SITT AL-MULQ: Sister of the Caliph al-Hakim – and the reputed object of his incestuous desires – she appears to have been almost as intimidating a figure as her brother. After his death, she reigned as Regent for four years, ruling with a savage efficiency, until she too mysteriously disappeared.

SMENKH-KA-RE: A shadowy and ephemeral figure, even by the standards of the Amarna period, it has even been suggested that he may have been Nefer-titi, reigning as Pharaoh under a pseudonym. More probably, however, he was the elder son of Akh-en-Aten, ascending the throne after his father's death, but dying himself almost immediately.

For the controversy surrounding his probable burial place, see Author's Note (p 427).

THOTH-MES IV: The father of Amen-hetep III. I have not invented his belief in the value of dreams. A stele found at Giza records how the Great Sphinx had appeared to the sleeping prince and promised him the throne if he would only clear the Sphinx's body of sand. Thoth-mes did as he had been requested, and duly became Pharaoh.

His tomb was discovered by Howard Carter in 1903.

THUA: Wife of Yuya, their joint tomb was discovered by Theodore Davis in 1905. The evidence for Thua's Nubian origins is exceedingly circumstantial.

TIYA: Wife of Ay and High Priestess of Isis, she appears to have been related to the Royal House.

TUT-ANKH-AMEN: Most probably the son of Akh-en-Aten and Kiya, he ascended the throne when he was only a child, reigning for some nine or ten years before his death of an uncertain cause.

Of all the mummies which were buried in the Valley of the Kings, only Tut-ankh-Amen's still remains in its original resting place.

TYI: The Great Queen of Amen-hetep III, she was exceptional both for her non-royal ancestry and for the extent of her influence over her husband. She was also evidently very long-lived, since a wall painting on a tomb at El-Amarna shows her with her son in the twelfth year of his reign.

Some of her funerary equipment was uncovered in Smenkh-ka-Re's tomb; Theodore Davis's attribution of that tomb to Tyi herself has been conclusively disproved.

HAROUN AL-VAKHEL: Fictitious character, whose adventures are largely derived from *The Thousand and One Nights*. The story of his expedition to Lilatt-ah is based on 'The Tale of the City of Bronze', and the account of his marriage to Leila on 'The Tale of Jullanar of the Sea'.

YUYA: The only nobleman to be privileged with a burial in the Valley of the Kings, his mummy bears a strikingly non-Egyptian appearance. The identification of Yuya with the Biblical Joseph was first proposed by Ahmed Osman in his book 'A Stranger in the Valley'.

AUTHOR'S NOTE

Most Egyptologists appear to thrive on controversy, but I have found that those who write on the Amarna period enjoy it even more than most. The network of relationships in the late eighteenth Dynasty is a particularly heated topic of debate, and if the family tree on which I have based this novel represents a cross-section of opinion rather than a consensus, then that is because consensus, in such a field, does not exist.

There is one other major minefield across which I have wandered with the insouciance of the amateur. Tomb KV55, first excavated by Theodore Davis in 1907 and assigned by him to Queen Tyi, remains to this day the most discussed tomb in Egypt after the Great Pyramid of Giza. In *The Sleeper in the Sands*, I have chosen to assign it to Smenkh-ka-Re; on the basis of all the conflicting opinions I have read, this seems to me to conform best to the facts, but readers should be aware that in its time the tomb has also been assigned not only to Queen Tyi but also to Kiya and to Akh-en-Aten himself. Fortunately for the purposes of this novel, the truth will probably never be known for certain.

Finally, I must offer profuse thanks to Fiona Burtt at the British Museum Society, for all her help, and to Lucia Gahlin, for showing me her photographs of the quarry

discovered by Carter and Newberry. Thanks also, as ever —
and they know it goes without saying — to Sadie, Patrick,
Andrew and Fil; and to my occasionally companionable,
Bastet-esque cat, Stan.

YOU'VE READ THE NOVEL, NOW DISCOVER THE TRUTH ABOUT ANCIENT EGYPT . . .

The British Museum's Egyptian collections are unequalled in the world for their range and quality, comprising objects of all periods from virtually every site in Egypt and Sudan. Many of these 80,000 objects are not on display, but joining the British Museum Society (the 'Friends' of the Museum) will give you opportunities for special access to the world of the ancient Egyptians. Private views after hours, penetrating lectures by world-class scholars and visits behind the scenes to the undisplayed collections are all enjoyed by BMS members. So, to find out more about Akhenaten and the histories of the ancient Egyptian dynasties –

JOIN THE BRITISH MUSEUM SOCIETY!

Members enjoy the following benefits:

- free and priority entry, with a guest, to all British Museum exhibitions
- free entry, with a guest, to monthly Evening Openings of the Museum
- the British Museum Magazine sent to you three times a year
- exclusive members' events programme, including performances, lectures, study days and visits behind the scenes of the Museum
- discounts in the Museum shops and restaurants

For further information about joining, please contact:

The Membership Officer,
British Museum Society,
British Museum,
London WC1B 3DG, UK
Telephone: 0207 323 8605/8195

THE VAMPYRE

Tom Holland

Legendary poet Lord Byron comes to life with incendiary brilliance in this spellbinding blend of gothic imagination and documented fact that paints an unforgettable portrait of the nineteenth-century romantic genius as the world's most formidable vampire.

Wandering in the mountains of Greece, Byron is drawn to the beauty of a mysterious slave; soon he is utterly entranced, and his fate is sealed. The supreme sensualist embarks on a life of adventures even his genius could not have foreseen; having chosen to enjoy powers beyond those any vampire has ever known, Byron enters a dark, intoxicating world, traversing centuries of long-lost secrets, ancient arts, and scorching excesses of evil. But his diversions – delicious and cruel – are suffused with the rich scent of doom. Byron's gift is also his torment: an all-consuming thirst that withers life at the root, damning all those he loves . . .

'Not since *Interview With The Vampire* was published almost twenty years ago has a novel of this genre appeared that's half as good as Tom Holland's *The Vampyre* . . . a powerfully atmospheric tale'
Company

'Vampire fiction gets a transfusion . . . a classical alternative to the traditional tale, Byron himself would have been pleased by such an eerie, erudite addition to his myth'
Time Out

'A tour de force of scholarship and gothicity'
Los Angeles Times

Warner
0 7515 1361 X

SUPPING WITH PANTHERS

Tom Holland

In 1888 Dr John Eliot returns to London haunted by the memory of a terrible expedition to a remote Himalayan kingdom, where he had uncovered horrors far beyond the frontiers of science. Yet Eliot's faith in reason is to be tested even further when the body of a friend, drained white of its blood, is dragged up from the Thames, and another associate goes missing. Eliot's quest to uncover the heart of the mystery reveals a deadly conspiracy, but then, in the lair of an enigmatic Eastern adventuress, he glimpses hints of a truth yet more extraordinary, of dark and terrible pleasures, of a whole new world . . .

Vampires and immortals walk the gas-lit streets of Victorian London, mingling with Oscar Wilde, Bram Stoker and Lord Byron, as Tom Holland meshes fact with fiction in this brilliantly imaginative novel of passion and suspense – which unveils at last the truth which gave birth to *Dracula*.

'Goes at a cracking pace with its wit, superb sense of humour and literary cross-references – this novel is an expert mix of the fantastical and the real'
Alice Thompson, *The Scotsman*

'In the tradition of the great English gothic novel – a ripping yarn'
Independent

'Meticulous about literary and historical accuracy – scarily bright'
Daily Telegraph

'High entertainment with a dash of romance . . .
genuinely chilling'
The Times

Warner
0 7515 1485 3

DELIVER US FROM EVIL

Tom Holland

Deep winter, 1659: a killer is abroad on Salisbury Plain.
Roundhead officer Captain Foxe fears that the horribly
mutilated bodies found at ancient pagan sites point to more
than mortal cause. A long-buried evil, from the very
depths of Hell, is awakening.

For Robert, Captain Foxe's son, the rising tide of darkness will
result in exile – from his home, from his family, from all that he
loves. His quest for revenge will take him from the dark
mysteries of Stonehenge to the ravishing temptations of
Restoration London, from the labyrinthine Ghetto of Prague to
the virgin forest of the New World. Weaving the fantastic
with scrupulously documented historical fact,
Tom Holland has once again created a wildly
imaginative work of dazzling storytelling.

'Anne Rice with added scholarship . . . frighteningly realistic'
Scotland on Sunday

'Thrills and spills'
The Times

'A wealth of good writing'
Express on Sunday

Warner
0 7515 1861 1

Other bestselling Warner titles available by mail:

The prices shown above are correct at time of going to press. However, the publishers reserve the right to increase prices on covers from those previously advertised without prior notice.

WARNER BOOKS

WARNER BOOKS
Cash Sales Department, P.O. Box 11, Falmouth, Cornwall, TR10 9EN
Tel: +44 (0) 1326 569777, Fax: +44 (0) 1326 569555
Email: books@barni.avel.co.uk.

POST AND PACKING:
Payments can be made as follows: cheque, postal order (payable to Warner Books)
or by credit cards. Do not send cash or currency.
All U.K. Orders   **FREE OF CHARGE**
E.E.C. & Overseas   25% of order value

Name (Block Letters) _____

Address_____

_____

Post/zip code:_____

☐ Please keep me in touch with future Warner publications

☐ I enclose my remittance £_____

☐ I wish to pay by Visa/Access/Mastercard/Eurocard

Card Expiry Date

☐☐☐☐☐☐☐☐☐☐☐☐☐☐☐☐   _____